P9-CCR-831

NEVER FAR AWAY

ALSO BY MICHAEL KORYTA

If She Wakes

How It Happened

Rise the Dark

Last Words

Those Who Wish Me Dead

The Prophet

The Ridge

The Cypress House

So Cold the River

The Silent Hour

Envy the Night

A Welcome Grave

Sorrow's Anthem

Tonight I Said Goodbye

NEVER FAR AWAY

MICHAEL KORYTA

LITTLE, BROWN AND COMPANY

New York Boston London

The characters and events in this book are fictitious. Any similarity to real persons, living or dead, is coincidental and not intended by the author.

Copyright © 2021 by Michael Koryta

Hachette Book Group supports the right to free expression and the value of copyright. The purpose of copyright is to encourage writers and artists to produce the creative works that enrich our culture.

The scanning, uploading, and distribution of this book without permission is a theft of the author's intellectual property. If you would like permission to use material from the book (other than for review purposes), please contact permissions@hbgusa.com. Thank you for your support of the author's rights.

Little, Brown and Company
Hachette Book Group
1290 Avenue of the Americas, New York, NY 10104
littlebrown.com

First Edition: February 2021

Little, Brown and Company is a division of Hachette Book Group, Inc. The Little, Brown name and logo are trademarks of Hachette Book Group, Inc.

The publisher is not responsible for websites (or their content) that are not owned by the publisher.

The Hachette Speakers Bureau provides a wide range of authors for speaking events. To find out more, go to hachettespeakersbureau.com or call (866) 376-6591.

ISBN 978-0-316-53593-9
LCCN 2020941165

Printing 1, 2020

LSC-C

Printed in the United States of America

For Ben and Jenn Strawn,
this story of an unorthodox but deeply appreciated family

Part One

THE END

I

They circled her car with guns in hand, orbiting but never intersecting, like twin satellites of death.

Nina sat with her hands on the steering wheel and her eyes straight ahead. The tears had dried on her face. The shakes had stopped but her jaw ached from clenching her teeth. She watched them move and listened to them talk and she didn't say a word. There was no point, and she understood this. They would make their decisions and then she would die.

They all understood this.

"Use the rifle and make it one shot," the taller man said. He was lean and had long blond hair that fell nearly to his shoulders. He carried an AR-15 loosely in his right hand. Behind him, the headlights showed the lonely bridge and the river beyond. The wind was still and there was no sound but their voices and Nina's rapid breathing.

"One shot?" the other man replied. He was a few inches shorter and layered with muscle, his hair cropped as tight as a military cadet's, but he might have been the taller one's brother. They looked eerily similar, in fact, as if superficial differences had been created simply to avoid confusion. They moved as one, spoke as one, breathed as one. "Why not open up, leave nothing but broken glass and shell casings behind?"

"Carnage," the long-haired one said with a sigh. "You always favor chaos where cleanliness would work."

They passed each other then, going in opposite directions, neither pausing to look at the other. Their eyes never left Nina.

When their paths crossed, they seemed to quicken by a blink. You could never see them together for long. You had to turn left or right to track them, which meant you had to turn your back on one or the other. It all played out like a choreographed dance.

Nina stared at the road in front of her.

"It's not chaos," the clean-cut one said. "It's a statement. That's the idea."

The headlights threw their shadows long across the cracked asphalt, turned them into supernatural figures that capered across the bridge and the surface of the water.

Nina wet her lips. Clenched and unclenched her hands on the steering wheel. Waited for them to choose.

"We weren't asked to make a statement; we were asked to make her dead," the long-haired one said. He had a nearly musical cadence to his voice, light and almost amused. Even as he circled, he watched Nina. She could feel his eyes on her, and she wanted to look away but refused to. *Just look straight. If he passes, look him dead in the eye and let him carry on.*

Until he was done carrying on. Until it was over.

"Single shot to the brain, then?"

Their shadows overlapped again. Nina could smell the river, the only cool thing in the stagnant Florida night. It was the loneliest road she had ever seen. A mile behind her was a sign that said the road was closed and the bridge was out. That sign was lying facedown now, sawed off at the base.

"It would be my preference," the long-haired man said. He paused, stood dead center between the headlights, and stared at Nina. His right hand lifted and the gun muzzle rose with it and centered on her and held. His gloved finger stroked the trigger. He studied her for a long moment and then nodded. "Clean," he said. "It would be clean and quick."

"There will need to be blood," the other one said, and Nina closed her eyes despite herself.

"Correct. Rather a lot of it too."

"I'm afraid so."

Nina forced her eyes open. Beads of sweat rose on her forehead, too cool, like the sweat when a fever broke.

They were standing as close together as she'd ever seen them. Not shoulder to shoulder, but aligned, at least temporarily, no more than a single pace apart. The river ran through their shadows. Neither of them moved and neither of them spoke. The sound of the river was a distant thing. Cicadas trilled and somewhere in the far distance there was a soft splash. An alligator, maybe.

"Your knife?" the long-haired man said.

His companion withdrew a knife from his pocket and flicked the blade open and passed it over. The long-haired man let the AR-15 muzzle drop again and walked toward the car at a leisurely pace. All the time in the world. He stopped beside the driver's door and reached out and took the handle and pulled it open. Knelt. Looked at her.

"It must be done," he said.

Nina nodded. She couldn't speak.

He sighed and leaned his rifle against the back door of the car. Then, holding only the knife, he used his free hand to sweep his hair back from his face and looked up at her with what could almost pass for tenderness.

"I can do it," he said. "Or—"

"Me." The word left her lips in a gasp. She breathed and blinked and said it again, firmer this time. "Me."

The long-haired man nodded. The other one had moved out of the headlights and stood watching from the shadows.

"I respect that," the long-haired man said, then he rotated the knife so he was gripping it by the blade and passed it forward. Nina finally released the steering wheel and took the textured black rubber grip of the knife in her right hand.

The long-haired man leaned forward and reached for Nina's

hand. Instinctively, she jerked it back. He waited, patient. She extended her left hand to him, trying to will the shaking away.

It didn't work.

He took her bare hand in his gloved hand, turned her palm up, and traced the fine blue vein that ran from the top of the wrist to the base of her middle finger.

"Cut deep, and across the track, not with it," he said. "The blade is sharp. It won't take much. Just remember to get to the headrest in a hurry. We wouldn't want to create confusion."

Nina's heart rate was triple-timing and her breasts rose and fell with shallow breaths. She felt a wave of dizziness and for a moment thought she might drop the knife. She looked away from him and out toward the river and spoke aloud but to herself.

"Hailey," she said. Then, after wetting her lips: "Nick."

No one said a word when she brought the gleaming, angled blade to the inside of her left wrist and cut a furrow through the skin and deep into the vein.

She cried out then despite herself, the pain rising behind the blood, and the long-haired man said, "Hurry, now, hurry," and she turned in the seat and reached for the headrest and held out her hand so her palm was open and skyward, like a desperate prayer.

The blood ran free over the tan leather and formed reservoirs and tributaries as it tracked down the headrest and chased the grooves of the leather back south. The dizziness returned and she started to pull away but he caught her by the elbow.

"More," he said softly. "It has to be enough. You know this."

She knew this. Hailey. Nick. Doug. She closed her eyes and let the blood run. Hailey and Nick, Nick and Hailey, and Doug was there, Doug was still there, Doug would always be there. She curled her hand into a fist and the open skin pulled farther apart and the blood ran faster.

"Good," he said, and then her hand was back in his and a

bandage was closed over the wound. He moved swiftly but gently, with the seasoned touch of a nurse. She felt her pulse against his thumb as he applied pressure to the wound.

"Up now," he said, and he guided her out of the car. She opened her eyes just as the clean-cut man lifted a small flashlight and thumbed the back and a brilliant beam pierced the blackness and illuminated the tan leather.

Ribbons of blood gleamed jewel-like in the light. It was darkest on the headrest where the flow had begun but the tendrils snaked down and out and found their own routes. There was more blood than she'd imagined was possible from a single cut vein.

The light went off.

The long-haired man's voice came from the blackness. "I don't think that's enough." He said it with sorrow.

"No?" The light returned, capturing the scene once more.

"No. The blood is there. The blood is fine. But I'm thinking of him...the man has seen many killings. Executions. You know this."

"You're right."

"Think blood will be enough for him?"

"Perhaps not."

Nina breathed through her nose and felt her pulse throbbing in the cut and looked from one of them to the other, her heart rate spiking again.

"Hair," the one who looked like a soldier said.

"A touch more than that," the long-haired man answered.

Nina's legs quivered, but she stood tall. Tried to betray no fear as she said, "What touch?"

The long-haired man sighed. "It would be most compelling—"

"And realistic," his partner put in.

"If there was a hank of hair that also seemed to have..."

"An attachment point," his partner finished for him.

Nina blinked. "What?"

"Flesh," the long-haired man told her, his blue eyes looking black with the light hidden behind him.

Nina tried to lock her knees, but the dizziness came on fast then, and she shifted and parted her lips and sucked in the humid night air.

"Think of a bullet," he told her.

"Of what it would do," his partner said.

"Even if you're gone, there's a bit more than blood left behind."

"Bone would be nice."

"Bone would be ideal, but under the circumstances..."

"It's a tough get."

"Exactly," the long-haired man agreed. "So we make do with what we have."

The whole time speaking as if they were alone on the road, as if Nina weren't listening to each terrible word. She stared at them, her eyes going from one to the other.

"May I?" the long-haired man said, and he lifted his hand. When she didn't react, he reached out and traced a small circle on the back of her head, his fingertip barely grazing her skin. "It would go like that. I know you're willing to go it alone, and as I said, I respect that, but it would be easier in this circumstance if—"

She handed him the knife. Said, "Hailey and Nick and Doug."

"Yes," he said. "Sure. Embrace whatever thoughts you need to have for your courage."

"Hailey and Nick and Doug," she repeated. The bandage on the back of her hand was already sticky. She lowered herself shakily to her knees, the pebbled asphalt biting through her jeans, and tried to draw up the images she needed. Her daughter's face, her son's, her husband's.

"I'm ready," she whispered, and bowed her head.

He cut so quickly that she scarcely felt it. For an instant, she thought that it was done and that it had not been so bad at all.

Then he yanked her hair.

It was a single, swift tug, and only as her flesh separated did she realize that he still had the blade to her head, was cutting and lifting even as he jerked.

Nina fell forward onto her hands and opened her mouth to let out a howl of pain and then a gloved hand clamped over her mouth and the long-haired man's voice was in her ear.

"Shh, shh," he cooed. "Can't be too loud. Just in case."

She saw red and black and a rotating world and sagged in his arms as he passed a hank of her hair and flesh back to his partner in exchange for an unwrapped bandage. He pressed it to Nina's head and held it there as she rode the current of pain.

The second man stepped up and leaned past them and Nina saw the nickel-size layer of her flesh swinging from her own hair like a miniature scalp as he draped it judiciously into the blood she had already shed.

"Do it quickly," the long-haired man said.

His partner drew a pistol from his belt and took aim and fired. The sound should have been loud but no sound could be loud against her pain. She sat on the pavement holding the bandage to her head and she smelled the cordite from the gunshot and blinked and refocused and saw the hole punched through the headrest.

The clean-cut man holstered the pistol and stepped back, tilting his head. Then he leaned forward again and nudged the small piece of Nina's scalp with his index finger, tapping it into a position that pleased him. "It's not great," he said.

"Less than ideal circumstances," the long-haired one said. "A bit of a time crunch."

"Indeed. Still, the man has resources. What would convince a local lab might not be enough. He can fact-check if he wishes."

"That's what we're here for. To discourage second opinions."

His partner smiled, and Nina watched him and shivered despite herself.

They were empty men.

She had needed two like them, though. Yes, she had.

The long-haired man released her and stepped back. "I'd wear a baseball cap for a time if I were you," he told her.

She put her palms against the pavement and pressed herself up, first into a sitting position, then all the way to her feet. The world spun. She waited. The world steadied. "Keys are in the car?" she said.

He smiled. The wind fanned his pale blond hair back over his shoulders. "Yes." He nodded at the river. "Right over the old bridge. You couldn't drive across it, but you can still walk it. Step carefully, though. I know he's supposed to think you're in the river, but it would be a shame if you actually ended up there."

Nina nodded. Looked at the two men with their knives and their guns and her blood on their hands. "Thank you," she said.

"Our pleasure."

"Happy to help."

Nina looked one last time at the blood-soaked headrest where her hair hung, then turned and walked into the night.

They watched her go. Only when she was across the bridge and the sound of an engine growled in the darkness did either speak.

"We would get more money if we told him the truth," the long-haired man said finally.

"His money and hers."

"Yes."

"She's of little use to us alive."

"None whatsoever."

They turned in unison and looked at the car. The shorter one thumbed the flashlight on again. The blood gleamed. The hank of hair with the circle of Nina Morgan's scalp dangled beside the gunshot hole.

"I'm curious, though," he said.

"Can we sell it. That's what you're wondering."

"Exactly."

"It was rushed work, yet…"

"Not bad."

"No. Not terrible."

"I can't say I ever liked the man either."

"The job in Mazatlán, for example."

"We weren't put in a position to succeed on that one, no."

"There's being considered expendable, and then there's being sacrificed."

"Very different situations."

"Indeed."

Silence. They studied the car.

"We'll have to call it in," the long-haired man said.

"Here's a prediction," his partner answered. "He won't pay us."

"Because she's in the river, and we weren't supposed to put her there?"

"Correct. He wanted to see her. So the bastard won't pay us."

The long-haired man gave a thoughtful nod. "In that case, the only sure money is Nina's."

"Unless we give her up."

"Unless."

"But even then…"

"He might not be happy."

"Correct."

The long-haired man removed his gloves. Studied the car. "It's an experiment," he said. "Can we sell it?"

"Why not try?"

"Why not?" the long-haired man agreed, and he took out his cell phone and dialed.

Part Two

GUARDIANS

2

The wasp flew into the back seat of the truck at night, unnoticed.

Doug Chatfield had lowered the window earlier when he was driving home with his thirteen-year-old daughter, Hailey, in the passenger seat and his eleven-year-old son, Nick, sprawled in the back amid a tangle of baseball bats, gloves, cleats, and stink.

The kids were arguing when Doug pulled into the winding entrance road of the subdivision. Hailey took issue with what she termed Nick's "totally rank BO." Nick responded by peeling off one sweaty sock, lunging forward, and dangling it under his sister's nose. That led to Hailey grabbing her brother's hand and bending it backward, mercy-style. That led to a shriek of pain.

At this point, Doug Chatfield said, "C'mon, gang," and cracked the back window even though it was just beginning to rain, fat drops sprinkling out of a nickel-colored sky behind clouds that promised more.

"Release your brother and let his stink blow south," Doug said in the formal tone of a royal proclamation. The voice amused Hailey. Nick's hand was freed, the sock fell onto the center console, Hailey swept it away with disgust, and the cracked rear window let the humid summer air pass over the fragrant cargo in the back seat. Not much air, though; Doug had cracked the window only about an inch due to the rain. Cracked it so little, in fact, that he didn't remember it was open at all by the time he pulled into the garage.

The wasp was already in the garage. It had flown in when

Doug exited the house to go to work at his accounting office that morning, and it was sealed off from its nest under the eaves when he put the door down. When the Chatfield trio climbed out of the truck, the wasp crawled onto a dusty blue plastic tub that held Christmas lights. By the time it finally took flight, the garage door was down once more, and escape wasn't an option.

Sometime around midnight, it found the cracked window.

On Saturday morning there was neither work nor practice nor alarms in the Chatfield house. No demands on the family until two p.m., when Hailey had tennis, and four p.m., when Nick had another baseball game—both activities weather-dependent. The storms that had rocked the Louisville area overnight had saturated the ground but hadn't broken the humidity, and there was a chance of more rain that afternoon. When Doug woke, the sky was dark, and on the back porch, where he stood with coffee in hand, the air was so thick it seemed to have texture, like passing through a curtain.

They'll be inside all day, he thought with confidence. *It will be a day of closed windows and air-conditioning and TV and video games and at least one battle between them, maybe two.*

Get things off on the right foot, then. A treat, a surprise. Doug was usually a big proponent of healthy breakfasts, the one meal he felt he had total control over on days that could so quickly devolve into chaos and crammed schedules. He was a big proponent of most things health-related, actually, because at one time he'd been a physician's assistant. Now he tried to pass himself off as a hypochondriac to explain away the medical knowledge that occasionally leaked out. "Degree from WebMD," he'd joke, and people would smile and accept it, because everyone knew that Doug Chatfield was an accountant and a widower. Who could blame him for being paranoid about his family's health? He was all alone in this.

A balanced breakfast was mandatory on most days, but this was summer vacation, it was Saturday, and his kids were looking at a rainout. There was a Dunkin' Donuts three minutes up the road. Hailey was a jelly-doughnut fan and Nick was a chocolate-anything kid. Doug could get to the Dunkin' and back in ten minutes, have the box waiting on the kitchen island whenever the kids woke and wandered downstairs.

What the hell. They called it *vacation* for a reason.

He left a note on the island just in case one of them woke while he was gone, unlikely as that was. One word, with an exclamation mark: *Doughnuts!*

He rarely left them alone, but they'd be fine, and it was good practice. This was, as he'd discussed with Hailey repeatedly in recent weeks, the summer he wanted her to take more of the responsibility she was constantly demanding. She was convinced that she was already an adult—*Thirteen going on thirty* was the tired joke in the bleachers at the tennis matches—and that Doug smothered her, was an overprotective, clueless dad.

Maybe she was not entirely wrong. Any parent knew the wicked risks this world held for children, but Doug could conjure up more creative risks than most. He had to push back against those fears, those memories. You couldn't bubble-wrap your kids against the world.

But you could give them treats.

Let it rain, and let them sleep late, and let them eat doughnuts.

He grabbed his keys and went into the garage. Started the truck and put up the door. Backed out, put the door back down, and pulled away. Only then did he hear the high whistle of air through the cracked window behind him and remember the body-odor battle of the previous day.

He shut the window without a glance in the back seat.

His house was a mile deep in the winding roads and culs-de-sac of a subdivision composed of brick homes striving for visual separation without much success. The speed limit was fifteen miles per hour inside the subdivision, and Doug adhered to it. You had to, with all the kids in the neighborhood. Kids did crazy things—chased Frisbees into streets, chased dogs into streets; hell, chased *cars*. They didn't understand risk. Not yet. So you drove slow, and you paid attention.

He was at the stop sign near the low stone fence bearing the neighborhood's name—Flanders' Woods—when the wasp crawled from the door panel of the back seat to the driver's-door panel in the front.

Doug didn't see it. His eyes were ahead, on the road. There was no stop sign for cross traffic, and people drove too damn fast on this stretch. The hill to the east was particularly problematic in the morning, when the rising sun glared down on the crest and made visibility difficult. He paused for several seconds, making sure that he was clear, and then turned left.

Now he was on Oak Ridge Road, where the speed limit rose to forty-five, except for the S-curves, where it dropped to thirty. One mile down this road, one more stop sign, and then he'd be on Fourth Street, and the Dunkin' Donuts would be visible.

He pressed down on the gas pedal.

An American wasp is adorned with bright yellow and black bands. The colors are frequently adopted by sports teams and even warships for a reason—it's an aggressive visual pairing.

It is supposed to be.

The colors are intended to sound an alarm and provoke a primal response. *Don't touch me. Don't even come close to me.*

For those who cannot see the warning, though, or those who see it and choose not to take it seriously, the female wasp is equipped with a second protective measure: a stinger. Unlike a bee's barbed stinger, the wasp's is smooth, capable of multiple stings. Only the female wasp has a stinger because she has the burden of protecting the nest, and she remains close to it.

Unless the world intervenes.

The wasp crawling along the armrest of Doug Chatfield's Dodge Ram was a female, and she was no longer near her nest. She was trapped, and her threatening colors had been overlooked, ignored. When Doug shifted his left arm, the sleeve on his polo shirt rode up, and he brushed against her.

She stung him once in the meat of his left triceps.

Doug shouted. The pain that rocketed through his muscular, nearly two-hundred-pound frame in response to the quarter-inch-long stinger was a blistering shock. He looked to his left, hurt and scared, exactly what the sting was meant to accomplish, and finally saw the wasp. She was still crawling along the door panel, still not taking to the air.

He shifted his left hand away from the steering wheel and swatted at her. Missed. The wasp flew between his fingers, stung him once more, piercing the webbing just below his ring finger, then clung to his hand.

He made a high sound of surprise and tried to do two things at once: lower the driver's window and shake the wasp off before she could sting again. She was capable of hurting him, yet she was still a trivial threat. Things would be fine if he could just fling her out of his world and into another.

He had both hands off the steering wheel when the horn from the oncoming Chevy Tahoe blared. He looked up and grabbed the wheel, seeing, as the wasp stung him again, that he was well across the center line. He had time to jerk the wheel to the right as the Tahoe swerved away, and for a half a second everything was back in his control—the wasp was gone from his hand and the collision had been avoided.

Then the truck flipped.

It rolled twice across the pavement before colliding with a hundred-year-old oak tree that offered enough resistance to pin the wreck above the steep grade below. The airbags deployed, dust hung in the air with the smell of cordite, and bits of broken glass and plastic tinkled down into Doug's hair and rode rivulets of blood along his neck.

Before the screaming started up on the road, and long before the sirens, the wasp found the shattered window and flew free. She buzzed there, alone above the carnage, and searched for a nest she could no longer find.

3

"Western wind, inbound, left to right. Approximately six hundred yards of open water ahead. Slight chop. Taxi check is complete."

"Good, good, and good. Next?"

"CARS. *C* means 'carburetor heat,' which is off. *A* means 'area ahead clear,' which it is. *R* means 'water rudders up,' which they are. *S* means 'stick back.' Which it is."

"Try it?"

"Why not?" Leah Trenton said, sitting in the cockpit of a Cessna seaplane, taxiing across North Woods waters. The prop spun with increased throttle. Dark water trembled ahead. The pines on either side of the window morphed from green to black as the speed rose. The stick felt light in Leah's palm. "First rise," she said.

"Good."

Faster, the pontoons still in contact with the water but only at a surface glide now.

"Second rise."

"Good. Tune for the step."

"Roger that."

Twenty yards, thirty yards, forty, and…water contact gone. Pontoons free. The catch in her throat wasn't fear; it was utter joy. The earth no longer had a claim on Leah Trenton.

She was alone with the wind.

Well, almost alone. Beside her, the seaplane's owner, Ed Levenseller, beamed.

"Terrific! That was perfect. You've got such a natural feel for it."

Leah smiled as the plane climbed above the lake and pines and angled into the late-afternoon sun, Mount Kineo falling below. She appreciated Ed's compliments, but the smile was one of amusement too, because what Ed was praising as a natural feel was far from natural. Leah had at least fifteen thousand more flight hours than Ed.

Well, her brain and body did. Officially, those flight hours belonged to a woman with a different name, a woman who'd been dead for just shy of a decade now.

She took the plane up to a thousand feet and circled Mount Kineo, an angry rock island that rose a sheer eight hundred feet from the surface of Moosehead Lake, jutting skyward as if furious at being surrounded by water. As she banked, she tried to seem just hesitant enough. After all, it was only the fourth time Leah Trenton had taken off at the controls of a plane.

She glanced to her right and saw Ed smiling back at her, his broad, tanned face framed by the shadowed angle of his headset. He touched her arm gently. "Pretty special, right?"

"Pretty special," Leah agreed, and it was. Oh my goodness, how special it was to leave the earth and soar above it. The water take-off added something. She was in tune with all the elements then, water and land and wind and her own brain and body and spirit joined into one.

That much she was able to talk about truthfully with Ed. She always felt a pang of guilt pretending to be a novice pilot with this kind, earnest man who'd been first a friend, then a colleague, then a lover. If there was one thing that Ed valued above all else in a relationship, it was openness, and his loving Leah meant he was loving a lie.

Most of the time, she could avoid discussing her backstory and be present. She talked of this—*Be present, be here now*—

with Ed as if it was a mantra for living, and it was, but it was also a method of being honest. *Ask me about today so I can tell you no lies.*

Here, she was happy. Content. Moosehead Lake spread beneath them in all of the awesome majesty that had captured Thoreau a hundred and fifty years earlier. Massive bays and hidden inlets and streams, dozens of islands, walls of granite rising with the randomness of indifferent glaciers. Tamed since Thoreau's day? Sure. Conquered? Not hardly.

Moosehead was tourist country, there was no question about that, but it was also hard country. Not as isolated as the Allagash Wilderness stretching to its northern side, which held Leah and Ed's destination for the day, but certainly not suburban. The cabins and cottages were filled now, the lake speckled with brightly colored boats, the inns and restaurants booked solid. By late fall, though, it would be a silent place once more, and by winter, when the northern wind howled down and ice augers growled through frozen feet to find the water's surface, it was a world unto itself.

Leah's world now. It was hard to believe she'd once been a Florida girl.

"Busy summer coming," Ed commented. A gusting wind rocked the plane as if offering a gentle but firm reminder of what forces were in control here. Ed kept a careful eye on Leah.

"I think the word is *chaotic,* not *busy.*"

The biggest difference between her forty years and his twenty-nine was the degree to which one was willing to be overwhelmed. What she'd embraced when she was Ed's age she now viewed through the prism of risk assessment. How much money would it cost, how much time would it take, what if it all went wrong? Of the many things she liked about Ed Levenseller, his young gambler's heart stood out. He wasn't reckless but he had a far easier time talking himself into a choice than out of one. Among the summer's choices: renovation of the six cabins they'd purchased in the deep, isolated Maine North Woods. Leah thought they'd make it through renovations on two of them. Ed was pushing for all six but was willing to settle for four.

Their long-term goal was a chain of cabins accessible only by seaplane, kayak, or canoe. They'd guide for those who wanted guides, and they'd facilitate access for those who wanted to go it alone. Rustic experiences were nearing a renaissance, Ed insisted. In a hyperconnected world, there was an appetite for escape. A week of cold wind and no Wi-Fi held appeal now. Ed and Leah could provide that escape, that unique taste of a part of the world that few people ever saw.

"No need to rush," Leah said, and though she was speaking of the cabins, she felt as if the words carried too large a meaning. If she asked Ed for anything, it was patience. While he charged forward, she circled, wondering how much to allow herself in this new life.

And how much to allow herself to ask of him. She wanted to tell him no lies and yet here she was, accepting his instructions on how to fly a plane she could have flown before he had his driver's license.

"Let's keep it contained to thinking about the kitchen of cabin one," she said. "I'm worried enough about that."

"You mean the kitchen of Trout Vista?" he said, and they both laughed. It had been an ongoing joke as they scouted properties and discussed possibilities that so many of the inns and cabins of the North Woods carried some odd animal-themed name. She'd laughed about it one night early in their relationship while they drank beers at a pub called the Stress Free Moose. "Who is coming up with these names?" she had wondered out loud, and ever since then Ed liked to tag their own cabins with absurd names.

"It's just doing some beadboard, some flooring, and adding

some butcher's block to the counter," he said. "Be done by the end of the month. I assure you, the warm hearth of—"

"Cabin number one."

"Caribou's Courage will be done by the first fireworks on the Fourth of July. Then I'll march triumphantly on, miter saw in hand, to conquer—"

"Cabin number two."

"Egret's Estate, yes. Even less work there."

"The roof is missing."

"The roof is *sagging*."

"Water goes right through it."

"That's the beauty of the sag—it directs the water to the center of the living-room floor," Ed said, making a funnel shape with his hands to demonstrate. "Without that sag, the place might be a wreck."

Leah smiled and shook her head.

"Four cabins ready by fall," Ed said confidently. "It's a lot, but—"

"It's less when I'm guiding all of your summer clients."

"Come on. You're guiding summer fishermen. Grandfathers and grandsons who'll be happy with bluegill." He gestured at the altimeter. "You're letting it creep."

Actually, she was not "letting it"; she was taking it higher by intent, but her intent ignored his guidance and fell back on the physical experience that he didn't know she had. Wasn't that often the case with young men and older women? Ah, the things you could not tell the sweet boys with the fragile egos.

"Beaming back to earth," she said and angled the nose down. Beneath them, two white sails glistened on the blanket of dark water—Hobie Cats racing across the lake.

"Nice work. You really should get licensed to fly," Ed said, and while he meant it supportively and with admiration, Leah's smile slipped.

"What?" Ed said. "You seem to *love* flying this thing. If we can double the pilots without doubling the pay..."

"I know," Leah said. "It just doesn't feel like my thing."

He was watching her with a furrowed brow, puzzled, because Ed Levenseller was young but intuitive, and he knew joy when he saw it. Leah could pretend to have only a passing interest in the plane, but her eyes and her body sent another message. She was not merely joyful up here, she was home.

"There's a difference between doing it for pleasure and doing it for money," she offered by way of explanation.

"I guess," Ed said. "But isn't the idea to do what you love? If someone is willing to pay you to do what you love, well, you're ahead of most of the world."

"Yes," she said. "You are. But I love to guide and I don't love to shoot. You know the difference there."

He didn't push it. The silence that followed was comfortable, not the product of disagreement, just a pause in a long-running conversation. They were both lost in their own thoughts but joined in the moment by the soft shudder of the aluminum shell that swept them over a wilderness that was so beautiful, you had to struggle to believe it had the capacity to harm.

Beautiful things always did, though. Somewhere just beneath them, north of Lily Bay, were the remains of a B-52 Stratofortress that in 1963 had left a Massachusetts air force base and crashed into Elephant Mountain. Several crew members had survived the crash only to perish in a blizzard. All this had happened while they were serving stateside during peacetime, flying with the lights of bucolic New England towns twinkling below them. Only hours later, they were freezing to death in subzero weather, still stateside but no doubt feeling very far from home and peace.

You never knew what was coming your way. All the same,

though, flying above this wilderness with the sun starting to gleam red behind Mount Washington? It was hard not to let the moment hold you.

Leah banked north, Ed's hand warm on hers, and they flew on alone, together.

4

A person can be in one place and span many. It is possible because the present is shaped by the past and the future, buffered by them like guardrails. Or the sides of a funnel.

This is Leah Trenton, asleep in the slanting sunlight of late afternoon, her lover's breath on her neck. This was Nina Morgan, in a hospital room in a Florida city, her second child in her arms, the baby's breath impossibly warm against her skin, the preternatural heat of newborn life pushing forward like wind on a fire.

While Leah slept in Maine, a dead woman's life called for her. The past left the earth, chased blackness through space along an invisible thread, found a satellite, angled back down, and pierced the present with a scream.

Leah jerked awake, the sheet falling from her breasts, Ed's body going rigid beside her.

"What is that?" he muttered, half asleep.

"Don't know," she said, but she did. Inside an Osprey backpack hung on a hook beside the front door, an orange satellite messenger blared, an awful tone somewhere between a cheap alarm clock and a siren.

Leah swung out of bed and fumbled for the clothes that had been discarded on the floor, clothes still damp with sweat and sawdust. A day of labor on cabin one had been followed by a welcome diversion that began in an ice-cold shower and moved to the ancient bunk that was now equipped with a new mattress and flannel sheets. Flannel in June. Summer in Maine. A day of hard work and loud laughs and clear eyes on the future.

The messenger bleated again, and even as Leah tugged on her tank top and buttoned her jeans she was thinking, *A cruel mistake, this is such a cruel mistake.*

Ed was rising, but she pushed him back. "It's mine," she said. "I've got it."

"Got *what*?"

"Low-battery alarm," she said, but she'd been monitoring and maintaining the batteries in the device for a decade, and she knew that it was not a low battery. The satellite messenger was outdated but functional. It could receive incoming texts from anyone who knew the number. There was only one person on earth who knew the number.

A mistake, she insisted to herself as she tugged the pack down and fumbled the zipper open. The messenger blinked green lights at her. She pulled it free, staring at the screen, where an outdated, pixelated display showed a phone number. The number was the only message, like you'd see on a pager from the 1990s.

A pause while she stared, and then it went off again.

"Batteries," she said as Ed propped himself up in bed, blinking at her in sleepy confusion. "Sorry. Go back to sleep."

She took her cell phone from the kitchen table and then opened the door and stepped outside, the satellite messenger in one hand and the cell phone in the other. Outside the cabin, Leah's dog, Tessa, whined and rose from her own slumber in a patch of sunlight, loose grass sticking to her fawn-colored coat. Leah had found Tessa under an abandoned barn five years earlier. The dog was of unknown breed origins, with a boxer's broad chest and stance, the muzzle and ears of a corgi, and legs that seemed to have been appropriated from an elk. Tessa, like Leah, had come to embrace a life of minimal electronic intrusions. The sound of the pager concerned her in the way no natural noise ever did.

"It's okay, girl," Leah said, but her voice was so wooden that the dog took no reassurance from it and instead hurried to Leah's side and pressed against her thigh, body rigid, tail stiff, whining through closed jaws.

"Let's check it out," Leah said, trying to lighten her tone. "Come on. Let's check it out."

She didn't rush. If anything, she moved more methodically. Walked down the dirt and gravel driveway and toward the lake, aiming for a point between two towering pines that threw long, angular shadows across the rippled water. That spot, where the browned fallen needles formed a soft pocket between the rocks, was the only place on the property that had reliable cell phone coverage. She waited until she was standing at the water's edge before looking at her phone.

One bar.

This was a luxury. Cabins two through six would have no bars. But here, she could make a call. All it took was the courage to dial the number.

Impossible. Cruel joke. Don't let yourself think of them. Don't let yourself believe it is about them.

Tessa whined again, high and insistent.

"We're fine," Leah said. "Just fine."

But down in the center of her chest, there was a fluttering like a hummingbird's wings.

The number. You're going to miss it, Leah, you're going to lose it and never know whether it was real.

The number was still on the display. Area code 502. Where was 502? She'd been through so many area codes over the years, and most weren't as broadly helpful for location as her current one, 207, which covered the entire state of Maine.

Her hand was shaking so badly that it took her two tries to enter the number.

Cool your mind, Leah. Cool your mind.

She took a breath, hit the dial button, put the phone to her ear, and waited.

One ring. Two. Three. Four, and this was wonderful because she would get voice mail and maybe that would explain the mistake without Leah needing to talk to—

"Hello?"

The voice was young, female, hushed. Whispered, almost, as if the speaker didn't want to be overheard.

Leah said, "Hailey?" and then she was sitting on her ass in the pine needles without knowing how she got there, legs slack, hands trembling.

"Aunt Leah?"

Leah knew the rules, knew how her children had been taught to think of her, but still, *Aunt Leah* was a lance of pain. *No,* she wanted to say, *I am not Aunt Leah, I am your mother. I brought you into the world. I have missed you every day with every fiber of my being, and if you could just call me Mom one time, just once, it would change my life. It would be all that I'd ever need.*

Instead, she said, "Yes, it's…yes, this is Aunt Leah." A bloodletting, those words. "What's wrong?"

"Dad told me I had to call you. I don't even know you, and Dad made such a big deal about it over and over, but I don't know why I am supposed to call you!"

Hailey wasn't supposed to call Leah. Not ever. Not unless…"Hailey, calm down, it's okay. What—"

"No, it's not," the girl said, the whisper falling away, her voice rising. "It is not okay! My dad is dead and I don't know who you are and none of that is okay!"

Dead. The word landed on Leah with a numbing sensation, more sedating than shocking. "Who killed him?" Leah asked. "Hailey, do you know who—"

"*What?* Nobody *killed* him! He was in a car accident. He was driving to get doughnuts and he…he…" She was starting to cry now, and Leah heard someone else in the background, a voice calling from the distance, calling Hailey's name. "We're alone,"

Hailey whispered between sobbing breaths. "He's dead, and we're alone."

"You're not alone. I'm here," Leah said. "And I'm going to make sure you're safe."

Again, the background voice called Hailey's name. There was a rustling, a muted cry of *One second, Mrs. Wilson!* and then a soft crunching that Leah identified as footsteps. She tried to picture the scene, to imagine where her daughter walked, what surrounded her, who surrounded her. What she looked like. Once, she'd had Leah's dark complexion and brown eyes and angular jawline and seemed destined to have her father's height. So long ago, now.

"Hailey?" she whispered. "You still there?"

"Why did I have to call you? I don't know you. Dad made me promise and practice and it was awful, because he always said, *If anything ever happens to me,* and I didn't want to imagine that anything could, could…" She stopped and then disintegrated into tears.

Doug really did keep his promise, Leah thought numbly. It would have been so much easier for him not to. "Your father was looking out for your safety," she said. "That's why he made you learn what to do. So you could take care of yourself and your brother if…"

If anything ever happened to him sat unspoken between them now.

Dead. Doug was dead.

Leah squeezed her eyes shut, her pain for her daughter a physical thing as she imagined the moment, imagined the thirteen-year-old girl—*child*—hearing the news of her father's death and still having the wherewithal to deliver on the instruction he'd given her.

"Is Nick safe?" Leah asked, and she could almost *feel* her infant son's warmth against her chest right then.

For a moment, she thought Hailey had hung up. Then her daughter's voice returned, softer and more controlled than before.

"He's safe. Daddy was alone." Then, as if embarrassed by using the more childish term, she corrected it: "Dad was all alone. And now we are too. My mom died so long ago I don't even remember her, and now my dad."

So long ago I don't even remember her.

Leah tried to speak and couldn't. She wet her lips, gathered herself. Sensing the agitation, Tessa licked Leah's ear, offering comfort.

"I'm so sorry, honey," Leah said. "I'm so, so sorry. But I promise I'll be there for you. You'll both be safe. I'm on my way."

"I don't even know you!"

"I understand that, and I'm sorry about it. I should have visited." These words were hard to get out; how badly had she wished to visit or simply watch them from a distance? "I know that I should have. But I'm going to come for you now."

"I don't need you to come for us!"

"Yes, you do," Leah said, keeping her voice as calm as possible even as her hummingbird heart intensified its wing speed. "Hailey, you really do. And you know that you do, because your dad made that clear, didn't he? He taught you how important this is. If he hadn't, then you wouldn't have called."

Soft sobs came but no words. At least she hadn't hung up, though, and no one had taken the phone from her—yet. Mrs. Wilson, whoever she was, didn't sound like the type who'd let the call go on for long, though.

"The number you called me from," Leah said, "is it a cell phone or a landline? Is it your phone or does it belong to someone else?"

"My cell phone."

"Okay. Perfect. That's perfect. I have your number now, and I will call you back. I'm coming to help. If you need me, use the first number again. I will always call back. Always."

"He's dead," Hailey said, the sobs returning. "He's dead, and we don't have anyone."

"You'll have me. I know that doesn't mean much right now, but if you can cool your mind and remember you'll have me—"

"What did you just say?"

"You need to remember—"

"No. You told me to cool my mind."

"What I meant was—"

"I know what you meant. Dad always said that. He told us it was my mom's expression."

The distance between them seemed greater now.

"It was your mom's expression, yes," she said. "It just stuck with me. When you're in trouble, you need a cool mind. Keep one for me now, okay?"

She managed to seal her lips before the rest of the words charged out, managed not to say: *And you need to watch out for strangers. This is the most important job you will ever have. Three strangers in particular. One will be tall and tan and have white hair. He'll probably be dressed very nicely, a suit and shined shoes. He wears glasses. Or he used to. He'll look like a kindly grandfather. The second one you need to watch for is a pale man with different-colored eyes. His left eye is green and his right eye is brown. He'll be younger than the old man, and he'll be shorter but much stronger. And then there will be the one we all called Bleak even though his real name was Marvin Sanders; he was just Bleak, period. I don't know how exactly to describe him other than that he will look like he deserves the name. If you see him, you run. You take your brother and run.*

But she couldn't say that. Those men wouldn't be coming for Hailey and Nick. Those men had no interest in the children of the deceased Doug Chatfield. They'd been interested only in a woman named Nina Morgan, also deceased, dead for almost a decade now.

Leah said, "You've already done such a good job, honey. You did exactly what you were supposed to do. And I'll be coming for you."

"It won't help. I shouldn't have called."

"Yes, you should have. You did exactly the right—"

Leah was not surprised when the girl hung up. She thought that made plenty of sense, actually.

My mom died so long ago I don't even remember her.

For a few moments, Leah sat in the pine needles with the phone in her hand, the wind freshening off the lake and shivering the boughs overhead. Tessa whined, and Leah lifted her hand and scratched Tessa's ears absently, attempting to soothe her. Tessa knew something was wrong, though. You couldn't fool a dog.

"Who was that?"

Leah turned to see Ed standing on the porch, shirtless, his lean torso scratched from a splintered shim that had sliced through his shirt that morning. That morning, back in the hours of laughter and Leah Trenton. An old life now.

Another old life.

"It was my—" She caught herself. "My niece." The word like bitter bile on her tongue. "There's been an accident, and my brother—my sister's husband—is dead. My brother-in-law is dead."

She would learn to say the words right.

She stood up and looked away from Ed, back to the satellite messenger, still astonished that it had been used. Doug had taught Hailey the plan. Had made her learn it, had driven its importance home so that even in the worst moments of her life, she had executed it.

For ten years, Leah had kept the batteries in the satellite messenger charged, just in case. It had been more ritual than reality. Each charging and each software update a communion, wafer on the lips, wine on the tongue.

Forgive me, Father.

Ed stepped off the porch and walked across the lawn toward her, grass clinging to his bare feet. "Oh, Leah. I'm sorry. Who is with them?"

"What?" she said stupidly, blinking at him.

"Who's with them now?"

"With…"

"Your niece and nephew."

She saw their faces so clearly, though all of the photographs had been hidden long ago. Her children. Her babies. She looked at Ed, processing his question in low gear, grinding through the crumbling soil of her thoughts, and said, "I have no idea. But I need to go to them now."

"Where?" he asked as he reached her.

"Area code 502," she said.

He cocked his head, stared at her with confusion and uneasiness. "You need to sit down?"

"No."

"Let's sit down," he said as he took her arm, talking to her as if she'd escaped an asylum and must now be returned to it. "You look…kind of in shock, okay? Just sit down."

"Do you know where that is?" she said, not sitting. The wind was blowing and the wind was cool and she was grateful for that. She needed it like ice on a fevered forehead.

"Do I know where area code 502 is? No." He shook his head, still holding her arm, still looking at her with that wariness. She closed her eyes and breathed the wind.

Cool your mind.

It was my mom's expression.

"I'll need to find out," she said, eyes still closed. "I've got to get back to town. Fast."

"You know where they are," he said. "Leah? You need to take a minute here. Get your thoughts—"

"I *don't* know."

"Yes, you do. You write them letters," he said in that soothing voice. "We've mailed them postcards. Remember Camden?"

Camden. Yes, of course. Camden, where she and Ed had

gone together last December. Camden, the coastal village with its perfect little library and perfect little harbor and the Christmas by the Sea festival where Santa arrived on a perfect little lobster boat and where Ed had said, *If I ever had kids, I would want to raise them in this town.*

Leah had wept that day, though not in his presence.

"You mailed them postcards from—"

"Yes," she said. "I remember." But she couldn't tell him that didn't help because the cards went to a post office box in Atlanta and were forwarded from there. She did not know where they went, only where they paused in transit.

She opened her eyes. "I need to get back to town," she repeated. "I'll need to go to them now. Quickly."

She couldn't tell if he looked more afraid for her or of her. But he nodded.

5

Area code 502 encompassed portions of Louisville, Kentucky, and Leah drove southwest through Vermont in the dark, traveling alone. Ed had wanted to come with her, but Aunt Leah needed to travel alone. She was sure of that. She'd even left Tessa behind with him, and she always traveled with the dog. She hadn't passed this way in years and was trusting her Jeep's navigation system to guide her. Granite mountains bordered the road but they were invisible now, and the darkness on either side of the highway soaked up her headlights, leaving nothing clear except the road ahead. Her children somewhere at the end of it.

No, no. Your niece and your nephew.

When Leah and Doug had made their agreement all those years ago, when the DeLorme emergency messenger number had been acquired and memorized, the two of them exchanging it more like a prayer than a number, there had been an unspoken acknowledgment that all of it was a stage play designed for Leah's benefit. The number represented the tiniest glimmer of hope that she might one day return to the only existence she desired. *We are going to wipe you off the face of the earth, but in exchange, you get this phone number with no phone attached. Sound good?*

But then Hailey had called.

I'm so grateful, Doug. So grateful that you prepared her.

Thoughts to a dead man. This felt more familiar than not. For all intents and purposes, he'd been a dead man to her for a long time. Their relationship had started two years before the marriage, and the marriage had lasted five years before Nina Morgan died in Florida, and Leah Trenton appeared in Maine.

You cannot hide from Lowery, Doc Lambkin had told her on the night that her life began to slip away. *Not all four of you, not from him.*

So then there would be three. One dead parent and three survivors. The surviving parent was preordained, because it was Nina they wanted to kill, Nina that they would pursue. So it was Nina who had been murdered and thrown into a river in Florida's backwaters.

She felt cold acid stir in her stomach, and her foot went heavy on the accelerator; the Jeep roared toward ninety miles per hour before she brought it back down. She set the cruise control so the car could fight back against its driver's worst impulses.

There is no way Lowery is still looking for you. No way he's still watching them, waiting.

But she couldn't be sure. He was still alive. She kept an eye on that. Followed the news about him, which was never much. For a man of such rare and terrible power and reach, he was relatively unknown. Mostly, what the Google News searches returned of J. Corson Lowery these days were references to his charitable contributions. He made many of them—to schools, to police departments, fire departments, libraries, gardens. His benevolent heart at work.

The man who'd founded what one senator had termed "Blackwater on steroids" had always excelled at keeping a low public profile. Even in the days when scandal simmered and federal investigators waited on Nina Morgan to make their case, Lowery had done a fine job of avoiding the press. He had a spokesman for his conglomerate of mercenaries masquerading as security professionals, of course. Had it been merely a matter of testimony and a few underlings sent to prison, Leah wasn't sure that she would have needed to change her name, let alone flee from her own family. But she'd been asked to bring the top man down.

"You come at the king, you'd best not miss," said Omar Little of *The Wire,* one version of an old saying, but Nina Morgan had learned that there was a worse outcome than missing: taking a shot at the king and hitting the prince.

He will not let you live, Doc Lambkin had told her on that awful night in the warm Florida breeze, the sound of the Gulf of Mexico a whispered soothing in the background, blending with the tranquil lighting on the patio to create an atmosphere so serene that it seemed mocking. *Here is one world,* the spring night promised her, *and you will never see it again. Soak it up. This is the last night of its kind for you.*

She'd resisted. Fake her own death and leave her family? Never. She ran instead, fleeing with her husband and children, hiding out in a cash-only cabin awaiting the new identities that would let them vanish permanently, cleanly. The Morgan family would cease to exist, but they'd remain together. Forever together.

Then the assassins arrived.

The family had been out of the house, thank God, but the security cameras picked them up. Two men dressed like contractors, tool belts on their waists and smiles on their faces. They rang the bell and paced the house and left, and Leah—Nina then—had sent a clip of the video to Doc Lambkin.

"Not sure about these guys," she'd told him. "But probably I'm just paranoid."

She wasn't just paranoid. When Doc called back, his voice was unsteady for the first time in her memory.

"We need to talk about this," he said.

"You recognize them?"

"I recognize them."

Doug and the kids went to a hotel, checking in with a stolen credit card, and she returned to Doc Lambkin's home. He'd poured her three fingers of single-malt scotch and told her about the men who'd visited her home.

By the end, her hands were shaking so badly, she dropped the whiskey glass. It shattered on the patio stones and some of the fragments fell into the cobalt water of the swimming pool and only moments later it began to rain. Still they had stayed outside, her hair plastered to her neck and her face awash with rain and tears as she had listened to him tell her the only way she could protect her family.

You have to die, Doc had said, and there might have been tears in his eyes too, or maybe it was just the rain. *You have to die one way or the other, don't you see? But if you die alone, your family is safe. He'll extract no pleasure from harming them, not without you there to see it and suffer.*

She'd told him they could run. She'd talked of South American countries and remote Pacific islands, and Doc had listened and sipped his whiskey as the rain cascaded down and he never spoke, just allowed her to talk herself out until she saw the futility in her own ideas.

I have to die, she'd said finally. *One way or the other, as you said.*

Doc had nodded.

Lowery will never believe it, she'd told him.

Doc paused. Chewed on his lip for a moment. Said, *There is one chance of convincing him.*

How's that, Doc? How in the hell will he be convinced *unless he sees my body?*

He trusts the men he hired to kill you. He knows how good they are. He knows that someone like you could never escape them.

She was staring at him, bewildered. Yes, the idea that she couldn't escape was the point; how was Doc missing that?

But I don't think they care for him, Doc said, speaking slowly and carefully. *And I know that they like a challenge.*

That was how Nina Morgan ended up on a roadside on a sultry Southern night with an assassin's knife tracing her scalp.

And it had worked. Clearly, it had worked.

My mom died so long ago I don't even remember her, Hailey had said today on the phone. Hailey was right; her mother was dead, which meant that Hailey had lived in safety. But then somewhere on a suburban Louisville street, Doug's blood had flowed across the pavement, ending his own life but reviving another's. Nina Morgan was born again, bleated into life through the chime of a pager.

I cannot let this ruin them, she thought, remembering Hailey's voice, the underlying maturity beneath the hysteria. How much had Doug told their daughter? It couldn't have been much. Enough to convince her to make the call, though. Enough for that.

Leah would take them, and she would keep them safe. It would not be easy—could not be, should not be—but it could be done. Time didn't heal all wounds, but it added scar tissue that dulled the pain. This Leah knew better than anyone. All she needed was her children and time.

This was all she had ever needed.

Just after she crossed the New York state line, her fear got the better of her and she made the call she'd promised not to make unless the situation was beyond all hope.

Doc Lambkin—"Dave" to those who didn't know him—lived on an island off the coast of Washington. Once he, too, had been a member of the Lowery Group. Unlike Leah, he hadn't been foolish enough to testify against them. Unlike Leah, he hadn't gone into hiding. He'd simply retreated, leaving her with an apology and a promise: *If he comes for you, call me, and I will help.*

There was no old-fashioned pager for Doc Lambkin, no secret system. Just his cell phone number, unchanged and—she prayed—unmonitored.

"Hello?" he said in that bedside-manner tone that had earned him the nickname. Well, the bedside manner and his unusual knowledge about everything from poisons to body-decomposition rates.

"This is L-Leah," she stammered. The name was hers now, and she was so used to saying it that she'd forgotten he might not remember. All he'd done with the name was arrange for it to be on the documents. "I mean, this is Nina from—"

"I know," he said softly. "How *are* you? It's so good to hear your voice. I've wondered…"

He didn't finish the sentence, but the rest of it would have been *if you were still alive.*

"Doug is dead," she said. "He is dead, and I am coming for my children, and I am so scared. Doc, I am so scared for them."

"How did you find out?"

"My daughter. She called. Just as we—just as Doug and I had planned."

A pause. "And you're going to them. You're going to take them."

"Yes. And once you told me that I should call if I ever needed you. They were probably just the words you needed to say at the time, but I—"

"You know better than that," he snapped, the bedside manner gone. She took comfort in the anger. He *did* care. He always had.

"He won't find out," she said. "Or maybe if he does, he won't care. It's been so long."

Silence. He was waiting for her to talk herself out of fantasy and back to reality.

"I know," she said. "If he learns, he will care."

"He doesn't forget promises. The terrible one he made to you…he certainly will not forget that."

"No."

She could hear his breath moving in and out like the tide, and she could picture his face, the way his mouth tightened at the corners and his eyes narrowed when he pondered a dilemma. He would nod his head slowly as if listening to options and opinions from voices no one else could hear.

"I shouldn't have involved you," she said. "There's no one to help me, not against him. Turn to the FBI again? No. He's too connected across too many layers, Doc. You know that."

"I wouldn't look for government assistance," he admitted.

"That leaves nothing. Because there is no one crazy enough to take him on. Not with the network that comes with him." *Black-water on steroids.* An international network of contractors, killers, spies, and informants. Diminished in strength now, perhaps, but wasn't that what people had said about the KGB? You presumed weakness at your peril.

"There might be someone."

"*Who,* Doc?"

Pause. "Maybe not anyone in a white hat, Leah."

"What does that mean?"

"There might be an option," he said gently. "*Might* be. But he's not the kind of hero that you have in mind."

"Could he protect my children? That's the *only* thing I've got in mind."

Pause. The soft breathing in her ear. Then: "Let me make a call."

6

Dax Blackwell was in Italy when the call came. The sun was just up and the streets of Bernalda were filling with sidewalk vendors for the weekend market. He'd come in pursuit of hot peanuts from the same vendor he saw every Saturday, and he was trying to contain his rage at the way the stooped old man made a point of shifting the bag of peanuts away from Dax's outstretched left hand and toward his right.

The old man thought this was a show of kindness. In the early weeks, Dax's left arm had been in a cast. The cast was gone now. The left arm, broken in seven places during an unfortunate morning when a woman had tried to run Dax over with a car, was getting better every day. The old man remembered it as a weakness, however, so he pushed the bag of warm peanuts toward Dax's right hand.

I could kill you with the left hand too, Dax thought. *I could kill you in twenty different ways with the right hand and maybe only a half dozen with the left at this point, but I could kill you nevertheless.*

Then the old man smiled and the phone rang and Dax pushed petty concerns from his mind. There was no profit in killing the peanut vendor, and Dax Blackwell wasn't a pro bono kind of guy. His was a family business, and while that sounded emotional, it was strictly practical.

Instead of killing the old man or even envisioning the best method for the task, Dax simply smiled and said *"Grazie"* and accepted the peanuts with his right hand. The vendor was almost a friend, after all; his peanuts were delicious and packed with protein and healthy fats. Restorative. Dax Blackwell had come to Bernalda to restore himself.

As he walked down the sun-splashed street toward the glistening Mediterranean, he shifted the bag from his right hand to his left, reached into his pocket, and grabbed his cell phone one ring before it went dead. After it rang twenty times, the caller would hear a dial tone.

Dax Blackwell didn't use voice mail.

"Hello?"

"Dax?"

The speaker's voice wasn't immediately familiar, but he'd used the right name, and he'd used it with the right hint of trepidation. "Who's asking?"

"Doc Lambkin."

Doc Lambkin. Dax had a vague recollection of the name, nearly none of the man. Once he had hired Dax's father and uncle for some work. Because Dax was a student of the killing trade, he'd been aware of his father's work since he was ten—and involved by the time he was fourteen. What he remembered of Lambkin was that Dax's father viewed him as a misplaced soul, a fundamentally moral man in a profoundly immoral business.

"We met in Perth, Australia," Lambkin said. "You probably don't remember. Your father brought—"

"I remember." Dax shook one shelled peanut into his mouth, cracked the shell with his teeth, and spit it out neatly. He'd become very accustomed to working with one arm now. When he was back to full strength with both, he'd be even more formidable. A man, like a bone, could strengthen along old fracture lines.

"I was a...mediator. A go-between. Not the client, but—"

"An ambassador of the Lowery Group," Dax said, and he smiled when he heard the sharp intake of breath on the other end of the line. Lambkin didn't like hearing the client's name said aloud. That was fine. Dax wasn't looking for work.

Also, his father and uncle hadn't particularly liked the Lowery Group. The Lowery Group had once protected their own operators while sending Dax's family members into a nearly suicidal situation. Suicidal work never intimidated a Blackwell, but they viewed it as poor form for employers not to provide them with the best possible intel beforehand. *Even the Alamo got a scouting report,* Dax's father had said. If Dax remembered correctly, J. Corson Lowery had also once refused to pay a bill. He couldn't recall the details of that one, but his family had spent many nights debating the situation and pondering recourses. They'd held off on killing the man, Dax remembered that. He'd been vaguely disappointed, but he understood the idea: a man had value when he could provide either money or protection, and there was a chance for Lowery to offer both in the future. Still, they'd been bitter about the situation, and as far as Dax knew, it remained the only unpaid tab on the ledger.

"Speak," Dax told Lambkin. "Unless you're going to deny the truth of what I just said, in which case don't waste my time."

"I was an employee of a security firm," Lambkin said, refusing to use the name. "Quite the memory you have."

"It's not so hard. Observe and think. Be considerate. Memory is about other people, when it comes right down to it. How much do you care? If you don't care, you don't remember."

A pause, and then a low, unamused laugh. "Your father's son," Lambkin said. "Yes, you are that. Your uncle was less...philosophical."

"Depended on the audience. He had his moments. You might recall that no one in my family worked for your *security firm* for many years. It was never a situation of high mutual trust. I'm surprised you think the circumstances have changed."

"I'm calling because I assume they haven't."

"Clarify that."

"I don't work for them anymore."

Interesting. Lambkin didn't strike Dax as the sort of man who'd go freelance. He'd been more of the vanishing kind. An off-the-grid move, perhaps, a retreat to someplace where he did nature photography or landscape painting and tried to forget old bloodstains.

"I'm also not looking for your services," Lambkin said. "I'm simply back in the mediator role. The *ambassador* role, if you prefer."

"But not for Lowery."

"No."

"Then who?"

"A woman who may find herself threatened by Lowery. A woman your father and uncle once rescued."

Dax stopped walking. Shook another peanut into his mouth, cracked the shell, spit out the shell. Waited.

"Did you hear me?" Lambkin said.

"Sure."

"No interest in that story?"

"I'm skeptical about your word choice," Dax said. "*Rescued*? If the woman wasn't family, and I'm quite sure she was not, then she probably paid for assistance."

"She paid," Lambkin acknowledged. "But not nearly as much as Lowery would have paid them to kill her."

This was the past-due bill, the one outstanding invoice. Dax felt his interest rise and tamped it down. Grudges were a fool's game. He'd been taught this from the beginning. "Can she outbid him now?" Dax asked.

"I...I don't intend to find out," Lambkin stammered. "The job is for her. Period."

Dax shook another peanut into his mouth. Didn't speak.

"It's a deal-breaker for you, then," Lambkin said. "Going up against that kind of outfit. I understand. The risk versus the reward is too high."

"That's your opinion of it?"

"It was my expectation, at least. It's one thing to work for them and something very different to work against them."

"And still you called."

"Wasted breath," Lambkin said resignedly.

"And still you called," Dax repeated.

"She's a good woman in a bad spot. She's alone. Just her and two children."

"Are you sleeping with her?"

"No."

"Prudent choice. You wouldn't want to be in bed with her when they come to murder the family."

"She's a good woman in a bad spot," Lambkin said again, "and all I promised her was that I would try. You're a clever young man. You understand that my options were limited. I shouldn't have called, though. It's too great a challenge. Any freelancer who took a job against an outfit with that reach and those resources would be on a suicide mission."

"You were hoping to send me on a suicide mission, then?"

"I was hoping to find someone who thought he'd at least have a chance of success. I don't think there are many with your family's...appetite for a challenge. Of course, you've seen the price of that now, so you know better."

Dax smiled. It was a tight, unpleasant smile. It had been a long time since his father and uncle died, and still he couldn't take remarks about their demise in stride. He didn't mind that, though. Why should you ever learn to take events of mortal consequence in stride? With your own loved ones, at least. That was the sticking point. He could make peace with events of mortal consequence for most of the world, himself included, but family? Family should be different.

This was how he had been raised.

"It's a good pitch," he told Lambkin. "I like every word of it. A little bait with the opponent, someone for whom I might already harbor feelings of resentment. Then an appeal to the heart—which was surprising, I have to say—with that reference to the woman and her children. The nostalgia of my family's past involvement. And finally, the taunt—saying that my father and uncle might've been bold enough for this job, but I am not."

"That's not what I was—"

"Come on."

Pause. "All right, the assessment is closer than I'd like. But it's not entirely accurate."

"What did I miss?"

"Sincerity," Lambkin said. "Every now and then, a bit of work will come your way with sincerity, Mr. Blackwell. The man in the middle won't have any skin in the game. He'll speak honestly to you, asking for the unique help that only a few people on the planet can provide. And if you accept, for one occasion at least, you'll have the pleasure of working with a clean heart if not clean hands."

"You wound me."

"I mean what I say. I've spent more decades in darkness than you know. There comes a time in our line of work when even a single clean day feels like a gift."

"Anyone who is in the crosshairs of people like Lowery is not living cleanly."

"You'd be surprised."

"I live in hope. But unfortunately, Mr. Lambkin, I'm not taking work at the moment."

"I'm not sure there is work at the moment. There may never be work. For that matter, she may already be dead."

"Happens to someone every day."

"Indeed. She understands this better than most. I said that I would make a call. I've done that, and you've declined to help. No one will be surprised. She probably had less faith in the possibilities than I did."

"It all sounds quite tragic."

Lambkin sighed. "Nothing more to say. You're declining, and I understand."

"Not exactly. You said there was no work yet. I said I wasn't working. So far, we seem to be meeting each other's needs just fine."

Don't toy with him. Don't leave the door cracked. Because a man like him will come back, and you know it.

On cue, Lambkin said, "So if I were to call again, you'd listen."

Dax rattled the peanuts. Stared across the bright street, the sunlight reflecting on pale stone.

"Yes," Dax said. "I will listen."

He hung up the phone and pocketed it. Opened and closed his hand, feeling the muscles work along the knitting bones. There was still a throb in the nerves near his elbow but it was a faint pain and he'd grown almost fond of it. It was the right kind of pain, the kind that didn't derail your future but didn't let you forget its point of origin either.

He shifted the bag of peanuts from one hand to the other and walked on down the dusty street toward the sea.

7

The first time Leah was alone with her children was in a grief counselor's office just down the hall from the courtrooms where custody was decided in cases where tragedy had struck the unprepared. Leah wasn't among the unprepared. Not on paper, at least. In front of the kids, though?

There was no preparation for that. They didn't know her, certainly didn't trust her.

"Why didn't you ever visit?" Nick asked. Nick, her sweet baby who had loved to reach for her earlobes with his chubby fist. He now had Doug's broad jaw and light complexion, a scattershot of faint freckles across each cheek.

"I should have," Leah said. "I know that, hon. It was a mistake, and I'm sorry. Your father and I didn't do a good job of staying in touch. But I should have visited."

"Yes," her son agreed. "You should have."

Beside Nick, Hailey kept a dubious eye on Leah. She didn't have any of Doug's features; she was all Leah. A lean face that could become a blade when she turned angry; dark embers of eyes beneath raven-black hair; the colt legs that Leah remembered from her own youth, that sudden summer of growth, what seemed like five inches in three months. Hailey was on her way to that now, standing only a few inches short of Leah's five nine.

"I think we should be able to stay with Mrs. Wilson or with the Copelands," Hailey said. "They actually *know* us. We know them. Mrs. Wilson is on the same street. She already said she'll take us!"

Leah listened, patient. The conversation was on a loop. It had been the same with the counselor, and now it was beginning to play again in their first minutes alone.

"Trust your father," Leah said. "You don't have to trust me. I haven't earned it yet. I will, I promise you that, but right now you need to trust your dad. He arranged all this because he loved you. Because he wanted to be sure you were always safe, always loved." She fought to keep the tremor out of her voice. "He established the guardianship agreement to protect you."

"He barely knew you! Our mom's been dead for ten years and just because you're her sister doesn't mean you have any right to...just *take* us."

"He established the guardianship agreement," Leah repeated.

"You could move in," Nick suggested. "Then we wouldn't have to move out."

Leah felt like she was flying, but there was no joy to this sensation. She was simply adrift, without touch or command.

"We will not be able to stay," she said. "I'm very sorry about that. But it isn't an option. We will be together, and we will be a family, but—"

"We are not a family!" Hailey snapped.

Her daughter was beautiful when she was angry. That intense face, those flashing eyes. Closer to a woman than a child now, but still with the same expressions she'd had as a little girl, the same—

Doubt. She has always looked at you with doubt.

Maybe not always, but it was the expression that Leah remembered most.

"You're all the family that I have," Leah said. "That means more to me than you know. It's sacred."

Hailey crossed her arms over her chest but didn't speak.

"You look like our mom," Nick said thoughtfully, tilting his head as if to consider Leah from a new angle. "Dad had a couple pictures. You look just like her."

Leah felt a momentary panic. Before she could answer, Hailey did.

"Mom's hair was fuller."

True. Leah's hair was quite thin along the line where a man had once torn a hank of hair and flesh from her skull. She wore it up almost always now, pulled back to hide the place where it would never grow again.

"She did have better hair," Leah said.

"And cheekbones," Hailey said, and then, flushing, "sorry, I don't mean—"

"It's fine." Leah suppressed a smile.

"They do look alike, though," Nick insisted, and Leah decided to redirect this conversation. The more time she spent under the microscope, the closer she would come to breaking down and telling them the truth. There would be a moment for the truth, but it was not now. It would come when they were ready. When she knew that they were safe.

"Well, we were sisters," she said. "There are always similarities, you know. What did your dad tell you about me?"

Nick answered immediately. "He said that you were the only person we should call if anything bad ever happened. And to do it fast."

Hailey shot him a reproachful look, but he didn't notice. He wiped his nose with the back of his hand and sat forward on the cheap sofa. "He said when we were older, we'd all get together then, but not until—"

"Nick, be quiet," Hailey said. "She doesn't get to just show up and ask questions."

"I do, though," Leah said, her voice soft but firm. "For better or worse, hon, I do, because for better or worse, I am your family. I know that is upsetting to you right now. But it's true. Your dad made sure you remembered who to call if you needed someone. That wasn't my instruction; that was *his*."

Hailey tried to pace away but the room was so narrow that she couldn't go far. There was a plastic plant in one corner of the room, a ridiculous imitation of a tropical tree, and Hailey leaned against the wall beside it as if seeking shelter.

"He told Hailey, mostly," Nick said. "I didn't get to practice the phone call."

Leah loved him so much for that undercurrent of petulance, the heartbreaking humanity of the little brother who didn't want to be left out. She was seeing the dynamic between them already, understanding it and loving it—Hailey the protector, and Nick wanting every privilege already granted to her, wanting the years between them to mean nothing.

"I saw you when you were young," Leah whispered to Hailey, who was still standing with her arms folded across her chest, her lithe frame almost trembling with fear and anger. "You don't remember it, but we were together, and I said that I had to go, and I promised that I would see you again sometime. I kissed your forehead. I told you..."

Her voice broke then, and a single tear ran from her left eye. She wiped it away and took a shuddering breath and tried to gather herself.

A small, sunburned hand touched hers. Nick reaching for her. Eleven years old and trying to comfort her. Leah had intended to project nothing but warmth and strength, but that single tear had thawed even Hailey, who pushed off the wall and took a step forward but didn't fully bridge the distance.

"I'm not trying to be awful," Hailey said, and Leah had to bite her tongue to keep the swell of emotion down.

"You're being so brave," Leah said, her voice thick. She cleared her throat. "You've both been so brave, and it's such a terrible time...all I can do is promise you that I am here to keep you safe. We will get through it together. Okay? Together."

Nick nodded. Hailey remained motionless.

"You need to trust your dad now," Leah said. "You know that he loved you. The two of you know that better than anything in the world, don't you?"

Silence. Nick nodding, Hailey watching.

"You trusted him," Leah said. "And he trusted me. I need you to remember that."

"Where are we going?" Nick asked.

Leah wondered about recording devices. It was supposed to be a grief counselor's office; why would they record? But you never knew. "We're going to my home," she said finally. "It will be your home now. You'll like it in time, I think. It is all going to take time."

Hailey finally broke her silence. "I don't want to go," she said. "I don't want to leave."

Leah gave her daughter a broken smile. "I know *exactly* how that feels. But sometimes we don't get a choice."

She tried to give them hugs then. Nick accepted, hesitantly at first, then squeezing her fiercely, and even though she understood that he would have hugged almost anyone on a day like this, it took her breath away. Her son. Her baby.

When she reached for Hailey, her daughter offered only a one-armed squeeze before pulling away, opening the door, and walking out.

Leah watched her go and thought, *That is fine. Because you called. You did the hardest thing. The rest is up to me.*

"We'll be okay?" Nick asked. A question, not even a hopeful one, just sincere.

"You'll be okay," Leah told him. "I promise."

8

She called Doc Lambkin, told him that she was safe, that the kids were with her, and that she'd seen no sign of trouble. Nonetheless, she said, was there any chance he'd made his call?

He had.

"And? If I need help—I mean, if I need...that kind of help..."

"I'm not sure."

She tried not to let fear creep into her voice. "I don't think I will need any. I think it is all behind me and will stay there."

"I think so too."

"It's just that, knowing the man the way I do, I wanted..."

"I know."

"Just for peace of mind. A break-glass-in-case-of-emergency option."

"My contact might still be that. I wouldn't rule him out."

"Who is he?"

Doc went quiet for a moment. "Very young, but experienced. A very...unique pedigree."

"Does he know Lowery?"

"Not personally. By reputation, though. He is not a fan. His family had some dealings."

That made her nervous. She did not like the idea of a family history, of any overlap. She trusted no one except Doc.

"What dealings?"

"Well...they helped you once," he said hesitantly.

For a moment, she was confused. Then it came in a flash— the men on the Florida back road, their detached dialogue, their absolute disinterest in her even as they arranged her hair and blood judiciously on the headrest.

"Those sociopaths?" she said, at once both afraid and, perversely, encouraged.

Because they *had* helped, hadn't they?

Still, she could smell her own blood and see their flat, affectless eyes.

"Not exactly. They're dead, in fact. But there's family. A young one who—"

"I won't need him," she said. "I won't need anyone who is at all like...like those two. I'm safe. The kids are safe."

"I suspect you're right. But if anything—*anything*—makes you feel otherwise? Call me and let's see if we can indeed break that glass."

That afternoon, she went to see their house. She went without the kids, because they were with friends and families of friends, with the supportive love of people they knew. Mrs. Wilson, for example, who had two older children, both in college, and was sincere in her offer to take Nick and Hailey in. She was petite and round-cheeked and spoke with a sweet Southern accent and looked as if she probably baked pies from scratch.

Leah hated her.

She'd had to meet these people, though. Had to linger long enough that taking the kids didn't seem like a kidnapping. After that, she'd gone to meet with the attorney who had filed the standby guardianship. He was a thin man of about fifty with wire-rimmed glasses and thinning sandy hair. He wore an out-dated suit and had University of Kentucky cuff links and worked alone in an office that his father had worked in before him. He specialized in estate and probate law and had no experience in criminal practice. Leah thought that Doug had made a perfect choice. Everett Spoonhour was a qualified and competent attorney but the furthest thing from the sort of man who might overlap with the Lowery Group.

He'd walked her through the process of executing the guardianship, assured her that he'd do what he could to expedite it, and said that he would see that Doug's assets were transferred into a trust for the children as his will required. He also asked for her home address.

When she hesitated, he looked up, one eyebrow raised. Not suspicious, just perplexed. The question shouldn't have stumped her.

"It's a post office box," she said. "That's the only address I have. So just put box three seventy-three, Greenville, Maine."

"For mailing, no problem," he said. "But I'm going to need to have a physical address so the necessary home visits can be done."

"Of course," she said, trying not to show alarm, trying to believe that it was completely unreasonable to imagine that J. Corson Lowery would even be aware of Doug's death, let alone look into it with such scrutiny as to find his way to these documents.

But she still couldn't bring herself to do it. Instead, she told him that she owned multiple homes in Maine—true enough, if you considered six collapsing cabins to be homes—and that she wasn't sure yet which would be the best choice for the children. "Let me call you with that, please? I just need a day or two to get my head wrapped around all of this. Look into things like school districts and…and everything."

Mr. Spoonhour nodded sympathetically and made a notation in his file.

"Could I see their house?" she asked.

"Pardon?" He looked up with that single cocked eyebrow again.

"If it's possible for me to just walk through or at least have a look at it before they're with me, I think it would help. Everything is new to me. I want to understand where they're coming from so I make decisions about where we are going to go. Does that make sense?"

"Certainly, Ms. Trenton."

And so off they'd gone to see the home where the man she'd once loved had raised their children. It was in a subdivision of brick homes with oversize garages and wide lawns and clean sidewalks. There was a neighborhood watch program and a dog park and mature shade trees everywhere you looked. The air was scented with flowers and freshly cut grass. She stood on the front porch, taking it all in. A place of safety, security, stability. A neighborhood where any mother would want to raise her children.

You did so well by them, Doug, she thought, and then she thought of her own house. It was nearly two miles from a paved road, and there was no neighbor in sight. A brook ran through the ravine to the north of it, but you couldn't see the water from the house because the pines grew so thick, so dark. The backyard wasn't an open expanse of grass for games or swing sets; it was a steep, granite-lined slope that offered majestic views of the valley below in the winter.

In the winter, when brutal winds blew snow down by the foot, all but the main arteries of Piscataquis County were closed to car traffic. Even on the open roads, you weren't going anywhere without snow tires or chains. Get farther out, and you weren't going anywhere without a snowmobile. She had literally no idea where the closest neighbors with children lived. She heated with a mixture of a woodstove and supplemental propane. Had Nick and Hailey ever seen a woodstove?

"Ms. Trenton?"

She shook herself out of her reverie and looked back at Everett Spoonhour. He was standing in the threshold, holding the door open for her.

"Thank you," she said, and she stepped into her family's home for the first time.

Ahead of her was an open-concept floor plan, the kitchen with its gleaming stainless-steel appliances and bright white cabinetry looking out across a living room with vaulted ceilings and a sectional sofa that wouldn't fit inside Leah's house. She didn't have a sofa, in fact. She had a recliner, a rocking chair, and a dog bed.

Everett Spoonhour was babbling about the home being lovely, complimenting the kitchen island and the range vent hood as if he were a real estate agent. At length he must have realized his nervous energy wasn't helping and he fell silent, following her from room to room rather than guiding her.

It was like visiting a place you'd dreamed of but had never actually seen. Familiar yet foreign, surreal and frightening. School pictures on the fridge. Children's handmade artwork on shelves. A trampoline in the backyard—with a net to prevent a harmful fall.

Safety. *Keep them safe, Doug, please, just keep them safe.*

And he had. For so long, he had.

Hailey's room and Nick's were large and separated by a shared bathroom with a double vanity, a shower, and a tub. Someone had painted a rainbow on the wall above the tub. She stared in at this time capsule of a life she'd never known, then cleared her throat and said, "May I see my husband's room?"

"Pardon?"

The authentic confusion in Spoonhour's voice jarred her back into the moment, and she realized what she'd said. "Brother," she amended and forced a laugh that came out too high and too harsh, echoing in the bathroom like a seal's bark. "In-law. Brother-in-law, that's who he was!"

Everett Spoonhour blinked at her and frowned. "Are you all right?"

"Fine, fine. Really." She waved a hand. "I'm just lost in my own thoughts. May I see my *brother-in-law's* room, please." Another forced laugh, this one closer to human.

He led her down the hall to where the master bedroom waited. She counted her steps as she trailed behind him, feeling like a death-row inmate on that infamous Green Mile. She knew the things in Doug's bedroom might be difficult to bear, all the evidence of a life without her, maybe photographs of other women, other loves. She could brave those for the one thing she had to see, though.

The bed was across the room, facing a bay window that would get the eastern light each morning. There was a nightstand next to it—but just one. She was embarrassed by how much this pleased her; he'd deserved love and she hoped he'd found it. She just didn't want to imagine it.

She crossed to the bed, and now she could smell him. There was nothing so powerful as sensory memory. If she closed her eyes and breathed deeply, she thought, she'd be able to taste him. But Everett Spoonhour prowled behind her and so she did the only thing she'd come here to do.

She walked around the bed to that lone nightstand, leaned down, and inspected the lamp. A length of monofilament fishing line was looped over the switch of the lamp, and on the end dangled a platinum ring with a small but sparkling diamond.

Nina, will you marry me?

She closed her eyes despite herself now, reaching out and touching the ring with her fingertips. She slipped it toward her left ring finger. It slid right on, the weight familiar.

Yes. I will—

"What's the story with the ring?" Everett Spoonhour said.

Leah opened her eyes and slid the ring off her finger and let it swing back and forth on the fishing line. "It was his wife's," she said. "My sister's. She died. He kept the ring on the bedside lamp."

She watched it arc, glimmering, and ignored Spoonhour's soft, sorrowful utterances about this crazy, unfair world.

The ring was their last promise, nearly as crucial as Hailey's phone call. The ring told her that Doug hadn't been afraid, that he'd had no reason to believe the family was in danger. There would be days when he'd feel otherwise, he had told her. He was sure of that. And if anything ever happened, she should look for that ring. If it was gone, he'd had reason to be concerned, and that meant that so did she. That meant that Lowery had come.

But the ring was there.

"Do you want to see anything else?" Spoonhour asked.

"Sure," she said, although in fact she didn't. It was time to leave Doug's bedside, though. The ring was swaying to a stop on its length of fishing line, pulling out of the sunlight and into the shadow, its sparkle gone.

She turned and left Doug's bedroom and did not look back.

They wandered through the rest of the house. While her movements were aimless now that she'd seen the ring, she wasn't merely killing time. She wanted to see it all, to know the place her children had called home. It was a beautiful house. In the basement, a bonus room was filled with toys and games and there were beanbag chairs and a video-game console and a Ping-Pong table. A suburban child's Xanadu.

There were pencil marks on the door trim showing Nick's growth, each mark labeled with dates and heights. The last one had been made a week before Doug's death. Nick was closing in on five feet. Leah traced the lines with her index finger and envisioned her own home in Maine through their eyes: The darkness she treasured because of the stars it revealed. The mournful call of the owl that lived along the ravine; the playful yips and yowls of the coyotes that passed through in the night. The winter mornings when the sun glared off cratered snowdrifts. All of the challenges and beauty that she'd embraced, alone, to forge a new life.

They would be terrors to Nick and Hailey. She looked at the video games and thought, *I can't even get Wi-Fi.*

Then she thought of the postcard that Ed had reminded her of. The one she'd sent from Camden, where the library stood sentry above the harbor and its waterfall, where she'd seen kids riding bikes on paths that wound through the waterfront, where charming New England homes lined streets with wide sidewalks.

"I will find the right place," she said aloud. She'd almost forgotten Everett Spoonhour's presence until the attorney spoke.

"I'm sure you will. Whatever help you need, my office is here to provide. I know that doesn't feel like much."

"Thank you. I appreciate it."

He looked at her sadly and said, "It's a shame about your family."

"Pardon?"

"Such a small family," he said, offering an awkward smile. "I grew up with a huge extended family. Reunions felt like stadium events. With it just being the three of them, and then you…" He lifted a hand. "I'm sorry, I don't mean to go on. I was just thinking that you must feel very alone right now."

"I've learned to live with feeling very alone," Leah told him. "What I've got to do now is learn to live the other way."

She chewed on her lip and looked at the room with all its trappings of childhood happiness.

"I will find the right place," she repeated.

9

There had been few constants in Doc Lambkin's life, but the sea was always there. Even when he'd lived in landlocked places, they'd merely been stopovers between him and a better boat. When the work no longer seemed worth doing, he'd find his way to a shipyard where custom teak was being shaped or sanded and he'd remember why money mattered.

Boats weren't cheap.

From his home in Friday Harbor, Washington, he could look out of nearly any window and see the gray expanse of the Strait of San Juan de Fuca and his forty-two-foot Catalina in the deep-water harbor and know that while not all of his choices had been good, at least he'd never lost the purity of wind and sea.

Today, he motored into the sound and then raised the sails. The wind was blowing at five knots, carrying him toward the sun. The boat heeled gently, fine spray touched his face, and he closed his eyes and breathed in the sea.

"Peaceful, isn't it?" a voice said.

Doc opened his eyes and saw the man in the black baseball cap standing belowdecks, looking up at him. His hands were in the pockets of a gray hooded sweatshirt, and while there was surely a weapon in one of them, his posture was casual and indifferent. He was young, early twenties at most, and looked younger. He had a quality that would have made Doc's mother compare him to Eddie Haskell on *Leave It to Beaver*. Doc's mother had been dead for years. Doc thought that he was about to join her.

"Young Master Blackwell," he said. "You are very good, aren't you? Very quiet." Doc had been on the boat for nearly an hour now, if you counted the time at the dock, and he'd been belowdecks twice. There wasn't much space down there, and Doc was a man who noticed things. He had not noticed Dax Blackwell.

"Don't feel bad," Dax said. "You've had a lot of quiet years. Out of practice. It happens."

Doc looked at him and felt the tiller under his palm and entertained the idea of knocking it hard to port and seeing if he couldn't upset the young killer's impeccable balance. What would it gain, though? Time enough for Doc to jump overboard and drown slowly instead of being shot fast? His escaping days were in the past. He left the tiller alone and sighed.

"You hung up after talking to me and called Lowery himself, is that the way it went?" Doc asked. "Now you kill Nina and you kill me and you make far more money. Bravo."

"Not true," Dax said. "And such a cynical outlook."

He had a handsome face with blue eyes that promised honesty, which was amusing in a family like the Blackwells. He had his father's voice and personality but he looked more like his uncle.

"Come on up here," Doc told him. "Talk to me in the sun. Or doesn't that suit you?"

"You've had too much sun," Dax Blackwell said. "I've got old boots that look better than your skin. Cancer's no joke, you know."

His right hand emerged from his sweatshirt pocket. It was empty. He used it to grasp the rail as he walked up the steep steps and onto the deck. He kept his left hand in the pocket. He came up onto the deck and stood facing Doc with an upturned lip, a 10 percent grin.

"You're scared of me," he said.

"You're a contract killer who was hiding on my boat. Yes, I'm scared of you."

"Put like that, it sounds reasonable." Dax crossed the deck and eased onto the bench seat on the port gunwale across from Doc. He did not watch his feet while he walked. That was unusual for a novice on a sailboat.

"How old are you?" Doc asked. He was trying to do the math. The last time he'd seen Dax had been in Australia. Dax had looked like a child but he had probably already killed a half dozen men. It was hard to say. His father would bring him into the business and then take him back out, and in between the kid was just a ghost. Nobody knew where he was or who raised him or how.

"'Old enough to party,'" Dax said. "What movie?"

Doc blinked. "Excuse me?"

"Google it." He crossed his legs at the ankles and leaned against the gunwale. His left hand stayed in his pocket. "You haven't called me back. Does that mean your friend is already dead?"

"I hope not."

Dax squinted at him as the sunlight angled off the water. "You really don't know?"

Doc shook his head. The mainsail needed to be let out and he started to reach for the sheet automatically, then stopped. "You mind if I move around a little?"

"Why would I mind? It's your boat."

Doc leaned down, flicked the sheet out of the cam, let out the sail, then cleated the sheet again. "If she needs help, she hasn't called me, which is why I didn't call you. And yet you're here. On my boat."

Dax shrugged. "I had time."

Silence. The wind freshened. Doc adjusted the tiller. They heeled slightly, and Dax shifted as if he'd anticipated the change. His left hand stayed in his pocket.

"You never named a price," Dax said. "Is there money to be had?"

"Whatever she has. It wouldn't be a sum that impresses you."

Dax nodded. His face was shadowed beneath the baseball cap.

He had stopped looking at Doc and was watching the receding shore of the island. "Did you call anyone else?"

Doc shook his head.

Dax's 10 percent smile widened to 20. "There's a reason you picked me. Go on and say it."

"I made a mistake. I'm sorry."

"I didn't come here to listen to you apologize. I certainly didn't come here to listen to you lie."

The smile was gone now.

Doc wet his lips. He watched Dax's left hand and wondered about the weapon it held. Gun or knife? It ultimately didn't matter. He would be very good with both.

"Lowery is an…unusual target," Doc said. "There aren't many people who would work against him, and there are plenty who would tell him that I'd inquired. I thought you might not fit into either of those categories."

"And? Keep telling me the reasons. I think there's one you're neglecting. Probably because you think that I don't know about it."

"I believe your father considered it an unsettled score," Doc said carefully. "Perhaps I was wrong."

"Considered *what* unsettled?"

"A bill, for one. He never paid them because they didn't follow his instructions."

"For one. What's the other?"

Doc met his eyes again. "Lowery set them up once. They were supposed to die."

Dax looked older and colder now. His gaze did not waver. "Then why didn't they die?"

"Because they shot their way out. They were very good. Very fast."

"And yet they are still dead now. Even being fast and good."

Doc acknowledged that with a nod.

"So it's not a job that would appeal to me for money or for simplicity," Dax said. "It would require deeper motivation. The betrayal narrative. Or, as you put it, the unsettled score."

Doc didn't speak. His hand ached from holding the tiller so tightly. He loosened his grip and breathed and waited. What would happen would happen and he was not going to stop it.

"If my father and my uncle cared so deeply about these betrayals, why didn't they try to settle that score? Years passed. Why didn't they take a shot at him?"

"I always expected they might."

Dax looked at the top of the mast. With his face exposed to the sunlight, a single thin scar was visible along the right side of his jaw. Too narrow to have been left by a blade. Glass, maybe.

"They killed for money or to protect themselves," he said. "Their minds were not clouded by anger or grudges or unsettled scores."

"I see," Doc said.

"Who is the woman?" Dax said, his eyes still on the top of the mast.

Doc turned this over in his mind. There was no reason to believe he wouldn't die here on his boat and thus no reason to give Dax the name, but there was also little reason for Dax to have come all this way just to kill him. If he'd come for the truth, then Doc's original gambit hadn't been a mistake.

"Her name was Nina Morgan," he said. "She was his son's pilot."

"Lowery's son. Brad."

"Yes."

"He's dead. Suicide."

"Yes."

Dax finally looked away from the mast. "What's the connection between that and Nina Morgan?"

What was the connection? Doc thought back on it and wondered how to condense months of madness into a concise explanation.

"Corson did not want the son to be anything like him except when it came to power," he said. "Corson would build the infrastructure of power, and he would use it to his son's benefit. I think that was the idea. But then it turned out the son wasn't that different from the father."

Doc thought that he needed to choose his words very carefully now. When you talked of fathers and sons with Dax Blackwell, you ventured onto thin, black ice.

"Corson Lowery lived for his son," he continued. "Every dollar, every deal, every leveraged politician. It was all about Brad's reach, Brad's power, Brad's future. The father's ambitions were the son's achievements. Joe Kennedy had nothing on Corson. Neither did Fred Trump. Pick your preferred political example."

"I'm firmly independent," Dax said.

"My point is, Corson believed he could raise a clean man within a corrupt house."

Those *eyes*. Those remarkable Blackwell eyes. How he remembered them. Dax's father and uncle had never looked at each other, it seemed. They talked—oh, how they would talk—but their bond was like wolves', an understanding so deep and innate that neither one ever needed to look at the other; they simply acted in tandem, each confident of the other's response. They moved through both physical space and conversations like deadly dancers. Dax had the same eyes, but he was alone, and so Doc did not have an excuse to look in another direction. He wished for one now but he made himself hold the stare.

"Nature versus nurture," Dax said. "Corson wasn't counting on what he could not influence. What was in the blood."

Doc waited.

"So the son is dead but the empire isn't," Dax said. "There was a federal investigation. It went away. Why?"

"Because the target was Brad, and Brad went away." Doc shrugged. "People need to maintain an appetite to see corruption taken apart. If there's a figurehead for it, and the figurehead falls, well…"

"People fool themselves into thinking something bigger was accomplished. Sure. Can an organization outlive its figurehead, though? That's a question of culture." Dax's 10 percent smile was back. Doc did not know if this was a good thing or a bad thing.

"It's an excellent question," Doc said uneasily.

"What about Nina? What was she a witness to?"

"A murder." Doc felt the old sadness rise. "A witness and the witness's children. Their car was hit leaving the airport. It was supposed to look like cartel work."

Dax sat and thought about it, then said, "The son's sins do not mean a thing to the father; all that matters is he was driven to put the gun in his mouth because of this woman's testimony."

"I think so," Doc said. He indicated the mainsail. "May I?"

"I keep telling you, it's your boat."

"Right." Doc adjusted the sail again and altered course, moving with the wind, farther offshore.

"How'd she stay alive this long?" Dax asked.

Doc took his time cleating the mainsheet. "I hid her."

"You did."

"Yes."

"Why?"

"Because she came to me for help." He cleared his throat. "Because I introduced her to the agents who were investigating Brad. Because I encouraged her to cooperate."

"I have this troubling sense that you're leaving something out, Doc. I've never liked ambiguous stories. You know the kind— where we walk out of the theater together and I think the ending meant one thing but you think it meant another?"

Doc smiled. "You're your father's son," he said. "That you are."

Dax did not smile, and his eyes showed that he didn't like the reference. "What are you leaving out?" Dax said.

"I never testified. Nina had my assurance that my cooperation would come in time. She was batting leadoff, and I'd come in as cleanup, you might say. But…"

"Right," Dax said. "But." He shifted his weight and leaned back again, still with the left hand in his pocket. "So your controlled situation spun out of control, and this woman, Nina, was left twisting in the wind. You helped her hide because otherwise, well, a man might feel guilty about the way things played out."

"A man might," Doc said.

"That has been a number of years now."

"Almost ten exactly."

"So how'd she come back on the radar? And why isn't she already dead?"

Doc told him about the husband and the two children and the aunt they'd never met but had been trained to call in an emergency. He told him about the way it had all unraveled in a one-car accident in Kentucky. Dax listened and did not speak until the story was done.

Then he said, "Nina's problem would seem to solve itself."

"How's that?"

"If Lowery is dead, her problem is gone." No change in his expression.

"Possibly. There are others, though. At least two who would be…quite motivated. The men who hit the car with the witness and her children flew back on Nina's plane. She identified them to investigators."

"Are they good?"

Doc understood what he meant. "They are very good," he said. "Bleak—excuse me, Marvin Sanders—is better than anyone I've ever seen."

"Who's the other one?" Dax asked.

"Randall Pollard. They're in prison, though. As far as I know, they'll remain in prison for a few years more, at least."

"Because of Nina?"

"Ultimately. They were the low-hanging fruit the feds had to settle for once Brad ate his gun. She got investigators to the right place for some surveillance videos, I believe."

"Those two didn't turn on Lowery? Why go to prison for him?"

"I suspect they'll find a friendly parole board someday and walk out as very, very rich men."

"Lowery remains their benefactor. I see. Then, ideally, you'd kill them whether they're in prison or not. You'd take all three of them out of the game to solve her problems. That's a lot of work. All to save a woman who got herself in trouble because you were hiding from it. And a woman who doesn't have enough money to pay for one fix, let alone three."

Doc didn't speak.

"She still trusts you too," Dax said. "You helped put her into the mess, but she still thinks you got her out of it."

The wind had changed, and while Doc didn't feel the need to ask for permission to adjust sails any longer, the bigger question loomed. "May I head back to the island?" he asked.

Dax smiled. "How else would you get home?"

There it was, floating between them. There was no reason for Doc to die out here, but Dax Blackwell might have other notions. The seconds stacked up and they sailed on, out into the open sea, the island fading farther behind.

"Take us home," Dax said at last, and Doc Lambkin exhaled from his very core.

"Thank you," he said.

"For what?"

"For...considering Nina's—Leah's—situation."

"Well, I'll need operating money. That will do for now."

"Operating money?"

"For the job."

"There is no job."

Dax Blackwell yawned.

"She might be fine," Doc said. "The job was to help if she needed help. But I haven't heard from her yet, so she might be absolutely—"

"Prepare to come about."

"What?"

"Aren't you supposed to say that when you turn a sailboat?" Dax Blackwell said. "You've got to turn the boat to go back to the island. And when you turn a boat, the boom swings. If you're not communicating properly, it could lead to a nasty accident. A captain must issue commands to avoid tragedy at sea."

Doc just stared at him.

"I'll say it, then," Dax said. He cupped his right hand to his mouth and then, in an Australian accent, called out, "Prepare to come about." He smiled at Doc, a broad, infectious grin, and nodded enthusiastically. "Do it, then."

Doc Lambkin brought the boat around and sailed for his island home.

"Do you know any sea shanties?" Dax said.

"I do not."

"No man should have a boat and not know a few sea shanties," Dax said. "It should be outlawed."

"I'm sorry."

"It can be fixed." Dax rested his right arm on a stanchion and broke into song. " 'Oh, I am not a man-o'-war nor a privateer,' said he. Blow high, blow low, and so sailed we. 'But I'm a salt-sea pirate, a-lookin' for me fee.' "

He had a gorgeous tenor voice. Soothing.

"Do you mind if I continue?" Dax asked. "It enhances the experience, I think."

"By all means," Doc said.

Dax smiled, picked up the jib sheet from where it rested in a neat coil, and ran the thin line through his fingers with the appreciation of a man who knew good rope. He looked almost blissful, sitting there with the line in his hands, crooning his soft, age-old song. Doc looked away from him, back at the open ocean, and watched the wake spread behind them as they sailed on through the sunlit sea while Dax Blackwell sang. He had a truly beautiful voice. Doc wondered if his father had taught him how to sing. He wondered if it would be foolish or dangerous to ask. He was still wondering this and Dax was still singing when the noose dropped over Doc's head and pulled tight against his throat.

He dropped the tiller and grabbed the line with both hands, but Dax was already drawing it back, the thin, strong rope so tight that it seemed to be of Doc's flesh now instead of encircling it. Dax was still singing. He hadn't even lost cadence.

"'Oh, I am not a man-o'-war, nor a privateer...'"

He hauled back on the line and Doc's feet went out from under him and now he was on his back on the bottom of his own boat, strangling.

Dax Blackwell stopped singing and smiled down at him.

"I have good news," he said. "I've decided to take the job. You're right—she deserves help. You may be right about one more thing—it could prove beneficial to do some work with clean hands. I don't think you're the man to tell me that, though. You betrayed the woman and yet you disguise yourself as her sole comfort in this cold world?" He shook his head sadly. "There's little honor in that, my friend."

Doc choked and clawed at his throat. His desperately searching fingernails carved bloody furrows through his skin. The rope didn't loosen. The breath he needed didn't come.

"If I take your advice," Dax Blackwell told him, "and attempt to work with a nice clean heart pumping nice clean blood to my nice clean hands, well, it simply couldn't be work I do for you, Mr. Lambkin. I'm sure you understand that."

Doc stared up at him. Begged with his eyes because he could

offer no words. Apologized with his eyes for the words he'd already offered. He had meant no offense by suggesting that Dax work with clean hands. He'd never meant to offend a Blackwell. He had lived this long because he knew better than to do such a thing. If he lived longer, he would not repeat the error. He stared at Dax and tried to convey all of this as the world went gray at the edges, as all eternity tunneled in on that smiling, earnest young face.

"So let's start clean," Dax said. "And see how it goes."

He put his boot on Doc's shoulder to hold him down while he hauled up on the rope, tightening it and tightening it until all that remained of Doc's vision went dark.

10

The sun was shining and a light summer breeze teased the pines when Leah and the kids arrived at her cabin, western Maine in all of its summer glory. Vacationland—the way life should be.

She turned off the paved road and onto the packed dirt that led into the forested hills. It was a dry day and the gleaming new Jeep was soon covered with dust that shimmered in the filtered sunlight.

"This is your driveway?" Nick asked with barely contained horror.

"No. This is the road," Leah said.

"What?"

"It's just a summer place. You know, for vacations. On perfect days like this," Leah said of her year-round home. A pine bough whisked across the passenger side of the Jeep, and Hailey leaned back as if it might puncture the window and snatch her.

"People save money for years to come up to a place like this in the summer," Leah said, trying again, and right then the Jeep found a moon crater of a pothole that knocked them all back in their seats. "They'll grade the road soon," she added. "Smooth it right out."

"What town are we in?" Hailey asked.

"Um...well, let's say Greenville."

"Let's *say* Greenville?" Hailey echoed. "Are we in it or not?"

"Technically, these areas are just numbered and lettered. Township and range. To everyone who knows the area, though, I live on the Caya Camp Road. To anyone who doesn't know the area, you'd just say Greenville."

She turned right, crunched through another pothole, and clawed up the rutted slope through the packed pines. Home sweet home.

"In Camden, you'll have your own rooms," she said. "Here, it's going to be a little tight. But it's just for a few nights. Just so I can show you the place."

For all of her warnings, the sensation of *home* that swept over her at the sight of the low-slung log cabin with its forest-green metal roof and long porch was a physical relief, as if her pores had opened up and stress flooded out. When she cut the engine and heard Tessa's sweet, familiar bark, for a moment she felt right.

Hailey said, "There is no signal here. Like—*none.*"

Leah looked in the rearview mirror and saw her daughter holding her phone with a horrified expression.

"I know," she said. "There are some spots up higher, where on a clear day…" She stopped before she did any more damage.

"Luke was going to call," Hailey said. Luke was the boyfriend. The fourteen-year-old heartthrob who played football and base-ball and somehow still managed to FaceTime Hailey on a nearly hourly basis.

"One night," Leah said. "Maybe two."

"It's fine," Hailey said, making more of an effort at enthusiasm than Leah had expected. "I'll just use the Wi-Fi."

"About that…"

"You're kidding? There *is* Wi-Fi. There's got to be—"

"In Camden," Leah said, "you will have Wi-Fi. We're just taking a break here, okay? That's all. A short break."

Nick said, "Is that your dog?" and Leah couldn't have been more grateful for the distraction.

"Yes," she said, opening the Jeep door and getting two muddy front paws in her lap as Tessa wagged her tail so hard, her entire back end joined the mix. "This is Tessa. Let's go say hi."

While Tessa occupied the kids, Leah went up the porch steps, unlocked the door, and stepped inside. The cabin had been her home for seven years and yet it was as if she'd never seen it before. She remembered her first entrance, the way the old man who'd been selling it looked her up and down and said, "It'll work for a wintah camp but I expect you're more interested in the summah."

Judgmental, yes, but not inaccurate. The cabin had intimidated her. She'd been more Nina than Leah back then. More summah than wintah.

She'd made it work, though. She'd remade the cabin and remade herself and somewhere along the way, the place ceased to feel foreign and started to feel like home.

Nails clicked on the hardwood as Tessa galloped up the porch steps, came inside, and leaned her weight against Leah's thigh.

"Hey, baby. I missed you too." Leah rubbed the dog's velvet ears. Tessa licked her hand. Then they both turned in unison and looked back at the two kids walking up the steps. "Our family," Leah whispered to the dog. "Can you tell they are mine? Do you know?"

She didn't rule it out. She believed dogs were more intuitive than people.

Nick and Hailey eyed the cabin as if it might be a trap, pausing at the threshold and waiting for Leah to beckon them farther inside.

"Come on," she said, and Tessa trotted away from her and back to the kids. Nick reached for her with a hesitant hand, and he got a lick too. Yes, the dog knew. Somehow, Leah was sure of it.

"I'll give you the tour," she said and then felt ridiculous—there were only four rooms, and with all of the doors open, you could see into them from anyplace in the main room. "It's not a big place. In Camden, you'll have more space."

"Who took all the pictures?" Nick asked, gazing at the framed photographs crowding the walls. Leah had long ago given up on any feng shui approach to hanging her art. She liked the pictures more than the proper arrangement of them.

"I did."

"Really?" He walked over to a close-up of a fox with a snow-dusted muzzle, then moved on to a black bear in the middle of a creek with one paw lifted, throwing a bright spray of water across the frame. "You were that close to a bear?"

"I had a good lens," Leah said, though in fact she had been that close to the bear.

"This is what you do for work?"

"Part of it," she acknowledged. She'd told them about the wild-life photography along with the guiding and the camps. She had not told them that she could abandon any source of revenue and exist without noticing its absence. Her association with the Lowery Group hadn't made her a rich woman, but it had certainly made her a financially independent one. A decade of rural Maine living during a bull market hadn't hurt either. Even without Doug's trust, they would be fine. How to explain this, though? How to explain any of her past? She wasn't sure what to reveal or when to reveal it. The biggest thing, the only revelation that mattered, being the hardest: *I'm your mother. I brought you into this world. I felt your first kicks, heard your first cries, watched your first—*

"Who is Ed?" Hailey said from behind them.

Leah turned and blinked at her daughter. "Pardon?"

Hailey held up a sheet of paper that was on the counter beside a vase of fresh-cut wildflowers. "He left a note."

"Oh. Thank you."

Hailey handed it over but repeated the question. "Who is Ed?"

There was a bristle to her, and Nick was watching, and Leah

suddenly felt as if she were aligned in their crosshairs. *They don't want anybody playing dad. They don't even want to be with me. But at least I'm...family.*

"He's a friend," she said. "He took care of Tessa."

The note was simple, nothing intimate, just a welcome-back. He'd filled the wood rack and changed the bedding. He hoped everyone was doing okay. He would come by when they were settled in.

She read the note and set it back on the counter beside the vase of asters. Hailey had drifted across the room to a framed map of Maine.

"We're on Moosehead Lake?"

"Yes. Near there."

Hailey located the big lake and placed her finger on it. Then she eyed the rest of the state. Everything that indicated civilization was down and to the right, crowded in southern Maine. Everything near her fingers and above it was empty, unbroken by highway lines or towns. Just lots of blue water and green forest. As Leah watched, Hailey began to trace the map with her fingertip, following the winding blue line of the Allagash River. Leah was confused; she was tracing it backward, moving north to south. Then she remembered that her children had known only the Midwest. Rivers there emptied southward, to the Mississippi and out to the Gulf of Mexico. Hailey had probably never encountered a river that flowed north.

"It's cold in here," Nick said.

Leah didn't think so, but she said, "I'll get a fire going. Warm it right up."

"But it's summer," he said, wandering to the window and staring out at the stacked pines beyond. "If it's cold in August, what is it like here in the winter?"

Breathtaking, Leah thought. *Brutal and beautiful. Up here in the winter, you remember just how small you are and how little you matter, and you find peace in that. You take your peace where you can find it, sometimes.*

"We won't be here in the winter, buddy," she said. "We'll be in Camden. Hailey, Camden is down on the right-hand corner of the—"

But her daughter had turned away from the map.

Leah set to work making the fire.

I I

The transfer schedule was for five prisoners, but just before the six a.m. pickup a change order came through, and five became two. They came from different cellblocks and were of different ages and one was white and the other was black and if you didn't bother to scrutinize their entire lengthy files, you would not know that they'd ever crossed paths previously.

The corrections officers at United States Penitentiary Coleman 2 in central Florida did not bother to look at the files, let alone scrutinize them. All they cared about was getting the men secured in the MG&L van and shipped off the property. No one cared much where they'd come from or where they were going. Prisoners were transferred in and out of Coleman every day. Most were bound for another cell or maybe a courtroom.

The COs who hadn't finished their morning coffee yet did not give a shit about the destination of Marvin Sanders or Randall Pollard.

The bulletproof MG&L van was a converted Ford Econoline with reinforced-steel grates separating the cargo area from the cab. There were three bench seats behind the grates, and aluminum bars ran alongside each seat at shoulder level and on the floor.

Sanders and Pollard were cuffed to the bars above and below. Chains allowed them to sit and granted about six inches of motion in any direction.

There was room for eight prisoners in the back of the van, but due to the change order, each inmate got his own bench row. They did not speak, did not exchange so much as a glance or a nod.

That boded well for the MG&L guys. It would be a nice, quiet ride. There were two representatives from the transport company, a driver and a guard. Both were white guys who looked like they'd just walked off the field following yet another year of failed tryouts for a pro football team.

They moved quickly through the process, though. No time wasted on small talk and no confusion with the paperwork. They'd done it before, many times. A lot of Americans believed the nation's prison system handled its own transportation. In reality, there were far too many inmates on the move for that. Private transport companies were the norm, and of late, private prisons were too.

MG&L vans passed through Coleman constantly. The driver and guard would be seen again, but they wouldn't be remembered as noteworthy.

Neither would Marvin Sanders or Randall Pollard. They had replacements en route. There were rarely empty cells.

Once the change order was processed and the transfer paperwork signed, the gates groaned open on heavy hinges, parting to reveal the road. The sun was a red band in the east, the humidity already so high the blacktop seemed to smoke in the rose-colored light.

The MG&L van headed toward the free world, the gates closed behind it, and Coleman prison went on about its day.

The van made its first stop in north Georgia. The driver exited the highway, turned onto a two-lane county road, and drove two miles to a truck stop. There he parked, killed the engine, and got out. The guard joined him. They spoke in hushed tones and smoked cigarettes and waited.

Ten minutes passed and then the door to the truck-stop diner opened and a tall man with thick, perfectly combed white hair and a golf-course tan walked out and crossed the parking lot in brisk strides. He moved well, far better than most men of his years. He wore jeans and a crisp white T-shirt under a lightweight blazer. His eyes were shielded by silver-framed Ray-Bans. He nodded at the MG&L driver and guard without speaking to them or slowing, then walked around the van to the far side and slid open the unlocked door. He leaned against the frame casually as he looked from one prisoner to the other.

"Randall," he said.

The white man was forty-four years old with a shaved head, stubble of beard, and corded neck muscles. His eyes were different colors, one brown and one green.

He nodded and said, "Good to see you, sir."

"Likewise. And you too, Bleak."

Marvin Sanders was thirty-nine years old, black, with a shaved head and no tattoos or distinguishing features whatsoever. He was utterly unremarkable except for his eyes, which were noticeable but for very different reasons than Randall Pollard's. Sanders's brown eyes matched perfectly, but they were so flat and unemotive that they somehow compelled immediate attention—and, often, immediate anxiety. Sanders, whom the white-haired man had called Bleak, did not nod or speak. He just waited.

The white-haired man smiled at this and seemed pleased.

"You ready to go missing?" he asked.

Randall Pollard chuckled and nodded. Marvin "Bleak" Sanders did not move or speak.

"It'll cost me," the white-haired man said. "You know that. Shit, we lose a few from time to time, accidents happen, and it's why you have insurance. But you boys? Yes, you two will cost me a little bit more. Insurance premiums might even go up. Wouldn't that be a bitch?" He sighed. "Such is the cost of doing business. We live in the age of liability. We protect ourselves the best we can."

The prisoners waited. They knew he wasn't through.

"I'll deal with the fallout," the white-haired man said. "Despite the cost. I may lose some money, and I may have to lose a few employees. Accountability matters. But I can handle that. Now, do either of you have a guess as to why I'm willing to take such risks for your freedom?"

They waited some more. Waited until at last he smiled a cold, empty smile.

"You get her," he said. "Lucky sons of bitches. You two drew *her*."

Silence. Randall shifted. Looked over his shoulder at Bleak. Bleak did not look back at him. Randall returned his attention to the white-haired man. When he spoke, his voice was lower than it had been before. "We get her, meaning we get..."

"Nina," the white-haired man said, and he nodded. "Yes, Randall. You get Nina."

"She's alive?" Bleak said, his voice soft but deep.

The white-haired man nodded, and the skin around his mouth and eyes tightened. "So it would seem," he said.

"Explain?" Bleak said.

A deep breath. "I monitored the husband and the children over the years. It felt necessary at one point because I'd never seen the body. But the years stacked up and she didn't visit and so I believed..." Again, the tightening around the mouth and eyes. "I trusted that the work that I'd been told was done had, indeed, been done. I took comfort in that. In knowing that she was dead. Last week, we received a death-index hit on the husband's new name. Those things can take weeks, I'm told, to reach the Social Security system." It was obvious how deeply he hated this fact—or any delay.

Pollard said, "Who clipped him?"

"No one. It was a car accident. But my curiosity was piqued. I arranged an inquiry into the whereabouts of the children. I understand that his sister took custody."

Pollard shifted. "So?"

"He didn't have a sister," Bleak said, and the white-haired man nodded.

"No," he said, his voice very soft. "He did not." He tossed a pair of black iPhones onto the seat beside Pollard.

"Details for the attorney who dealt with her are on the phones. Read and delete."

"Is she close?" Pollard asked.

"I'm not sure. Point last seen was Louisville."

"How fast to find her, do you think?"

The white-haired man shrugged. "Unknown. That's why it's you two."

"I ask only because it's a difficult thing, doing a job and disappearing at the same time."

"That's why it's you two," the white-haired man repeated. "If you don't think you can handle it, I can make sure the van delivers you back to prison, where things are less challenging."

"That won't be necessary."

"I thought not." The white-haired man nodded in the direction of the highway. "The boys will see to your escape up the road. You'll have a three-hour start and a clean vehicle. Licenses and passports are in the vehicle. Registration will come back to a construction company in Atlanta. Anyone asks, you're carpenters."

"No problem," Randall Pollard said. "I've used a hammer plenty of times. A drill too. Seen Bleak here make nice use of a miter saw once."

He laughed. Bleak didn't join in.

The white-haired man said, "Don't fuck it up."

"We won't."

"Hope not. You find her, and you call me. I want to be there at the end. I was supposed to be there the first time, and I will not— under any circumstances—trust someone who tells me that the job is done. I will do it myself. Understand that?"

Silence while he looked from Pollard to Bleak, confirming that they understood.

"That's all, then. Enjoy the fresh air, gents."

Pollard said, "Thank you, Mr. Lowery." Then he added, "We'll get her. No problem."

Bleak didn't utter a word. The white-haired man gazed at him for a few seconds, taking in the endless depths of those unblinking dark eyes, and then he smiled. "It's good to see you again, Bleak. It truly is. You were always the best of them."

Pollard didn't object to this assessment. Bleak didn't respond to it.

The white-haired man slid the van door shut, nodded once at the two employees of MG&L Security Transportation Solutions, a subsidiary of the Lowery Group, then walked back across the parking lot.

A black Range Rover was waiting, the motor already running.

12

Ed came by on the kids' second afternoon at the cabin, and Leah had never been so glad to see his battered Dodge Ram rattle up the drive and into the yard.

"This is my friend Ed," she said as Tessa bounded in delighted circles, herding him up to the porch of the cabin.

"Right—the *friend,*" Hailey echoed. Quiet scrutiny. That was Hailey.

Ed shook Leah's hand without visible affection. He seemed to read the situation easily enough; everything was new to the kids, and he was the newest thing, don't overload any emotional circuits.

"Good to see you, Trenton," he said.

Trenton? Trying too hard, maybe, but it was hard to blame him.

"You too," Leah said. "Thanks for watching Tessa."

"She watches me."

As if in affirmation, the dog gave his hand a playful nip.

Leah smiled and went through the introductions: "This is my niece, Hailey, and my nephew, Nick."

Hailey offered Ed a nod and a peace sign, a gesture Leah had never seen her make before and one that seemed more like a hex, warding him off. Ed returned the nod without stepping toward her. Nick charged forward, regarding Ed curiously.

"You're the hunting guide?"

"That's right."

"Do you have a gun with you?"

"It's not hunting season."

"So...no?"

"So no." Ed's grin seemed to draw Nick in.

Nick jutted a thumb at Leah. "She says you've killed moose and bears."

"Yep."

"She says she doesn't kill moose and bears. *Or* bears, I mean."

Ed shot Leah an amused glance from beneath his dusty Cabela's cap. "She finds them, though. She's better at that than me. If she wanted to start shooting something other than pictures, she'd run me right out of business."

Nick gazed at Leah with newfound respect. "Really?"

"Facts," Ed said. He leaned against the porch rail, more at ease now.

Leah nodded at the door. "Come on inside."

"Too nice of a day for that," he said. "I'm going fishing. Figured I'd see if anyone wanted to join me."

"Yes," Nick said at the exact moment Hailey said, "No, thank you."

Ed looked at Hailey first, nodded, then turned to Nick. "We'll hit the lake for a couple hours, get you a trout, Mr. Nick. Sound good?"

"Sure."

Hailey, reproachful, said, "I don't think he should go alone. He doesn't know you."

Ed, lounging against the railing, waited on Leah.

"You want to fish?" Leah asked Nick. He nodded emphatically. "Okay." Looking at Hailey, she said, "He'll be safe. Ed's a professional guide and the weather's great. I'll stay here with you."

Her daughter's stare seemed laced with tumbleweeds.

Hailey said, "Then we'll all go. I don't need to fish. I can just hang out, right?"

"Sure," Ed said. "I need someone to haul the anchor. My shoulders get sore." He waited until Hailey shot him an uneasy look before he smiled. "Kidding. You can get some sun and relaxation while your brother gets his fish. Sound fair?"

"How big is the lake?" Nick said. "I've only fished on rivers."

"It is the biggest lake east of the Mississippi that is—"

"That's a lie," Hailey interjected. "Superior is the biggest lake east of the Mississippi."

Ed gave that slow grin again. He liked Hailey, Leah realized. There was something in her contentiousness that he appreciated. She granted no free passes, and he respected that.

"Biggest lake east of the Mississippi that is contained *entirely in one state,*" he said. "How is that for obscure trivia?"

Hailey gave a grudging nod, but Leah guessed that she would probably fact-check him.

"Put Nick in a life jacket," Hailey said. "If it's that big, it's probably deep."

"I can swim!" Nick cried indignantly.

"Put him in a life jacket," Hailey repeated.

"Yes, ma'am," Ed said. "I have enough aboard for everyone. State law."

"I'll get my sunglasses," Hailey said and went back into the cabin. Ed looked at Leah and raised his eyebrows. Leah just shrugged. Her daughter didn't hand out trust. It had to be earned.

And you're undermining it, she told herself. *Every second of every day, you're undermining it. Your life is a lie.*

"I'll get my sunglasses too," she said, because she didn't want anyone to be able to look into her eyes right then.

Moosehead Lake was stunningly beautiful, and, yes, it was the largest lake east of the Mississippi that was contained entirely in one state. It was populated with islands, dozens of them, and when the sun settled over the western mountains, the land was as perfect as anyplace Leah had ever been. There in the isolated mountains she'd actually made more friends than she had intended to when she'd arrived seeking solitude. Maybe it was because the region was so sparsely populated that you couldn't stay anonymous even if you tried. Or maybe it was because she'd grown tired of seeking anonymity. The years passed, she stayed alive, and her children stayed safe with their father. One life had faded behind her but there was still daylight ahead. Time didn't heal, but it moved you forward, whether you liked it or not. The current of time respected no anchors; it swept you along, indifferent to your sorrows or rages or fears. The current of time had swept Leah here. She'd still thought of her old life daily, prayed for her children each night, wished death upon J. Corson Lowery each morning…but time had worked on her with its relentless power. The past receded with each sunset, never forgotten but always farther away. She'd begun to find a true identity of her own. The first new skills. The first real friendships. The first romantic relationships. Nina Morgan faded; Leah Trenton emerged.

It was a fine afternoon. Leah loved the lake and Ed's humor and warmth, the way he took time to explain the difference between a brook trout and a lake trout to Nick, the way he accepted a reel with a backlash and showed no trace of annoyance, simply talking in his low, unhurried pace while he unraveled the snarl. He didn't leave Hailey out but was wise enough not to push her, too. The only thing she displayed any interest in was Mount Kineo. The steep rise of granite on an island in a freshwater lake intrigued her, and she asked questions seemingly despite herself, interested in the stories Ed told about the early American Indians who'd come there for the stone to make tools, the old hotel that had at one time been the largest waterfront hotel in the United States, and the golf course.

"There's golf here?" Hailey asked.

"It's Maine, not Mars," he said good-naturedly. "Golf's every-where. Give Mars a year or two and they'll get a course up. You play?"

"Not really. My dad was teaching me, and we'd do the driving range or Top Golf." That was where she began to shut down again. When Leah tried to nudge the conversation forward, mentioning that there were courses near Camden, the only curiosity she aroused was from Ed. It was the first she'd spoken of Camden in front of him.

Hailey was as relaxed at times as Leah had seen her. At one point, she stretched out in the bow and propped her long legs up and leaned her head back and soaked in the sun as the Ranger bass boat rocked in the lake's grasp.

She could learn to like it here, Leah thought, but then memories of winter crept in, the isolation, the lack of peers. Leah knew better. She had seen the house in Louisville; she knew how Nick and Hailey had been raised. When Leah came to Piscataquis County, she'd been an adult seeking not only solitude but penance. Her children had asked for neither and deserved better.

The day wore on, the sun kept shining, and Maine offered up its impossibly blue sky. Leah wondered how many summer people that sky had lured into trying a full-time move north. She didn't have to wonder how many had stayed. The population in Maine was declining, not growing; the state had the oldest citizens in the nation per capita. Maine attracted visitors but not residents. Somewhere along the line, as mills closed and railroads went dormant and shipbuilding drifted south, Vacationland had become more of an identity than the state desired.

Still, it was her state now. She didn't want to leave. She could accept leaving the western mountains—fine. Head to the coast—fine. She wasn't inclined to leave Maine entirely, though. She thought again of that Christmas in Camden, of Ed saying, *If I ever had kids, I would want to raise them in this town.*

In the stern, Nick laughed as he reeled in a smallmouth bass scarcely larger than the Rapala lure it had attacked.

"That little bass had big eyes," Ed said. Nick thought that was funny. Leah knew the truth, though—bass would eat their own young. They were voracious predators. Big eyes indeed.

By the time the sun was sinking behind the western mountains, Nick had caught a handful of sunfish, a pickerel, and two trout. Ed had just turned on the winch to lift the anchor when a floatplane passed overhead. He pointed it out to Nick and Hailey.

"Your aunt can fly one of those," he said.

"What? Seriously!" Nick was enraptured, and even Hailey slid her sunglasses down her nose to look at Leah over the top of them.

"My mom was a pilot," Hailey said.

Leah felt a pang of fear, irrational but visceral. "No," she said. "I mean, yes, your mother was. My sister. But I'm not a pilot. All I did was pretend a few times. Ed was nice enough to let me do that."

Ed regarded her curiously. This was the first he'd heard of her dead sister being a pilot.

"Mom was a professional," Nick said. "Hailey used to watch the conrails—"

"Con*trails*," Hailey corrected.

"Hailey used to watch the contrails in the sky and pretend our mom was flying past. She'd make up stories about where our mom was going and what she did. They were good stories. It would feel like Mom was really up there, you know? Like she'd never died. She was just somewhere else. And we would wave up to her, like she could see us."

Leah couldn't draw a breath.

Ed came to her rescue. "There's a fly-in at this lake every year on Labor Day," he said, breaking the silence. "They have contests, do races, simulate rescue operations, things like that. There will be planes and pilots from all over."

"Do you fly in the races?" Nick asked.

"I make an attempt," Ed said.

"What are you best at?"

"If your aunt is helping, I'd say the canoe race."

"The canoe race?" Nick echoed, confused.

Ed nodded. "She paddles a canoe into the middle of the lake, and then I fly in and land. We lash the canoe to the floats and then take off and run a course. It's all on the clock, you know. But the person in the canoe has to be as good as the pilot."

"I don't know about that," Leah said.

"Hailey could do it," Nick said. "She'd win it."

"Yeah?" Ed said, distracted, peeling tendrils of weed off the anchor and tossing them back into the water.

"She's awesome in a canoe," Nick said. "She could definitely win."

"What's that?" Leah asked, sitting up straighter.

Hailey looked annoyed, as if Nick had let a secret slip.

"She's really good at canoeing," Nick said. "She started in camp a couple years ago but then she took classes that even had some rapids."

The earnest pride in his voice was enough to thaw Hailey. "Class-three rapids," she said quietly. "Not that big of a deal."

"Still a big deal," Leah said, excited at this knowledge of something she shared with her daughter. The feel of the paddle and the rush of the water. Leah in Maine, Hailey in Kentucky, but joined across the distance. It felt both lovely and eerie, the sense of nature versus nurture. In her life as Nina Morgan, she'd never been in a canoe. Then she'd arrived in Maine and built a new life, and canoeing became central to it, professionally and emotionally. On the water, she found a part of herself that began to restore her sense of identity, and the notion of her daughter taking up the same pursuit thousands of miles away in a state where Leah had never lived felt magical, destined. The two of them paddling together beneath the contrails of unknown aircraft, linked by the stories they told themselves.

"We'll need to go out and run some rivers together," she said. "We should go to the St. John and Kennebec. The Dead River. There are some class-four stretches in that one too. If you like white water, we definitely need to—"

"I don't think I'll want to do that for a while," Hailey said. "That was something I did at home."

They all fell silent for a moment. Finally, Ed said, "Let's get another bass in the boat before we call it a day, all right, Nick?"

"Sure. Different lure, maybe?"

"Yeah, let's change it up, throw something new at them and in a new spot."

Ed was speaking to Nick but looking at Leah. She forced a smile, then imitated her daughter—sunglasses on, legs stretched out, face to the sky. They roared on across the lake, and Leah closed her eyes and breathed the world she knew and loved. Mountain air, pine trees, and fresh water. Soon, it would be the smell of the sea again. Different from Florida—the North Atlantic had little in common with the ocean you saw from Florida beaches—but still a world apart from Maine's western mountains. Eyes closed, she pictured the house she had rented, walked through it in her mind. The right place.

It occurred to her then that until Ed mentioned flying, there had been a few blissful hours when J. Corson Lowery hadn't crossed Leah's mind.

Except for the little bass with big eyes, maybe. Yes, he'd crossed her mind then.

13

J. Corson Lowery owned an apartment on Central Park West and homes in Siesta Key, Florida; Martha's Vineyard, Massachusetts; and Red Lodge, Montana.

Red Lodge lay just twenty-five miles east of the site where Dax Blackwell's father and uncle had died, and while thirty minutes of searching the internet had told Dax that Lowery was currently in Florida, it was to Montana that Dax traveled first.

There was preliminary work to be done.

He had never allowed himself to come this close to the place where they'd died. There was no point in blaming the land where they'd fallen. A place couldn't carry any spirit or soul. A place was made of bits of dead stars. There was nothing more to it than that. Space dust and coincidence, dying stars that had burned hot, gone cold, and then allowed for the existence of something that simpler humans viewed as sacred and spiritually formed, created out of love by a higher power for a species deserving of nothing.

He had no fear of treading anywhere in the dust of dead stars.

He flew into Billings and rented a truck and drove southwest through the plateaus toward Red Lodge and the Beartooth Highway, a snaking road of sheer cliff sides that curled through Wyoming and Montana. He knew that on top it would crest eleven thousand feet in Wyoming and then dip back down to about eight thousand across the Montana state line, where Cooke City and Silver Gate waited. Old mining towns. Those towns had smelled of smoke from fires many times before and they would again. They sat on the edge of the largest active volcanic caldera in North

America, about thirty-four by forty-five miles of molten magma that churned beneath Yellowstone and considered its options. The smartest geologists in the world had no idea if, let alone when, it might erupt again. They knew only that it could. If it did, the western Rockies would be buried beneath three feet of charred earth, and cities on both coasts would see ash fall like snow. A few inches in New York and a few in San Francisco, depending on wind and weather. No one would miss it, that was for sure.

A majestic power. People poured their life savings into making trips to that park and walked across the ground unaware of what it might do to them if it chose to.

Dax liked the idea of it as a choice. Liked the idea that the chambers of magma down there were coiled like a snake and had eyes that watched the world and a forked tongue of flame that flickered out now and then in teasing flashes, incinerating a California town here, a Canadian forest there. Just teasing, tasting.

Waiting.

He drove and he thought and, from time to time, he argued with a voice in his head that sounded vaguely like his father's.

Why Lowery? For so little money. If there's money to it at all.

Why not Lowery? I've got to step back into the game somewhere. Why not with him?

So little money and so much risk. A fool's errand.

That would hardly be a first for the family.

There were reckless choices made a time or two but never grudge matches.

This one is different, and not because of any grudge—or not only because of that—but because of what it might build. The mythology. Touch the untouchable, and people take note. The family brand could use a revitalization. A reminder that the Blackwell business is doing just fine.

He was now off the highway and onto a dusty road broken occasionally by cattle-guard grates that he rattled over. He put the windows up to keep the dust out of the cab. The sun was descending and he could see the sparkle and shine of the Yellowstone River ahead. Lowery owned a few hundred acres and nearly a quarter of a mile of Yellowstone River frontage and yet it was unclear how many days he spent in this place.

Good for him.

The entrance to the ranch was as clichéd as they came, featuring a wrought-iron fence and a high arch and even a name, the L-C. Cute. One of the most famous ranches in this part of the West was the L-T (that was pronounced "L *bar* T," and a sure sign someone was a tourist was asking why people called it that). Hemingway had fished and stayed at the L-T. He'd written some of *A Farewell to Arms* there. Dax had enjoyed that one more than he had most of Papa's work. Reading had been important in his family. *You must have a curious mind and an empty heart,* his father would say. *When it comes to matters of the human race, the one who questions the most and fears the least is the one who thrives.*

The Blackwell School for Curious Youth. Shooting classes mandatory. Knife work encouraged but not required.

Dax drove beneath the arch and started up the winding dirt drive. He could see the house in the distance. One of the houses, at least. A long, low building of sprawling wings and wide windows set in massive logs. A rich man's vision of the West, oozing with a hilarious blend of money and machismo. Refined testosterone. Decor that said, *I might have been in a bar fight once, but if I hit anyone, it was with a bottle of fine cabernet.*

He smiled at the thought, but he knew that Lowery had plenty of men and women on his payroll who'd been in much worse than bar fights.

He hadn't made it even a quarter mile down the drive before one of those employees arrived. The guard drove an ATV with a roll bar and a spotlight. Dax put the truck in park and rolled down the window and waited until the ATV roared up alongside. The driver was dressed in black tactical gear and wore a sidearm and there were two shotguns in a rack across the back and one rifle in a custom slot that kept the stock near the driver's hand. Well armed for a little jaunt from the barn.

"You miss the private-property signs?" the man said.

Dax shook his head and looked chagrined. "I seen 'em, but I figure I ain't got much chance of meetin' Mr. Lowery unless I come onto the property."

He thought his Western drawl sounded good, but his aunt had always cautioned him to be careful with accents. It was far easier to convince yourself of their authenticity than it was to convince the locals.

"And what do you need with Mr. Lowery?" said the over-armed security guard. He was not a local and made no effort to speak as if he were.

"Lookin' to get paid."

"This is the wrong way to do it. No jobs, kid. Sorry."

Dax nodded and kept his forlorn expression while he looked away from the guard and out past the barn where three horses were visible in the paddock. He had never liked horses; he didn't trust any animals with eyes on the sides of their heads. He preferred cats, creatures of speed and agility and silence who could terrify with a single stare. Or taunt.

"You hear me, chief?" the guard said. "No jobs. Roll on down the road now."

"Problem is, the job's already been done," Dax said, keeping his eyes on the paddock.

"What's that?"

"There's a past-due balance."

"Mail a fucking invoice, then. Don't drive your dumb ass up here and get into trouble."

Dax turned and looked at him.

"If he's here," Dax said, "I'm talking to him. Just for a minute."

The guard seemed to ponder how much fun to have with this opportunity, the opportunity being an ass-kicking and the extent of fun being how long he wished to administer it.

"He's not here," the guard said, "and he's not going to hire you, and there aren't any horses to break or hogs to wrestle or whatever the hell it is you do."

Dax nodded sadly. "Fair enough," he said. "I figured it was too pretty a place for all of that, anyhow. Just tell him I passed through, all right? I'm telling you, mister, he's heard of me."

The guard leaned over and spit in the dust beside the ATV. "Sure, I bet he'll be awfully impressed when he learns you passed through. What's the name?"

"Blackwell," Dax said.

Nothing.

Nothing at all. Blank-faced. How was that possible? It had been a few years, yes, but...

Time to refresh the brand.

"Blackwell," the guard repeated. "Great. I'll be sure to pass the word."

Dax stared at the guard and wondered if he ever thought about the Yellowstone caldera. Of all that heat and pressure building up beneath his boots, of an ash cloud settling onto distant seas.

"Thanks," Dax said, and he turned to reach for the gearshift, then stopped himself and said, "Oh yeah—I'll need to leave the old invoice with you."

"I'm not taking your stupid—"

Dax drew a suppressed pistol from the console beside the gearshift, lifted it, and shot the guard once in the forehead. The pistol made a soft sound that was lost immediately in the vastness of the countryside. The guard made a slightly louder sound when he crumpled to the dirt, but not enough to carry far.

Dax set the gun on the dashboard, stepped out of the truck, and removed a folded piece of paper from his back pocket. He used his foot to roll the dead guard over, then he withdrew a slim knife with a five-inch blade with his right hand while he unfolded the paper and centered it on the guard's chest with his left.

He buried the blade just below the base of the guard's throat. He sat back on his heels and watched the blood ooze and then leaned forward and adjusted the dead man's head so that the blood would not drip down across his chest and render the note illegible.

The note read:

Past-due balance: $250,000
For: Murder of Nina Morgan
Plus interest in amount of: $250,000
Outstanding total: $500,000

Please remit payment at your earliest convenience.

Regards,
The Blackwell Company
Independent contractors, family-owned and -operated, unlicensed, uninsured

When he was satisfied, Dax climbed back into the truck, drove under the L-C sign and arch, off the ranch property, and down the dirt road to the pavement. The Beartooth Mountains loomed in the deepening twilight in the west. He turned east and put them at his back and drove away.

He could have sworn he smelled smoke on the wind.

He kept the speed up all the way back to Red Lodge, ready for sirens and flashing lights but doubtful they would appear. Anyone who carried guns for Lowery probably knew better than to make the local police the first call.

The mile markers passed by, and no sirens or lights appeared in either direction. It was a quiet trip back to Billings. He found a hotel close to the airport, a place called the Northern, that had clean rooms, a well-stocked bar, and a good amount of the nation's cowhides nailed to the walls for a charming atmospheric touch. He reserved a room for one night, put his bags in the room, then came back down and walked through the ornate old lobby that had welcomed so many ranchers and oilmen in its time—and probably still did—to the long, dark bar in the restaurant. Steaks were on special. He had a feeling steaks were usually going to be on special here.

He ordered an old-fashioned with Maker's Mark. The bartender carded him.

"Sorry," she said. "It's just, you know, I gotta go through the motions when somebody looks as young as you. Trust me, you'll miss it one day."

"I bet," Dax said, and he gave her a smile and a New York driver's license identifying him as twenty-six-year-old Thomas Levy.

"Good deal, baby face," she said, passing him the license and reaching for the Maker's Mark.

He sipped the old-fashioned, opened his laptop, and logged on to the internet. He didn't use the hotel Wi-Fi, because hotel Wi-Fi was about as secure as mirroring your computer screen on a Times Square billboard. He used a mobile hot spot with satellite-based coverage instead, and he would change the hot spot in the next state. He expected the next state would be Maine.

Mixed feelings about that. An ache in his arm, a memory of ruby taillights and the glitter of broken glass. At least he had the memories, though. Full knowledge of a lived experience. That was better than it had been out at the Lowery ranch near Red Lodge, looking into the mountains where his family had perished and not being sure of how exactly it had all come to pass.

Once he was connected to the hot spot, he set about finding Nina Morgan, aka Leah Trenton. He began with a phone-number lookup and discovered that both Nicholas and Hailey Chatfield had their own cell phones. Kids these days. What could you do?

A bit more probing revealed that the phones were on the AT&T mobile network and were active. Unless Leah Trenton had thought to send the phones elsewhere as a ruse, the phones were traveling with the kids. Dax hoped Leah had had at least this level of foresight, but he remembered what Doc Lambkin had told him: she was not an operator. She was a civilian who'd been in the wrong job at the wrong time.

He thought about it for a while and then selected the boy, Nicholas, as his first target. Eleven years old, armed with a smart-phone, and traveling away from home? He could probably use some distractions. A little something to put a smile on his face. Dax sent the boy notifications with download codes for a free game app and a free streaming app that promised a series of still-in-theater releases. Bootlegs, yes, but they were usually high quality and could be enjoyed on a phone screen. He wasn't sure that kids cared much about movies these days, so he put more faith in the gaming app. You never knew, though. Nicholas Chatfield could be a young Marty Scorsese.

Once he'd both texted and e-mailed the bait advertisements for his unique apps, he went to see what he could find about the two men whom Doc Lambkin had mentioned, Randall Pollard and Marvin Sanders.

He did not need to invest much time in the search. There were news alerts from national and regional media. It seemed Mr. Pollard and Mr. Sanders had been involved in a van accident while in transit from Coleman Prison in Florida to a prison in Terre Haute, Indiana. The driver had been injured but survived. Pollard and Sanders had escaped. They'd be wearing distinctive orange prison garb and handcuffs and should be considered dangerous, the news reports warned.

Dax suspected that only one of those three things was currently true.

The prison van's driver seemed awfully fortunate. Surviving a crash like that with two prisoners and emerging largely unscathed? That was good luck indeed. He was an employee of a transport company called MG&L that had contracts with numerous prisons. A company spokeswoman touted the impressive safety statistics even while she apologized for the unfortunate accident. There was no detail about the company beyond its name, its apology, and its impressive run of safe transit before this regrettable incident. Curious about this fine institution that had suffered such a bad day, Dax ran MG&L through a corporate-profile search. MG&L, it turned out, was a subsidiary of a company previously known as the Lowery Group.

"Fascinating," Dax said.

"What's that?" the bartender asked. She was leaning against the bar with her back to him, checking Instagram on her phone. Dax was one of two patrons in the entire place.

"I'm reading an article," he told her. "Really interesting stuff."

"Yeah? Hit me with it." She still didn't turn or look up from the phone.

"Did you know," Dax said, "that the Yellowstone Caldera could blow this entire state right to hell? This article says that there's an active volcano down there, been sitting dormant all this time, but ready to just…ka-*boom*."

She looked up at him then. Studied him for a moment. Then said, "Probably bullshit. Like how we're always supposed to be *just* getting missed by meteors or asteroids or whatever and then it turns out they're really, like, ten million miles away."

Dax smiled at her. "Yes," he said. "It's probably just like that."

14

The afternoon following their fishing trip, Leah told Ed that she was taking the kids to Camden.

He came by just after four, having worked a half-day fishing trip. Nick seemed pleased to see him, wandering out in the yard to ask him about the fishing, and Hailey seemed carefully indifferent. She waved but didn't come down off the porch, where she'd spent most of the day seeking futilely for a cell phone signal and reading a book that she'd taken a greater liking to than the Annie Dillard she'd tried the first night. It was Cormac McCarthy's *All the Pretty Horses*. The orphaned John Grady crossing the border into Mexico, homeless and in a strange land with only one trusted companion.

Perfect. Leah wished she would return to Tinker Creek.

They'd been at the cabin all day except for a trip into Greenville for lunch. The rest of the time had been spent packing. Leah was trying hard to seem nonchalant about going to Camden, to the unseen but already rented house. She was, she realized, acting very much like Hailey. *I am not afraid. I will not show you fear. I will not break.*

She wished she could be like Nick—open and honest and not afraid of cracking right in half. But that was a child's right, not a mother's. There was no fear more contagious than a mother's.

You're just Aunt Leah, though. Go on and embrace it. Crazy Aunt Leah can be scared of leaving the little house in the big woods if she wants!

She'd worked through the day sorting and packing, and she did not put the handgun in the car until she was sure neither of them could see her. Then she'd put it in the glove box and locked it.

The rifles and shotguns would have to stay behind. She would have no need of them in Camden, of course. Not the long guns and not even the pistol. Still, she left the pistol in the car.

When Ed arrived, she stayed in the garage while he talked to Nick and tossed a Frisbee for Tessa. At length he extricated himself from boy and dog and crossed the yard and joined Leah in the garage. He studied the back of the Jeep, which was already crammed with bags and boxes.

"Their stuff from home?"

"Some of it. Most of that is still in storage." The storage center had been located and the movers retained by Everett Spoonhour. Leah owed him a few e-mails and a phone call. He was following up constantly, reminding her of the court's requirements. High on the list was a site visit of the home where the children would be raised. Leah thought she should get keys to that house before she shared the address.

"Doesn't look like you're *un*packing it," he said.

"No." She closed the tailgate, leaned against the back of the Jeep, propped one foot on the bumper, and faced him. He was standing with one hand resting on the lip of the overhead garage door. The sun was behind him, so his silhouette loomed beside Leah's, as if to make up for the gap he was carefully leaving between them.

"They'll need a different place," she said. It wasn't the first time they'd spoken of it, but it was the first time in person. Always before, it had been on a phone call, and it had been brief.

"Seemed to enjoy the day yesterday all right."

"Absolutely. It was also a lake day in perfect summer weather."

Ed acknowledged that with a nod. "Be different in February."

"Be different, yes. Too different. They're used to travel base-ball teams and private art lessons. We must FaceTime with Luke,

Hailey's boyfriend, and play video games with Jerome, Nick's best friend. This requires fast Wi-Fi and an omnipresent cell signal."

"Everything we were going to help people escape from when they wanted to," he said, and smiled.

"Right."

"Emphasis being *when they wanted to,*" he said. "Those two haven't been given a say, let alone made the request."

He understood what she was saying without making her say it. Somehow, that made the whole situation worse. "That's my concern," she agreed. "They're upside down now. Everything they knew is gone. I can't fix that, but I can at least be someplace that resembles their home. Someplace where they've got at least a touchstone of the lives they knew."

His face was turned from her when he said, "Where is that place?"

"I'm not sure, but I'm starting with Camden."

He nodded slowly and kept his body half turned. "It's a good spot to try. It feels safe. Might not feel familiar to them, but I think it will feel safe."

"Yes."

He turned to look at her. "Everything we'd talked about…that's not going to be a practical fit for you, is it?"

"Not this summer. Not this fall, I guess. I just need to get them settled first."

"I know it. But what I'm saying is, I don't see when that'll become practical for you."

"I'm sorry."

"Stop it. You kidding me? Your brother-in-law died and suddenly you're a mother. You think you need to apologize to me for anything?"

She said, "I am their mother." The words painful and sweet simultaneously. Four words that gave her an identity, made her whole.

Ed said, "Exactly. That's the way you've got to think of it now. You're not their aunt any longer when it comes to decision-making. You've got to think like a mother."

She hadn't expected him to misunderstand, although it was reasonable that he had, and for a moment she stammered without getting any words strung together. Finally, she said, "Right. *Think* like their mother."

"So, Mom goes to Camden." His chest rose and fell and he said, "Don't stress about the rest of it, okay? Not now. You have to at some point, but not now. The cabins aren't going anywhere. I'm not going anywhere."

"I'm not asking you for patience," she said. "I appreciate it but...no expectations. I won't do that to you."

Ed leaned against the garage-door track, his baseball cap pulled low, shadowing his stubbled face. He looked away from her, down to the creek. You couldn't see the water in the oncoming darkness but you could hear it. In the yard, Nick laughed and Tessa barked and Hailey made no sound.

"Going to be quite a life change," Ed said. "Just...boom, raising two kids." He brought his hands together as if imitating a collision, having no idea just how accurate that was. Doug's truck had collided with a tree and knocked the past right into the present, spinning Leah's world until the future faced backward.

"There's really nobody else in the family to help out?" This was as close as he would come to asking prying questions, challenging questions. He was a private man with respect for a private woman, and it was that nature that had brought them together.

"No," she said.

"You know where you'll be staying in Camden?"

"Yes. There's a rental house that seems like a good fit. Just a mile outside of town, so you can walk to everything, and there are kids around."

He gave a small sideways smile. "Walk to Cuzzy's?"

They'd once gotten very drunk at a bar called Cuzzy's. It had been a foul-weather day and the rain kept pouring and the bartender kept pouring and they'd gone back to the hotel across the street and made love in the middle of the afternoon like college kids.

A stranger had died and Ed's life had changed. It felt unfair and yet she knew he would never let himself feel this way. He wasn't a big believer in ideas of fairness. He was interested in right and wrong and just and unjust but not in fair and unfair. She realized, not for the first time but certainly the most intense, how badly she would miss him.

"I hope you'll come over when you can," she said.

"Couldn't keep me away. The land of lobster and lounge chairs? Book me in."

"Adirondack chairs."

"Sure, but there's no alliteration in that." He smiled at her and there was just enough sunlight on the side of his face for her to see his sadness. "It's the same damn state," he said. "You're right down the road. Don't act like it's far."

"Feels far," she said. "Doesn't it?"

"Nah."

"A long drive."

"You should find somebody with a plane, then."

She laughed. "You can commute."

"Exactly. Put her down on Lake Megunticook or whatever it is over there, taxi right up to your new place."

"Just that easy," she said, and although there was still laughter in her voice, somehow the words brought the exchange to an end and put both of them back into silence.

"You take care," Ed said, "and holler if you need me, all right? I'll be there right away."

"Thank you," she said. "And I'm sorry that—"

"I said stop it with that. Please."

He crossed the garage to her and leaned down and put his hand on the small of her back and kissed her slowly. She reached up and grasped the back of his head, and he put his free hand on the leg she had propped up on the bumper. They broke the kiss and he rested his forehead against hers and they stood there for a moment in shared silence. Then he kissed the top of her head lightly and stepped away.

"I hope the house in Camden is what they need," he said.

"Me too."

Part Three

WHERE THE MOUNTAINS MEET THE SEA

15

They settled into the house in Camden like hostages, not visitors.

But they weren't visitors either, Leah reminded herself. The stay wasn't temporary. This was home.

It sure didn't feel that way, though.

Leah had talked the town up enthusiastically during the drive. She'd told them about the schools, the ocean, the old-fashioned schooners that sailed past the Curtis Island lighthouse, told them about skiing at the Camden Snow Bowl and walking to the library and eating ice cream on a bench in the harbor. She sounded like a spokeswoman for the conventions and visitors bureau.

They took Route 1 south from Belfast, chasing the coast down through Lincolnville, where the ferry waited for a run to Islesboro and lobster boats floated at moorings, then drove up into the wooded Camden Hills, then back downhill and straight into the town.

Camden. Home.

She'd been so busy talking about all that awaited them there that the arrival felt too abrupt and the town too small. Sure, there was the beautiful library overlooking the harbor, and there was the cascading waterfall where the Megunticook River emptied into the sea beside a bucolic park, but then they passed those things and the tourist shops that flanked Route 1 were gone and the GPS was instructing her to take a right turn onto Washington Street. Maine had plenty of blink-and-you-miss-it towns, but Camden had begun to feel outsize to her as she'd made her plans, and the swiftness with which the heart of the village came and went was jarring. She made the right, and then quickly the beauty of the harbor was behind her and they were driving past an old textile mill that had been renovated and turned into restaurants and apartments. She remembered this area only vaguely, from a skiing trip years ago.

"That's Forty Paper," she said, still in tour-guide mode. "It's a little Italian restaurant with a great happy hour."

A great happy hour? Gather 'round, kids, we've got to discuss the best cocktail prices in town. This was her attempt at mothering? Well, maybe it preserved her identity a little bit better. Aunt Leah the Lush.

"There's a river up here," she said, trying to move on from the happy-hour observation and remembering the map she'd studied on sleepless nights in Louisville, "and then there's a lake. The lake is supposed to be pretty special. It's a—"

"We've seen a lot of lakes already," Nick said, and the fatigue in his voice silenced Leah. He wasn't wrong. They had seen a lot of lakes.

"I'm excited about the house," she said.

No one answered.

The home was a two-story yellow Colonial over a walkout basement with an oversize deck facing Mount Battie. Leah pulled in and killed the engine.

"What do you think, Hailey?" she asked.

"I don't like yellow," Hailey said.

Strike one. Leah nodded. "Good news, then—there's no yellow paint inside."

They climbed out, and Tessa promptly ambled across the property line to the neighbor's yard, squatted, and shat.

Beautiful. I'll get to meet the neighbors with a poop bag in hand. But first I'm going to have to unpack some poop bags.

Tessa trotted back when Nick whistled, and the four of them

gathered outside the door as if three of them were waiting for the dog to take the lead.

"Do you have a key?" Hailey said. "Or is someone supposed to meet us here?"

"It's a code. Let's hope it works."

She put the code into the electronic lock and opened the door. "Home sweet home," Leah said, and her voice echoed. The house had hardwood floors and high ceilings—selling points that the agent had mentioned repeatedly—but all of that lent a cool hardness to the space rather than welcoming warmth. It felt undeniably like the rental it was. Clean and cute and furnished tastefully but cheaply. *Ikea Presents: Maine Cottage in a Box!*

The kids walked through the house in near silence, with Nick gawking in all directions and inspecting knickknacks with curious fingers and Hailey walking behind, hands in her pockets, shoulders tight. Her eyes took in the new space but she didn't engage with it in any way. It was as if she wanted to pass through the walls and fade away for good, ghostlike.

Just like her mom did, Leah thought. *The only difference is Hailey actually wants to disappear.*

"Let's go see your bedrooms," Leah said. "You each have your own."

"We'd better have our own," Nick said. "I don't want to live with a girl."

"If you're real quiet I bet you can hear the applause from relieved girls everywhere," Hailey muttered.

Leah smiled. That was a mistake; Hailey saw the smile and shut down again, determined not to waver in her silent disapproval.

They went up the steps as Tessa barreled ahead. She hadn't been in a house with a long run of steps before, and she struggled to find her stride, making them all laugh, even Hailey. They watched the dog with her high, swinging hips moving like a girl in her first set of heels. Leah breathed easier, hearing the laughter.

At the top of the steps was a small hallway with rooms in all directions. Bedrooms and bathrooms, nothing else. The kitchen, living room, and dining room were downstairs, and all the bedrooms were upstairs. It was a large home, but somehow the partially cracked-open doors of all the bedrooms seemed to squeeze Leah as she stood in the hall. She remembered picking out the nursery in their old house in Florida, remembered the way the baby monitor had lived on her nightstand, tracking every sound these two had made. How could they not remember her?

"Who goes where?" Nick asked.

"Hailey gets to choose first."

"Why?" Nick demanded.

"She's the oldest," Leah said, because she was lost in a memory of holding her firstborn in her arms. Her daughter. Sweet, beautiful Hailey. Leah had taken a long maternity leave for Hailey. The Lowery Group had been very good about that, very understanding. A wonderful place to work, so much better than any commercial airline. It wasn't until Leah went back to work that she began to fly exclusively for Brad Lowery. Lots of trips, lots of VIPs picked up on private airstrips. He was the chosen one. Congress, then Senate, then a run at the top. There was no doubt in anyone's mind back then, back before he'd gotten a leaked look at the affidavit of one Nina Morgan and loaded his Smith & Wesson.

Nick said, "Okay, Hailey, you get first dibs. Which one do you like?"

"I don't care," Hailey said in the tone that Leah was getting to know well. It wasn't insolence—that might have been better—but distance. A voice that promised the real Hailey was in there under lock and key, and good luck getting to her.

"You don't want to be here," Leah said, "and I understand that. But I want you to pick whatever room might make you happier."

"I will only be happy back in my room in—" Hailey stopped and shook her head. Another consistent habit. Any time the expected rage about the loss of all that she'd known seemed ready to burst to the surface, Hailey would swallow it. Unlike Nick, she never raged and only rarely lamented the things she missed. She internalized, internalized, internalized.

"My room is no more," Hailey said softly, a flat statement, not a dramatic one. "So I guess I'll take the one with the best view. That would be the mountain view."

It was some level of effort, at least. Not a complete refusal to choose. Leah was grateful. "Mount Megunticook," Leah said. "That's the highest mountain on the Eastern Seaboard that isn't on an island, believe it or not. Doesn't seem so tall, but…"

Hailey walked past her without speaking, went to the window, and turned the rod that shut the blinds, blocking the view of the mountains.

Leah nodded. Fair enough.

"So I get this one?" Nick said, wandering into the room across the hall. It was larger than the northern bedroom that Hailey had chosen, with new furniture that made it a proper bedroom but a sterile one. All the right furniture but none of the clutter of life. Hopefully, Nick would fill it up with that soon enough.

"Is it okay?" Leah asked.

He inspected it, pacing the space, peering out the windows. He was wearing an oversize Indianapolis Colts shirt and a cap that was too big for him and rested on his ears, pushing them out to the sides. His freckles had darkened in the sun at Moosehead. She could see Doug in him.

"Yeah," he said. "Yeah, I like it. There are a lot of trees."

Hailey made a soft sound that might have been mistaken for exasperation about his observation of the trees but that Leah knew was really driven by his willingness to say *I like it.*

"I hope you'll like it," Leah said. "It's a great town and a nice neighborhood. The rental agent told me there are some kids around your age. In fact, there's a boy right next door who is just about Hailey's…"

She turned back to look at her daughter, but Hailey had vanished into her new bedroom and closed the door behind her.

16

There was a family in the yellow house.

This was discouraging to Matt Bouchard. The yellow house was technically next door to his own but separated by a three-acre expanse that was neighborhood green space. The green space was Matt's personal territory. Most of the neighbors viewed it as just trees and rocks, but all the stormwater funneled down through it and out to a retention pond before entering the Megunticook River, and in heavy spring rains, that stretch could look like a waterfall. The place was pretty cool—and great for practicing wilderness skills, as Matt often did—but Mrs. Wilkes up the road was always prattling on about the dangers of the pond and the *liability* of it all.

"She's concerned," Matt's mom would say.

"She's fearmongering," his dad would respond.

Matt could avoid Mrs. Wilkes—frankly, it seemed like most of the neighbors tried to—but her house didn't afford any view of the green space. The yellow house looked right out across it, which meant the people in it would have a view of all his liability-risking excursions.

He watched them move in through binoculars. He already knew what to expect. The woman's name was Leah Trenton, and the kids weren't her own kids but her niece and nephew. Mrs. Wilkes had told Matt's parents this, because Mrs. Wilkes liked to share other people's business. *Gossip and bullshit is all that charges that lady's batteries,* Matt's dad had said.

According to Mrs. Wilkes, who had heard it from someone

who had heard it from the property manager who handled the house, Leah Trenton was a registered Maine guide who worked up around Moosehead Lake and the Allagash Wilderness.

How cool was *that*?

There were some jobs that sounded cool but really weren't once you dug beneath the surface. Matt's mother, for example, was a private investigator. A real-life PI! Sounded awesome, legit badass, but Matt had had too much time *seeing how the sausage was made,* as Mom said. She didn't do stakeouts and she didn't have tracking devices or cell phone bugs or any of the cool stuff. She definitely didn't have a gun.

Leah Trenton, though, actually went into the wilderness, went on moose hunts and bear hunts and took floatplanes to isolated lakes where she'd paddle even farther into the unknown to catch trophy fish on a fly rod.

Legit badass.

She didn't look much like a wilderness guide. She was wearing jeans and a tank top and looked physically fit, but you could look physically fit from an exercise bike, too.

The boy was maybe eight or nine years old. Possibly older than that and just small. He was wearing a hooded sweatshirt and an Indianapolis Colts baseball cap.

Not going to make many friends up here in that hat, Matt thought, and then the girl climbed out and he forgot about the cap.

She was the one who was Matt's age, Mom had said. Going into seventh grade this year, like him, or maybe eighth. Mom hadn't been sure. The girl was tall, wearing jeans and a fleece jacket— *Why is she dressed like summer is over?*—and had long dark hair that fell just below her shoulders. To say that she looked like her aunt was an understatement. It was uncanny. The girl even did the pause-and-look-around thing like her aunt had. When she looked up, past the house and into the mountains, she seemed to stiffen a little, like the sight of them intimidated her.

They're from somewhere in the Midwest, Matt's mother had said.

The Midwest was flat. Maybe she'd never seen any mountains? Still, it was a strange reaction. Everything about her response to the place was strange, actually. She stood there rigidly, looking at the trees as if they hid a sniper. The thought was almost enough to make Matt lower his binoculars.

Almost.

A soft, cool breeze rode up the river and through the green space slope. It rustled leaves, fanned through the grass, and then eddied around the Trenton family. The girl's dark hair swept across her face, and she took one hand out of her pocket and pushed her hair back over her ear, and Matt's throat felt tight.

She was going to be the most beautiful girl in school. Libby Nielson was in for a rude awakening after Labor Day.

Seventh grade, Matt implored the heavens silently. *Please, please let her be in the seventh grade.*

The woman said something in a voice too soft for Matt to hear out in the woods, across the retention pond where frogs chirped, and then the whole group walked down the driveway, up the steps, and into the house. The front door closed, and they were gone. They'd been in sight for only the brief moment, none of them touching one another or speaking, let alone expressing any of the celebration or enthusiasm you might expect from two kids showing up at their new house.

Maybe they don't want to be in Maine at all, Matt thought.

Something was off with them. He wondered what exactly it meant that the kids weren't living with their parents anymore. Had someone died or gotten sick or gone to jail? There were so many bad things that could happen.

He needed to ask his mother. *She should call them,* Matt thought. *Be neighborly, show a little kindness.*

And find out that girl's name.

17

The strangers arrived in Everett Spoonhour's office just after
five, walking in mere minutes after Linda, his receptionist,
had left for the day. Usually Linda was the last to leave, but on
Wednesdays she hosted a Bible study and hustled out, which
meant that on Wednesdays, Everett tended to host a bourbon at
his desk before heading home himself. He could always use a
bourbon after a day of minding the affairs of the dead.

He was minding the decanting of exactly one and a half ounces
of Blanton's into a tumbler glass when he heard the office's front
door open and close.

"Forget something?" he said without turning, maneuvering to
block the bottle and glass from Linda's view with his body. He
didn't *care* that she saw what he was doing, necessarily—he was
the boss, after all—but he didn't want to advertise it either.

"Mr. Spoonhour?"

The voice was masculine, with the faintest whisper of Boston in
that closing *r.*

Everett turned in surprise and saw the white man and then,
behind him, the black man, who closed the door so softly the
latch's click was nearly inaudible. The white man was wearing
gray Carhartt work pants and a long-sleeved shirt open over a
white T-shirt. He was about forty, several inches shorter than
Everett's six two, and muscular, with a week's worth of beard.
The black man was taller and leaner and possibly the same age
but somehow harder to define, with a presence so quiet that he
seemed less distinct, as if you had to squint to determine his exact

silhouette, let alone any features. He was wearing a Carolina blue T-shirt, black jeans, and khaki-colored boots that were so clean, they seemed to glow.

Everett Spoonhour was the furthest thing from a racist—you could ask anyone about that. Even though his grandfather had been in the Klan, Everett was absolutely *not* a racist...and yet the black man scared him more than the white man.

"May I help you?" he said, walking to the open door of his office.

"I sincerely hope so," the white man said. He'd stopped at the empty reception desk, and the black man stepped up at his side and nodded politely, and Everett began to feel foolish for that momentary fear. "Sorry to be bothering you so late in the day, but we've been on the road since six and we're headed to the airport first thing tomorrow, so we had to try to catch you before heading back to Texas."

"Texas?"

The white man nodded and extended his hand. "Name is Scott Mason, sir. My colleague is Reggie Taylor."

Everett shook their hands. Strong grips, both of them, but while the one named Scott looked around the office when he spoke, the one named Reggie never took his eyes off Everett. It wasn't an aggressive stare; in fact, it was so calm that Everett felt himself relaxing. He was a student of human nature, and he could see that there was no hostility in Reggie Taylor.

"What brings you here from Texas?" Everett asked, thinking that he hadn't worked a case with any overlap in the Lone Star State in many years.

"Missing children," Scott Mason said.

"Pardon?"

"Missing children," Mason said again. "Not your Amber Alert kind yet, although we think they should be. We think you probably agree."

"I'm not following."

Mason reached into his breast pocket and withdrew two items. One looked like a passport, and the other was a four-by-six photograph. He opened the passport first and handed it over.

It turned out to be a private investigator's license. Everett gave it a long, scrutinizing look, even tilting it back and forth so the light hit it at different angles. This was all show, of course; he had not the faintest idea what a Texas PI license should look like.

"All right," he said, passing it back. "No jurisdiction in Kentucky, though. With all due respect, PIs don't really have any jurisdiction anywhere."

Mason gave a thin smile. Reggie Taylor did not.

"Correct," Mason said. "We can't do a damn thing except ask questions, and that's all we're here to do. With the full understanding that you don't have to answer them."

"Glad we're in agreement there."

"But we hope you're concerned with the safety of the children," Reggie Taylor said.

It was the first time he'd spoken. His voice was soft but grave, like wind before a storm.

"My concern for safety is joined with my concern for confidentiality," Everett said, striving to find the entitled evasiveness of the esquire.

Mason held the photograph up. Two children were in the picture, an older girl who was maybe thirteen or fourteen and a boy a few years younger.

"Her name is Hailey Chatfield. His name is Nicholas Chatfield. Correct?"

Everett had drawn up the standby guardianship for those children a decade earlier, though he remembered Doug Chatfield only as young, physically fit, and nervous. Nervousness wasn't uncommon in Everett's office. Even the most virile could grow a little green around the gills when you were signing and notarizing documents pertaining to their demise. Doug's overriding concern had been the creation of an ironclad standby guardianship.

Everett had done his job.

He hadn't seen the man again. He'd never seen the children. Years passed, clients came and went, and Everett's memory of Doug Chatfield dimmed. Then Doug Chatfield's truck had flipped, and Everett's phone rang, and suddenly there was one Leah Trenton in his office, a tall, lean, muscled woman with intense dark eyes and a copy of the document that Everett had drafted all those years earlier. Leah, the legal standby guardian.

I believe this is the triggering event, she'd said, and Everett had somberly conceded.

"Is it true?" Mason asked him now. "Did you make custody arrangements for these children?"

Everett wasn't confirming that to strangers, but he certainly wasn't going to deny it. Only two types of men denied the truth: liars and fools.

"You guys understand that I can't discuss the situation," he said.

"You're bound by client confidentiality, yes. But the problem, Mr. Spoonhour, is that your client is dead. His children are not."

"That doesn't mean they're in harm's way."

"We disagree."

"If they're in danger," Everett said, "then law enforcement should be involved. I may be able to talk to them, but I can't talk to private investigators. I can't get into this without a court order compelling me to do so. Not even if I wanted to."

"Understood and appreciated," Mason told him. "Likewise, I hope you understand and appreciate this: those kids *are* in danger. My guess is, you already sense this."

Everett found himself giving the slightest nod in response. It seemed to be enough for Mason, because he finally lowered the photograph and returned it to his pocket.

"We've had no leads on this," he said. "I'm being honest to the point of embarrassment. If we had other options, we wouldn't be here, Mr. Spoonhour. We don't need the backstory from you or even any details. But those children…they need someone. If we had the faintest idea where to go from here, well, that might make the difference between a healthy and happy future for them or something terrible."

Time passed. No one spoke.

"I don't know where they went," Everett said at last. "That has been a problem for me. You're adding to the problem, not fixing it. I can't fix yours either."

"No idea where they went. Okay. What about means of contact?"

Everett shook his head.

"No address?" Mason said. "No phone number? Nothing? The man died and you stepped in to handle his affairs but you've got no way to contact his children? How do you intend to see that they get insurance money?"

Everett stayed silent.

"You have a contact for her," Reggie Taylor said. It was a flat, empty statement. None of the questioning or pushing that Mason tried. Just assertion.

Everett had an e-mail address and a phone number, but he couldn't share those. He thought about the children, thought about his professional and ethical code, and measured the distance between them.

"I'm sorry," he said. "I can't help you. I wish that I could."

Mason nodded. Taylor did not. He just stared. Somewhere behind Everett, ice cracked softly as it melted in the bourbon.

"You need to send the right authorities my way," Everett said. "Someone with child welfare who has jurisdiction. That shouldn't be hard, because if it is as bad as you say, they will want to move aggressively."

"We'll be in touch with them," Mason said. "But I have less confidence in the good faith of government, sir."

"You'd be surprised."

"I hope so."

Mason looked at Reggie Taylor. Unspoken communication passed, and then Mason nodded.

"We'll let you go, Mr. Spoonhour. Thanks for your time. We knew it was a long shot, but..." He tapped the breast pocket where the photograph rested. "We had to take it."

"I understand," Everett said.

They left his office then. When the door was closed, Everett realized his heart was racing. He was not a nervous man, and yet the two of them had triggered his adrenal system like the buzz of a rattlesnake.

He went into his office, closed that door, too, then sat behind his desk and drank his bourbon. It went down faster than usual. He replayed the bizarre conversation in his mind, thinking about what he'd said and what he wished he'd said. Something bothered him about those two, something more than Reggie Taylor's cold eyes and empty voice. He was almost certain that they weren't private investigators, not in Texas, not anywhere.

"Speculation, Everett," he said aloud. "Strike it from the record."

He almost reached for the Blanton's again. He knew better, though. Willpower bred contentment. He put the bottle back on the wet bar shelf, rinsed the glass, and walked out of his office.

They were waiting in the reception chairs.

Neither of them reacted when he jerked to a stop and let out a little sound of surprise. They just sat there, watching, both with feet flat on the floor and hands flat on their thighs. He couldn't believe that he hadn't heard them come back in. Then he remembered the way Reggie Taylor had closed the door the first time. Almost soundlessly, and studying the latch as if learning it for later.

He was able to say "What the hell are you doing?" before the first blow.

Taylor exploded off the chair with speed most men couldn't

muster coming out of a sprinter's crouch and hit Everett once in the throat and kicked him in the side of the knee and then Everett was dropping, choking and gasping and falling, beaten in a blur, never so much as getting a hand up. He might have had time to feel shame about that if he'd made it to the floor, but he didn't. Mason caught him, spun him, and sealed a forearm around his throat.

"Office," he said. "Walk."

Everett was having trouble staying upright, let alone walking, but Mason bore most of his weight. They trundled out of the reception area and into Everett's private office and Taylor closed the door behind them. Soundlessly, of course.

"Desk," Mason said, and for a moment Everett took it as an instruction for him and started forward. Mason held him tight, though, and Taylor went behind the desk and opened drawers, moving quickly, checking for a weapon, most likely. He'd donned a pair of thin black gloves for the task.

"Clean."

The pressure on Everett's windpipe loosened. Breath still didn't come easily, the pain continuing to constrict his lungs, but there was reassurance in the physical freedom.

I will do what they want, he told himself, *and I will live.* It was that sad and that simple. Sometimes you could fight. With these two, there was no hope of that. He needed to do what they asked.

"Where do we find her?" the one who called himself Mason said. By now Everett understood that all names were lies.

"I honestly do not know. There is a post office box in Greenville, Maine. That is all I have."

"Think harder," Reggie Taylor said. His name also a lie, of course. Lies stacked on lies that ended lives. Everett offered the truth. What harm could the truth do now?

"The post office box and her e-mail address are all that I have. The rest is in her file. His file, I mean. Doug Chatfield's file."

"And where are the files?" Mason asked.

"Hard copies in the cabinet and the rest in the computer," Everett said, his voice a rasp from his swollen throat. "That's all of it."

"Good boy," Mason said in the tone of someone training a puppy. "Which cabinet, which drawer?"

"Middle cabinet. Second—no, third drawer. Alphabetical." He rubbed his throat. Breathing was easier now, but he was more aware of the pain in his leg where the kick had landed. He had his weight on the left side because his right knee felt loose, untethered, as if a tendon had detached.

Reggie Taylor went to the cabinet, opened the third drawer, and scanned through the files, searching for Chatfield. Found the accordion folder and removed it. He didn't check the contents, just took the folder and closed the drawer.

"What's on the computer that's not in this?" he asked.

"E-mails."

"You need to log in?"

"Yes."

"Then do it. Move slowly. Hands above the desk."

The instructions were pointless; Everett had no choice but to move slowly, limping around the desk and favoring his wounded leg. He fell heavily into the big leather swivel chair, feeling a pop in his knee. Taylor stood behind him and Mason stood across the desk while Everett logged in to his computer, pulled up his e-mail, and found the exchanges with Leah Trenton. There weren't many of them, and they were mostly one-sided queries from Everett.

Reggie Taylor used his phone to take pictures of the screen. Everett, uninstructed, hit Print. The printer glowed, chimed, and then hummed as it went to work. Mason looked at it, laughed, and said, "Good boy," again.

They were silent until the printer was done. Then Mason walked over, collected the documents from the tray, folded them, and put them in his pocket. "That's all?" he said.

"That's all. Really."

"Why you saying *really*? Think we don't trust you, Everett? That's not a nice thought to have."

Everett knew better than to argue or fight or beg or plead. He knew better than to do anything, and yet he found himself asking a question. "Who was Doug Chatfield?"

He was starkly aware of two things when the words left his lips: these men would not answer, and he would not live. That was why he had asked the question. Because it felt unfair to die without even knowing why.

"He's unimportant," Mason said, and Everett expected him to leave it at that, but instead Mason added, "He married the wrong woman, that's all."

"There was no wife," Everett said, suddenly hopeful that he could disappoint them with this enough to send them from his office. "By the time I met him, she was dead."

Mason reached into his pocket and withdrew a photograph. Everett was expecting to see the shot of the two children again, but instead there was a woman in the frame. She was dressed in a flight suit but there was no military insignia. She was standing beside the wing of a plane, a small jet, and she was smiling into the sun. Tall and lean, with an angular face, her suntanned face split into a smile, dark eyes gleaming.

It was Leah Trenton. An old picture, but a clear one.

"That's not his wife," Everett said. "That's his sister-in-law."

Neither Mason nor Taylor spoke, and in their silence, Everett understood his own mistake.

Mason looked at Reggie Taylor and smiled. "Tell us where to find her, Everett."

"I've told you everything I know."

"You're sure?"

"I'm sure."

"Then I guess we've got nothing more to gain from you," Mason said conversationally, and he started for the office door.

Everett watched him go and thought with relief, *It is over, they are going to leave.*

He was right about both things, and wrong only in his relief.

Without looking back, Mason said, "Your turn, bleak." The phrase was curious and Everett was just about to say that he didn't understand what that meant when Reggie Taylor stepped forward with a knife in hand and sliced Everett's throat. The blade was in and then out and then Everett's hand was finally raised but it was too late and instead of defending himself against the blade he was closing his fingers around a geyser of hot blood.

In his last thought he understood the phrase that had confused him before.

Bleak was the man with the knife.

18

Labor Day weekend came and went, the weather so beautiful that it seemed determined to reassure Leah, the warm breezes whispering, *You are safe here, they are safe, it will all be fine.*

The house helped. She'd known that it would. Nick had already made enough of a mess in his room that it felt occupied, not so sterile. Hailey, however, refused to leave so much as a crease in the sheets to indicate her presence.

They watched TV and rejoiced at the presence of Wi-Fi. Nick had an endless array of bizarre YouTube videos that made him laugh. The laughter was loud in the house and Leah was grateful for it. She now had about a hundred more streaming options than she'd ever known existed, with Nick adding app after app.

"They're all gonna be free for a while," he'd told her.

For a while. Reassuring. She knew this was a mother's moment—enforce some rules, don't just sit back and let them take control—but she was so happy to see him lounging on the couch with mismatched socks on his feet and a smile on his face that she didn't give a damn about policing the TV. They'd been through real tragedy; she wasn't afraid of what the TV could do to them.

They went shopping in Rockland, returning with a carload of items deemed essential. To Nick, for reasons unexplained, this involved strings of outdoor patio lights that he hung from the bedroom ceiling. He was entranced by the tiny Edison-style bulbs, and Leah loved the delight he showed when the sun went down and he could finally see his new, softly glowing room.

It was his now.

Hailey had requested a stop at Home Depot, where she walked through the paint aisle with purpose and came back with a small can of black paint that said it had a chalkboard finish.

"Do you care about the basement wall?" she asked.

Leah had barely thought about the basement. It was an unfinished space, although the walkout doors and nicely trimmed windows suggested the builder had entertained bigger plans for it at one point. The floor was bare concrete and the ceiling was exposed joists. The walls were primed but not painted.

"I do not care about the wall," she told Hailey, and they bought the paint. There was an art-supply store in Camden (it seemed there was an art-supply store in every town in Midcoast Maine; if one could survive solely on art supplies, scented candles, and lobster-themed trinkets, one would never need to leave), and they stopped there at Hailey's request and bought chalk.

"What's your plan here?" Leah asked.

"The paint works like a chalkboard," Hailey responded as if speaking to the world's dumbest human. "That's the whole point."

"Understood. But what will you put on it?"

Hailey just shrugged. That night, while Leah helped Nick hang his patio lights in the bedroom and offered crucial advice about collision points between the bulbs and the blades of the ceiling fan, Hailey descended into the basement with the paint, a roller, and some tape. When she was done, the wall looked like a black hole, something with depth, something you could pass through. Leah found the effect strangely unsettling, but Hailey was pleased.

After all three coats of the paint had dried, Hailey got to work with the chalk, and Leah learned something new about her daughter: She was an artist. Not just an artistically inclined kid, but an *artist,* with very real talent. The sketches that went up on the chalk wall were intricate, vivid, and precise. They were also of a frightening theme—monsters that glowered, snakes with wings, demonic caricatures of men with leering smiles and sharp teeth. When she first saw the artwork, Leah said, "So how did you come up with these things?"

"I didn't come up with them," Hailey said. "Writers did." She pointed at one monster. "Neil Gaiman." Pointed to the tall old man with the fang-like teeth. "Joe Hill." On to the next. "Chuck Wendig. Paul Tremblay. Dean Koontz. Stephen King." And so on.

Her artist daughter was also, evidently, a voracious reader.

"I didn't know you liked books that much," Leah said lamely, although how had she missed this? Back at the cabin, Hailey had cycled through Leah's books with the only real enthusiasm she'd shown for anything.

"How would you have known?" Hailey said, and though her tone wasn't unkind, it was still painful to hear. Leah was on the steep part of the learning curve, and it was a constant reminder of all that she had missed.

You loved Paddington Bear, she wanted to say. *The old book, the copy from when I was a child. You loved it. And the silly little drum that your dad bought you. You'd sit on my lap and bang away on that and you would laugh and I'd look at him and say, "What have you done, why would you give her something to make her* louder?" *and then we'd all laugh.*

Unable to relive these memories with Hailey, she instead endeavored not to miss any more. The next day they went to the gorgeous harbor-front library and got cards. Nick left with one book—and Leah had the distinct impression that he was taking it out just to please her. Hailey, though, left with a stack that had to be distributed among the three of them just to get the books back to the car. Driving home, Leah considered asking Hailey why on earth she hadn't expressed her desire to go to the library sooner, but she already knew the answer. In Hailey's eyes, it would have been a double failure: it showed a need for Leah and allowed Leah to gain a better understanding of her, a glimpse behind those walls.

Everything in those days felt like progress, with one crucial exception: Ed.

Leah had missed the fly-in at Moosehead for the first time in years. She'd talked to him on the phone briefly afterward. He'd finished second in one of the races, a timed rescue simulation, losing to the pilot from Quebec who beat him every year. She asked who his partner was in the canoe race, and he named a woman they both knew and said she was not an ideal replacement since she was scared of the plane. They laughed about that but already Leah felt the distance between them growing.

"First day of school for them tomorrow?" Ed asked.

"Yes."

"Nervous?"

"Terrified. But everyone says they're great schools, and the counselor I met with was excellent, so I guess I shouldn't be."

"I meant are the *kids* nervous," Ed said with a low laugh.

"Ah. Right. The kids. They have to be, but they aren't showing it much. In fact, if I had to guess, I think Hailey is looking forward to it. The daily routine, the purpose, the..." *Chance to get away from me.* "Just the return to normalcy," she said. "Nick is probably more nervous."

"He'll do fine."

"I hope so."

"Do you miss the woods?"

"There are woods here. I'm staring right out at Camden Hills."

"Camden Hills is a park with roads and public toilets."

She laughed. "Doesn't count, I get it. I *will* miss the woods. I just haven't had much time to yet. But they're not far away, right? I can get to them in a hurry. And I will soon."

They both understood that they were talking about more than the woods, but Ed wasn't going to pressure her to visit. Pressure was not his style.

Later, after hanging up with him, she stood on the deck cooking burgers on the grill and turned his question over in her mind. Did she miss the woods? Nina Morgan had been uncomfortable in the woods when she'd arrived in Maine, but Leah Trenton had no such past. Leah Trenton was nothing but a future. She'd become obsessed with that idea. She asked herself what intimidated her most about Maine, and the Southern city girl who'd once been Nina Morgan answered immediately: the winter and the wilderness.

So she'd found a two-week course that taught winter woodcraft in the Allagash. There'd been times—snowshoeing through gale-force winds, scraping a tent site out of snowdrifts, chipping ice away from fishing holes because it was so cold they'd kept refreezing—when she'd hated everything about it.

But there'd been good moments, too. A below-zero dawn when the sun crested above her camp and lit the snow-filled valley. A day on snowshoes when a hare ran beside her, keeping pace with her as if she were a natural companion. Lighting a fire in a howling wind in the dark without needing to use a flashlight. Pulling up a rainbow trout from beneath twenty inches of ice, its speckled body glistening like a ruby in the winter light.

Moments of beauty, moments of triumph. Small victories each day.

That spring, she'd signed up for the professional guiding course. Maine regulated its guides to ensure that anyone who took money to lead strangers into the wild was qualified to do so. She was delighted to learn that Maine's first registered guide had been a woman, Cornelia "Fly Rod" Crosby, certified in 1917. Fascinated by the idea of a woman being the first licensed guide in a field so dominated by men, Leah had read up on

Crosby and come across a quote that pleased her immensely. "I am a plain woman of uncertain age, standing six feet in my stockings…and I would rather fish any day than go to heaven."

Leah Trenton, who stood five feet nine inches in her stockings, had never fished a day in her life until the winter when she'd pulled the trout from the frozen lake. In the spring, she landed a three-pound smallmouth bass on a dry fly. There was a moment, with the bent rod trembling in her hand and the trout a silver streak in white-water spray, when heaven descended briefly to earth and joined it, and Leah was there between the two.

She finished the guiding course in a year and went to work in Rangeley the next spring. Now when people asked why she'd come to Maine, she had an answer: for the wilderness.

She hadn't anticipated how deeply she'd fall in love with the solitude and the beauty and the relentless, irrepressible creativity of the wilderness. The way that standing alone in a forest or dipping a kayak paddle into a cold river could produce a healing that seemed to come from the inside out.

The lessons of the Allagash went beyond hopefulness and found grace. You had to fight for every inch, nothing was easy, but all of it was beautiful. The rivers and woods held all you needed to be nourished and sheltered as well as all you needed to be wounded or killed. They swirled together there, danger and beauty and threat and triumph. In the wilderness, Nina Morgan became Leah Trenton.

Do you miss the woods?

She turned and leaned against the deck railing and looked through the windows into the living room. Nick was stretched out on the couch, and Hailey was curled up in the armchair. They were watching a movie together, and Leah could've sworn it was the new Marvel movie, one that was still in theaters. Was her son watching bootlegged films? Surely not. She thought about asking him, but who gave a damn if it was bootlegged; they were happy. They were laughing. She closed her eyes and listened to that sweet sound.

No, she did not miss the woods.

19

School started the Tuesday after Labor Day. Hailey Chatfield took the bus.

Matt Bouchard was planning on biking to school but he was struck by a desire to change this transportation choice on the first day of seventh grade after catching sight of Hailey standing at the top of the steep driveway with her backpack on, her hair pulled back and knotted in a sort of loose ponytail, sunglasses shielding her eyes. Matt walked his bike back to the garage and ran inside to tell his mother he'd opted for the bus.

She looked at him as if he were insane. Riding his bike to school had been a point of contention all last year, a valiant battle finally won by forces of good and decency and Matt's relentless text messages regarding the Camden crime rate, or rather the lack thereof. Being allowed to bike to school had been seen as a win for freedom and independence everywhere. Now he was trading it for the bus?

"The new neighbor kid is out there, and her aunt asked me— and *you* asked me—to be nice to her or whatever." He tried to seem put-out by the idea, as if grudgingly succumbing to his better nature. His mother's surprise morphed into a smile, though, and he felt heat rise in his cheeks. *"What?"* he said. "Didn't you ask me to be nice to her?"

The smile remained as she nodded. "I certainly did. So you just saw her standing out there and felt so bad you decided to do this on the spur of the moment, eh? That's considerate of you, Matthew."

"I thought so," he agreed. "I probably won't do it again, but new kids get nervous on the first day, you know? So just this once."

"Just this once," his mother echoed. "Be polite," she called after him. "She's probably a nervous girl today." Pause. "And a cute one."

"Mom." He shut the garage door hard enough to be emphatic but not so hard that he would get into trouble for slamming it.

Up the hill, Hailey Chatfield had her head down and her phone in her hand. She'd pushed her sunglasses up on the top of her head. This was a small thing, and yet it made her look impossibly mature to him, impossibly cool.

Her focus on the phone was so intense that she didn't hear him approach. His own fault; years spent perfecting his silent walking techniques in the woods were coming back to bite him now. *Couldn't be clumsy if I tried,* he thought. "Hey," he said. He'd tried to deepen his voice, but it came out sounding more like a guttural grunt than a friendly hello. She snapped her head up and took a startled step backward. When she moved, her sunglasses slipped from their perch on her head and fell to the ground.

"Crap!" she said.

Matt rushed forward and bent to pick them up, praying that the lenses weren't cracked. In his hurry, he didn't see that she was bending over too. Their skulls met with a bone-on-bone *clack.*

"Ouch!" She stepped away, rubbing her head, face twisted with pain.

Couldn't be clumsy if I tried, Matt thought again, and he wanted to laugh and cry and run back to the house all at once. Take his bike to school after all. Skip school, maybe.

"Sorry," he said. "I'm really sorry." He picked up the sunglasses, brushed the dirt off them, and offered them to her. "They're not broken, at least."

She hesitated before taking them from his hand, as if afraid that he might follow the headbutt with a karate chop to the throat.

A bad start. A very, very bad start.

She inspected the sunglasses carefully. The lenses weren't cracked, but when she put them on, they canted to the left.

"They're bent," she said. "Damn it, they're bent!"

She was almost shouting at him, and when she tugged the gold-framed sunglasses off her face again, he saw with astonishment that there were tears in her eyes. She could get *this* upset about some stupid sunglasses? He felt less embarrassed now and more irritated. Who cared if she was new and pretty? She was also pretty shallow.

"I said I was sorry. But it was an accident. I mean, *I* didn't drop them."

She wiped her eyes furiously with the back of her hand and Matt saw that the anger wasn't because of him, or at least not entirely. She was mad at herself for showing so much emotion, it seemed.

She's probably a nervous girl today, his mother had said. Maybe Matt had underestimated her anxiety. She looked so cool, so calm, so mature, that the idea of her being nervous about anything didn't make sense. But then again, everything was new to her. Being tall and pretty and smart didn't keep you from being an outsider on the first day of school.

"It's okay," she said. "It's just... my dad gave them to me, that's all. It's fine. It wasn't your fault." But the tears were coming again.

"I can fix them," he said.

"Don't worry about it." Her voice was thick and she avoided eye contact, but there was a single tear leaking down her cheek. She wiped it away with a ferocious swipe of her hand, like she was swatting at a mosquito.

"Here, let me see."

"It's no big—"

But he was taking them from her, and she didn't resist. He held them gingerly in both hands, lifting them and studying the balance. They were Ray-Bans with dark lenses and thin gold frames. At the point where the left earpiece met the frame, the metal was bent and the tiny screw that joined the two pieces together was pushed up.

"This will be easy to fix," he said. "I promise. My dad's got little screwdrivers for stuff just like this. It'll take me two minutes." He was already in motion, hurrying back to his house.

"You don't need to!" she called after him.

"It'll be easy!"

"But you're going to miss the bus!"

He looked back and saw that the bus was indeed approaching, making the turn up the hill and onto their street. He couldn't fix the glasses now and ride the bus with her too. He hesitated, then said, "I usually bike anyhow. It's faster." Both statements were lies.

"You don't need to—"

"I'll find you in school and give them back. Do you know your homeroom?"

"Mrs. Houseman."

"Oh. Okay." He hoped she didn't see his deflation. Mrs. Houseman was an eighth-grade homeroom teacher. Hailey was a year ahead of him. Hopelessly far away from him, in other words.

She was already hopelessly far away after you headbutted her and broke her sunglasses.

"I'll find you," he said, and then: "My name is Matt."

"I'm Hailey."

"I'll find you, Hailey." He turned and ran back down the road and up his driveway. He watched his feet while he ran. It had been a long time since Matt Bouchard had tripped over his own feet while running, but today, with Hailey Chatfield watching, anything seemed possible.

It took him five minutes to find the set of eyeglass screwdrivers on his dad's workbench in the garage and then another fifteen to remove the earpiece, carefully bend the metal, and reset it with the tiny screw. He wasn't happy with his first effort, so he did it a second time, and then he set the glasses on the workbench and studied them to see if there was any tilt. They looked even. He found a level and rested it gently across the top of the frames. The bubble floated to the center.

Success.

He held the glasses up and put them close to his own eyes, studying the lenses to see if there'd been any faint scratching that he could buff out. The lenses looked fine. Holding the sunglasses this close to his face, he felt as if he could smell the faintest trace of perfume or shampoo. He leaned closer, inhaled...

"*Matt!* What are you doing?"

His mother's shout surprised him so much that he came terribly close to dropping the sunglasses again. He held on, though, and looked back to see her staring at him from the door to the house, her car keys in her hand and her bag slung over her shoulder.

"I had to come back for a minute," he said. "Hailey dropped her glasses, and she was all upset because her dad gave them to her, and I knew I could fix them, so—"

"School started five minutes ago!"

He glanced at his watch, his beloved Garmin that told the altitude, barometric pressure, and compass bearing as well as the time.

She was right. The first day of school had officially started without him. But Hailey's sunglasses were fixed. You had to count victories and losses.

"Get in the car," his mom said in a low, warning tone that brooked no discussion. "Now."

And so he arrived at his first day of seventh grade not on his bike or on the bus but in his mother's Subaru, fifteen minutes late by the time he climbed out, holding the sunglasses as gently as if he were transporting a kitten.

"We'll talk this afternoon about your approach to punctuality," Mom said.

"It was one time."

"I sincerely hope so."

He walked into school thinking that he'd be surprised if being tardy on the first day was detention-worthy...but regardless, he was already tardy, so could one be tardier? Late was late. Better to look to the future and start fresh by being on time for English.

Also, with no reason to rush, he could wait outside Mrs. Houseman's room.

The bell rang ten minutes after he arrived, and the hallway flooded with students. Almost all were familiar faces. Camden-Rockport was far from the smallest school around—Islesboro had just fourteen students in seventh grade this year—but it also wasn't so big that there were many strange faces. You knew almost everyone by seventh grade. He exchanged a few nods and hellos with classmates, but he was on the hunt for the one face that would be unfamiliar to all of them. She was nearly the last one out of the room, walking with her head down, eyes on her schedule.

"Hailey?"

She looked up, surprised that anyone knew her name, then recognized him. "Oh. Hey."

"Hey." He held the sunglasses out. "I fixed them. You can check, but I think they're fine."

She took them out of his hand, slid them on...and smiled. "Wow. You did it."

The smile weakened his knees, but he nodded with what he hoped passed for calm confidence.

"Sure. Like I said, it was easy. You just need the right tool, that's all."

She took the sunglasses off, handling them carefully, pulled a case out of her backpack, and zipped them into it. Matt waited, and one of his friends, Danny Knowlton, passed by and gave

Hailey a look and then Matt a look, one eyebrow raised. Matt just shrugged. He knew he'd hear about this soon enough. He'd get plenty of questions about the new girl by the end of the day.

"Okay, since you're such a big help, can you do me another favor?" Hailey asked.

"No problem." He was ready to agree to build her a car if she asked for one, but she just handed him her schedule.

"Where's my science class?"

"I'll show you."

"You won't be late for yours?"

"Nah." He laughed. "I was already late for school, so I'm not too worried about it."

She fell into stride beside him, the two of them walking upstream against a swarm of students. He loved the feel of walking beside her, but he wished he were taller. She also had the extra year on him. But she was walking with him, and he'd fixed her sunglasses, and her mother had asked him to keep an eye on her. By that calculus, he was already the best friend she had. It might last for a week or two.

"You were late?" she said. "You rode your bike?"

"No. My mom took me, and I was still late."

"Is she pissed?"

"Not too bad. I'll find out when she gets home from work, I guess. If I'm lucky she'll be really busy with casework crap and she won't have the whole day to think about it."

"Casework?"

He nodded. "She's a private investigator."

Hailey stopped walking. "Seriously?"

"Yeah. It's not as cool as it sounds, though. She doesn't do any of the interesting stuff. She pretty much sits at a desk all day using computer databases. It's not like your aunt, who's—"

"There's a private investigator in Camden, Maine?" She looked incredulous to the point of suspicion.

"She actually works in Rockland," Matt said, but it was evident that Hailey didn't distinguish between the two.

"As an investigator," she repeated with what seemed to be growing fascination.

"Yeah, but the boring kind. Trust me, she's not doing anything cool."

"But she researches people, finds out who they really are, things like that?"

Matt was used to dismissing his mother's profession as boring and nothing like TV, but there was something to the intensity of Hailey's interest that told him not to do this. Anything that interested her was something he wanted to encourage.

"Yeah," he said. "That sort of thing. Background checks and stuff like that. Tracking people down."

"Background checks," Hailey said. Someone bumped into her but she didn't react. She just stood there, one thumb hooked in the pocket of her jeans, her dark bangs swept across her forehead, staring at Matt as if truly seeing him for the first time. He liked the feeling. A lot.

"Yeah."

"So if I gave her, like, a name and a birth date, she could tell me about that person? She could find stuff that doesn't show up on Google?"

Matt Bouchard hadn't reached the age of thirteen without developing a few finely honed instincts. He had good *emotional intelligence,* a teacher had told his parents. As he looked back at Hailey right now, emotional intelligence met a healthy dose of hormones and produced genius.

"I could do that myself," he told her. "She's shown me how to do basically everything that she does."

"Seriously?" Hailey looked both dubious and hopeful.

"Sure," Matt said. "She let me job-shadow her."

This was true. He'd job-shadowed his mother for exactly one

day. He'd spent most of the time playing games on his phone but he knew better than to mention that. "If there's anything you want to find out," he said, "just let me know."

"Okay," she said. "Cool. Let me...let me think about that."

"Sure. I mean, I'm right next door, so just come by the house, or find me here in the hall, or whatever."

The hall, as it happened, was rapidly emptying. They both seemed to realize that at the same time and Hailey said, "Where's my science class?"

"I'll show you. Hey, why don't I get your phone number and you can just, like, text me the name or whatever and I'll find out everything you want to know." Casual, as if having her number didn't mean the world to him.

"Okay," she said, and just like that, he had her number. Just like that, the day went from good to great. He put it into his phone, sent her a text that said, Hey, it's Matt, now you've got my number, then pocketed the phone as they reached her classroom door. She made it in as the bell rang, leaving Matt alone in the hall, late for the second time that day. But walking to his English class, he didn't care about the tardiness one bit.

It was less than an hour before she texted him: Douglas Louis Chatfield, DOB 08/12/1979.

He'd responded to the text with nothing more than a thumbs-up emoji. Professional investigators didn't ask more questions than they needed to. Certainly not of clients. You nodded knowingly, as if you understood everything already, and you went to work. In today's society, the thumbs-up emoji was the equivalent of the knowing nod.

Matt Bouchard had a PI client, and she was gorgeous.

Bring on the seventh grade.

20

For a few blissful hours that night, all news was good and Leah's focus was on the future. The first day of school had gone well for both Nick and Hailey. Nick had a lot of news that excited him: There would be a field trip on a three-masted schooner, which was *way* cooler than any field trip he'd taken in Kentucky; there was another Nick in his class who looked so similar to him that other kids joked about them being clones; he'd won races in gym; the food was better here than in Kentucky; his teacher was funny. Small things that were huge in the world of an eleven-year-old boy, and the accumulation of positive experiences filled Leah with hope.

Hailey spoke less and with a more reserved demeanor, but her reports weren't discouraging. She thought she was ahead of the math class she'd been placed in but said that was okay because she didn't want to have to stress over it this semester. The kids were okay. The teachers were okay. Everything was okay, fine, neutral. She wouldn't condemn anything or praise it. She just wanted to close her bedroom door and FaceTime with her friends back home.

There were no complaints, though, which was good.

Then, after dinner, an e-mail arrived from the law office of Everett J. Spoonhour.

> As we deal with the sudden and tragic loss of Everett, we hope that you will understand the gravity of the situation and remain patient. Recommendations for new counsel are available upon request, and we will work to expedite as necessary. As the staff and family deal with this tragedy, please reach out with questions only if they are urgent. We greatly appreciate your patience and your sympathy.

Leah blinked, read it again, and said, "What in the hell happened?" aloud. She was sitting at the desk in the small library room off the living room, and the doors were closed, but the doors were glass, so the kids could see her. She looked to her right and saw Nick's feet protruding from the end of the recliner. He was facing the TV. Hailey, however, was on the love seat, staring directly through the glass doors at Leah.

"Everything okay?" Hailey called, loud enough that Nick turned and leaned over in the recliner until Leah could see his face too.

Get it together. Act normal, and remember you're not alone in the house, Leah!

"It's nothing," she called, offering a dismissive wave of the hand to prove the point. "Some silly stuff with the...with the guy who checks in on the cabin when I'm gone."

"What happened with the cabin?" Hailey was sitting straight up now, looking at Leah intently.

"Oh, nothing. The generator might be broken, and the generator is almost new, so I can't believe..."

Can't believe I keep lying to my own children.

It was the right thing to do, though. For their protection. The truth would terrify them more than any fiction she could spin. For the time being, silence was better.

It's not just silence, Leah. It's active, not passive. You're lying to them.

"Did it blow up?" Nick said, sounding almost hopeful.

"No. It did not blow up. I bet it's just the battery." She waved her hand again. "Anyhow, it's no big deal, guys. Sorry."

Nick, satisfied by the explanation if disappointed by the lack of an explosion, faced the television again. Hailey kept her eyes on Leah. She always seemed to be watching. That shouldn't be a problem, except that...

You're lying to her, and you don't want to get caught.

Except for that, yes. Lying was a bad thing but still the right thing. Lesser of two evils. She would tell them the truth in time.

Right now wasn't the time. Right now, she wanted to get away from her daughter's watchful eyes.

She closed the laptop and went upstairs to her bedroom, where the iPad waited. There, out of sight of her children, she opened the e-mail again, read the client letter once more, then opened Google, went to the news search page, and entered Spoonhour's name.

Heart attack, car wreck, hunting accident, please let whatever awful thing it was be an isolated awful thing...

The results loaded, and Leah's blood seemed to thicken and slow in her veins.

Louisville attorney Everett J. Spoonhour, 52, was found dead in his office Wednesday night, and the Louisville Police Department has termed the situation an active homicide investigation.

Spoonhour's body was discovered in his office shortly before midnight, after a coworker unlocked the door following a call from Spoonhour's wife, who was concerned that he hadn't come home. The coworker found Spoonhour dead at his desk and summoned police.

LPD detective Richard Jackson stated that Spoonhour had died from a knife wound to his throat and that the weapon was not present at the scene.

"It was a brutal crime," said Jackson.

Security cameras that show the building's lobby entrance were apparently either malfunctioning or disabled. While police have declined to say whether there are initial suspects in the case, Detective Jackson acknowledged that investigators will "likely" be in contact with "clients or potential clients."

Spoonhour, a Louisville native who took over his father's practice, did not practice criminal law. According to his website, his areas of concentration were real estate and probate.

Leah's heartbeat was steady but loud in her ears, a bass drum building to a crescendo.

"Nothing to do with me," she whispered. Of course it had

nothing to do with her. It was a tragedy, but tragedies happened everywhere, every day.

You've got exactly one lawyer, Leah. A man who specializes in real estate and probate and dusty old deeds, and he's been found at his office with his throat cut. How many of Spoonhour's clients were involved with the throat-cutting kind of people, do you think?

She felt bile in the back of her throat and swallowed it. Questions rose up and vanished in her mind like road signs along the route of a speeding driver: How many clients did Spoonhour have? How much were the police legally allowed to learn about the clients? How would they attempt to make contact with clients? Would they be content with a phone call?

The only number that Spoonhour had for her went directly to the satellite messenger. She'd given him that simply because she'd had to give him something. The messenger wouldn't ring, of course, but she'd told him she preferred text messages. If he'd sent any, she hadn't gotten them, because the messenger had been forgotten once Hailey and Nick were with her. They were the only ones for whom it had ever existed, and the kids wouldn't be using it again. The magic talisman had served its purpose and she'd not bothered to look at it since.

She set the iPad down, rolled onto her shoulder, and removed the DeLorme messenger from the top drawer of the nightstand. The screen showed several notifications: a low-battery alert and four messages. Four phone numbers to which she'd never responded. She scrolled through, recognizing the first three: Spoonhour, Spoonhour, Spoonhour. Dead man, dead man, dead man. The fourth, though, the most recent, was an unfamiliar number with an area code that wasn't Kentucky. She reached for the iPad, intending to look the number up. That was when Hailey spoke.

"Is that how I got you?"

Leah swore and fumbled the messenger and the iPad, dropping the first onto the bed and the second onto the floor. She whirled around and saw Hailey standing on the other side of the partially opened door.

"My *goodness,* you surprised me," Leah said, trying to recover her composure while her mind whirled with questions. How long had Hailey been standing there? Was the murder story visible from that angle? "You've got to learn to knock. It's the polite thing to—"

"Is that how I got you when Dad died?" Hailey said.

Leah fell silent. Looked at Hailey and then down to the messenger, which rested on top of the comforter. She picked it up, then leaned over and grabbed the iPad from the floor. It was still open to the browser, the headline Louisville Attorney Murdered in Office in bold font.

She flipped the cover shut.

"Yes," she said. "This is what you called. I'm very glad you did."

"What is it?"

"An emergency messenger. It relies on satellite so you never have to worry about a cell phone signal. When you're in Maine, not having to worry about a cell phone signal is pretty important." Leah forced a laugh.

Hailey didn't match it. Just stared at Leah with those ever-scrutinizing eyes. "But you've got an iPhone," she said. "And an iPad and a laptop and an Amazon Fire Stick. You're not using old-fashioned stuff. Why is *that* thing the number I had to call?"

"Like I said, cell signal where I lived could be pretty—"

"I didn't know your other numbers. I didn't know your address. I didn't know anything about you except for that one number. And why did Dad make me *practice* calling it? I had to memorize it, and I knew it wouldn't ring. He made sure I understood that. He made sure I knew that I would have to leave my number and press the pound key and hope that you called back."

Leah held the DeLorme tight in her palm, looking back at her daughter and feeling the distance that lies and secrets had built between them and was threatening to widen now. There was no way to close it except with the truth, but—

Louisville Attorney Murdered in Office

The truth needed to be delivered at the right time.

"Your father and I were not particularly close," she told Hailey at last. "But we were family, and it's such a small family that you have to plan for the worst because...well, because there just aren't many of us. He wanted you to call me because he knew that I would take care of you and Nick. He was right." Her eyes searched Hailey's. "Do you understand that?"

Hailey said, "What did my dad do?"

Leah pulled her head back. "What?"

Hailey took a half a step into the room. "He did something, didn't he? Something bad, I bet. And nobody wants to tell me."

Leah was shocked. She'd never thought suspicion would boomerang back to Doug. "He didn't...no, honey. He was a very good man. Your father loved you and he was—"

"*I know he loved me!*" Hailey snapped. "I don't need *you* to tell me that! I didn't ask if he loved me. I asked what he did."

"He didn't do *anything*. I promise."

"Something is wrong here. You know that."

Leah was looking at her with slightly parted lips and the truth waiting just behind them when there was a clatter of nails on hardwood and then Tessa burst into the room, tail wagging, snout raised, tongue dangling. The dog looked from one of them to the other with a goofy *Why didn't you guys tell me there was a party?* face. Immediately after the dog's arrival, Nick shouted, "Where is everybody?"

"Upstairs, hon!" Leah called, trying to keep her voice light. She stood up, slipped the satellite messenger back into the open nightstand drawer, and grabbed the iPad with her free hand as if afraid Hailey might snatch it, flip back the cover, and find the murder story.

"We will talk about everything," she said in a low voice. "I promise you, Hailey, we will talk when the time is right. Until then, I need you to work with me. And the one thing you need to remember is that your father was a good man who loved you."

"What about you?"

"I love you. Of course I do."

"That's not what I meant. Are *you* a good person?"

"I certainly try to be."

"We have a lot of secrets for a family full of good people," Hailey said.

A rush of footsteps on the creaking stairs, slapping tennis shoes, and then Nick was shoving into the room behind Tessa, wrinkling his nose and staring at them in confusion. "What's wrong?"

Leah waited. Hailey waited. Tessa whined, as if sensing the tension. Finally, Hailey spoke.

"Nothing's wrong," she said. "Don't you know that, Nick? Nothing is ever wrong in this family. We are all just good people. It's a shame that there aren't more of us, considering what good people we are."

She walked away, leaving Leah standing in front of the nightstand clutching the iPad with its bloody news.

21

The lights went out one by one in the Trenton house, but Dax Blackwell maintained his watch in the dark rain.

Someone had to. Leah Trenton seemed determined to push her kids out into the world and ignore the risks. Dax appreciated this. There were two ways to live when there was a high probability of finding yourself in someone's crosshairs: boldly or fearfully. Only one allowed you to have much fun.

The only problem with Leah Trenton was that Dax didn't believe that she really appreciated those risks. Her protective measures were minimal at best—renting the house under a business name instead of her own, for example, and buying new phones for her kids—and she did not seem willing to draw the children into the game. That was a shame, Dax thought. The family unit was so much tighter and the emotional bonds so much greater when everyone understood his or her role. When danger was present, it should be acknowledged, and then the lessons could begin. Constant threat was a unique gift, one that enhanced every experience and certainly provided an impetus for swift learning.

Perhaps Dax should open a charter school. They were popular in some places these days, and tuition was sky-high for the elite academies. Dax Blackwell's academy would be very elite. *I want you kids to understand that at any hour of any day, someone may be considering ways to kill your family. Now, let's talk about the survival probability of low-IQ humans versus high-IQ humans, with a particular focus on problem-solving abilities. Shall we begin?*

You had to coddle these kids, though. There probably wasn't

a school around, private or public, in which the book *Countering the Threat of Improvised Explosive Devices* was required reading. What a loss. Dax had learned a good deal about basic chemistry and physics from that starting point. His aunts and uncle had been sticklers for the STEM side. His father had been more interested in the humanities and had a particular fondness for philosophy.

Another required text, *Kill or Be Killed,* had been the first of many primers on hand-to-hand combat, although Dax had favored one titled *The Little Black Book of Violence.* He believed that *should* be mandatory in every child's education. It showed the reality of fighting, the gravity of injuries that could be inflicted with a simple exchange of punches, the way lives could end or be forever altered by physical conflict. Dax thought there'd be fewer fistfights in middle schools if kids were required to read that book. If he were on social media, perhaps he could be one of those ballyhooed influencers. Really change the system from the outside in. Alas, social media wasn't ideal for his line of work.

He stood in the rain, listening to the water sluice through the needles of the fir tree above him, and watched as the lights went dark in the house. It took a long time for Leah Trenton to shut off the faint blue light in her room. It was probably from a computer or a tablet. What was she reading? Dax wondered. What was she planning?

If she was planning to stay alive, she was doing a very poor job of it, with one notable exception: she'd made the call that led to Dax's arrival.

What better choice could one make?

As baffling as her behavior seemed for a woman on the run, it was less perplexing than that of Marvin Sanders and Randall Pollard. At least when it came to Leah Trenton, Dax could understand why she trusted in her safety—she'd vanished ten years ago and had been safe for all that time. The children were now in her care, and nothing bad had happened. Easy—albeit foolish—to believe that would continue. She wasn't an operator, Doc Lamb-kin had said. She was a civilian who'd crossed paths with some dangerous folks.

Marvin Sanders and Randall Pollard, however, *were* operators, men who knew the killing game well, and yet they hadn't found their quarry yet. That was surprising. The task hadn't been hard. Nicholas Chatfield had downloaded both the streaming app and the game app he'd been sent. He'd been rewarded with access to expensive pirated content on both fronts, and Dax had been pleased to see him enjoying the latest theatrical releases and the FIFA soccer game. In exchange, Dax had been rewarded with the ability to monitor the entire family. Nicholas's phone had granted him access to the router, which Dax had infiltrated to gain access to the cameras and smart speakers of any device in the network.

Simple stuff. Quite literally child's play. And yet Mr. Sanders and Mr. Pollard hadn't arrived at the same solution, it seemed. They'd been slicing a lawyer's throat in Louisville, an absolutely needless crime. Even with that achievement under their belts, they somehow hadn't made it to Camden. What was taking them so long?

Lightning strobed and illuminated the stormwater running down a steep, rock-lined ravine into a holding pond at the base of the slope. The running water was a beautiful sound, like a con-versation between rocks that were usually silent but now seemed happy to raise their voices together and catch up on all that had passed since they last spoke. Dax swiveled his head slowly, taking in the quiet, tranquil neighborhood.

Perhaps he was giving Sanders and Pollard too much credit. They were pros at the killing game, yes, but that didn't require the same skill set as the hunting game. Their competency with automatic weapons did not mean they were proficient at electronic-tracking techniques. Once again, a failure of education. At the

Blackwell Academy, one would not be allowed to graduate until one had demonstrated a varied and versatile range of skills.

The culprit might be standardized testing, Dax mused as the rain kept falling. *If teachers aren't given a chance to really take ownership of their product, things are bound to fall between the cracks.*

If they'd followed the trail from the lawyer, they'd be in Maine soon. The first addresses they'd find affiliated with Leah Trenton would lead them to Greenville, and from there they'd determine where she owned property with Ed Levenseller, and they would head through the wilderness checking those locations, which was a sad waste of their time but not an entirely foolish choice. Dax could wait. He was a patient man.

He withdrew his phone from his pocket, shielded the screen with a gloved hand, and checked the video feeds from the Trenton and Chatfield devices. Nick was asleep, his phone charging—and watching—from the nightstand. Hailey's phone was on the floor, but Dax could hear her regular breathing. And Leah Trenton lay awake, shifting from side to side in the bed, as if searching for comfort.

"Relax, my dear," Dax whispered. "I'm right here."

She turned onto her other shoulder.

Where, oh, where might the Lowery boys be?

En route, Dax knew. He pocketed the phone. They were late, but they were undoubtedly headed this way.

22

There were plenty of things Becky Conway had come to loathe about Greenville, Maine, during her two-year tenure as post-master, but the most prominent among them was the residents' overwhelming tendency to use the word *moose* when naming a business.

From her counter at the post office, she sorted parcels for the Moose Mountain Lodge and the Moosehead Vista Motel, the Cozy Moose Cabin, the Stress Free Moose Pub and Café, and Crazy Moose Fabrics. Within a block of her, there was the Moosehead Historical Society, the Moosehead Marine Museum, and Moosehead Motorsports. After work on a Friday, with her head pounding, she'd go into the bar and look at the specials board advertising a moose-cow mule cocktail.

We get it, people, she thought. *Enough with the friggin' moose.*

Maine had more moose than the rest of the Lower 48 combined, and that meant that assholes from away liked to venture up to see them, and that meant you worked a *moose* into your seasonal business name if at all possible.

Try sorting *that* mail. Her eyes would be blurred by moose-names by the time she finally settled onto a stool for her moose-cow mule. Screw it, she'd just order the vodka neat. Get right to the point.

Becky, originally from Vermont, had found her way to Maine courtesy of an absolutely worthless boyfriend and then stayed for another one. At least then she'd been closer to Portland, where you could get a decent meal and hear a good band play without driving two hours. When the fine people of the United States Postal Service offered her a promotion that sent her to Greenville, she should have researched the area a bit better before accepting. She'd been ready for a change, though—a bad relationship choice or two had stung her in Portland—and when she went to Greenville to interview, it was July and the place was pretty enough and she'd said why not. She hadn't really thought through the winter yet. Or realized that she was really moving to Moosington Center, capital of Mooseville, Mooseland.

We have other animals, she thought now, dumping a stack of letters into an outbound bin as the door chimed and two men walked in.

Strangers. This wasn't uncommon in the summer, but Becky knew most of the people who came in after Labor Day. Plus, one of these guys was black. She definitely knew all of the black guys in Greenville. Which wasn't saying much, considering she had more fingers on one hand than Greenville had black guys.

"What can I do for you?" she said cheerfully. Her voice was always cheerful. This was one of the reasons she remained employed and placed in front of people. She could be in a miserable damn mood and still sound perky as hell, just as happy as you wanted to believe. Becky Conway's lyin' voice was her greatest attribute. *And my ass,* she thought. *Definitely.*

"We're a little lost," the white guy said. He wasn't bad-looking, muscled up and a little rough around the edges, which was how Becky liked her men, but there was something off about his eyes. She squinted and figured it out—they were different colors. Weird. She looked at the black guy, and his eyes seemed absolutely colorless. What was that kind of paint that didn't have any shine to it? Matte? That was this dude's eyes.

"Head south," Becky said. "If you're lost, trust me, south is the right direction."

The white guy smiled a little at that. "I bet. But I don't mean *lost* as in we don't know which way to drive. I mean *lost* as in we're here and we don't know where to go next."

Becky slid the outbound-mail bin across the table and turned back to face him, cocking an eyebrow. "Is that supposed to make sense?"

"We're looking for someone who didn't provide us with a street address," he said. "Just the PO box. Which is here." He glanced sideways, taking in the bank of locked boxes. "Think you can help us out?"

"Wouldn't be legal of me to," Becky said. "But gimme the name just for giggles."

The hell did she care who they were looking for? Only thing Becky was looking for was a transfer. Maybe getting fired was the fastest route out of here before the snow flew.

She seemed to be entertaining the white guy, who was grinning at his buddy, but the buddy was not smiling. He was one poker-faced son of a bitch. Kind of seemed like a cop, whereas the white guy kind of seemed like he'd go out of his way to avoid a cop.

"Leah Trenton," the white guy said. "Box three seventy-three."

"Don't know her," Becky said, which was a lie, and she certainly knew box 373. She was forwarding the mail in box 373 every week. Premium priority forwarding, which was a royal pain in her ass, and expensive.

The black guy took out a phone and set it on the counter. A photograph was on the display, and Becky was about to shake her head and say she didn't know the woman in it, but then she stopped herself, cocked her head, and took another look. It was an older photo, but she did know the woman. She was Ed Levenseller's girlfriend...maybe. Anyway, they went around together. Becky had never been clear on the exact formality of the relationship and didn't particularly care. Ed was one of those guys who never seemed to loosen up much around Becky and would stick to beer when you wanted him to have a bourbon. Leah Trenton was around Greenville less than Ed but still a fair amount. She'd be there at all times of year, coming and going and occasionally checking her mail. She hadn't done that for quite some time, though, because her mail was being forwarded.

"Why you looking for her?" Becky asked.

"You do know her, then?" the black guy said. He had a voice with no treble, just bass.

"Why you looking for her?" Becky repeated.

The white guy smiled at her. "You're not a bullshitter," he said. "I like that."

"Do you, now," she said. "Well, you can imagine how that makes my day." He thought he was charming. Figured he was slick enough to impress a hick postal worker, at least. But Becky had dated a lot better than him.

And a few worse.

He leaned on the counter. "Uh-huh. Smart as you are, I bet you don't really need to ask that question either. Couple of guys show up from out of town with a PO box and a name but nothing else, what's *your* guess on why we're looking for her?"

Becky looked him in the eye and leaned across the counter herself. Got close to him. Held his attention for a moment before whispering, "You want to murder her." Then she straightened up and laughed. It had been a pretty good line, she thought. The white guy laughed with her. His black compadre did not. He just put the phone back in his pocket.

"Debt collectors?" Becky said.

The white guy's smile widened. Up close, his mismatched eyes weren't so weird. In fact, they were kind of intriguing. The green one was pretty. Shame he didn't have two of them.

"Got us," he said. "Your pal in box three seventy-three is running a little late and low these days."

"She's no pal of mine."

"Thought you didn't know her," the black guy said.

"That's right."

"You know she gets mail here, though," the white guy said. "And you probably know that a lot of them come with stamps that say things like *final notice* or *urgent.*"

Actually, Becky didn't recall any of those arriving for box 373, but she'd met debt collectors before, and there was no doubt in her mind that these boys were here about something that was past due. Intuition was one of her strong suits. Like her voice. And her ass.

"You guys know I can't answer that," she said.

"Does she come in and pick them up? Tell me that much?" the white guy said, still smiling but looking plaintive now, like a bad dog nosing for a treat he doesn't deserve.

"She might somewhere," Becky said, eyeing the clock, which showed it was two minutes to closing time on Friday afternoon. Bring on the stool and the mule. "But she doesn't do it here. I can tell you that much."

"It just stacks up and nobody gets it?"

Becky shrugged. Said, "That's one option."

They thought about that. It was the black guy who got it first.

"Forwarded," he said. "This one's just part of the chain. She's got more lined up."

Becky didn't answer.

"Where's it go from here?" the white guy said. "Please. Hook us up. We're sick of driving around here. We need to head south, like you said."

"If it goes somewhere from here," Becky said, "I don't know what happens to it. I'm just telling you, you'll be wasting your time if you hang around waiting for her to walk in that door." She pointed at the door theatrically. "And I'm about to walk out of it, fellas. Quittin' time. On Friday. The math does itself. I've got a date with a moose-cow mule."

That made her laugh but neither of them joined in. They were looking at each other as if they were trying to decide what to do next.

"Moose cow," the black guy said. She waited to see if he would laugh. He did not.

"I was nicer than I needed to be," she told them sweetly. "But that's all I got, okay?"

"I could use a drink myself," the white guy said.

"She's talking about a drink?" the black guy asked.

"I thought so," the white guy said. He turned back to Becky, fixed the brown eye and the green eye on her, and said, "Let us buy you a round for your trouble?"

She looked from him to the black guy, who was standing there so motionless it was like he'd been bolted to the floor, and tried to imagine him ordering a moose-cow mule. The thought of it made her lips curl into a smile. She pointed at him. "This one has to order whatever I want him to," she said. "Is that a deal?"

"Sure it is," he answered in that all-bass voice. He looked like you could zap him with a Taser and still not get a reaction.

"All the moose down in Mooseville liked moose quite a lot, but Becky, who lived north of Mooseville, did not," Becky told him in a deadpan voice.

He didn't so much as blink. Just gazed back at her. She snorted.

"You are some piece of work. But I'm gonna make you laugh, buddy. Better believe that."

"I look forward to it," he said. Tone of voice like he'd just scheduled a colonoscopy.

"I bet you do," she said, coming around the counter and walking toward the door. "Go on and get out of here. I got to close up. You don't want to stand in my way. Neither rain, nor sleet, nor snow."

The white guy smiled. "You wanna tell us where to find you for that drink and the laugh?"

"I'll give you a hint," Becky Conway said, opening the front door and waving them out. "There's a moose in the name."

Naturally, they went to the wrong place first. They tried the Stress Free Moose before finding her at the more respectably named Moosehead Brew House. There, they bought her four drinks before she told them that box 373's mail was now being forwarded to Camden. She didn't remember much of what she said after the fifth or sixth drink. They kept buying; she kept knockin' 'em back. Hell, it was something different, and in Greenville, Maine, after Labor Day? Something different was always a desirable night.

She got the white guy to dance with her. She did not get the black guy to dance. He sat on a barstool in the corner, back to the wall, eyes on the door, like some sort of old-time gunslinger. She gave up and tried to force him to pick a song on the digital impostor of a jukebox that had been blaring bad bro country for most of the night.

"Something that suits your personality," she said, by then expecting absolutely no reaction. She was surprised when he actually got up and went to the jukebox. Then she choked on her drink when Tupac's "California Love" came blaring through. The wild energy of the song couldn't have been less like him, this unblinking dude who looked like he had a resting heart rate of thirty and an exercising heart rate of thirty-one.

"That's funny," she told him as he took his barstool and leaned back against the wall again.

"Yes," he told her.

Now let me welcome everybody to the Wild, Wild West…

"What's your name?" Becky asked. Slurred, maybe. She was getting ahead of herself a tiny bit. Better slow down. But a fresh copper mug of moose-cow mule was being pressed into her hand by the white guy.

"They call me Bleak," the black guy said, and Becky laughed

again, laughed hard. He was funny, this guy. *They call me Bleak.* Now that, unlike the song, actually seemed to fit him.

Fresh out of jail, California dreamin'...

She danced with the white guy again. The bar was crowded and she was spilling her drink. She wasn't sure what number drink it was. She wasn't sure how or why she got to talking about Leah Trenton, explaining that she was some kind of hunting guide but probably thought she was better than everybody because she wasn't big on socializing, just kept to herself, and she'd been completely MIA for most of the summer and then began having her mail forwarded to Camden. She wasn't sure why she got to talking about Ed Levenseller, let alone writing his address on a cocktail napkin beneath her own number. She was better with addresses than phone numbers. Perks of the profession.

She knew she was drunk, but it felt different than usual. Higher and faster, her head floating at thirty thousand feet while her heart hammered back down on earth. How many drinks had she had? Better question: How many of her drinks had she watched them handle? You had to be careful, taking drinks from strangers. You had to be careful or you ended up feeling like...

Like this. Down on your hands and knees in your own living room looking for people who'd just been there with you but now seemed to have vanished as if they'd been imaginary the whole time. Her head drifted higher and her heart pounded faster and she looked for help but couldn't find it. Her friends were gone.

They weren't your friends.

No, maybe not. She needed a friend. She needed one real bad.

Where's the phone? Find the phone.

She fumbled at her pockets, but the phone wasn't there. Pockets too small, jeans too tight. Where was her purse? The couch, maybe? She smelled vomit and didn't remember getting sick. Her head floated higher, higher, higher. Heartbeat thundered lower, lower, lower. She crawled for the couch, made it about ten feet, and fell onto her side. The room spun around her and she thought she saw the two men for just an instant, standing in the hallway, watching her with unblinking eyes, but then they were gone and the spinning went on and darkness crowded in at the edges. She tried to remember what to do, where to go, who to call. She couldn't find answers for any of those questions, though. The only thing she remembered clearly was that she hadn't gotten the black guy to laugh after all.

Matter of fact, Becky realized as blackness washed in and over her like an eternal tide, she didn't think he'd even smiled.

23

While they waited for the bus that morning, Matt Bouchard told Hailey he had a good start on the research and that they should meet in person to discuss it.

"Can't you just e-mail it?" she asked.

Good thing he was prepared for this question. He hadn't spent the entire night online and wasted valuable lawn-mowing money on a Genealogy.com subscription just to hand his intel over without some face time.

"Nope," he said with what he hoped passed for an air of disappointment. "I wish. But when the information is confidential and privileged, it's such a risk. I've got a Gmail account, and..." He paused, made a show of considering, then shook his head. "I just don't trust the security on that. One hacker could cause a lot of trouble for Google, you know? So what we do— I mean, my mom and the other pros—what they do in this business is stick to hard copies. It's safer, because you can destroy them."

Hailey cocked an eyebrow at him as if she didn't completely buy the reasoning but then shrugged. "Whatever. Where do you want to meet up?"

"You tell me."

"Someplace where nobody is listening," she said. "Not school or my house or anyplace like that. Someplace private."

Excellent. Privacy was good. Privacy with Hailey Chatfield was a wonderful idea. "You have a bike?" Matt asked.

"Yeah, my aunt got me one, but I don't ride it. I'm not ten."

Matt nodded, trying to pretend that he wasn't embarrassed. "I'm only on mine for business. It saves time, you know."

Hailey's lip twitched. "Sure," she said. "Okay, so if I ride my bike for *business,* where would I go?"

He was all too ready for this question, because he'd spent two summers imagining where he'd take a girlfriend if he actually had one.

"Rockport Harbor," he blurted out. "There's a park right by the harbor, but there's also a trail that goes up to a waterfall, and almost nobody uses it. It's real pretty up there and, like, totally private."

There was the lip-twitch smile again. "You do a lot of business by the waterfall?"

She was only a year older than him, but she had a way of asking teasing questions that made him feel as if she believed she was twenty years older.

"Not a lot," Matt said, refusing to take the bait of the question or back down from his chosen meeting place. "It's a good spot, though. For your needs."

"For my needs," she echoed. "Great."

Then the bus arrived and Hailey went straight to the back seat. Matt fell into the middle of the bus, not wanting to follow her. Kids nodded at her, but that was all. She was interesting to everyone because she was the new girl and everyone thought she was pretty because...well, because that was an objective fact. She popped her AirPods into her ears on the bus, as if she wanted to build a wall between herself and the rest of the kids.

Matt sat with Danny Knowlton and listened to Danny's theories on the New England Patriots, trying hard to pretend interest and not glance repeatedly at the back of the bus. Yesterday, Danny had asked Matt if he could see into Hailey's bedroom from his house, and everyone had laughed when Matt hotly said he had no idea. His friends were all equipped with teenage-calibrated lie detectors. Everyone already knew he had a crush on her, and none of them thought he had a chance.

They also did not have a meeting scheduled at the waterfall, however. *Bouchard 1, losers 0.*

24

When the kids left for school, Leah sat down at the computer, determined to do some research into the death of Everett Spoonhour and work proactively to either address her paranoia or lessen it. Something about the computer in the new house bothered her, though. She was suddenly conscious of things like IP address tracking and, damn it, cell phone tracking. She wished the kids didn't have phones but it hardly seemed like something she could take away from them now. *Let me have your only link to the friends and world you left behind. We're not going to use them anymore.*

No, she wasn't going to do that. But all the same, she missed those days out by Moosehead where Hailey had hunted for a cell signal in vain, and Nick had expressed dismay over the lack of Wi-Fi.

It was safer there. You made a mistake, bringing them to Camden.

But what could she do? Keep on the run for the rest of her life, without even knowing whether she was truly being pursued?

When the doorbell rang, she almost screamed. Instead, she let a long breath out through clenched teeth and chastised herself.

No panic. We will not panic, damn it. Cool your mind, Leah.

The doorbell again, its cheerful chime an intrusion.

She rose from the desk and went to the front door. Started to check the peephole before realizing that the man outside was standing at the bottom of the steps, watching her through the windows that flanked the door. He'd pushed the doorbell and then retreated.

Not Bleak, not Randall, not Lowery. He looked like a college student.

If he offers to mow the lawn, I'm going to scream, Leah thought as she rotated the dead bolt back and cracked the door. "Yes?"

"Hi," he said brightly. "Hope I'm not intruding."

"Well, actually, I was in the middle of—"

"But I wanted to be the first member of the Windward Ridge Homeowners' Association to welcome you." He beamed. He was dressed in charcoal hiking pants and black boots that matched his black baseball cap—good boots, she noted, Lowa Renegades, an excellent backcountry boot—and a long-sleeved T-shirt that was fitted to showcase his lean, chiseled torso. He was probably a runner and definitely a hiker with boots like that, and she suspected he was also a rock climber. She'd met plenty of climbers, and they all seemed to share two things: a minuscule BMI and an annoying-until-it-became-infectious enthusiasm. They were also often young or dumb or both.

He looked like he was both.

"This is not the right time for—"

"Completely understand," he said, lifting both hands, palms out. "I won't bother you. I just wanted to drop by when the kids were gone, you know, because I didn't want to freak them out with..." He gave a little between-you-and-me glance around and lowered his voice. "Their safety concerns."

Leah stared at him. "What did you say?"

"Safety concerns," he repeated calmly, and she pulled the door a bit wider, as if she were about to burst out of the house and run at him. Then she stopped, thinking of her gun, suddenly afraid, because a Lowery man wouldn't let her go back for the gun...

"You okay?" he asked, gazing up at her with a bemused smile. He might've been older than she'd originally taken him for; maybe he'd just retained that bright-eyed boyish look that some women would find adorable and some would find intolerable.

Regardless, too young to be a Lowery man. The company hired only experienced hands.

But you *were bright-eyed and young. When you started, at least. By the end, though…*

"The pond," he said.

Leah blinked. "Pond?"

He lifted his left arm to point east, then winced a little, as if the gesture pained him, and nodded his head in that direction instead.

"The green space," he said. "You're an abutter."

Leah's heart was pounding pavement at about a hundred and fifty beats per minute and her hand was tingling for the feel of a gun grip and cold trigger, and this little prick was talking about…a neighborhood pond?

"I really do not have the time to—"

He lifted his hands again. "It's not going to be me that shows up to cause them trouble. You know that."

Something about the way he said that gave her pause. She tightened her hand on the doorknob.

"Excuse me?"

"You *know* that," he said again, and his blue eyes twinkled with mirth that made her want to slap him.

"Who will it come from?" she said, each word dull and wooden in the crisp morning air, and she knew the name before he said it.

Lowery. It will come from J. Corson—

"Mrs. Wilkes," he whispered. He gave another nod to the east. "You know the one."

"I have no idea what you're talking about."

"Oh!" He leaned back and laughed, embarrassed. "My bad. Ouch. Shouldn't have let the secret slip. Anyhow, there's, like, one lady in this neighborhood who is…" He sighed and lowered his voice. "I wouldn't trust her when she walks down here with a smile on her face, is all I'm saying. And she will. Mark my words, she will. But, hey, good news, right? I'm here first. That's good for the kids." He grinned, showing a dimple. "Safety first."

"This is a bad time for me," Leah said. "Truly. If you could come back…"

"Okay, okay, I'm sorry. I'll get out of your hair. But when they show up? Just remember I was here first and could have helped."

He laughed and turned away. She looked up the drive and saw that there was no car at the top of the hill. He'd come on foot.

"What's your name?" she called.

"Marvin Corson."

Time stopped. Blood stopped. Then he turned and gave her the grin again.

"Just ask anyone to point you to the Carson house up the hill," he said, waving a hand in the direction of the birch trees across the road. "Everybody knows us."

Carson. Carson, not Corson, Leah. Get your shit together. "Carson," she echoed, and her voice cracked. She wet her lips. Tried to breathe.

"Yeah," he said. "My dad's Scott Carson. More people around here know him."

"Thank you," she said, because he was staring at her so intently that she felt she had to say something.

"Don't need to thank me," he said. "It's a family thing. I've got to do it."

This time, he did not smile, and he did not laugh.

She watched him until he was out of sight, then she closed the door, locked it, picked up her computer, and jammed it into a laptop bag. She needed out of this damn house.

25

She found a place called the Camden Deli that looked out across the harbor and had enough tables filled with tourists that she didn't feel as if she stood out. There she sat down with coffee and an omelet for which she had no appetite and opened the laptop and got to work.

She returned to the Google News page and put Everett's name back in, thinking today might bring a new, more detailed story, but the only things she found were rehashings of the initial news stories. If the police had any real information, they were playing it close to the vest. The good news was that she also didn't find any additional comments about the theory that one of his clients might have been responsible. In fact, the only addition was a quote from someone saying that Everett "didn't practice the kind of law that brought you in contact with killers. This is someone very sick who probably didn't know Everett at all."

She hoped the source was right, awful as it sounded to wish that a man had been murdered by a sociopathic stranger. Better that than anyone with an agenda or questions.

She forced a bite of the omelet down. The coffee was gnawing at her empty stomach. She returned to the search page, hesitated, and then entered a new name: *Lowery Group*.

She knew what she'd find, of course. References to some charitable contributions made, J. Corson Lowery being the benevolent good neighbor that he was. The strings attached to the donation were likely not to be clear in the article. Most of Lowery's motivations floated under the radar. She was paranoid, and the best evidence of that was this morning's odd exchange with the neighbor, who'd said Carson but Leah had heard Corson because she was so damn paranoid and hearing only what she—

The page refreshed, news results loaded, and Leah's throat constricted.

Prisoners Still at Large After Transit Van Accident.

There was only a teaser line of text below the headline, but it was enough. More than enough.

Marvin Sanders, 42, and Randall Pollard, 39, remain missing five days after they escaped following an accident during a federal prisoner transport in rural Georgia.

The teaser text didn't even mention Lowery, and it didn't have to. Leah knew. She understood exactly how this had played out.

He handpicked them, she realized. *Two men I would know. Two men who would know me. He could have sent anyone, he didn't need to risk arranging an escape, but it was worth it to him because they know me, and because they terrify me.*

Her throat pulsed and her stomach stirred and suddenly she was rushing past people in line at the counter, fighting her way to the tiny bathroom. She slammed the door shut behind her and leaned over the sink, preparing to retch.

Her gorge held but sweat sprang from every pore. Cold, clammy sweat, drenching her tank top, dripping from her hairline. The sweat of sickness, of fever, or of fear. She hung there, gasping and shuddering, a full-body tremble, and then eventually the nausea passed and she was able to turn the cold water on and rinse her face. She dabbed her skin dry and took a deep breath and opened the door and went back into the restaurant. A few people turned and watched her go by uneasily, and she felt like telling them not to worry, the omelet was fine.

She took her seat facing the wide glass windows that showed the waterfall cascading into the harbor and looked at her laptop screen once more, this time with a cool mind.

They're coming. All these years have gone by, but he didn't forget. He kept watch, just in case.

But had he? J. Corson Lowery was a dangerous man and certainly a man who held grudges, but would he have actually kept surveillance on Doug and the children if he'd located them? It felt off somehow. Not impossible but not probable either.

Coincidence, Leah? The attorney who handled the only dealings between you and Doug has been murdered, Randall Pollard and Bleak are free, and you're saying it's a coincidence?

Bleak. The name conjured the man, and Leah's stomach clenched again and the world swirled gray at the edges. She remembered the first time she'd heard his name. Rae Johnson, the first of the potential witnesses against Brad Lowery, had explained it to her. Leah could picture Rae in that tiny but immaculate little house in St. Petersburg, just past the Chattaway, where they'd met for a burger and a beer. Rae was a petite black woman with an easy smile and gorgeous eyes. On that day at the Chattaway, she'd looked into the face of a woman named Nina Morgan and said...

Bleak. That's all. Just Bleak. Nothing else to the nickname. He's not a big guy, not intimidating—at least not physically. Some of the guys they hire, the ones who did the bloodiest tours, they'd get to kind of like it, you know? Or anyway, they'd get a high off it. Adrenaline, testosterone, whatever. Marvin Sanders, though? He just seemed...indifferent. Apathetic. They'd all tell stories about him, talk about how fast he moved and how well he shot, talk about how he never said anything but what he needed to say. They steered clear of him too. I noticed that pretty early. People kept their distance.

He was from Cleveland. St. Claire Avenue, on the east side. Played wide receiver in high school, played it well, got scholarship offers, but never so much as made a campus visit. Enlisted in the army right out of high school. By the time Rae met him, in Kabul in 2005, where she was deployed with the air force, he'd graduated from Ranger school and earned a reputation for being unflappable under fire and unapproachable anywhere else.

Rae had joined the air force to get through college, the same as Leah, but without the interest in flying planes. She just preferred their pitch and their benefits. She was in the reserves on 9/11 and was called to active duty three years later. She'd been part of an intelligence unit, and eventually that put her in close contact with some operatives of the Lowery Group, back when they were just starting to secure major government contracts. She liked soldiers, she told Leah, particularly the special ops guys. They were courageous, elite, and, for the most part, decent men.

She did not like Marvin Sanders.

Empty, she told Nina Morgan. *I don't mean he could create emotional distance between himself and the job, because all of them can do that. Have to do that. I mean just what I say: he was empty, like a body without a soul.*

The nickname came from Marvin Sanders himself. In retrospect, Rae thought that was the only way he'd have gotten one that would stick or at least one that anyone would say to his face. It was during a midnight ambush on a raid that had gone bad in a hurry. Four Rangers were killed, five injured. One of the dead had been in charge of communications. He'd taken three rounds to the face and went over on his back, bone and blood where his eyes and mouth had been, his radio still crackling, Bagram asking him about the need for air support. When he didn't answer, the edgy commander from Bagram shouted for an update, the radio capturing his fear and fury, a guy miles away from the firefight yelling that he needed to know—how did it look out there?

Marvin Sanders had picked up the radio and responded with a single word: "Bleak."

Then he'd put the radio back down, crawled forward on his belly, and opened fire. His comrades dead, his entire unit and his own life in peril, and all he'd said was "Bleak." The nickname took hold fast, and while Marvin Sanders was surely aware of it, he didn't comment on it. He did not comment on much.

All of this, Rae had told Nina years later. They were colleagues then, all four of them—Rae and Nina and Bleak and Randall Pollard, the man with the mismatched eyes. The Lowery Group paid each of them more than double what the U.S. government had paid them to do basically the same job. Rae still scheduled flight plans and analyzed security concerns. Nina still flew planes in and out of isolated airstrips. Marvin "Bleak" Sanders and Randall Pollard still vanished into the night wearing full combat gear, the only difference now the lack of insignia or dog tags. If they died out there as independent contractors, it was very important that they were clearly civilians. There were multiple reasons for that, of course. One hurt the enemy, it being less impressive to boast of killing a civilian security contractor than a special operator in a Ranger or SEAL uniform. It was less impressive because the nation they were fighting took less interest, and that was even more important to the Lowery Group.

They wanted anonymity, not credit. The corporate culture could be distilled down to a single word: *silence*.

Anyone who didn't grasp that wasn't Lowery material. Nina Morgan learned that early. Another pilot had been posting photographs on his private Facebook page. They were innocuous shots of mountains and desert airfields, but he was still fired for the transgression.

It wasn't hard to buy into the need for silence, though. In fact, it made some sense when you were part of the mission. As the lines of the Lowery Group and the U.S. military blurred and wavered, as Nina began to fly people with official insignia alongside those in the trademark black of the Lowery Group, the mission began to feel very important indeed. Never mind that she didn't understand much of it. Who in a war really did? Winning a war was about doing your job. Incremental gains became cumulative successes. Fly safely, land safely. Do it again.

Strange as it was to say now, it had felt like a family company at the time. J. Corson Lowery—Mr. Lowery; nobody called him anything else—was actually around. He'd come and go frequently, and he made a point to know everyone. His recall for names was remarkable. His son was usually at his side, looking like a carbon copy but with dark hair instead of white, the two of them tall and trim and impeccably dressed. *Crisp*—that was the word for their look.

And they were kind, even. They exuded a sense of warmth that made you glad to work for them. When the owner of a billion-dollar operation looked you straight in the eye and smiled and called you by name, you felt a warmth for him, felt both impressed and grateful.

The old man was the boss—and there was no doubt about that, not even a whisper—but the son was the public face. Brad was the future, and not just because he was the heir apparent. His résumé was polished, his look perfect. Princeton undergrad, Harvard MBA. Army reserves. Worked in intelligence during his one brief deployment. Manager of hundreds of millions in capital and friend of a dozen senators, and only thirty-five years old. He would run for something. Everyone knew it.

In the beginning, he was just a different kind of cargo to Leah. Fly him out, drop him off, pick him up. He always called her by her first name, and he always asked after Doug. She requested stateside work when she became pregnant with Hailey and was granted it. By then, there was stateside work. Plenty of flights across the border in Mexico, but even those were short trips, and she could start and end each day in her own bed.

You could believe it was all normal. You learned not to think about the vagaries you used when explaining your own job to strangers. Sometimes, you recognized familiar faces on the television news. You'd see them later in Iowa, New Hampshire, and South Carolina. They'd usually be touting their foreign-policy expertise, the committees they'd served on. Committees that awarded contracts. You knew that Brad Lowery would be out there soon enough himself. Maybe not the next election cycle, but certainly the one after that.

You didn't really care. You had your own life to worry about—a career, a husband, a daughter, a son.

You had all of those things back then.

Leah put a new search in on the laptop, but this time she knew the result before it came up. She'd looked at the photograph a thousand times. It was the one the family of Rae Johnson had included in her obituary. In it, Rae was sitting in a pile of leaves with her two sons, Dante and Durrell. They'd been nine and six at the time of the picture, sitting shoulder to shoulder with her in a bright scatter of autumn leaves, mouths wide with laughter. The younger one was in a Batman T-shirt and his older brother wore a LeBron James jersey. Rae was wearing a simple white tank top over jeans and looked young and fit and fearless. There was a single maple leaf, red as a nicked vein, trapped in midair between them.

They'd been visiting her family somewhere near Philly when the photo was taken. Leah had never met the family. By the time Rae was buried, Leah was already in hiding.

It had been Rae's death that brought the investigators to Nina Morgan's door and, eventually, brought the pistol to Brad Lowery's lips.

The hit, Doc Lambkin had told her, wasn't supposed to involve the children. Just Rae.

This information came only after Leah flew the woman to her death.

Leah hadn't understood any of it back then, of course. She'd been unaware of the investigations, let alone that Rae was considering giving testimony. There wasn't a soul outside of the deepest reaches of the federal government who was supposed to know of those things. That was why, when Rae was invited to use the Lowery family's island home on Isla Mujeres, off the coast of Cancún, she'd apparently taken it at face value. Or, rather, she'd taken it as an opportunity to show them that her conscience was clear, that her unflappable loyalty wasn't compromised.

Her children hadn't been on the flight manifest.

They'd arrived at the private airport outside of Tampa with her, carrying bags loaded with flippers and snorkels and sunscreen, those two boys with their stunning, infectious smiles, off for an adventure. Rae smiling as well, because the pilot was Leah, a favorite and a friend. One long weekend on the company dime.

Rae had had to go, Leah realized later. She'd had to sell it as if she weren't afraid of a thing. On the flight, it had seemed as if she *wasn't* afraid of a thing. She trusted her protection from the feds.

Brad hadn't known about the children. It was supposed to be just Rae. In some perversion of his mind, that had evidently mattered. Kill Rae? Sure. Wipe out a family and risk being exposed for that? Apparently, that was a bridge too far.

In a strange way, Leah had been glad to hear that he'd killed himself. Glad to believe there was some shred of human guilt left in the man. She'd had a lot of years to think on that one. Her theories—hopes? Were they still sad, rationalizing hopes?— would never be proven or disproven. All she knew was that she'd flown Rae and those two beautiful children to a beautiful island

and waved goodbye to them as they piled into the rented Range Rover and headed off for their dream weekend, and then she'd waited on the tarmac for an hour before picking up her return-flight passengers: Marvin Sanders and Randall Pollard.

She was home by the time she heard the news about Rae and Dante and Durrell. They were dead, killed in a triangulated exchange of gunfire, although the explosion that resulted from the shots led investigators to wonder if the Range Rover had been rigged to blow up regardless of the shooting.

Cartel violence, law enforcement said, and the American media was all too ready to run with that narrative. Beware the beaches of Mexico. You don't know the evil that lurks south of the border.

The first investigator to visit Leah had carried a photograph of Dante and Durrell with him. She remembered staring at their faces while she fumbled out answers.

Yes, I can tell you about the flight. Plans were changed. It was Mr. Lowery's idea—Brad's, I mean—and I wasn't expecting the kids. It was supposed to be Rae and her sister, arriving on different flights. Then the kids came.

Yes, I brought passengers back with me. I can tell you their names too. Marvin Sanders and Randall Pollard.

Less than forty-eight hours later, Brad Lowery made a two-minute phone call to his father, and not long after he disconnected, he was dead by his own hand, and Nina was back on the phone with investigators, trouble headed her way.

Now, in Camden, Maine, two thousand miles and one lifetime removed from those events, trouble was headed her way again.

She closed the laptop, sealing the photograph away.

"I made a mistake," she whispered to herself, looking out those wide glass windows to the harbor beyond, the old wooden schooners sitting at moorings, the postcard-perfect park and shipyard and island. She had made a mistake coming to Camden. She was scared now, and she was scared for good reasons, but one of them had been self-inflicted: she had left the den. Foolish. She'd placed herself in a location that gave her no natural advantage. In the woods north of Moosehead, on the isolated logging roads and in the endless empty forests, she had built a woman capable of meeting and defeating all comers. Why was she pretending to be anything else, and why was she risking unfamiliar terrain?

Bleak. That's all. Just Bleak. Nothing else to the nickname. He's not a big guy, not intimidating—at least not physically.

He was on his way. Had been for days now, and Leah hadn't even been aware of that, because in her attempt to create a blissful bubble of existence, she'd denied herself the right to wariness. The right to fear.

She was afraid now, but that was all right. She was coming back into her own. Maybe not too late. Maybe not.

She left the deli, walked out into the crisp September day, and went to her Jeep. Unlocked the glove box and opened it and pulled out the Glock semiautomatic she'd brought with her, checked the magazine. Fully loaded, chamber empty. She set the gun in her lap and turned the car on and for a minute she sat staring up the street past the old Methodist church and the library and on out to Mount Battie with its stone tower built to memorialize fallen soldiers. Then she called Doc Lambkin.

He didn't answer. He always answered, but not today. His voice mail in-box was full, a robotic voice informed her.

No help from Doc. Not today.

She disconnected. She took a deep breath, leaned over, and put the gun back in the glove box, but this time she left the glove box unlocked. It was time to stop pretending she could live a life without guns close at hand. It was also time to get the hell out of this town. They would find her here soon, and they would find her children, and she wasn't prepared for them here. She would take her children and head north into the places that she knew and they did not, and there she would make the preparations that needed to be made.

If Pollard and Bleak chased her north?

Well, God help Pollard and Bleak then.

They thought they were pursuing Nina Morgan, and they were not prepared to meet Leah Trenton.

She was a very different woman.

26

Dax was having coffee at Marriner's when Leah Trenton went into motion. He was disappointed to hurry out because the coffee was excellent and he particularly liked their place mats, which were throwbacks to another era, when businesses actually advertised on such things. Evidently the approach was still useful in Maine when one offered snowplowing or tree-cutting services. Who knew? With a single place mat, Dax could have his yard excavated, his trees cut, his driveway plowed, his computer repaired, his boat stored for winter, and even take a seaplane tour. It was good to see that the internet hadn't yet spoiled Maine's print-advertising market. Did anyone actually call these businesses, say that they'd been reading about the company on a place mat, and ask for a quote? Perhaps *he* could advertise. *Murder and witness-extrication services, good references, family-owned!*

He was smiling over the potential of this when Leah Trenton pulled away from the curb and headed north, up Route 1 toward Belfast. Dax took his time following because he'd already installed a GPS tracker on Leah's Jeep. No need to rush.

When he left, he took the place mat.

He found Leah Trenton in Lincolnville, just a few miles north of Camden. She was talking on her phone and pacing the sidewalk that ran along the short stretch of sandy beach. Dax parked his rented Toyota Tacoma in the lot of someplace called the Whale's Tooth Pub and then walked to the water's edge and pretended to have great interest in the sea. It wasn't hard to pretend, because it was a stunning day and the wind over the water smelled clean and salty. Islands dotted the bay and far out beyond them you could see Mount Desert Island, near Acadia National Park. A beautiful place, Maine. All the same, he didn't care for it. He'd nearly died here once, and the clean, cold smell of the North Atlantic seemed to make his arm throb.

While he pretended to take cell phone photos of brightly colored lobster buoys, he watched Leah Trenton. She hung up her own phone, walked briskly down the pier, and entered the ferry terminal. She was inside for seven minutes and emerged with what appeared to be tickets in hand.

Dax frowned. The island might make sense to Leah, but it was so utterly impractical to Dax that he struggled to envision it. He didn't like to poison his own mind with someone else's bad ideas. Maybe she had a friend on the island, someone she trusted. Maybe she was proud of herself for buying paper ferry tickets with cash in a place that required no personal information, just payment, as if she were boarding a train in 1950.

But still…an *island*? Oh, Leah. Be better than that. Be best, as Melania Trump had said. Dax smiled at that thought. *Be best*. You laughed or you cried, right?

He pretended to ignore her and watch a pair of absurdly expensive sailboats pass by, flying Bahamian flags. Northern cruises in the summer and head south in the winter. The good life. He wondered how many people on those boats were bored with the good life. He wondered how many of them had once called someone in his family for a little assistance protecting their good lives. Yacht money rarely came without enemies.

He thought that J. Corson Lowery might have a boat. A man who owned an entire ranch that he rarely visited felt like a man who'd own a crewed boat he never sailed on.

I believe your father considered it an unsettled score, Doc Lambkin had said.

Dax gazed at the boats, breathed in through his nose, out through his mouth, and told himself that he felt nothing at all. There was nothing personal in this for him. There was never anything personal to the Blackwells.

Clear eyes, empty heart, can't lose.

When he turned back to the parking lot, Leah Trenton's Jeep was gone.

She'd driven away from the sea and into the hills, abandoning Route 1 for the back roads. Dax kept his distance, trusting his GPS tracker. Leah had been alerted to threats and he suspected she wasn't likely to miss any car that lingered in her rearview mirror. The green dot that indicated her Jeep finally came to a stop at the end of a dirt road called Fernald's Neck that led through the pines and dead-ended near Megunticook Lake. For the first time, Dax wondered if there was any chance he might have been seen. There was absolutely no way to go down the dead-end road without chancing a direct encounter, and maybe that was precisely what she wanted to provoke.

He pulled off the road in front of the Lincolnville general store and waited for the dot to move. It took a while. Twenty minutes passed, then thirty, and he began to grow more curious about Ms. Trenton's motives in the woods. He was considering a foot pursuit when, finally, the green dot returned to motion, tracking southeast and making the turn onto Route 105.

She was headed home.

What had the stop been about, then?

He drove to the end of Fernald's Neck as she had. The dirt road ended in a parking area for a local land-trust preserve. Signs indicated there were hiking trails ahead. Dax was all in favor of a nice walk in the woods to clear one's mind in times of crisis, but he found the idea of Leah Trenton going for a stroll unlikely.

She was in action mode today, and while some of the pieces made sense, others did not. Why the stop at the ferry terminal, and what in the world had she been doing at the lake?

"Interesting, Leah," he said aloud. "And no disrespect meant when I say it's about time."

He didn't know what Leah Trenton had in mind, but he was fairly certain she intended to be on the move soon.

27

The day dragged on interminably, and Matt never saw Hailey. He moved from class to class thinking of the limited information he'd been able to uncover about her father and wondering how to spin it in a way that suggested progress. It had been a single night's work, after all, and even a good PI needed a reasonable amount of time. Especially a PI who still had a curfew and a bedtime.

They sat separately on the bus ride home, and only when the bus pulled away and Danny Knowlton's leering, freckled face vanished from the window—he was waiting to see if Matt would try to talk to Hailey—did Matt speak.

"This afternoon still good?" he said.

"Yes. You still want to go to the waterfall where you have your business meetings?"

"It's the best spot."

She smiled a little and then it was quiet and he felt awkward.

"So you want to meet me down there?" he asked.

"Can't we just go together?" She said it like it was the obvious choice. As if the idea shouldn't have accelerated his heartbeat.

"Sure," he said. "That's what I meant."

Her lip twitched and she nodded. "Okay. I'll go get the dumb bike, then."

"Me too," Matt said of his beloved eighteen-speed.

He dropped his backpack off in the kitchen, ran upstairs and grabbed the folder marked *Confidential and Privileged Data,* ran back down, pushed his bike to the top of the driveway, and waited.

A few minutes later she appeared, pushing what seemed to be a new bike. Most of her things seemed to be new. He thought about her sunglasses again and the way she'd reacted when she thought they were broken. *My dad gave them to me.* Was that the only thing she had from him? What had happened to everything in her house?

"What?" she said as if sensing that he was assessing her.

"Nothing. So, uh, it's mostly downhill," he said, just to say something.

"Good," she said. "With no cross-country this year, I'll probably die going up hills."

He pedaled off, she rode beside him, and all was momentarily perfect with the world. The air was warm but not hot, the sky a blue so bright and cloudless that it seemed like computer effects had been used to deepen and brighten the color. Leaves not changing just yet, but the promise of fall was trapped in the deceptively warm air. Maine in September.

They rode out of the neighborhood, turned onto Washington Street, and headed toward town. Washington was all coasting, a glide toward the harbor. Halfway down there was a clear view of the bay, a cluster of sailboats moored in the sparkling water, Curtis Island just beyond. The little rise was something you didn't even notice in a car, but on a bike you felt your stomach drop a little, and there was the exhilaration of speed that came when the road crested and leaned steeply toward the harbor. Matt thought a lot of the best things in town could be missed from inside a car.

They passed the old Knox Mill, then cut through a parking lot, the Megunticook River churning beside them, and came out across from the library and the harbor park. Camden Harbor drew more visitors than Rockport, which was precisely why Matt was headed for Rockport.

They biked uphill, past the French and Brawn market, then stopped to walk their bikes across the street. Matt glanced over and saw that Hailey was smiling. He hadn't seen her smile like this before—not in sarcasm or teasing but just a wide-open, having-fun smile.

She saw him looking and seemed to catch herself, as if she regretted the smile. Then she shrugged and said, "I haven't ridden a bike in a few years. Downhill is really fun. I kind of forgot that."

"Yeah. It is, isn't it?"

Traffic stopped for them, and they waved and crossed the street. From here they rode along Union Street, out of Camden and into Rockport, passing beneath the big arch that announced the town name and snaking toward the harbor marine park. It was smaller than the Camden Harbor and set down below the town with a handful of lobster boats moored among the sailboats and an ancient train locomotive called the Vulcan resting on an island of track laid in the grass. It was quiet and beautiful and looked like every postcard of Maine. Girls from Maine might ignore it but he thought it would impress a girl from Kentucky.

When they paused above the harbor park and looked out to the open bay beyond, the smell of the sea came in on a warm breeze and Hailey tilted her face up to take it all in. Matt would have been content to hold that moment for the rest of the afternoon. He didn't want to be caught staring, though, so he turned away.

"This is the place?" she said. "I don't see a waterfall."

"It's back there, where the old quarries are. Follow me."

They biked down a narrow trail that wound through crowded pines that deadened the road noise and dropped the temperature, creating the sensation of a secret realm, cooler and quieter than the world they'd left behind. The area had once been a lime quarry, and mounds of white rock flashed bright on the other side of the dark pines.

When they finally reached the picnic tables by the falls, Matt was a little out of breath and trying not to show it. Hailey didn't seem to have broken a sweat.

She sat on the picnic table. Not on one of the benches but right up on the table, which presented Matt with an awkward choice— sit up there with her, side by side, or sit below.

Sit next to her, dummy.

But he didn't. Instead he sat on the bench and halfway down the table, keeping his distance. "Okay, so what I did was run the name you gave me through a few databases," he said, trying to sound professional. "It took more time than I expected because there are more Chatfields in Kentucky than you'd think, but I've got a list."

She leaned down to look, her body putting a shadow over the pages. When she reached out to separate the sheets with her index finger, her hand grazed his arm. He was still fixated on that brief touch when she said, "None of this helps."

He blinked. "Huh?"

"I don't know any of these people."

"Well, I thought they were family, maybe? I mean, they're all connected."

"To my dad?"

They'd never flat-out acknowledged whose name she'd given him before. He hadn't asked, and she hadn't volunteered the information.

"Um, I'm not sure yet," he said. "I didn't have that much time. But I figured you'd recognize some of them?"

"I don't. But this also isn't what I meant by finding out who someone was. I didn't want a family tree."

"Well, it sounded like you did," Matt said, a bit indignant considering his financial investment in Genealogy.com. "You said you wanted to know who he was."

"Yeah, who *he* was, not which relative came to Kentucky from Virginia in 1826."

Matt, who had been proud of the 1826 discovery, was now embarrassed enough to become flustered and defensive. "Well, he was *your* dad. What was I supposed to find out about him that you don't know?"

The silence that settled between them then seemed to press his shoulders down and squeeze his lungs. The idea that anything resembling a smile had ever been present on Hailey's face seemed impossible now. She didn't look angry; she looked devastated.

"Forget it," she said softly.

"No," he said, earnest. "*What do you mean?* I don't understand what you want me to find. If I understand, I'll figure it out. I promise."

She shook her head and didn't answer, just turned and sat staring at the waterfall, the spray reflected in her sunglasses.

"Sorry," she said, and her voice was very soft.

"You don't need to be sorry. I just don't know what you're looking for. I thought it was for his family."

"I thought so, too." She swallowed, and when she spoke again, it was in a whisper. "I should recognize some of those names, right? I should have grandparents, like everyone else. Aunts and uncles and cousins. Don't you have all of those?"

"Yeah."

"I don't. I had a dad. That was all."

"What happened to your mom?"

"She died when I was really little. Right after my brother was born. I don't remember her, though. The only family I ever had was him."

"And your aunt."

"But she wasn't around. Not ever. She'd send these notes and birthday cards with money but we never even knew how to write back to thank her. She didn't do anything normal, like call or text or e-mail. She communicated with us like she was a hundred years old or something. And my dad almost never talked about her."

"I couldn't find a birthday for either of them." This was painful to admit. "I can find a birthday for almost everyone else, even the really old names. But not your dad or your aunt."

"My aunt? You looked her up also?"

He flushed. "Not really. I mean, just to try to figure some things out."

"She doesn't have a birthday?"

"Well, she's got one, I just couldn't find it. Or his. It was weird. According to the computer, they're both, like, ten years old."

He laughed but she didn't join in. She was staring at him with an intensity that made him grateful for her sunglasses, as if without them, her eyes would burn him.

"What do you mean, ten?"

"I was joking. It's just that they didn't really show up on anything until a few years ago."

"A *few* years or *ten* years?"

She was leaning forward now, voice rising, and he felt almost afraid of her.

"Ten," he said. "Why does that matter?"

"It doesn't."

"No, you're not surprised by it. Why are you looking up your dad, anyhow? I thought maybe Douglas was your grandpa or uncle or something."

"I don't have those."

"You have to."

She gave a strange, high laugh. "I know! But I don't. He said his parents were dead."

"Maybe they are."

She shook her head angrily. "Then why didn't he talk about them? Why didn't he talk about *anyone*? The stories he told us about being a kid…he'd always, like, cut himself off in the middle. And my aunt doesn't tell the same stories. Not exactly. She has the same general details, the town and the school and things, but it just…it feels different. It feels like she's trying too hard to remember. Does that make sense?"

"No," Matt said honestly. "I think I know what you mean, but it doesn't make any sense."

"Welcome to my life. There's something really weird with Leah. She gets so private about some things and tries too hard with others."

"It has to be strange for her too," he said.

"This isn't just strange like she's not used to having us there, it's…" Hailey gave an exasperated sigh and turned her palms up. "I don't know how to explain it other than it's *not right*. There's something she is not telling us. I think it's probably about my dad. And the way he taught me to reach out to her if anything ever happened…that wasn't normal. It was scary, and he made a big deal out of it. I had to call Aunt Leah *immediately* if anything ever happened. He made me practice it, like I wouldn't remember."

"It doesn't sound like he had anyone else for you to call," Matt said. "Not family, at least."

"Right. Fine. But wouldn't a normal family just have her phone number? Not some weird messaging thing where I had to put in my number and wait for her to call back?" Hailey was talking quickly now, leaning close, color darkening her cheeks. "Then she showed up so fast. We'd never seen her, not once, and all of the sudden she shows up and we go off to Maine? There is something wrong with my family. None of that is normal!"

She was almost shouting. Matt stared up at her and didn't answer. What was there to say? She was right; none of what she described was normal.

"She's keeping secrets," Hailey said, "and so was my dad."

Matt realized with a mixture of astonishment and terror that she was starting to cry. "Hey," he said. "It's…don't do that."

The tears ran beneath her sunglasses and she wiped them away with her thumb and then more came. Matt stood and put his hand on her back and she didn't move away from the contact.

Give her a hug, you idiot. She's crying.

But he stood there, frozen and frightened, realizing just how little he understood about Hailey Chatfield.

"Why can't you just ask your aunt about all this?" he said. "You live with her now. Just ask her."

"She'll lie. Or at least not tell me everything. They had some secret, both of them together had a secret, and I think it was really bad. I think it was...I think my dad probably did something really bad."

Her voice trembled, and another tear ran down her cheek, and this time he didn't hesitate before hugging her.

For a moment, she went still, and then she wrapped her arms around him and hugged him tight, there in the cool pines above the waterfall. It was so close to the scene he'd imagined and yet terribly far away, a funhouse mirror version of what he'd hoped would happen here.

"I think we're hiding from someone," Hailey said, her breath warm against his neck. "I think we've always been hiding, but I don't know why."

She pulled back from him abruptly and stared at him. The waterfall reflected in her sunglasses, helping to hide her dark eyes.

"You can't tell anyone about this," she said. "Please, Matt? It's serious. What I'm telling you is serious."

"I won't tell," he said.

For the first time, he wished he hadn't found someplace so private. For the first time, he wished this had happened someplace where they might be overheard.

Then she hugged him again, and whispered, "Promise?" into his ear, and he said yes, of course he promised. They would find out the secret, and he wouldn't tell anyone.

"I don't know where to start, though," he said. Her emotion had disabled all of his efforts at bravado. "I don't know how to find anything like this out. My mom might be able to help, but she'd probably want to talk to your aunt."

"No!"

"Well, then, I don't know where to start!" he repeated.

"I think I do," she said quietly.

"Where?"

"She gets stressed out when she reads her e-mail. She looks at us differently sometimes afterward. Whatever she sees there scares her. She always closes it down, though, and everything has a password. She deleted the e-mail app from her phone, even. Isn't that weird?"

He nodded.

"But it's there on the laptop. It has a password, and if I can figure that out…I guarantee you, there's something on there." She wiped her eyes. The tears were drying, and her voice was hardening again, the emotion fading beneath strategy. "And maybe something in the safe at her cabin by the lake."

"The safe?"

"It's in the garage and it's mostly full of guns," she said.

Matt felt a prickle along his spine. His parents were a little nuts about gun control. If they knew Leah Trenton had a whole safe full of them, it would definitely weird them out.

"She is a hunting guide, though," he said, speaking almost more to himself than to Hailey.

"I don't care about the guns," Hailey said. "I bet there's other stuff in there. Paperwork, folders, things like that. I want to know what's in there."

"Can you guess at the password?"

She shook her head. "I tried on the computer a couple times but then I got scared it would lock me out. I don't even know enough about her to guess." She pushed her sunglasses up on her head, wiped her eyes again, and then stared at him. Her dark eyes reminded Matt of the way a deer looked when it heard the snap of a branch in the woods.

"Do you have any ideas?" she asked him.

"Yes," he said, and this time it wasn't a bluff, not like it had been with the PI research. "To get her password? Yeah, I can do that."

He knew that he could, too. It was a sneaky trick, but he'd used it once before and hadn't gotten caught. Of course, he'd just been playing then. It had all been a game, not something involving a strange adult who had no birthday and a safe full of guns.

"Really?" Hailey said, and she looked so hopeful—no, she looked so *desperate*—that all Matt Bouchard could do was nod.

"Yeah," he said. "I can do that."

28

Hailey got home before Nick each day and usually went directly to the basement, which she'd claimed as her private lair. Today, though, on the afternoon Leah most desperately wanted to know exactly where her daughter was, she'd gone for a bike ride.

While Leah waited for Hailey's return, she listened to Nick complain. The Wi-Fi was out, and because there was only one bar of cell phone signal on this side of the mountain, he couldn't watch videos, couldn't get online, couldn't do *anything*. A crisis of epic proportions.

Leah promised to call Spectrum and see what the problem was. In reality, she'd killed the breaker to the router. She couldn't make herself invisible to the world, but she didn't need to help Bleak and Randall either. All she really understood about internet tracking was that it could be done. Thus, no internet.

Finally, Hailey returned. She started upstairs immediately, but Leah called her back down. "I've got a surprise for you," she said.

"I want to take a shower," Hailey said. "I'm sweaty and gross."

Be patient, Leah, be patient. Do not show your fear. "Just make it a quick one, please."

The shower lasted ten minutes longer than it normally did, a passive-aggressive response that Leah should have anticipated. Hailey would object to the big surprise, there was no question about that, but Leah could weather the objections. Nick, she thought, might actually be excited.

When Hailey finally came back downstairs, Leah was making a risotto on the stovetop and trying to keep her head down so she wouldn't be caught constantly looking at the road, watching for any passing vehicle.

Or, worse, a vehicle that did not pass but turned into the drive.

"We're eating already?" Hailey said. "It's not even five."

"I know. But we've got an adventure tonight, so we have to eat early."

"I've got a ton of homework to do tonight."

"We'll figure it out," Leah said, stirring with her head down. "Nick, come over here, please?"

He wandered over to the kitchen island, still grumbling about the Wi-Fi.

"There's no power to the router at all," he said. "It's like the whole thing burned up."

"I'll have Spectrum take a look. Hey, guys? We're going up north for the weekend. Back toward my cabin. A little farther north this time, though."

"Cool," Nick said. "Can I fish?"

"Absolutely."

He scratched Tessa's ears absently. "We driving up on Saturday morning or Friday night?"

"Neither," Leah said. "We're leaving tonight."

He looked up from the dog. Hailey turned from the window.

"It's Wednesday," Hailey said.

"Correct."

"We're going to miss two days of school."

"I understand that. I've already called the schools to let them know."

"That's not right," Hailey said. "We can't just skip school to go fishing."

"We're not skipping school to go fishing," Leah said, ladling risotto onto plates and trying to keep her expression neutral. *Show no fear, and do not rush. Cool your mind, cool your mind.* "We're missing two days because I have a business to run and it needs some attention. I understand that it's not ideal, Hailey, but you guys also understand that we all have to make adjustments. You've had to make most of them, I know. This one is…this one is all about me. I'm sorry about that. But I need you to bear with me, okay?"

Nick said, "Doesn't bother me. Miss two days and go fishing? Doesn't bother me at all. Especially with the Wi-Fi out."

"Excellent," Leah said. "I appreciate the cooperation, sir."

Nick saluted.

Hailey just stood and stared. Leah waited for the questions and objections, but none came. Her daughter was taking stock of something Leah didn't understand. Actually, maybe Leah *did* understand it. Hailey was cooling her mind. Managing her temper and picking her battles. Her daughter.

"So when you've finished eating, pack enough stuff to last through the weekend," Leah said. "We'll be leaving pretty soon. I think it will be a fun trip for you. It's an adventure."

Running for our lives. It's an adventure!

Hailey said, "Aren't you hot?"

"Pardon?"

Hailey pointed. "You're wearing that big fleece and it's like seventy degrees in here."

Shit. Could she see the gun? No chance. But if Leah took off the fleece, Hailey would see the gun. Definitely.

"It won't be seventy degrees on the lake," she said. "So layer up before we leave, okay?"

Hailey's frown suggested she was considering a real battle, the first direct conflict, an end to the cold war she had been managing. "I'm going to be behind in every class. Before the first week is done, I'll be behind."

"You told me you were feeling good about your classes, remember? You were ahead, not behind. I'm sure you'll do great.

Regardless, it's my fault, and I appreciate you being understanding and patient with me."

Hailey sighed, nodded, and pulled a stool up to the island. Leah exhaled. One battle avoided. More on the horizon.

She looked out the window, up the road. No cars in sight.

Yet.

At some point they'll show up. They'll keep coming too. They won't quit.

She felt the cool granite of the island countertop beneath her palms and tried to use it to anchor herself. Shouldn't she be calling the police? Didn't that make sense? She wanted that to make sense. Wanted to be able to go back not to her old life but to an older version of that life, one in which good people who were in trouble called the police and were then protected from bad people, one in which distinctions were clear—good and bad, hero and villain— and the two sides didn't intersect, overlap, soak into each other.

She wanted, in other words, to be like Rae Johnson on the morning before Nina Morgan flew her and her children off to be murdered.

Leah took her hands off the island and stepped back.

"Put the dishes in the dishwasher when you're done," she told her children, "and then hurry up and pack. We need to leave soon."

29

The GPS tracker activated as the Jeep left Leah Trenton's driveway. When she went down the hill and across the harbor, an iPhone chime alerted him.

At a waterfront restaurant called Rhumb Line, Dax Blackwell set two twenty-dollar bills down on the worn wooden table and put a water glass over them to keep them from blowing into the harbor. Then he walked up the hill to his rented truck. He was pleased that she was in motion, because that afternoon she'd disabled her Wi-Fi and removed his eyes and ears from the house.

He was waiting to turn north on Route 1 when she passed, heading toward Lincolnville, where she'd picked up the ferry tickets earlier that afternoon. He let two cars go by to provide a visual barrier between his truck and her rearview mirror, then followed. All on schedule but moving toward a dilemma: the ferry.

According to Dax's information, the ferry had departed for its last trip of the day two hours earlier. It must have returned from Islesboro now and tied up at the wharf. Leah Trenton couldn't take the ferry anywhere, and if she intended to pick someone up from that last trip, she was taking her own sweet time doing it.

Route 1 curled northeast and the island-dotted waters of Penobscot Bay stretched out ahead of them and there was the ferry at rest. The lot was empty. Leah Trenton pulled into it and parked. Dax cruised by and turned into the same parking lot he'd visited earlier in the day, at the Whale's Tooth Pub, each motion already rehearsed.

The Trenton Jeep sat and no one got out. They were waiting. On what?

Dax picked up his iPhone and opened the Uber app, curious if there were any drivers approaching. There are no Ubers in your area, the app informed him. Stunned, he exited and restarted it. The message was the same: not a single Uber in the area.

Maine. The way life should be.

He was ready to leave this place.

When he looked up from the phone, he saw a pale blue sedan waiting to turn left into the parking lot. It had traveled southbound from Belfast and looked to be thirty years old; the tailpipe coughed gray smoke as it idled, waiting on the northbound lane to clear. The doors were emblazoned with the slogan ANNIE'S MIDCOAST TRANSIT, DOOR TO DOOR!

Dax didn't know exactly what to think of this development. No Uber available, but Annie's ghost cabs were on call? How had Leah Trenton discovered this? It must have been on the place mat at the diner, he thought, and almost laughed. Almost, because what was happening now was too unanticipated to allow for full amusement. Leah's family was piling out of the Jeep and into the ancient sedan, and this meant he would have to follow Annie's vehicle because he had no tracker on it. Annie might well miss the Toyota in her rearview mirror, but he had a feeling Leah Trenton would not.

Not tonight.

He watched as the car doors closed and the Trenton family was hidden from view and then he started the Toyota and drove out in front of them. There was only one destination he could anticipate, and if he was wrong, it would be a problem.

He was not wrong.

Two minutes after he reached the Lincolnville general store, Annie's pale blue ghost cab passed by.

Leah Trenton's odd afternoon detour was gaining clarity. She'd left her car in a place that would mislead anyone who found it, and Dax was willing to bet that she'd purchased tickets for the morning's first ferry. They would be pedestrian tickets, promising anyone who came looking for her that she was on the island and on foot. Hardly a sophisticated ruse, but not awful.

Annie's Midcoast Transit was now going to deposit Leah and her children at the nature preserve trailhead. Fernald's Neck. She would have a story to explain it to both the driver and the kids. Annie's cab would drop them off, and if it could actually make it back down that dirt road with the deep potholes without dropping the transmission or cracking an axle, the Trentons would be alone in the woods in the deepening twilight.

Then what?

He sat and waited and thought. Remembered the map of the lake and tracked its shores in his mind's eye as if with a drone camera. The lake fed into the river and the river fed into the sea. It wasn't navigable, though, not unless Leah Trenton intended to kayak over a few dams and beneath some bridges and then shoot the waterfall and land in the harbor. The lake was no better than the island would have been. There were houses all around it, but the houses were better reached by road than water.

Someone was going to drive in here and pick them up. That was the only logical option. All this effort for so little ultimate reward. He felt a surge of disappointment. He hadn't wanted Leah Trenton to be stupid. *Be best, Leah.*

The blue car appeared again in the dimming daylight, now wearing a skin of dust from the road to the trailhead. The car was empty save the woman behind the wheel. The Trenton family was either hiking to the water's edge to meet a boat or waiting in the parking lot to be picked up by another car. Neither option was smart. He sighed and started the truck and drove toward the lake, dismayed.

He was just heading down the rutted dirt road when he heard

the low whine of an engine. At first, he merely noted the background noise, his subconscious filtering through possibilities and dismissing them—car, lawn mower, boat, chain saw; no, no, no, no—and then he cracked the window and the whine deepened in pitch and he looked skyward just in time to see the glint of red pontoons passing overhead.

A seaplane.

Dax watched it descend, and he smiled. *Well done, Leah. Well damn done.*

She would lose him now. She would lose anyone who might have been behind her. Only briefly, yes, only a delay, but nevertheless a fine one. He appreciated that.

He pulled the truck into the weeds beside the road, climbed out, and ran for the water. The trail led through a field and into the woods before it returned to the water and he knew that he did not have that kind of time. Instead, he fought his way through the brush and the slapping branches and went straight for the water.

When he reached the shore, he paused only long enough to remove his boots and roll his jeans up over his knees, then he waded out. The rocky bottom was rough against the balls of his feet and the water was chilled without the sun's warmth. He splashed out until the water was beginning to reach the denim and he had a clear view of the plane. He stopped there, knee-deep in the lake, and memorized the details.

Red plane body, red pontoons, single propeller. An old plane but in immaculate shape. White trim that matched the paint for the tail numbers. He shielded his eyes with his hands and squinted into the darkness. A lean man in an olive field jacket was helping the kids aboard, and the dog was barking and dancing in the shallows, sending spray over them, but Dax did not focus on the man. He focused on the plane's tail numbers. It was too far away and it was too dark to make it out clearly, but the mind filled in shapes even when the eyes couldn't, and so he worked on the shapes and the combinations that might make them.

The first part was easy: *N*. All aircraft registered in the United States started with *N*. Focus on the following sequence—*29T?* That looked right. Don't get cocky with the letter, though. It could be an *F*, maybe—*29F?* Or *29P?* He thought the last number was the same as the first and his mind could find no other shape that fit. The first number was most likely a *2*, with an outside chance of a *7*. The last letter was either a *T*, an *F*, or a *P*.

The passengers were all boarded now, and the prop was turning. The load-up process had moved quickly, which suggested that the pilot was aware of the urgency.

The mind was filling in the missing shapes for him. The plane began its taxi and pulled farther and farther from him before losing touch with the water, and as it joined the air, Dax was nearly certain that it was NFR292.

He waded back to the shore, brushed the water off his legs, and put on his boots. As he laced them up, the plane passed overhead again, having banked around the lake and angled back in the direction from which it had come, flying northwest.

Dax waved. He doubted they could see him in the gathering shadows, but all the same, it seemed appropriate.

Catch you soon, old friends. Catch you soon.

30

The text messages didn't arrive until after the Trenton family was gone. Matt Bouchard was confused as his phone began to chime and chime and chime, stacked up messages finally filtering through.

> Hey, something is weird here. We are going away for the weekend? Leaving now? I don't get it. She never said anything about this and she seems tense or nervous. She says it is about her cabin.

> Damn it, my phone isn't working. Crap signal, and now no Wi-Fi. Router is dead. Are you getting these?

> ?????

> Stupid cell phone doesn't work in house. We are leaving now. On a seaplane that my brother thinks is cool and I think will probably crash. It is my aunt's friend, Ed. She says we will be gone three days up north of Moosehead Lake. ☹

> You can get in the house, though. The code to the door is 4540. If you actually think you can figure out her computer, it is on the desk in the little library room. She left it. She usually uses the iPad. It would be AMAZING if you could really do this. Thank u!

> OMG this plane is scary. Not cool!

Matt scrolled frantically through the messages, horrified that he'd missed so many. It wasn't his fault that his phone worked and hers didn't, but still...

He pecked out a quick response, but the blue line indicating the message progress froze three-quarters of the way across the screen. He tried it again as a text message instead of an iMessage. Nothing. "Damn it," he whispered to himself.

"What's that?" his mom said, looking over from where she sat curled up in the love seat, reading the new Alafair Burke book. Matt was on the floor, his dad sitting on the opposite side of the room in the recliner, watching an old Tom Hanks movie called *The 'Burbs* on Netflix. His dad loved that movie. Matt didn't get it—the effects were super-cheesy and old-fashioned—but he liked the scene where Bruce Dern fell off the roof of the house. His dad seemed to like everything about it, watched it over and over and over again.

"Nothing," Matt said. "Talking to myself."

"Keep your own counsel," Dad said. "Very prudent." Then Bruce Dern put his foot through the porch step and dropped the plate of brownies and Dad was laughing, sputtering on the old-fashioned he made most nights. One old-fashioned, one old movie, one old chair. That was the routine. Matt's mom was more varied, more interesting.

She was also more observant, which was a problem right now. She was looking at him suspiciously.

"What's got you upset? And what did you really say?"

"I'm supposed to check on the new neighbors' house," he said. "That's all."

"Pardon?" She set the book down. "What do you mean, *check* on it? Aren't they over there?"

"Gone for the weekend, I guess."

"It's Wednesday."

"I didn't make the choice!" he said indignantly. "I'm just supposed to go over and check on it."

His mom watched him. "Ms. Trenton asked you to do that?"

"No, one of the kids told me to."

"Which kid? Niece or nephew?"

"What does that matter?"

She smiled. "Answer me, please."

"The niece! Gosh." He sounded like Napoleon Dynamite. Another movie his dad could watch a hundred times. They never started anything new. Movie night was the same stuff on repeat: *The 'Burbs, Cool Hand Luke, Napoleon Dynamite, Shawshank Redemption, Jaws.* Endlessly *Jaws.*

"Ah. The niece. Hailey, was it?"

"Yeah."

"She texted you?"

"What does it *matter?*"

"I'm a curious woman. It's my job."

"Yes, she texted me, so whatever, be curious, but I still have to check the house."

"Check it for *what?*"

He felt a rising panic. Hailey's message was clear in its request to break into her aunt's computer. If his mom asked to see the message... "Her aunt wants two lights left on," he blurted. "One upstairs and one downstairs. Like it's a high-crime neighborhood or something."

A return to form; Matt knew the Camden crime statistics. They were essential to most of his arguments for freedom. His father generally found this more amusing than his mother did.

"She wants lights left on all night? That's strange."

"I don't know." He lifted his hands, palms up, appealing to the heavens. "She's new here. Can I just go over and turn them on and be done with it?"

"How are you supposed to get in the house? Is it—"

"Oh, for the love of all things holy, let him go turn the damn lights on so we can all be quiet and watch the movie!" Dad said.

"As if you'd miss something new," Mom responded dryly, but her eyes had moved from Matt to Dad, which to Matt felt like having interrogation lamps turned off.

"Hey, you learn something *every time* with great cinema," Dad said.

"Great cinema?"

"*Great cinema!* Did you ever notice that the garbage man is wearing a McCarthy button? Subtle social commentary. Lost on an undiscerning audience."

"I don't think that's true."

"You watch and see. I'll pause it. If you look closely, you'll see it."

"And that makes it great cinema?"

"Overlooked cinema. Overlooked excellence."

Mom rolled her eyes and picked her book back up and nobody was watching Matt when he stood up.

Bless you, Bruce Dern, he thought as he slipped out of the living room and then out of the house. All he had to do was work fast—and remember to turn two lights on like he'd said he would. The rest should be simple.

He had an Arlo wireless camera that his father had purchased for "home security," which was code for "a toy." His mother viewed it as a creepy invasion of privacy with its always listening microphone. She'd unplugged it and dumped it into a box in the garage. The Arlo was a great option for viewing Leah Trenton's computer while she typed in her password, but it also required communication with a base unit. Hailey had assured him that if he put the base unit on one of the shelves in the basement, nobody would notice it.

I'm the only one who spends any time down there, she'd said. And back at the waterfall, in the daylight, with Hailey next to him, Matt had happily agreed that it was a good option.

Things changed fast when you were alone in the dark.

Gonna get your butt in a lot of trouble, he thought as he hurried down the street, wearing a backpack that contained the Arlo. He hadn't been prepared to put the thing in the house by himself. Hailey was supposed to be at his side, impressed by his ingenuity. Now, walking through the cooling dark toward the house, he didn't feel impressive. He felt guilty and a little bit afraid. *Doing the right thing. You are doing the right thing. She's scared, and you're going to help.*

Help by breaking into an adult's laptop. Help by committing a crime. It had seemed like a simpler, cleaner idea this afternoon. He might've chickened out or at least delayed it if not for his lie about turning on the lights as Leah Trenton had requested. Now he *had* to go in the house.

The front door's keypad lock glowed a dim green in the gathering dark. Out on the lake there might still be traces of sunlight, but down here the house was screened by the mountains and the trees, and the night seemed to arrive early, broken only by shafts of twilight blue.

He punched the code in, wondering if he was supposed to hit another button to unlock it. Maybe Hailey had left out a step and the door wouldn't open for him, and he'd be able to walk back home and text her and say—

The dead bolt made a grinding sound as it ratcheted back. Unlocked. Open.

"Crap," he whispered, and he turned the knob and stepped into the house. He fumbled to the left of the door and could not find a light switch. That scared him enough that he almost backed out of the house, but he steeled himself.

"Don't be a baby." His voice echoed loud and high in the hallway, with its tiled floor and bare walls, and it sounded even more babyish than he felt. He shuffled forward and deepened his voice. "Don't be a bitch." Better. Danny Knowlton liked to say that. Of course, Danny Knowlton had cried when a fourth-grader kicked him in the shin.

The light switches were on the wall to the right. Matt could see them. He took a breath, let the door swing shut behind him, and crossed the entryway in a hurry, flicking the switches up as he went. The house flooded with light, and immediately he felt both relieved and embarrassed.

"Come on, tough guy," he whispered, and then he took three steps toward the living room before remembering what Hailey had told him—the library that her aunt used as an office was to the left. He pivoted and saw the room behind a glass door. Rows of built-in bookshelves with a small desk. A MacBook on the desk.

He went in and then turned to look at the shelves that lined the wall. Just as Hailey had told him, they were filled with books, mostly paperback mysteries or tourist guides, things that had been read by renters over the years or collected at the library book sale. All that mattered was that there were lots of them, which would make his job easier. If not for the cluttered shelves, he'd have no place to put the camera.

He opened the laptop and watched the screen fill with the password-protected prompt. No surprise. He kept it open so he could see the screen's position while he studied the bookshelves, looking for the right vantage point.

He arranged the camera with the lens peering out from between two Michael Connelly paperbacks and then stepped back to assess his work.

Not bad, but not hidden, either. If you faced the shelf, you might notice it. If you just walked into the room and went for the computer desk, though, the way most people did, the tiny camera lens wouldn't catch your eye.

Now, he just had to set up the base unit.

He sighed. One trip to the basement. Just one.

He left the library with the base unit in hand and walked through the house, searching for the basement door. His path took him past the granite-topped island in the kitchen. He saw something glistening in the decaying light there. Hailey's gold-framed Ray-Bans, the gift from her father, the pair that Matt had both broken and fixed.

He picked them up, feeling uneasy that she'd left them behind. She cared about them too much to leave them behind. She'd been hurrying, though. The trip was a surprise, a rush. A panic?

He tucked the glasses in the inside pocket of his fleece, where they rested against his heart.

She needs help. Needs your help.

He turned away from the island and saw the door to the basement. There was no trace of daylight remaining down there, and he hesitated at the top of the steps.

You are thirteen years old. You are not scared of the dark. What's the matter with you?

Nothing was the matter with *him,* but something was the matter with the house. He could feel it in the small of his back, where tiny muscles tightened and twitched.

He touched the sunglasses again, tapped them against his heart. "I'm no baby," he said. "No bitch."

His voice, too high, echoed again. The shame of the sound drove him forward, out of the living room. He was halfway down the steps before he realized there had to be a light switch at the top of the stairs. He didn't go back for it, though. As he went farther down, traces of nickel-colored light from the basement windows allowed him to see well enough to move.

He came out into an unfinished room facing a bank of dark windows and a set of double doors leading to the wooded backyard. The trees loomed in massive shadows on the other side, seeming bigger than they should have, like some prehistoric forest. To his right, a wall had been painted black and then covered with bright chalk sketches.

Distracted from both his focus and his fear, he turned toward it, studied the display. The drawings were beautiful and creepy, featuring monsters, laughing skeletons, and figures with gleaming eyes and curled lips over jagged teeth. He fumbled in his pocket, found his phone, clicked the flashlight app on. He panned over the images. These were really, really good.

He sidestepped to the left, entranced. As the images took on greater clarity, his eyes were drawn to a figure on the far left, a gaunt man in an old-fashioned, formal overcoat, a hat tipped low over his face, obscuring but not hiding his predatory smile. He was from a book or a comic, Matt thought, and he was pretty sure it had been made into a TV show. Something on AMC about a man who abducted kids in a Rolls-Royce. Scary stuff. Mom liked the scary shows; Dad liked the dumb comedies. This one his mom had watched, he was almost positive, because he remembered her talking about the book. He wanted to be sure, though, so he could watch the rest of the show and read the book. Impress Hailey with his knowledge. He stepped closer, lifted the light, and saw the shadow.

It was overlaid across the grinning figure, and it was hard to see against the black paint, but it was definitely there, a subtle teasing of dark on dark. How had she done that? The shadow looked almost like a man. In fact, there were two shadows. One shorter, one taller. Almost as if one shadow was Matt, and one shadow was…

The man standing behind him said, "Do not make a sound."

Matt disobeyed, but it was unintentional; he dropped the phone. It fell to the bare concrete floor and cracked and sent diffuse rays of light across the pink insulation that hung from the ceiling. Before he could release the scream that was rising, a strong hand in a glove was clapped over his mouth and an arm encircled his chest and hugged him tight.

From the darkness to his right, another voice spoke.

"If he's home alone, she and the sister can't be far behind." A second man, stepping out of the furnace room, speaking in a low voice.

The hand across Matt's mouth mashed his lips into his teeth. He could taste blood. On the chalkboard wall in front of him, the twin shadows had merged into one, Matt's smaller form absorbed by the larger one, as if it had never existed.

"No car pulled in," the man holding him said. "Mom's not

letting him walk home alone in the dark while she drives the sister."

His voice gave Matt no sense of his identity. It simply rose from within the shadow, and the menacing chalk figure with the tipped hat and the wicked grin felt like an accomplice to it all, watching and smiling.

Matt knew better than to fight against that strong arm squeezing his ribs and that hand crushing his lips into his teeth. Fighting would bring only pain. Maybe something worse than pain. Pay attention, then. Track the words. Remember the words because they would matter, they were hope, they were the only hope. Mom missing. Sister missing. No car. Those were the words, and none of them made sense, because Matt's mom was next door, she was in the living room, and he had no sister, and why would his mom have driven him down here to…

Realization rose behind the fear and the pain then: these two men waiting in the darkened basement thought he was Nick Chatfield.

No, no, no, Matt thought. *I'm not the one you want.*

But his bleeding lips couldn't part to say a word.

"Let me see him," the second man said, and Matt was twisted to face him. The light from his cracked cell phone on the floor offered just enough illumination to show him that the man was white with a square jaw covered in stubble. He wore jeans and a black sweatshirt and a black knit cap. When he leaned closer, Matt saw that his eyes were different colors, one green and one brown. He studied Matt for a long moment and then said, "Oh, fuck."

"What?" the one holding Matt said, his voice low.

"That's not the right kid."

Matt tried to nod his head. It was hard, with the way he was being held, but the man with the different-colored eyes seemed to understand that he was trying to agree. He said, "Let him talk. He won't scream. Will you?"

Matt tried to shake his head. After a pause, as if he were reluctant to do it, the man who'd grabbed him removed his hand from Matt's mouth. A line of Matt's blood was on his glove.

"Who are you?" the man with the odd eyes said.

"I live next door." The words left in a gasp. "I'm not one of the ones...I don't live here."

The man studied him. "Not the ones?"

"I don't live here," Matt repeated, and as his voice rose, the man holding him gave a twist of the arm that worked as an unspoken command. When Matt spoke again, it was in a quavering whisper. "I live next door. My parents are waiting for me. Please, just let me go home. I don't—"

"What are you doing here?"

"Just...turning on lights."

"Turning on lights. No. You're carrying this around, not turning on lights." The man picked up the Arlo base unit and looked it over. "You putting cameras in their house? What're you, some kinda pervert, looking to get your rocks off? Is that it?"

"No."

"Then what?"

Matt didn't answer.

The deep-voiced man behind Matt said, "We gotta make a choice here."

Make a choice. Matt didn't like the sound of that. He was already sure that them letting him walk back home wasn't one of the choices.

"We will," the man with the different-colored eyes said. "Once he tells me what he's doing."

"Don't matter what he's doing, he's the wrong damn kid."

Instinct took over then, a voice in Matt's head screaming at him to make this choice harder on them.

"They're somewhere up north of Moosehead Lake," he blurted out. "They left on a seaplane tonight."

Silence. The man with the mismatched eyes smiled at him. It was almost a kind smile. Almost.

"North of Moosehead Lake," he said. "And a seaplane. That's no guess, kid."

Then the man holding him said, "You seem to know a little bit about our friends. How much you know?"

Matt wasn't sure how to answer that. His legs had started to shake. Only his legs, because his torso was being held too tightly. The legs shook and he felt tears in his eyes and the man said, "How much you know?" again.

"That they're scared," Matt whispered. "I know that they're scared."

3 I

The only cabin that was remotely ready to host the guests that Leah and Ed had envisioned was cabin number one—or Caribou's Courage, as he'd jokingly named it—but they passed over that and flew farther north as the sun sank to their left side.

Ed was silent, focused on flying and, Leah knew, taking stock of what she'd told him on the phone that afternoon. It hadn't been much. She'd told him only that she needed the pickup and that Nick and Hailey were in danger. The rest, she'd promised, she would tell him in person.

He hadn't hesitated. It was trust she didn't deserve.

In the seats behind them, Nick and Hailey were silent. Initially, Nick had kept up a stream of questions about the plane. As the towns and houses fell away and the endless forests replaced them, the trees looking black in the gathering darkness, even Nick had run out of talk. Tension thrummed through the plane like another engine.

They were running out of daylight fast, and Leah knew that was weighing on Ed. It was legal to land a seaplane in the Maine North Woods in the dark but it was also foolish, the sort of thing you did only in emergency situations. His spotlights would illuminate water seconds before touching down on it, and something as simple as a floating limb could mean disaster.

The sun was nothing but a thin red line lacing the western mountains. Everything to the east was already dark. The safest landing—and the most habitable cabin—was behind them. She'd told him she wanted to push as far north as possible. Push to someplace where not even a Jeep or a lifted pickup would make it through.

When they'd passed over Moosehead, all she could think of was the wreckage of that B-52 on Elephant Mountain, and then she'd made the mistake of looking back at her children and giving them a reassuring smile and from that moment on she'd had to dig her fingernails into her thighs to keep her hands still. She wanted the stick, wanted control. Ed was an excellent pilot, but she was better.

No. Nina was better. And Nina never had to land on the water in the dark up here.

Still, she wanted control.

The Allagash spread beneath them in all its glory. Even from overhead, it could look impenetrable, a half a million acres of forested wilderness fed from the veins of rivers, dozens of lakes, hundreds of ponds and brooks and creeks. It would be more active now than at other times of the year; it was moose season, after all. If you stayed off the logging roads, as Leah intended, it was unlikely that you'd even encounter a hunter. They were headed to Martin Mountain Pond, a small body of water that fed into a narrow, unnamed brook before it found a swirl of rapids that deposited the brook into Lower Martin Pond, and from there it was a simple paddle to the Allagash River itself. Then the river ran north, into the St. John and on out to the sea. It was beautiful, it was cold, and it was isolated.

It was, she believed, a place where she could buy some precious time.

"We're going to put her down now, guys," Ed said. His voice was absolutely level, no trace of nerves, but she could see a muscle twitching in the corner of his jaw. He was grinding his teeth. "It'll be nice and smooth. So smooth that I'll have to tell you when we actually hit the water, because I don't want you to miss the landing. But check those seat belts anyhow. We do things right in my plane, even when it's going to be smooth."

Leah turned back to look at them. Nick tapped his seat belt and nodded at her. Hailey didn't touch her seat belt and did not nod. She just stared at Leah as if something she'd long suspected was being proven.

"It'll be fine," Leah told them.

Neither responded. The plane angled down and there was a moment when that faint line of fading sunlight seemed to brighten. Then it was gone and they were descending into pure dark. The pond looked like ink spilled on asphalt. The spotlights caught the water but offered nothing more than a liquid shimmer, and each of the dancing shadows seemed a threat. A branch, a beaver dam, an overturned canoe—she could see them all, was so briefly certain of these imagined shapes that she nearly cried out to Ed, *Pull up, pull up, please take us back up before it's too—*

A thump and a shudder. Nick gasped. Then he said, "We're down?" in an uncertain voice.

"We're down," Ed said, his own voice soft and tight. He didn't take his eyes off the water ahead as he cut the speed and taxied.

They'd just landed more than two hundred miles northwest of Camden, flying toward the setting sun and away from any sign that Maine had ever been touched by human hands. There were exactly three ways to reach Martin Mountain Pond: by seaplane, by canoe along a route that required challenging portages, or on foot across the desolate miles.

Leah let out a long breath and whispered, "Thank you."

Ed glanced at her for the first time. He nodded without speaking, his blue eyes studying her in the dim cockpit, unspoken questions dancing in them. Then he looked away.

"I don't see any cabins," Hailey said, the only words she'd offered since they boarded the plane. "You said we were checking on a cabin."

"It's right up ahead," Leah said.

And there it was: a low rectangle of ancient logs with a dark green metal roof. The roof was new. It was the only thing they'd done to this cabin so far. For decades it had belonged to a family from Presque Isle, a paddle-in retreat for two generations that had eventually reached a third generation whose members had no interest in paddling anywhere so remote. They'd sold it for ten thousand dollars cash and had seemed pleased to do that well. Leah and Ed had laughed ruefully about that afterward. Even their aggressively low bid had apparently exceeded expectations.

It's beautiful, the grandson of the original builder had told them. *But it's damn hard to get to, and it's lonely.*

His words came back to her now like a promise, as soothing as a hymn. *Damn hard to get to, and it's lonely.* That was everything she needed.

Ed beached the plane just past the cabin. After the silent, seamless water landing, the crunch of the pontoons on gravel felt like a savage impact even though it wasn't. The prop slowed and then stopped. A loon called, the mournful sound loud.

"Okay," Ed said. "Let's get unpacked."

He was trying to keep his voice light, but it wavered. Leah thought she knew why. He was thinking about the rifles she'd asked him to bring.

Leah got out first and helped the kids out one at a time. Tessa bolted out between them, splashing through the shallows, head high, tail erect. A million fresh smells to take in. When Nick and Hailey were standing on a large, flat rock on the shore, high and dry and safe, Leah went back to help Ed unload their gear. She was almost to the plane when Hailey spoke.

"Is that a canoe?"

For a moment, Leah thought she'd spotted someone on the water. Then she realized that Hailey was looking at the plane's pontoon, where a sixteen-foot ultralight Wenonah canoe was lashed.

"Yes," she said. "It's a canoe." It would be their only means of transportation when Ed flew out in the morning, but as she looked at the craft's bright yellow sides, she remembered that lazy August afternoon when Nick had told her about Hailey's interest—and skill—in a canoe. "We'll take it out tomorrow."

Hailey didn't respond. Ed, wearing a headlamp, tight-roped his way down the length of the pontoon and handed Leah her own headlamp.

"Getting dark fast," he said, the first reference to what he'd surely been worried about the entire time.

"It was a perfect landing," Leah said, putting the headlamp on.

"Let's not ask me to do it again," he said, and though he tried to inject levity into the statement, his tone undermined it.

"Let's not," she agreed, and then they got to work unloading the plane. While the two of them carried the gear from the plane to shore, Hailey and Nick stood on the bank, watching. They were standing very close together, their breath fogging the night air. Only September, and already the evening temperature here was in the low forties. The nearest town—which wasn't really a town in any traditional sense—was in Canada. Lac-Frontière, a French name that meant "Lake of the Frontier Border." An appropriate name.

She forced her mind away from that before the inevitable question rose behind it: Where next? Have Ed fly them into the Northwest Territories, raise her children among the musk ox? No. The running had to stop, and the running could not stop until Lowery was dead.

This was the truth that she had to accept. If he knew she was alive—and he did—then he would have to die. There was no alternative now. No future where Doug raised them safely without her. No future where silence masqueraded as innocence.

"I'm sorry it's already dark," she told the kids as she unshouldered the duffel bag at the cabin door and spun the combination lock that was closed over a stainless-steel hasp. "I wish you'd been able to arrive in the daylight and see how beautiful it is. But in the morning, you'll see. We'll take the canoe out and you'll see what's so special about this place." She unfastened the lock and pushed open the door, and their headlamps illuminated the cabin's interior.

The rough-hewn log walls looked virtually the same on the inside as they did on the outside. The bunks on the far wall were just planks, no mattresses, no pillows. Hooks made out of antlers hung on the wall to their left. The woodstove and the single window were to their right. Otherwise, the space was barren. The wall art was a topographic map of the Allagash Wilderness Waterway and a calendar from three years earlier.

"This is it?" Hailey said. "We're supposed to stay here? All of us?"

"The three of you," Ed said from behind them. "I'll be in a tent. But I'd always be in a tent, if I had my way."

He was trying to reassure, trying to soothe, but falling short.

"Let me build us a fire," Leah said. "By the time we get the sleeping bags out and a fire going, it'll feel cozy."

She stopped talking then and busied herself with the fire. Nick sat on the edge of the bunk tentatively and didn't move to take off his boots or his jacket or even his backpack. Hailey crossed the room, seeking privacy the way she did at the house. There was no basement here, though, no door to close. She settled for standing with her back to Leah, facing the topographic map on the wall. She touched it with a fingertip—she seemed to want to touch any type of art, as if the lines and colors spoke to her—and traced the river very carefully, from the place where they were now all the way down to Moosehead Lake, the place where she'd been before, her first stop in Maine. Leah saw that she was doing it backward again, the way she had at the cabin on the first day. Hailey trusted the rivers to flow south, the way they did in Kentucky, slow floats to warmer climates. She had no idea that up here they actually led north, led through places that were only colder and more isolated before dumping you into a hostile frigid sea.

Leah didn't want to tell her that. Let her think that all the rivers of the world flowed south, meandering back down to the Ohio River, drifting right into Louisville. Let her believe that all rivers and all roads led home eventually.

As she cracked kindling and stacked it in the narrow woodbox of the ancient iron stove, Leah knew once more the thing she'd chosen to deny for so long, the thing that had led her to Maine in the first place: She was no one's mother. She'd brought lives into this world, yes, but that was all. A mother provided safety; Leah invited harm.

This was the reason she had left all those years earlier. A mother who drew harm toward her children rather than guiding it away from them deserved nothing but exile. At *best,* she deserved exile.

She removed a lighter and a cube of WetFire from her pack. She tore the wrapping off the WetFire and scraped the tiny white cube with her thumbnail, peeling flakes of it free. Then she sparked the lighter and lowered it, watched the flame catch the fire starter and spread to the kindling, felt the first traces of warmth on her face, and remembered the day Nina Morgan had died for her children. She felt that she'd done the right thing for them.

A mistake.

Dying for them hadn't been enough. She knew now what she should have known then: A good mother didn't die for her children.

She killed for them.

Part Four

FOLLOW THE RIVER

32

The kids fell asleep early, which amazed Leah. The unfamiliar place, the rapid transitions, the absence of creature comforts, and still they slept.

She couldn't take much reassurance in that, though. They were exhausted and they were learning to adapt to days of disruption. Ever since Doug had died, their lives had been a collection of curveballs and changeups. Everything you did not want for your children.

And still she was putting them through it.

Now wasn't the time to worry about mistakes already made, though. Now was the planning hour, a time for cool minds and steady hands.

And loaded guns.

She could see the outline of Ed's tent, lit by the soft glow of a flashlight or headlamp. He'd set up camp along the shore and he hadn't returned. She knew he was waiting on her. Waiting on the truth. She added wood to the stove once more even though it was warm in the cramped cabin now, then looked at her children, watching their breathing patterns. Slow and steady. Lost to sleep. Nick's hand trembled and his leg twitched. Deep sleep, she hoped, and not nightmares.

She opened the door and slipped out into the night. The brushstroke smears of the Milky Way had the clarity you saw only when you were removed from all sources of urban light. She'd learned to love it but once it had scared her and she held that memory close now, imagining this place as her children saw it. For a few seconds she stood outside the cabin with the door cracked and breathed the night air and listened. The kids did not stir, not even when the loon cried again, the haunting call echoing from within the blackness.

Leah closed the door behind her and walked down to the shoreline to tell someone the truth of her identity for the first time.

Ed's headlamp moved within the orange and gray Kelty tent and then there came the soft rasp of the zipper and he pushed through the fly and crawled out of the tent. He turned off the headlamp before he looked at her. She didn't know how to take that; was it a courtesy, not wanting to blind her with a harsh glare, or was it that he didn't want to see her face?

She sat on the grass beside the tent, the ground cool and damp beneath her, and pulled her knees up to her chest. He sat beside her in almost the same position. For a time, they simply sat and looked at the sky and did not speak.

Finally, she said, "Thank you."

"Sure," he said, as if the favor he'd done had been routine.

"And I'm sorry," she continued. Her throat was thick and she had to swallow and wait to speak again. He gave her the time, silent, his head leaned back so that he could see the stars. "I am sorry, Ed," she repeated.

"Don't ever apologize for needing help." He looked at her then. "But that's not what you're apologizing for."

"Not just that," she admitted.

He nodded and looked skyward again.

"How bad is it?" he asked.

"Bad. I'll keep you out of it, though. I mean, from here on out." She felt ridiculous, saying that. Keep him out of it? He was the only person on the planet who knew where to find her. "I've got to trust you with the truth. I should have earlier. I think. There is a part of me that's still unsure about that, but it has nothing to do with you. There's a part of me that has been unsure about everything that I've done since Hailey called." She paused, considered, and said, "And many of the things from a long time before Hailey called."

Ed said, "They're your kids, aren't they?"

He stated it so flatly that she found herself merely nodding in the darkness. "They are. How do you know?"

"I'd wondered since the first time I saw them. Hailey, in particular. She looks so much like you. Carries herself like you. Everything tucked away, hidden."

This observation brought the shock that the previous one should have. "That's how I seem to you? Hiding things?"

"You're…a bit more than private. Let's just say that. I always thought I'd get through the walls and the defenses in time and that when I did, there'd be a story there. I expected something about another man. Insecurity, I guess. But then I met the kids, and…" He shrugged.

"And you knew that I was lying to you," she said, her shame a physical thing, a weight behind her breasts like a cold stone.

"I didn't *know* that. I wondered, that's all. Until today, I wondered."

"Why'd you come, then? Why did you help?"

"Because of you. Because of them."

She closed her eyes, sealing out the starlight. "I didn't know what else to do. I could have driven, but I was afraid of the car. I could have flown commercial or taken a bus or a train, but…same problem. No trust, lots of fear."

"It's that serious?"

"Yes." She opened her eyes.

"What did you do?"

"The right thing after the wrong thing," she said. "That's what it felt like at the time, at least. And then it was all the wrong things. For a lot of years."

He waited for her to make sense of it for him. She sat and

breathed the breeze off the lake and tried to remember Florida and Doc Lambkin and Rae. Tried to remember her husband and her children and how they had been and how she had been.

It was harder than it should have been to remember those things.

"There is a man who wants to kill me," she said. "A few of them now. They've wanted to kill me for a very long time."

Ed rocked a little but didn't speak.

"You don't believe me?" she asked.

"I believe it. You called and told me to fly you up here and to bring guns and not say a word to anyone about it. Yeah, I believe you, Leah."

"Nina."

"What?" He faced her in the dark.

"My name is Nina," she said, and then she shook her head. "No, it's not. It was, but it isn't anymore. I don't even feel like it belongs to me now. I'm Leah, but I was Nina, and Nina is the problem. She was then, and she is now. She's a threat to those kids." She felt pressure behind her eyes and she hugged her knees to her chest. Talking of herself in the third person made it more real, somehow. More personal. The weight of bad decisions mounting. "I don't know how to tell it," she whispered.

"The way it comes out," Ed said. "Just get started and let it come."

She closed her eyes and told it.

Talk of Corson Lowery led to talk of Bleak and Randall Pollard and then she was talking of her husband, dead now, gone so long to her but *really* dead now, and then she was explaining Doc Lambkin and then she was with Rae Johnson and her children on the last flight of their lives. Images rose and fell and she tried to explain each one and in the explanations she found more images and they all scattered out before her like the stars, some clear, others blurred, some joined in a pattern, others adrift.

Ed let her talk. He sat with his arms wrapped around his knees and he rocked and watched the night sky and did not say a word until she fell silent, exhausted and overwhelmed.

Then he said, "There is truly no one you trust to help? No agency, no department, no—"

"There is no one," she said. "I have called the only people I believe I can trust. You and Lambkin. He won't answer now."

Silence.

"I know it sounds impossible," she said. "But if you knew the *reach* Lowery has, Ed…"

"I understand," he told her, but of course he did not. He couldn't. That wasn't his fault.

"So I ran," she said. "Again. With your help, I ran. The only difference is…this time I took them with me."

"When will you tell them?" he asked, as if it weren't a question of whether she would tell them, only when.

She pressed her palms together and bowed her head, supplicant to the night sky. "I don't know. I want them to be safe first. I do not know if I can ever keep them safe."

"You're sure these men are coming for you?" he asked. His tone not disbelieving but not convinced either.

"They're coming," she said. "It will take them a while, I think. But probably not as long as I hope. When they get here, I'll need to be alone."

"That's insane."

"No." She shook her head. "I'll need to be alone."

"To do *what,* Leah?"

She raised her head. "To kill them," she said. "Or to die. It will go one way or the other. I don't know which. I just know that I won't make it easy on them."

Even in the blackness, his shock was evident.

"Hailey and Nick can't be here," she said. "They never should have been. I knew that then and I should have known it now, but when she called and told me that Doug was dead, when she told me they were alone…" Her voice broke. She breathed cold air in through her nose and out through her mouth. "I made a mistake then. I should have known better than to risk…infecting them."

"They were orphaned. They'd have gone to…I don't even know. They had no one."

Orphaned. How that word could cut.

She shifted, loosening the muscles of her lower back, which had tensed while she was telling the story. Orphaned. Yes, they had been.

But could she send them away? It seemed unbearable. It would be worse now than it had been then, and that had been the worst thing of her life. Maybe she wouldn't be able to bear it this time. She wasn't sure, but she didn't know that it mattered one way or the other.

"I rushed," she told him. "Hotheaded and afraid. I did not slow down and cool my mind when I needed to. I rushed and I made a mistake, but I can fix that. Up here, I can fix that."

She told him what she needed then. It would take two trips for him. Neither would take long: she needed a satellite phone, and then she needed him to fly her children away from here.

Away from *her*. The place was not the problem.

"The plane has a radio," he said. "You don't need a sat phone. We can make radio contact."

"I can't use the plane for contact, because I need the plane to be gone," she said. "I need to be alone. Just me and the satellite phone." *And the guns,* she thought but did not say.

"Who are you calling from the phone?"

The tears rose again and her throat constricted but she willed the words to keep coming. "There is a woman they know and love in Louisville," she said. "Her name is Mrs. Wilson. How perfect is that? So Midwestern, so trustworthy. So safe. I met her. I loved her too. She baked me cookies." She tried to laugh but the laugh was a sob. "I will call her, and I will tell her where they will be, and she will come for them, I think." She paused and shook her head. "No. I don't *think* she will come for them; I *know* that she will. She wants them, and they want her. They all want that for each other. I was wrong to take it away. I can fix it, though. I can still fix it."

Ed said, "Leah—" but she lifted a hand and cut him off.

"I will call her and tell her to come for them and she will do that. Then you'll take them out of here, take them to her, and I will stay behind." She felt a tremor in her jaw muscle, her body rebelling against the effort of remaining rigid. Remaining strong. "Then I'll make my second call."

"Who?" he whispered. "Lambkin? Or someone else?"

"Someone else," she said, and she left it at that, because she knew he would object to the plan if he heard it, and she loved him too much to fight over what had to be done. She had asked too much of him already. He did not need to know that when she was sure the children were with the lovely Mrs. Wilson, Leah would call J. Corson Lowery directly and tell him where she was.

Let him come then.

Let them all come.

A mother would fight, a mother would kill, a mother would die if she had to. All of those things could be done; all she knew was that she would not fight from desperation in front of the den, the last defense. If she died, she would die alone.

"Will you help me again?" she whispered. "I have no right to ask, but…will you help me again?"

He touched her leg, and in the touch was the answer. She put her hand over his and it was only then, when warm dampness from the back of his hand met her palm, that she learned he had wept at some point.

The tears he'd wiped silently away in the darkness dried against her skin.

They sat like that and finally she said, "I'll have the morning with them. Don't rush back, please. Take a little time coming back. Let me have the morning with them."

"What will you tell them?" he asked softly. "All of it?"

"Not all of it," she said. "Just...enough."

He didn't ask her what enough was, and she was grateful for that, because of course she did not know.

33

The man with the deep voice who'd grabbed Matt drove while the other one rode shotgun. Matt was in the back seat, and to anyone who passed by, he'd look normal enough, because no one could tell that his ankles were tied and there was a thin cord binding his right hand to the door panel.

There weren't many passing cars, though. It was full night and they were somewhere north of Bangor.

The car was a Tahoe with a deep tint to the windows. It was a comfortable car and it was late and the road rolled softly beneath them and the two men up front did not say much. He almost felt like he could sleep, which seemed impossible. They hadn't given Matt many instructions once they'd gotten him in the car, which had been parked in the lot at Shirttail Point above the river, a straight shot from Hailey's backyard. On the fast walk down to the car they'd given him plenty of instructions, telling him not to run or scream, telling him what would happen if he did.

They didn't need to say much once he saw the back of the tailgate, where shotguns and rifles waited. They were ready to fight an army.

There is something wrong with my family, Hailey had said.

Yes. It seemed like there was.

He'd cried for a while between home and Bangor. He'd tried to do it quietly to avoid angering his captors, but even when they heard him they didn't say anything. They didn't seem to have any interest in him at all, which was almost more terrifying in its own way. He hadn't thought that he could stop crying or shaking at that point, but then they drove on through the night and eventually the tears dried and the trembling stopped.

He tried to notice things then. Tried to observe anything and everything that he would need to tell the police.

You'll never talk to the police. They're going to kill you, and you'll never talk to anyone again.

But they hadn't killed him yet.

As even the little towns fell away and darkness overwhelmed the road, he began to actually wish that they would talk more. Listening gave him a distraction. In the silence he had nothing to do but imagine what lay ahead.

He thought he knew the place, at least. They were headed up Maine, toward the Allagash. All he knew about Hailey's destination was that it was north of Moosehead, but the men who'd kidnapped him seemed to understand more than that. They seemed to know exactly where they were going.

Behind him, the big guns clinked beneath the folded blue tarp that hid them from sight.

The man in the passenger seat, the white man with the two different eyes, had done most of the talking, but the driver seemed to be in charge. Matt wasn't sure why he felt this so certainly, because that man did not say much at all. Maybe that was why. When he spoke, it mattered. The other man would sometimes fill the air with talk but the driver never said anything unless it was a point of action. *I am going to turn off here. I don't want to stay on the highway.* Things like that, dispensed rarely and briefly.

The white man had said a name at some point, but Matt had been crying then, and he'd missed it. It had reminded him of something silly, but he couldn't put his finger on it. They'd been talking about *making the call* and at first he'd thought that meant a decision on whether to kill him or let him live, but then he realized it was an actual call, a phone call. By the time he understood that, the name had come and gone and he was left with only that vague sense of a silly association that he could no longer remember. The name had started with an *L,* he thought. He hoped that they would say it again.

The roads were narrower here, flanked with trees. He'd made a few trips to the perimeter of the Allagash Wilderness with his parents, once for a rafting trip and once to *have an experience,* as his dad had said. The experience they'd had turned out to be two flat tires on a logging road and it had ended with a protracted silence between his mother and father. That was the farthest Matt had ever been into the Allagash.

Thinking of his mother made him remember his rules for trouble. Notice things, that was rule one. Be observant. Pay attention to details.

He tried, but there was not much about the car that seemed unique. He knew the make and model and that it was black. The seats were leather. It smelled strange. Not like a new car, but sterile. A rental, probably. There was nothing in the back seat and in the third row there was nothing but the guns and the blue tarp. They'd made a point of letting him see the guns. That had been the driver's choice, actually. He'd been the one to pull back the blue plastic tarp and let Matt take a long look at all of those glistening rifle barrels and curved triggers, the scopes and the bolts and the magazines. He had watched Matt see all of this, and when he was sure that the message had been absorbed, he pulled the tarp over the guns and smoothed it with his hand. Everything he did was efficient, crisp. Silent.

They'd taken Matt's phone from him but not his watch. He didn't want to illuminate it and draw their attention, but it was too dark to make out the hands. He tilted it to face the road and waited for an oncoming car.

And waited some more. Just when he was about to give up on their ever passing another car, headlights finally rose. In the instant before they flashed by, he saw the watch face. It was 10:48.

His parents would have gone looking for him at least two hours ago. By now, they would have called the police. If the police had been called by nine or even nine thirty, what would the neighborhood look like now? He imagined the scene with flashing colored lights and crime scene tape and roadblocks. It probably wasn't like that at all, though. It was probably just the police chief, Adam Thomas, and a couple of his officers calling Matt's friends and walking the streets, telling his parents to calm down, kids ran away sometimes.

Why had he gone into the house? Why hadn't he waited until daylight? Or told his parents the truth and asked for help? He felt tears threaten again. He didn't like imagining his parents. They'd be terrified. He squeezed his eyes shut and tried to will a message to them: *I am alive. I am in trouble and I am scared but I am alive.*

It was nice to imagine that it might work.

When the driver spoke, it made Matt's eyes snap open. The sound of the man's voice was completely commanding, though it was not loud.

"Do they have to file flight plans?"

The other man, the white guy riding shotgun, seemed as startled as Matt. "Huh? What're you talking about?"

"A floatplane," the driver said. "It doesn't have to land at an airport, but it's still in airspace. They've got to have contact with the tower, right?"

It was a good question, Matt thought. He had a feeling that the driver wouldn't ask any questions that weren't good.

"I dunno," the man in the passenger seat answered. "I doubt it, since they don't need to land at an airport. I mean, our helicopters didn't talk to anyone, but that was different."

He laughed, and it was an unkind sound. The driver did not join in the laughter.

"Maybe not so different," the driver said. "She's a pilot. She knows the game. She could have told him to go on visual flight rules and keep off the radio."

"Think he understands enough to actually follow the instructions?"

"Maybe. Have to consider it."

"Well," the passenger said, "he'll either be there or he won't. If he's gone, we deal with it in another way."

"Yes," the driver said. "If he's gone. I still think it's speeding up, though."

"What is?"

The driver just looked at him.

"Ah," the passenger said. "Got it. You think we're getting to the shooting."

Matt's breathing seemed to stop. The shooting?

"We owe the old man a call," the driver said. "We were asked to let him deliver the finale. I think it's coming fast."

Matt knew he was one of the reasons things were speeding up. One of the threats to their patience. He felt a foolish urge to pipe up and tell them not to rush, not to worry about him at all, please, please, do not worry about Matt Bouchard, he was nothing if not patient.

"I'd like to have a location guaranteed before we call," the passenger said. "Lowery won't like that unknown."

There it was! That was the name, Lowery—it sounded like the seasoned salt Matt's dad used when he was grilling. He put it on everything. Somehow, that memory made the tears threaten again. How silly was that? The image of his father sprinkling seasoned salt on a steak, that was the thing that would make him cry?

His lip trembled and he bit down on it hard enough to taste blood. He wouldn't cry again. He needed to pay attention.

"The pilot boyfriend doesn't have skin in the game," the driver said. "Enough to let an innocent be killed? No."

"Gotta find him to make that case."

"I'm not worried about finding him."

The passenger gave a low laugh and said, "You're the best in the game, bleak."

The driver glanced at him then. Just a glance, but Matt could see his face, and he saw the anger in it. Reproach. He thought the passenger had just made a mistake.

Bleak.

Like a name? Bleak?

They drove on in silence, and Matt thought about what he'd just heard.

Let an innocent be killed.

There was only one innocent in this car.

34

When dawn broke in rose hues across Penobscot Bay, Dax pounded on the front door of a house in Owl's Head. A man stumbled to the door. He was wearing gym shorts and no shirt and was bleary-eyed, his hair lifted with static and one cheek still showing the imprint of a pillow.

"What's the matter?" he said. Pronounced "mattah."

"Are you Andy West?" Dax asked.

"Yeah. What's the matter?"

Dax held up his place mat from the diner. "I saw your advertisement for seaplane tours."

West blinked twice, slowly, as if hoping the second effort would make Dax vanish. "Are you high?" he said. "You gotta call the number, man, not show up at my house." It dawned on him that his address wasn't on the place-mat ad, and he cocked his head, looking more aware now, and said, "Who told you where I live? It's not even six in the friggin' morning, and you're showing up asking for a tour? Get outta here. Sincerely, I don't know what in the hell you—"

With his other hand, Dax held up a stack of hundred-dollar bills. Let them both hover in the air. One place mat, one stack of cash.

"I'd really like that tour," he said.

Andy West looked at him for a long time. The screen door creaked in the breeze. "What's going on, man?"

"There's a point to asking that question," Dax said, "but there's also a point to avoiding it. All you *really* need to know is that I'd like a pilot. Do you feel you *need* to know anything else?"

West considered, then shook his head.

"Excellent choice," Dax said. "We've lost privacy in a lot of the world. I'm glad to see you Mainers still respect it."

"How much money is that?" the pilot asked.

Dax appreciated that question. Pragmatic man. "Ten thousand. I suspect it's more than your going rate."

"Not enough for me to be a friggin' idiot and fly a criminal around."

"Harsh assessment of a stranger."

"Nobody offers money like that unless they're in trouble. I don't need trouble. Not even for ten grand."

Dax nodded, lowered the cash, and put it back in his pocket. He folded the place mat and put that in his pocket as well, and then he drew his knife and flicked the blade open.

"You were so close to making the right choice," he said. "Now you've lost ten thousand dollars and the opportunity for more. See how foolish that was? You could've negotiated. Now you can't."

West stared at the knife, then back to Dax's face. "I don't want a problem. Please, dude."

Dax said, "You've got an ex-wife named Ashley who lives in Exeter with your ten-year-old daughter. Do you want to fly me up north, come back home, and be done with this by noon, or do you want me to leave you bleeding out on your porch while I drive down to Exeter to see Ashley and the kid?"

Andy West said, "What the fuck."

Dax said, "Exactly."

Ten minutes later, they were on their way to the private airport in Owl's Head, not five minutes from West's house. West was driving, and Dax was at his side. The Knox County Regional Airport was quiet in the early morning. It was probably quiet most of the time. A few commuter planes down to Boston, a few private jets, and the occasional sightseeing craft.

No one stopped them when they walked from the car to West's

plane, which was bright yellow with black trim. It looked, Dax thought, like a hornet or a wasp.

Dax still had the knife in his hand but kept it hidden against his thigh. He was wearing a backpack that contained all of his own gear and carrying a flight bag that contained Andy West's identification, cash and credit cards, and both of the guns in Mr. West's legal possession. The shotgun was a cheap twelve-gauge pump, but the handgun was a quality Glock semiautomatic. Unfortunately, Andy had no ammo for the Glock, a sin for which he would have paid dearly at the Blackwell School for Curious Youth. Nevertheless, Dax had learned long ago that even an unloaded gun could be a persuasive weapon, so he'd brought it along.

"I'm embarrassed to admit this," Dax said as they approached the plane, "but I thought it would be on the water. I mean, I wasn't sure a seaplane would have wheels. Dumb, right?"

When West spoke, it was in a whisper, as if he thought someone on the empty stretch of tarmac might be eavesdropping. "Where do I need to take you?"

"I think it's called the Allagash," Dax said.

West stopped walking and rested one hand on the yellow wing of the plane. "Who are you running from?"

"I'm not running from anyone," Dax said. "All I need you to do is fly me up there, drop me off, and fly on back here. Then you go home and get back in bed and you do not tell anyone about this exciting plot twist in your life for, oh, one week. Sound fair? You'll have quite the story, and you can share it with the world one week from now; I won't mind."

"The Allagash is a big friggin' place. You don't care where I drop you?"

"Oh, I have a destination," Dax said. "But let's get off the ground before we discuss."

He let the blade catch the sunlight again.

"Okay," West said.

They got in the plane. The single prop started easily and ran smoothly. Dax listened while West spoke to the tower and nodded approvingly when the pilot kept his voice neutral. They taxied, took off, and flew toward the rising sun, then angled back in the opposite direction. Beneath them, the water was colorful with lobster buoys. Boats were already out. A fisherman's day started early. Good clean work.

"You'll do the right thing for your daughter, won't you?" Dax asked.

"Stop talking about her."

"It's a matter of motivation. You need to be motivated for me to trust you. Understand?"

West's face was tight with fear, but his hands were steady on the yoke. Another good sign. Dax didn't like jittery pilots.

"The wheels retract," Dax observed as they flew northwest. "That's what I wasn't considering. It seemed like a choice to me, that you'd have either wheels or floats. But you've got the best of both worlds, don't you? It's not a seaplane. It's an amphibious plane. Much more sophisticated."

West said, "You told me that once we were in the air, I'd learn my destination."

"The destination is a place called Roman Island Lake. You know it?"

The pilot nodded.

"Great," Dax said, settling back into the seat. "Fly on, Mr. West."

Roman Island Lake interrupted the Allagash River's flow like a blood clot. It was north of any property that Leah Trenton and Ed Levenseller owned but Dax had decided to start north and work his way south. He believed Leah would have sought her outermost point of security, which was on Upper Martin Mountain Pond, but he also suspected that she'd be highly attuned to the sound of approaching aircraft.

Dax didn't want to frighten anyone.

Andy West had an inflatable Zodiac dinghy stored in a bag beneath the plane and a 9.9-horsepower Mercury to power it. A bonus. Dax wouldn't need to waste time stealing a boat.

"I wish you hadn't said anything about my daughter," Andy West murmured.

"You should've taken the money, then."

The North Atlantic had fallen away behind them and the low mountains of the Camden Hills were gone. A decent-size town came and went. Bangor? Too far east to be Augusta, too far north to be Portland, and there weren't any other decent-size towns in Maine. The world was giving way to forest now, an interminable stretch of pines, and I-95 lay below them, straight and glimmering, like a single plowed furrow in ground that had proven to be untillable, inhospitable. Then the plane banked northwest, the highway was gone, and only the forest remained, pockmarked with lakes and frothing ribbons of river.

Dax's left arm ached. He did not like the view from here. Dax rubbed his arm and faced the pilot. He did not need to see the woods and the rivers. He needed to watch the human beside him, learn the mistakes specific to this unique specimen, and merge those lessons with all the other mistakes of other humans he'd watched.

Clear eyes, curious mind, empty heart. Recipe for success.

"What?" Andy West said, feeling the presence of Dax's stare.

"Just fly. The rest will take care of itself."

They flew. The forest seemed to gain depth as they pushed north, the trees sealing in on one another until the woods had a textured, overlapping look from above. As the sun rose, the hues of green brightened but the blackness was never completely gone. It would be a very dark wood from the ground, Dax realized, and it would be hard traveling.

A mountain with a hint of snowcap on the peak rose to their left.

"Is that Katahdin?" he asked.

"What's *that* matter to you?" Surly.

"I'm a curious man and I'd hate to miss this opportunity to learn a little," Dax said. "The chance might not come again."

West shook his head and didn't speak. Dax sighed and leaned toward him with the knife. "The place mat promised tours," he said.

West wet his lips and said, "Yes, that is Mount Katahdin."

Dax leaned back in his seat. "Excellent. We're now north of the end of the Appalachian Trail. The terminus, if you prefer to be more technical. Which word do you like, Mr. West? *End* or *terminus?*"

Nothing.

"Or *conclusion,*" Dax said. "We could say *conclusion* instead of *end,* couldn't we? The *outcome.* The *endpoint.* The *expiry.* Which term do you like?"

"*Stopover,*" West whispered.

Dax laughed. "That's very good," he said. "I enjoyed that one."

But West was not laughing, and he didn't appreciate the banter. This was one of the things Dax hated about traveling alone. He could be at peace alone, but it would be so nice to have a companion who understood you. What his father and uncle and aunts had had.

His left arm throbbed. Phantom pains from bones that had knit back together long ago. He shifted in his seat, seeking relief from the constant shudder of the aircraft. Even phantom pains could be loud presences.

Katahdin was out of sight and the big lakes were vanishing but the rivers were widening. Andy West brought the plane's nose down, and through the shimmer of the spinning prop, Dax saw an elongated lake between stretches of river, like a knot someone had forgotten to untangle. "This is the place?" Dax asked.

West nodded once. His face was turned away from Dax, angled down and to the left, scouting the island. Looking for a landing zone, presumably. But Dax didn't like his expression. There was a touch of the conniver to it.

"You been here before?" Dax asked.

"Roman Island?"

"Yes."

"Only in a canoe. Never flown into it."

From within the throb deep in that damaged bone, a voice rose up like the Yellowstone Caldera come to pay a visit: *Remember that he's not as useless as he seems, Dax. He's a bush pilot, even if he gives cute little tours during the summer months. Has a gun and a Zodiac and has used them. He's got some resourcefulness. Maybe he's got something in him that you don't see.*

It was easy for him to imagine that the voice was his father's. To remember the sound and cadence and the lessons left behind.

Roman Island clarified in front of them. Dax watched the odd tangle of lake in the center of the river widen to greet them, the island stuck there in the middle, and suddenly the warning voice was gone and that song from *Reservoir Dogs* was in his head: *I got the feeling that something ain't right.*

"Don't land by the island," Dax said.

"What? You said put it down at Roman—"

"Instructions have changed. Cope. Adapt. And do not put me down by that fucking island."

West looked pained, and that expression told Dax he had made the right choice, although he wasn't yet sure why. West had been too pleased about the descent to the island, and Dax believed that he'd lied about visiting the place only once and in a canoe. There was something down there that appealed to West, something more than merely the chance to get rid of his passenger. Dax didn't know what it was, but he knew that it was true, felt it in the way he felt the ache from that perfectly healthy but once broken arm.

"Go north," he said. "Far end of the lake. Far out of sight of the island."

"There's nothing wrong with landing at the—"

"Thought you hadn't landed there before."

West opened his lips, closed them, then tried again. "I know the water. I can just put us down there like you wanted and then—"

"Do I sound like I'm open to opinions?"

They flew over the island at about five hundred feet and kept pushing north. Dax studied the place as they passed. Maybe a dozen camps in all, if that. Some with signs of life, but others appearing to be shut tight for the season.

Several boats. Faster boats than the Zodiac, if he needed to steal one.

The island vanished behind them and the lake opened its cold gray arms ahead and Andy West said, "Put it down or circle?"

"Put it down."

"It's all rock on that shoreline, man. I can't taxi up and drop you off, not like I could have on the island."

"I'll live with it."

West shrugged and prepared to land. When they were about thirty feet off the surface of the lake, West brought the nose up slightly. The floats met the water, and West brought the throttle all the way back, idling the engine. They were now down on the lake with about two hundred feet separating them from a long low esker of rock.

"Would you have done that if the wind was blowing harder?" Dax asked.

West frowned and stared. "Done what? Landed?"

"Idled the engine. If the wind was really blowing, wouldn't you have wanted some power?"

West considered him as if seeing something new—and possibly more alarming. "No," he said. "I wouldn't have with the wind. Then I'd take a powered flare. But to do that, I'd need to eat up more of the lake."

Dax nodded, pleased with both West's explanation and himself for understanding it.

"Very good," he said. "I appreciate the insight. Take us over to that far cove." He pointed to an area where a horseshoe-shaped cliff surrounded the water.

"That's nowhere to get out. It's all—"

"Take us."

West taxied toward the cove. He was using the water rudders to steer, and because there was a current to this lake, which was really not so much a lake but a swollen section of a river system, he seemed to take a wider curve. Dax watched that and thought that taking off with current and a crosswind would be a complex task indeed. All the same, he might need to try it. You had to be prepared. The water landing, he thought he could replicate. Takeoff would be a different story. The runway hadn't taught him anything about takeoff from the water.

Maybe it was worth keeping Andy West alive.

A long curve of gravel appeared ahead, just past the horseshoe-shaped cliff. There were jutting boulders at both ends but nothing marring the approach.

"Could you beach there?" Dax asked.

"I could, assuming there aren't any snags under the surface."

"I thought you knew the water up here."

"I know it by the island."

"Where you've never landed the plane?"

West looked over at him, chewing on the inside of his lip, and didn't answer.

"Try to beach it," Dax said.

"Might do some damage to the plane."

"I'll reimburse you for any damage, of course. I thought that was in our contract." He looked down at the knife and then slapped his forehead with his free hand. "Oh, that's right. We agreed to proceed on the honor system."

West adjusted the water rudders and throttle and brought them in. He shut off the engine about a hundred feet from the shore and steered them under the remaining momentum. The plane rode lightly over the surface and then the floats crunched over the pebble shore, no rougher than a snow shovel on a driveway.

"I don't think that did much damage," Dax said.

West ignored him. "I've got to get out to turn it around, okay?"

"By all means. Allow me to help."

They both opened doors and stepped out onto the floats. West was watching Dax, and he seemed discouraged by the way Dax moved nimbly down the pontoon floats and leaped to shore. Balance was a priority to Dax, in all ways.

Andy West waded out into the shallows, took the plane by the tail cone, and pulled it around until the tail protruded over the low stretch of beach. Then he walked back across to the pilot's door, opened it, and reached beneath the seat.

"If there's a gun under there, you'll die," Dax said.

West froze. "A rope," he said. "It's just a rope. To tie her off."

"Okay. Come back up with a rope in your hand, please."

The knife was gripped now in a throwing position, and Dax had no doubt that he could bury the blade in Andy West's throat before the pilot got a shot off if he indeed had a gun.

He came back out with the rope, though, no weapons. He tied one end to the aft cleat and then walked up the beach, past Dax, to the nearest tree. He looped the free end of the rope around the tree and secured it.

"Beautiful," Dax said admiringly. "It looks regal, don't you think? Nothing in sight but woods and water, and it's facing into the wind, ready for action."

West didn't say anything.

"Did you name it?" Dax asked.

"What's with the friggin' questions? Just do whatever you came here to do and let me go, okay?"

"Questions are crucial, Andy. They are crucial to a well-lived life," Dax said.

West gave an exhausted head shake. Dax was approaching him slowly, and if West felt threatened, he didn't show it. That was an advantage of Dax's cheerful countenance and youthful face. Eventually, men began to let down their guard around him, even when he was armed.

"The thing about being curious," Dax continued, "is that you never know when you're in the presence of an expert. Sometimes a humble, quiet person is actually the smartest person in the room. You don't want to miss that opportunity."

"Okay, man."

"You haven't asked me very good questions," Dax said. "You've told me things, and you've made requests—the *Don't hurt my daughter* stuff—but we had a good long flight together and you didn't take advantage of it."

He stopped a single stride from West. The pilot turned all the way around and looked at him. Dax raised his eyes and nodded in an expectant way.

"I'm sorry," West said, because he knew by then that he had to say something.

"What would you have asked?" Dax said. "If you had the opportunity again, what would you have asked me?"

A pause. The front of the plane rocked faintly in a light breeze. The line from the aft cleat to the tree tightened and held.

"Who are you?" Andy West tried finally. "What are you doing?"

Dax sighed. "The right questions aren't the big ones, Andy. Start small. Be specific. Here's one for you: Why am I holding the knife in my left hand when before it was in my right?"

Andy West looked down at the knife. When he did, Dax punched him in the throat with his right hand, then he grabbed the back of the pilot's head, drove his forehead down, and hammered it with his rising knee.

The pilot slumped into the gravel, unconscious.

Dax looked down at him and said, "I changed hands as an

excuse to ask the question, Andy. Then I knew you would look at the knife when you shouldn't. That made things easier on me. If you'd been asking the right questions all along, you wouldn't have needed to do that. See my point?"

Andy West couldn't answer. It would be a few minutes before he'd be able to mumble, let alone speak, and by then he'd be in the cramped cargo hold with zip ties at his wrists and ankles and tape over his mouth. Still, Dax was hopeful that he'd take his time in the dark to reflect on what he would do differently next time.

No experience was wasted on a curious man. Not even a painful one.

Especially not a painful one.

Dax set to work removing the inflatable Zodiac dinghy and its small outboard motor from the cargo hold. When he had those secured on dry land and had inflated the boat, he unloaded the guns and then his own backpack. From his backpack he removed the zip ties and duct tape. He also had black electrician's tape. That would be useful, because the Glock was all black and so was the outboard motor casing.

Andy West was just beginning to stir when Dax slammed him into the cargo hold, closed the hatch, and locked it.

35

E d wanted to leave at first light, but Leah had pushed him to stay through breakfast. She wanted the sense of calm—a false sense, yes—and feared that if the children awoke to the sound of Ed's plane departing, it would shatter that.

She had enough shattering to do today. Let them wake to it at their own pace.

They were up early, though. Not much past first light. Primal biology, the parts of your mind and body that hummed to life here, where it was quiet enough that you could hear the woods and water and sky without straining.

The day dawned beautifully, but there was a shelf of gray massing to the southwest, an arcus cloud, the leading edge of a storm. Leah stood on the lakeshore and watched it and tried to determine whether it would come their way.

It was too far away for her to tell with certainty. Everything directly above was crystal, and everything to the north and east glittered with golden light. What wind there was came in soft, sporadic breaths. The water was so still that when a fish jumped, the ripples could be seen for a long time.

She'd planned on making breakfast on the woodstove in the cabin, but Ed built a small campfire, and while Leah walked Tessa along the shore, the kids emerged from the cabin and went down to join him. Nick was asking Ed questions as Hailey stood and faced the lake and the rising sun, tall and elegant and beautiful, a promise of all she could be.

Mrs. Wilson will take good care of her, Leah thought, and then she had to stop and pretend to study some withering wildflowers so she wouldn't approach her children with tears in her eyes.

She hadn't even reached the fire when Hailey turned and spoke to her.

"Good morning. May I use the canoe today?"

Leah was momentarily speechless. Hailey rarely initiated a conversation, and she never asked for anything.

"Of—of course," she stammered at last. "Of course you can use it."

"Great," Hailey said. "Thank you."

"Of course," Leah said for the third time. "It's a nice one. Ultralight. It's actually made out of—"

"Kevlar," Hailey said, and she smiled. "I know. The Wilsons have one like it."

The Wilsons. Leah felt her smile waver and fought to preserve it. Ed looked up at her, concerned. She nodded at him, trying to project calm. "Good morning, sir."

"And to you, ma'am."

"Sleep all right out here?"

"Dreams of trophy trout." Ed was kneeling beside the fire, stirring freeze-dried scrambled eggs and peppers with a long fork. Nick, next to him, was unconsciously—or maybe consciously?—mimicking his movements, though he was poking the fire with a stick, stirring smoke into the air. Ed didn't stop him, though. Everyone was patient this morning.

She looked at the arcus cloud again. It seemed stagnant, but she knew that was an illusion. The storm was in motion and headed her way.

"You like the ultralight canoes?" she asked Hailey.

Hailey nodded, walking toward the fire. "They're responsive. If you had to portage with one, I bet it's great, but I've never had to do that." She looked down at the fire, then back up at Leah. "Have you?"

"Yes," Leah said, thinking, *I will not call Mrs. Wilson, I will not let you go, I will beat Lowery somehow and we will all stay together, safe and together...*

"I'd like to try it sometime," Hailey said. "A portage trip, I mean."

"Anytime," Leah replied, her voice soft because she didn't seem to have any moisture left in her mouth.

Hailey wrinkled her nose and pointed at the eggs. "I would rather *not* try those."

Ed grinned. "Don't judge 'em until you've tried 'em."

"I can *see* them. I can *smell* them."

"Only one sense matters," Ed said, ladling some of the eggs and peppers onto a tortilla and offering it to her. "Taste."

She hesitated but finally accepted the tortilla, folded it, and sniffed.

"Gross."

"Taste," Ed repeated.

She took a tentative bite, chewed, and wobbled her head. "Not hideous? Is that what you're going for?"

"Wait until you've portaged a canoe," he said with a smile. "That breakfast will go from not hideous to downright delicious pretty fast."

"I'll take your word for it," Hailey said, but she continued eating.

Leah sat on a flat stone near the fire as Ed distributed the eggs and tortillas. They all ate in silence. A loon cruised by thirty feet from the shoreline, silent, studying them.

"You were all talk last night," Ed told the bird. "Where's the swagger now?"

The loon dived and vanished as if in response, and both kids laughed. Leah looked at them, sitting on the ground with Tessa between them, and suddenly she was having trouble swallowing the breakfast.

Why today? Why did Hailey pick today to begin to loosen up?

Ed wiped his palms on his jeans. "All right, guys. I've got to get airborne. Be back by, oh, midafternoon at the latest." He leveled a mock stern stare at Nick. "You'll have caught your limit of trout by then, hombre?"

"There's a limit?"

Ed smiled. "Poachers," he said. "You guys are everywhere."

"Why do you have to leave now?" Nick asked.

"Because duty calls," Ed said, and he rose. Leah was grateful that Nick accepted that nonanswer.

Hailey looked from Ed to the plane. "Can Nick and I watch you take off from the lake?"

"Cold swim, but sure thing."

"Not swimming. In the canoe."

Ed looked to Leah. She nodded. "Sure," she told them. "Just give him plenty of distance."

"I'm not going to paddle in front of him," Hailey said, exasperated. "I just thought it would be cool for Nick to see him fly over us."

"Yeah!" Nick said, shoving another egg-filled tortilla into his mouth and then talking around it. "Let's do that."

Grateful for the distraction, Leah told them where the life jackets and paddles were and then walked away with Ed. He'd doused the fire, and steam trailed behind them.

"Good moods this morning," he said.

"Yeah."

"Killing you, isn't it."

"Yeah."

He smiled sadly. "I'd like to be back by one o'clock at the latest. Don't want to rush you with what…what needs to happen here, but…"

"But you're thinking of how fast things could go wrong," she finished.

He nodded.

"One o'clock it is," she said, looking at the sun. It was nearing eight now. She would have fewer than five hours alone with her children before she had to call Mrs. Wilson in Louisville and ask her to do the unthinkable.

Behind them, Tessa barked and splashed in the shallows, trying to assist with the canoe launch. Hailey was attempting to send the dog back up the shore.

"She can get in," Leah called. "She loves the canoe, actually. She'll sit still."

Hailey looked dubious. "Can I try it without her the first time?"

"Come on!" Nick cried. "Let her come. She's—"

"I just want to try it first, Nick," Hailey said. "Once I get a feel for it, Tessa can come."

"That's fine," Leah said, and she whistled. Tessa whirled, her coat throwing spray, and galloped toward the plane. Leah turned back to Ed as the kids got into the canoe, Hailey moving with grace and confidence, Nick clambering awkwardly.

"Wish I could do something to help," Ed said softly.

"You kidding me? You're doing a *lot*. More than I should have asked of you."

"I mean here. With the...the talk."

"Ah." She shook her head. "Nobody can help me with that one."

"Right."

They stood together near the plane and watched as Hailey dipped her paddle with confidence and sent the canoe into the lake. It was a bright yellow with the Wenonah name scripted in black along the side. She was in the stern, and Nick sat in the bow, paddling too aggressively and changing sides too frequently. Hailey didn't shout at him, though; she merely adjusted her own deft movements to compensate for his chaos and keep the craft straight. Leah felt a thrill of pride. It was as if somehow Leah's own lessons had crossed time and space and found her daughter. As if they shared this thing.

"See you at one," she said to Ed. "Different moods then, probably."

"Probably," he acknowledged and gave her arm a brief squeeze. "Good luck."

"Thank you."

He stepped away from her, tight-roped down the float to the pilot's door, opened it, and climbed in. A minute later the engine growled and the prop spun and the water shivered beneath it. Leah immediately checked the location of the canoe. They were safely away and still paddling. Hailey had listened to Leah's warning and taken it to heart, giving Ed plenty of room. She was doubling down on safety, in fact. Good girl.

Ed leaned forward, caught Leah's eye, then pointed at the canoe and gave her a thumbs-up. She returned it and then made an A-OK gesture, indicating he was good for takeoff.

The motor's pitch deepened, the prop speed increased, and then he was off, gliding across the surface. The water was so glassy that the plane would feel sluggish to handle. It was counterintuitive, but some chop was good, as it created air pockets between the floats and the water and made the plane more nimble. More responsive, as Hailey had said of the Kevlar canoe.

After a long run, the plane seemed to simply separate from the water, no sign of a struggle, a peaceful mutual parting. Ed was airborne.

Hailey and Nick had paddled to the north to get out of

his way, which meant that he hadn't flown over them at all. He banked the plane and brought it back around, intentionally giving them the experience they'd been seeking. Hailey and Nick lifted their paddles and waved at him, the water spray bright in the sunlight, and Ed wobbled the plane slightly left to right, the wings returning the wave. Even from this distance, Leah could hear Nick's cry of delight. Then Ed brought the plane around and flew south. Leah scratched Tessa's ears and watched him go, watched until the plane was a distant dot in the bright sky, and then the dot was gone, and the sound with it.

She looked back at the canoe, expecting to see them coming in. They were actually farther away now. Hailey was coaching Nick even while she compensated for his mistakes. She was very good on the water. Leah eased down onto one of the glacial boulders that rimmed the shore and watched her daughter and son and tried to determine how she would start the explanation and when in the course of it she would say *I am your mother.*

She'd dreamed of it for years. Meeting them, holding them, telling them. But the rest of what she had to tell them loomed like the thunderheads to the southwest. *I am your mother and I cannot keep you safe. If you are with me, you are in danger. It is the opposite of the natural world. I draw harm to you.*

She lowered her head, closed her eyes, and listened to the light breeze and Tessa's soft panting. Thought of J. Corson Lowery's face and imagined it in the crosshairs of the scope of her rifle. She hated the rifle, but she could use it damn well.

I will make him come to me. I will wait for him, and I will kill him.

The rising sun was warm on her neck. She took a final, long breath and then lifted her head again and opened her eyes.

The canoe was farther away still. Out in the current now, where the pond funneled into the brook. Hailey was poised in the stern, a posture that was at once athletic and elegant.

There was nothing in the brook that would threaten them, but still Leah didn't like it. She got to her feet. "Hey, guys!" she shouted. Her voice echoed across the pond, and Nick looked back, but Hailey didn't.

Leah went into motion, walking down the shoreline with a fast stride, but she was still outpaced by the canoe. "Guys! You've got moving water out there! Hailey! Bring it back!"

Nick stopped paddling but Hailey didn't. She leaned forward and said something that spurred him back into action. Leah stopped and stared. What in the hell was happening?

They're running away. That's what is happening. You've made your plans and they've made theirs.

Running where, though? Into the empty wilderness? That seemed unlikely even for her daughter.

The memory of the map rose then. The way Hailey had traced the river's path with her index finger, moving backward, oblivious to the difference between here and Kentucky, and now Leah understood perfectly: Hailey thought she was going to pick up the river and ride it south, all the way down to Moosehead Lake and the towns she knew were there.

What would she do then?

Call Mrs. Wilson, probably. Do the same thing that Leah planned to do.

She was moving the wrong way for that. There were no phones where she was headed.

Leah broke into a run, leaping from boulder to boulder until she was on the high ground, and then the pine boughs were raking at her as she ran and screamed, *Come back! Come back, damn it!*

They paddled on, into the glistening brook where the current strengthened and pulled them ahead. The plane was gone and they had the only boat and Leah was on foot, hopelessly outpaced. She stopped running, caught her breath, cupped her hands around her mouth, and shouted, *"It goes north, Hailey! Up here, the rivers go north!"*

They were too far away, though, and her voice was too faint. The thing she had not said when she'd had the chance couldn't be heard now.

36

The flight from Martin Mountain to Greenville was a short one even in a small, single-engine plane, less than an hour, and when Ed Levenseller put the plane down on the calm waters of Moosehead Lake in front of his cabin, the area was still waking up, the water empty save for a few fishing boats and the pontoon ferry to Mount Kineo. It was amazing how things emptied out after Labor Day.

There was someone waiting on his dock, though. He didn't notice the man until he'd reduced power and begun to taxi because all his attention was on the plane during landing. Once he closed in, he finally saw him there, a lean black guy standing at the end of the dock, staring right at Ed's plane as if he'd been waiting on it.

Cop, Ed thought, but that was probably just paranoia. A cop didn't sound all that bad to him, actually, no matter what Leah had said. *Trust no one* was a hard ideology for a man like Ed to accept.

The stranger wasn't dressed like a cop. He was wearing jeans and a white T-shirt and sunglasses. Average height, ropy, muscular build, shaved head. He wore sunglasses and stood with his hands in his pockets and did not move at all as Ed floated up to the dock. Even when Ed opened the door, climbed out, and tied the plane off, the stranger didn't move. Just stared.

"How's it going?" Ed said.

For a long moment he thought that the man wasn't going to answer. Then he finally spoke, his voice soft but deep.

"Ready to head back north?"

Ed blinked at him, the paranoia returning. Suddenly, he wished there were someone else within view of the dock. His beloved isolation no longer felt comforting.

"Excuse me?"

"We're going back north. You need to fuel up or anything first, or can we just go?"

"I'm not flying anywhere," Ed said slowly. "You want to explain what you're talking about, or maybe just go on and let me do my…"

His voice trailed off as the man stepped forward, knelt, and extended a phone to him.

The phone's screen was lit up, a FaceTime application running. In the center of the frame was a boy Ed had never seen before. He was a pale kid with dark hair and his hands were tied and someone just outside of the frame was holding a rifle to his head.

"Please," the kid said, his voice high and tinny on the phone speaker. "Please do what he tells you."

It was only then that Ed Levenseller realized the terrified child was sitting on Ed's couch, in Ed's living room. A photograph of a winter sunrise was just behind the rifle. Leah had taken the photograph. It had been a Christmas gift.

Ed stared at the kid on the phone screen and didn't speak. The kid stared back, waiting on him. Ed had an absurd thought that if he responded to the kid, he would make it real, but if he didn't, it would never be real, there would be no child sitting on Ed's couch with a rifle leveled at his skull. He wanted to believe that.

Then the kid spoke again. "My name is Matt," he said. "They are telling me that if you fly them, I can…" His voice wavered, and he swallowed and then tried again. "If you fly them, then I can stay alive."

Before Ed could respond, the phone was gone. The black man pocketed it but didn't straighten up, remaining in the casual kneeling position with his arms resting on one knee, looking for all the world as if he were asking Ed a few questions about the plane the way any tourist might.

"It is not about you," he said. "Remember that. It's not about you or that kid or Nina's kids. Leah's kids—whatever you call her. It is only about her."

"Let him go," Ed whispered. "Whoever he is, just let him go."

"Thatta-boy. Thinking about the innocent ones. Just like you need to." He looked from Ed to the plane. Spoke again in the same monotone, a voice devoid of humanity. "So," he said, "do you need fuel, or are we good to go now?"

37

Moving water is alive with hope and threat. A river can sustain life or drown it, and a river hides its secrets. The one who sees what the river has hidden will be rewarded. The one who is satisfied with the river's surface will be punished.

Dax's father had told him that once, and the lesson lingered. Dax both loved water and respected its threat. He was thinking of this while he piloted the pirated Zodiac south out of Lower Martin Pond and into a narrowing brook, moving against the current toward Upper Martin. He was focused on the water, watching for its secrets, when a yellow canoe blazed into sight against the dark pines, headed into the rapids below.

There were two people in the canoe. The one in the stern knew what he was doing but the one in the bow did not, and that was trouble even before they made the fatal mistake and trusted the promise on the surface of the water, underestimating all that ran beneath. It was a simple eddy, a Z-shaped riffle on the surface, but the surface current surged forward into a deep pool that halted momentum, as if the river were in the midst of an argument with itself.

The resulting argument created a whirlpool that nudged the canoe sideways, toward the rocks.

The paddler in the stern saw it first, which was a problem. The bow seat offered the best scouting view, but the paddler in the bow was still trying to angle left even while the river told him to go right. In the stern, the second paddler saw all of this developing and shouted a command that went unheeded. Dax couldn't hear the words, but he understood the instruction: the paddler in the stern wanted to run the rapids solo, without having to compensate for the flailing of the partner in the bow. This made absolute sense to Dax. It was better to be competent and alone than to be hindered by a hapless teammate.

The canoe swung broadside, struck a rock, and upended as it shot between a trio of boulders at the base of the Z-shaped drop.

The paddlers screamed when they went into the water. High-pitched shouts, not the calm reactions of pros. They had no business being alone on this river, and yet there they were.

Dax listened to the shouts and smiled. You never knew what might come your way. "Precocious," Dax said aloud, twisting the throttle on the tiller and angling upriver. "They are precocious kids."

It wasn't Leah, just her children, and the idea that Leah's children were downriver and alone suggested that Leah wasn't in charge of this little adventure.

They had no idea just how fortunate they were to have over-turned in a stretch of a river where a competent man with a competent boat happened to be. The yellow canoe righted itself and drifted by, as if determined to demonstrate that it was the paddling team that was to blame, not the craft. It hurried past like a dog ashamed of its master.

"You know what you're doing," Dax told the empty canoe. "Easier to go it alone sometimes. Safe travels, Wenonah."

Wenonah rode the river on by and Dax focused on the children in the water beneath the boulders. They were both at the surface and swimming well enough to shout, which meant they swam well enough to make it to shore without drowning. Fortunate on all counts, because if they'd dumped in a recycling rapid with a strong current that could pull them back under and hold them in the deep or bash them against the rocks, the mistake they'd made might have been fatal. Even here, in this relatively calm stretch, they'd imperiled themselves. The Allagash was cold and lonely. It would be easy to die here, even beneath a bright sun.

Good news, though—they were not alone.

Dax brought the Zodiac in alongside the child who'd been in the bow and discovered that he'd made a regrettable error—he'd assumed the paddler in the stern, the one who knew what was going to go wrong before it did, was the boy. The boy, it turned out, was the one who'd been in the bow. Gender bias, no excuse for it, and certainly not a mistake that Dax should make, considering that the only broken bones he'd ever suffered had been caused by a woman.

"Quit crying and grab my hand," Dax told the crying child who was grasping a tree limb. "Hurry, now. I won't turn around to give you a second chance."

The boy took his hand. Dax hauled, grateful that it was his right arm, and the boy belly-flopped into the bottom of the Zodiac like a boated bluegill.

"You need to listen to your sister," Dax told him. "She might've coached you through."

Dax returned to the tiller, twisted it for more throttle, and steered toward the girl. She was already sitting on one of the boulders, catching her breath.

"You okay?" Dax called over the sound of the churning water, bringing the Zodiac in broadside to the boulder.

She stared at him, hesitant, but nodded. She was soaked, her long tangled dark hair dripping.

"That could've been bad," he said. He could see that the girl was crying, and so despite himself, he added the gentle truth: "If your brother had listened to you, I think you'd have made it. He needed to just stop paddling and trust you, didn't he?"

She nodded again. She was soaked and shivering and too distracted by adrenaline and fear to appreciate the compliment.

"Climb in," Dax told her. "You kids are lucky. Most days, this stretch of the river is empty. But here I am."

38

*C*ool your mind.

So many times, Leah had counseled herself with that three-word phrase. So many times, she'd been able to follow her own advice.

This was different, though. She'd grabbed her backpack and .30-30 Winchester with a Leupold scope, and as she jogged through the densely packed pines at a pace fast enough to cover ground but steady enough not to sap her reserves, she knew the difference as something that boiled up out of the blood.

You didn't tell a mother to cool her mind when her children were threatened. Or at least, you didn't tell her twice.

Leah wanted to lash out, wanted to be savage, wanted to paint the pines with the blood of her enemies. It was difficult to admit that the enemy ran alongside her, ran within her. The enemy was the truth that she had buried for so long. Buried with the best of intentions, but what did intentions matter when the innocent ones suffered?

Beside her, behind her, and occasionally out in front, Tessa galloped with an enviable ease. The dog would run all day if given the opportunity, and usually she ran with an undisguised joyfulness, but now she had her ears pinned back and she looked at Leah often. She might not know the source of Leah's tension, but she certainly knew it was there.

Leah wanted to go faster, but there was no such thing as a simple step in the Allagash, where limbs lashed faces and grabbed arms, rocks and roots turned ankles and tortured knees, and the soil would shift from a splashdown pool to a spine-thudding stone in a single stride. Everywhere, the trees obscured the sun and mocked your sense of direction and of space, even your willpower. Maine's terrain lacked the soaring elevation changes that made hipster hikers head west to Colorado where they could bag a fourteen-thousand-foot summit and be back to a craft brewery by evening, but every year Maine's terrain ate up some of those same hikers and then a guide had to come haul their foolish asses to safety. A guide like Leah.

She ran with fear but she ran with confidence, a contradiction that only those truly prepared for danger could understand. You knew that trouble would come, period, and in that acceptance came the confidence.

She knew this place so much better than she knew her own role. *Protector? Mother? Attacker? Aunt? Prey? Predator? Living? Dead?*

The possibilities came with each breath, inhaled and exhaled and lost to the lonely woods, and no answers arrived. Not yet. They would come eventually.

She felt pain and she felt fear and she felt peace. For the first time in so many days, she felt peace. Her children needed rescue again, but this rescue she was prepared for. They were lost in the wilderness and this was a condition that Leah Trenton understood.

Fix it, then. Fix this one thing and then endure whatever came on its heels.

The map, Leah. See the map, be the map, run the map.

The brook from Upper Martin Mountain Pond fed into Lower Martin in a stretch of short but tricky white water. Then, across Lower Martin Pond, the brook ran wide and smooth and deep and poured into the Allagash, where Roman Island Lake was the next stop. It was late in the year and the water was low, so the canoe wouldn't carry them as far and as fast as it might have.

She splashed through a bog that threatened to suck the boots from her feet and then clambered up across a rock scree and dodged a tangle of roots and ran on, slinging muddy water with each stride. She pictured the river and she thought she knew where she would find them. There was a Z-shaped chute above a deep pool, and the third point of the Z created a backing current that would throw a boat against the rocks.

They would strike the rocks and either overturn or bang their way through, and regardless, she thought that Hailey would seek safety following the chute. There was a wide gravel bank on the northeastern shore that could be reached easily even if they were swimming, because they'd been wearing the life jackets, she'd seen to that much, so they'd be afloat and—

Life jackets, yes; helmets, no. What if their heads meet the rocks? What then?

They would pause on that bank to assess the situation. She would find them there, she would find them and she would cry out to them and tell them all that she had hidden and then they would…they would…they would…

She ran on.

The rifle banged against her back. She'd have run faster without it, but it was better to be prepared.

Up ahead, obscured by the trees and hills but audible now, the rapids waited. Or was that her own ragged breathing? She tried to imagine it as the rapids, and the space between gasps as the stretch of bucolic gravel bank, and her children resting safely there.

I'm coming. I am almost there.

Mom is almost there.

39

The children had never been taught how to start a fire, Dax discovered, but he wasn't dismayed by this because primal lessons were rarely regarded as practical in these modern times.

Patient as always, he built the fire for them so they might dry out and warm themselves. They were appreciative of the warmth and the rescue, but they remained wary and he struggled to entice them into conversation.

A shame.

He'd put the Zodiac ashore on a gravel bank. Their yellow canoe glimmered on the far side of the pond, riding like a fishing bobber, drifting across the still waters and toward the river. Perhaps it would wash up on Roman Island or perhaps it would continue all the way out. Dax liked to imagine it reaching the sea, but he'd always been a romantic.

He sat on a sun-bleached limb that had washed onto the gravel bank and watched as Nick and Hailey huddled close to the fire, acting as if they'd left the river and entered a Jack London tale rather than a gorgeous fifty-degree day. The water had to be cold, though. He had no clothes or blankets to offer them, but the sun and the fire would do the work in time.

"So, I'm not one to pry," he said at length after their shivering subsided and they seemed to be steadying, "but it would be neglectful of me *not* to ask where you came from and where you're headed."

The boy and girl looked at each other. The boy waited on the girl.

"It's private," she muttered. "Sorry. Not trying to be rude, but...you're a stranger."

"A stranger who saved your stupid butts."

She looked at him uneasily, and he smiled. "Just teasing," he said. "You were going to be fine. *You* knew what you were doing. Just because you ended up in the drink doesn't mean you were incompetent. Failure is a necessity of adventure. You never appreciate that in the moment, but when you look back on things, you'll remember. Give it time."

"Okay," she said. "Sure."

"Wherever you're headed," Dax said, "it would seem difficult to get there without my help. Your canoe is well out in front of you now. I haven't done a lot of hiking around here, but it doesn't look like easy country. So you'll probably need a ride."

Silence. Dax smiled. Patient.

"You were headed north. Where to?"

Hailey shook her head. "South," she said. "We were headed south. To Moosehead Lake."

"It's an interesting way to get there, considering the river flows north."

She stared at him. Nick turned from the fire and looked over his shoulder at Dax, concern on his face.

Dax nodded sympathetically. "North. Wrong direction."

He could tell the girl was rocked by this news.

"I think we can all agree that it was a good idea, poorly executed," Dax said. "It happens to the best of us. Don't let it get you down."

She looked away from him, back to the river. He watched her study the river and then turn skyward and locate the sun, and he was proud of her for that choice and for the chagrin that passed over her face as she oriented to east and west and then returned her attention to the river and saw that he was right.

"If we can further agree that things are no longer proceeding as planned, since you intended to ride a canoe south and instead you went north and then lost the canoe…well, maybe we can come back to that question of what to do now. I've got to take you guys somewhere." He shrugged. "Or leave you here. I mean, it's none of my business."

Nick leaned toward Hailey and stared at her. He didn't speak, but his face said plenty; he wanted to take the ride. Help from a stranger was dangerous, but it was a far sight better than no help at all. Nick was the pragmatist, Dax decided. Hailey was more intriguing, governed by complex, conflicting emotions and a bone-deep desire not to seek help.

"I don't have too much time," Dax told them. "I could run you back to your camp or wherever you came from. I could call for someone to get you. But I certainly can't take you all the way to Moosehead Lake. I'm not even sure that's possible from here. I don't know the map all that well. I just know which way is which."

Hailey glared at him.

Dax lifted his hands. "Apologies. Not trying to poke the bruise. Just saying, I'm not sure that Moosehead can be reached by the water from here, and I absolutely do not intend to try. The choice is yours."

The girl looked at the river. Pushed a lock of damp hair out of her face and gritted her teeth. He wanted to applaud her. She was absolutely determined to do it alone, to recover from her mistakes without help.

"I suppose we could give it a little bit more time," Dax said as the silence lengthened, "and wait on your mother. I'm sure she's not far behind. If she didn't see you leave with the canoe, she's certainly figured out that's what happened by now. Mothers are never far away, am I right?"

"You're wrong about that," Nick said.

"I don't think so."

"Yes, you are," Hailey said. "It's none of your business, but you are."

Dax arched an eyebrow. "I'll bet you one hundred dollars," he said, "that I am right and that if we wait here long enough, your mom is going to show up."

"I'll take that bet," she muttered, and he could see that there were tears in her eyes.

Poor kid. Wet and cold and hurting, and all because she'd been protected from the truth. It was a terrible way to raise a child. The Blackwell family had never shielded someone from a hard truth just because he was young.

A good woman, Doc Lambkin had said of Nina Morgan in the moments before Dax had killed him. Perhaps that was true; Dax didn't measure human value the way that others did. But for a good woman, she was a terrible teacher.

Dax reached into his pocket, withdrew a damp hundred-dollar bill, and held it up in two fingers. It fluttered in the breeze, smoke swirling around it as the wind shifted.

"One hundred bucks," he said.

Hailey Chatfield watched him. Her eyes narrowed. Then she leaned forward and snatched the bill from his fingers.

"Whoa!" Dax cried. "You can't claim the winnings before we've seen how it all plays out."

"Yeah, I can. Our mother died ten years ago. She is *not* showing up."

Dax smiled at her through the smoke. "You're wrong about that, Hailey."

She was starting to object when she realized that he'd said her name although she'd never volunteered it. She froze with her lips parted and stared at him in terror, and Nick whirled from the fire, and Dax drew his gun from within his jacket and rested it on his thigh.

"Good news, kids. I've not only saved your butts from the

river, but I can summon your mother from beyond the grave. Aunt Leah is not your aunt. She is your mother, and I am almost positive that she's on her way. More good news? I've come here to save her life."

He looked from one to the other, smiling. "How about that? Good trick, right? This is what you might call a lucky break."

40

Before they left the dock but after Matt's hands and feet were bound, the man named Bleak got out of the plane again and went up to the car and came back down with the bags of guns. Randall kept the muzzle of his pistol pressed against Ed's skull while Bleak loaded the guns into the cargo hold. He moved as if already familiar with the plane. No hesitation, no questions. He loaded all of the guns and then he came back down with a phone that was attached to a small box by a thin, curled cord. It looked like an old-fashioned car phone Matt had once seen in a flea market with his mother.

The good guy, the one they'd trapped, was in the pilot's seat with a sick expression on his face. His name was Ed. Matt was in the back with the one Bleak had called Randall. Bleak and Randall had guns in their hands. Matt had hard plastic zip ties binding his ankles and wrists.

You can crash the plane if you'd like, Bleak had told the pilot while fastening the ties, *but the kid will die. Remember that. Seems like a nice kid. You'd hate to be the one who killed him, wouldn't you?* He had said that casually, indifferently. *The kid will die.*

The pilot started answering questions then. Told them that Leah was waiting at someplace called Upper Martin Mountain Pond. Told them how far it was and how many people were there—nobody else, he said, and even when Bleak hit him above the eye with the gun and opened a line of blood that had only just now started to dry, he'd stuck to that story. Told them how many guns she had. Told them there was a dog. Told them that Leah would trust his plane because she was expecting it to return. They'd seemed pleased by that.

Matt watched Bleak out on the dock and swallowed. It hurt his throat, which was sore from crying.

Someone answered the phone. Bleak spoke. His voice was soft but so deep that it carried, and even inside the plane, Matt could make it out. "Mr. Lowery. Yes. We do not have visual yet but it should happen shortly. Physical will be quick then. Where do you want her? There are contingencies we will have to account for." Pause. "Civilians. No threat. One helpful bush pilot, and one boy, maybe ten years old."

Thirteen, damn it, Matt thought, strangely irked considering the circumstances.

"I understand," Bleak said into the odd phone. "You're right. Zero-sum belongs only with Nina. I believe my helpful pilot will accommodate that."

Zero-sum. Matt knew that term; it meant, at least to him, "take no prisoners." His dad liked to say *zero-sum* whenever they played a game. His dad usually lost. Watching Bleak stand there, lean and strong and relaxed, Matt thought that this man probably did not lose many games.

If it was only zero-sum for Hailey's aunt, though, then the rest would live.

Matt watched the man and thought, *He is lying. He is lying so the pilot cooperates.*

He hoped he was wrong.

"Helicopter would be my recommendation," Bleak said. "Expect confirmation within the hour." He disconnected the call, loaded the strange phone in with the guns, and closed the cargo hold. The passenger door opened and Bleak stepped off the dock and into the plane with casual grace. He looked at Ed.

"Cleared for takeoff," he said.

Ed didn't answer. Just started the engine.

41

Nick scrambled to his feet when Dax broke the family news, his hands clenched, pale face stricken.

"Sit down," Dax said.

"Who are you?" Nick shouted.

Dax lifted the gun an inch. Hailey said, "Nick, sit down right now."

Nick sat.

Dax lowered the gun and said, "Thank you. Now, I'm open to questions. I don't want you to think that I'm some maniac who would make a bold statement and not back it up."

"You're a liar," Nick said.

"What did she do?" Hailey asked. Her voice was soft.

"Your mother?"

"Don't call her that. Leah."

Dax sighed and rolled his head theatrically. *"Ask better questions,"* he implored, eyes on the blue sky above. Mostly blue. To the west, a bank of dark clouds massed. "This is a special opportunity, kids. One you might not have again. Do not waste it."

Sticks crackled in the fire. No one spoke. Dax faced the sky and stroked the grip of his gun with his thumb.

"Why should we believe you?" Hailey said at last.

"Because you're intelligent," Dax answered, looking back at her, holding her gaze. "You know the situation is strange. You've always known that. And you know that you look just like her. It's absolutely uncanny. Even a child couldn't miss it."

She stared at him. Didn't speak.

"But the question is a good one," Dax said. "And because of that, I'll continue to indulge you if you have others."

Nick shifted away from the fire, moved closer to his sister. Dax didn't comment. Hailey reached out and put a hand on her brother's arm, but the gesture was distracted. All of her attention was on Dax.

"What did my father do?" she asked.

"I have no idea. I thought he was—oh. *Oh,* I get it. You're wondering if he did something bad, if he's the reason for the family dilemmas. As far as I know, your father never did anything to court the current crisis. Your mother, however, was presented with a very difficult choice."

He went silent. Waited.

"What choice?" Hailey said, and he smiled.

"There you go. Asking good questions. She was given the choice between leaving her family to keep them safe or staying and placing them in harm's way. She chose to leave. I can't imagine it was easy, and I personally think it shows a narrow-minded understanding of options, but…" He shrugged. "I'll be the first to acknowledge that my upbringing was unique."

He leaned down, and they both pulled back.

"Just adding some wood to the fire, guys. Relax. If I wanted to kill you, you'd be dead."

He holstered the gun, broke branches, and fed dry wood to the fire. If either kid had the thought of trying to run, neither acted on it. Nick looked like he was frozen by fear, but Hailey seemed to be anchored by shock. She believed what Dax was telling them.

When the fire was back to full life, he returned to his seat on the log and unholstered the gun once more.

"You're lying," Nick whispered.

"No," Hailey said, her hand still on her brother's arm. "I don't think he is."

Dax said, "There's no money in it for me. In lying, I mean.

There's some money in keeping your mom alive, but not as much as I'd like. She's not worth a lot."

"She *paid* you?" Nick said, disbelieving.

Dax waved a hand. "It doesn't matter. Business issues shouldn't be the topic of the moment. I'm curious to hear your opinions on her conduct. What do you think of her?"

Silence. The fire caught some dry pine needles, flared, then died back down, smoking and fragrant. The wind was pushing west to east, so the smell was unlikely to alert anyone who had come after them. Nevertheless, he liked having the gun in his hand. Pursuers would be coming soon.

"Why did anyone want to kill her?" Hailey asked.

"She flew a woman and her children down to Mexico to be murdered. One thing led to another. People got emotional." Dax yawned. "My understanding is that the police weren't considered a viable option. I might have found a workaround, but…" He shrugged. "Again, we return to the different upbringings."

"My dad told us she was dead," Hailey said, and she seemed more wounded by this than anything Dax had said. It made sense; her father had been the guide and guardian.

"This is my point," Dax said, shifting the gun from his right hand to his left and leaning forward so that he could feel the heat of the fire on his face. "In their quest to protect you, they set you up for more harm. Not physically, perhaps, but…" He tapped his forehead, then his heart. "Am I right?"

Nick looked over to his sister. He didn't want to believe Dax, but he could see that Hailey did. He was looking at her when she said, "How many people want to kill her?"

It was a child's question and yet, as with so many questions posed by children, it contained the most essential concern, the one that adults would be slow to consider, let alone voice.

"Excellent!" Dax said. "We move on to practical matters. I am aware of three specific men, but I can't speak to the total."

The wind rose and blew smoke into his face but he didn't look away from the fire. Hailey Chatfield was staring at him. She was, he realized, still stuck on her father's role as a collaborator. Dax had shattered her illusion of the trusted parent.

"There is no such thing as an innocent man, Hailey," he told her. "That's the sad truth of our condition. We've all made our concessions. We've all tried to pick the right wrong thing."

"What? The *right* wrong thing?"

"Yes."

"I don't know what that—"

"Sure you do. You ran away from your aunt. You stole her canoe. You put your brother's life in danger. Why did you do all of those things?"

The fire crackled and smoked. Hailey watched him from beneath the shadow of her damp bangs.

"Let me ask it another way," Dax said. "Would you have killed Aunt Leah?"

"No!"

Her response was immediate and horrified and it made laughter bubble up from Dax's belly.

"I love it," he said. "I absolutely love it. You would lie, you would steal, and you would imperil others, but you would not kill her. Hailey Chatfield, you are an iconic specimen of the human race."

Her face darkened and her jaw trembled. She did not like to be laughed at.

"You don't like Leah," Dax said. "That's the truth, right? You don't like her, you don't trust her, and you don't want to be with her. You don't want to live in Maine with a stranger. You want to be home among your friends. Am I wrong?" He looked from Hailey to Nick, eyebrows raised, waiting. "Well?"

Nick shook his head.

"No," Hailey whispered. "You're not wrong."

"Okay," Dax said, the smile gone now. He leaned forward again, closer to the fire, his face lit from the flames below. He stared at them with the earnestness that they deserved for the question to come.

"If you want," Dax said, "I will kill her for you. And then you can go home."

Silence. Smoke and wind. Nick stared at Hailey. Hailey hadn't looked away from Dax. He gazed back and nodded.

"It's your choice, Hailey. Remember that this woman abandoned you once already, she's lied to you, and she's put you in danger. If you go back home, maybe to stay with that nice neighbor, Mrs. Wilson? Back there, it could all be over. Not forgotten, of course, but *done*. All I need is your instruction. Just say the word."

Nick whispered, "Hailey," and tugged at his sister's damp shirtsleeve. She didn't react. She just watched Dax through the blowing smoke.

"I'll need to have an answer," Dax said, "because she's on her way. In fact, I suspect all of them are on their way to us."

As if in confirmation, there came a faint, high hum from the south. Nick looked skyward, searching for the plane. Hailey didn't look up. She was still staring at Dax. Still thinking.

"We're growing short on time," Dax told her. "I don't mean to rush you on such a crucial decision, but…"

She looked at Nick. He was watching the sky. Searching for help. She seemed disappointed by that, Dax thought.

"My father had an expression for moments like this," Dax said. "Moments in which the forces of antagonism mount and choices must be made."

The tremor in her jaw was scarcely noticeable. She was a tough one.

"What was his expression?" she asked.

His face split into a delighted grin. His father would have liked this girl. She had spirit, but better still, she had a hint of moral curiosity. A willingness to explore questions that others would avoid, to consider all options.

"'The crucible looms,'" Dax Blackwell said. "That's what my father would have told you. Do you know what that means?"

She paused, then said, "I think I get the idea."

Dax laughed. "Yes," he said. "I think you do."

Nick said, "I see a red plane. Hailey? I think it's our plane."

Dax glanced skyward. The boy was right. The red plane was there, tracking north by northeast, riding against a crosswind. There was nowhere to land in the immediate vicinity, but just to the north, a skilled pilot would find options.

Another sound, so soft it was easy to miss, came from ground level. Somewhere in the woods to the southwest, a dog barked. Not so much a bark as a baying cry, the sound of a hound alerting a hunter.

If the children heard it, they gave no indication. All of their attention was on the plane.

"The crucible looms," Dax said again, and he could swear it was his father's voice right then and not his own. Deeper and darker and more confident. A ghost made whole.

He closed his eyes, stroked the gun with his thumb, and breathed deeply of smoke and fire.

42

The man called Bleak broke the silence.

"Is that smoke?"

Randall leaned forward, peering through the windshield. "Ed, buddy? You need to stay engaged in communication. Is...that... smoke?"

"Where?" the pilot said.

"Two o'clock. Upriver. Yes—it's smoke."

They all turned to look together. Well, everyone except Bleak. He didn't move at all. Matt had never seen his head move, and yet he was the one who'd spotted the smoke. The man named Randall was leaning across Matt's body now, smelling of stale sweat, which made Matt's stomach roil. The gun in Randall's hand was some kind of pistol with an oversize magazine. Weren't guns like that illegal? How many bullets did it hold?

Too many. That was for sure.

"Yeah, it's smoke," Randall said, and Matt looked numbly out the window in the direction Randall was staring. He didn't see anything. Just the woods and the river.

"That where they're waiting for you?" Bleak asked, and the pilot shook his head.

"No. That's northeast of the cabin."

"How far?"

"A mile, maybe. Not far."

"The cabin is at my ten o'clock?"

"Yes. Upper Martin. The smoke is coming from Lower Martin, or close to it."

"But they shouldn't be there."

"No."

Silence except for the whine of the propeller.

"Check the smoke out, Ed," Randall said. "Check it out, then circle back to the pond. Stay high enough that she won't see you on first pass. That she can't be sure it's you, at least."

The pilot banked to the right but didn't descend. Matt leaned closer to the window, curious despite himself, frustrated that he still hadn't seen what they all had. Everything was green or blue.

There it was. A white wisp that rose against the blue sky, thin but undeniable. He couldn't believe how easily the man named Bleak had picked it out.

"Campfire," the pilot said. His voice was hoarse. "Just a campfire."

"Early for lunch, late for breakfast," Bleak said.

"People camp on a river and they light fires. I don't care what time it is."

"Ed, I'd appreciate you watching your tone when you speak to my man Bleak," Randall said, and he tapped the pilot's skull with the gun.

The pilot didn't answer. He was a tall, strong-looking man wearing a frayed baseball cap pulled low, the curved bill shading his stubbled face. The muscles in his forearms stood out in cords as he gripped the steering wheel—not a wheel, it was a yoke, Matt remembered—and Matt thought that ordinarily this pilot named Ed was exactly the type of stranger he would want to come across when he was in trouble. He looked confident and capable, the kind of man who could fix a problem. Matt didn't think Ed could fix the problems in this plane, though.

He was pretty sure nobody could do that.

"If it's people camping," Bleak said, "we should be able to see a campsite. Tent, kayaks, whatever. Take us down, Ed."

The pilot angled the nose of the plane down. Matt got a clear glimpse of the river below. They were pointed at a bend in the river where the blue water turned white.

The pilot went lower still and then leveled out and they passed over the smoke.

"Nobody by the fire," Bleak said. "Burning on the gravel bank on the right, untended. It's a campfire. No equipment in sight."

Matt realized that Bleak was holding a small pair of black binoculars to his eyes. When had he gotten those? When had he even moved? It was as if they'd just appeared in front of his face, like a card trick.

Without the binoculars, Matt couldn't see anything of the fire except for the single plume of smoke, which rose almost like a signal, the kind people made when they intended to send a message. If Leah Trenton had brought the family here to hide, as Ed had told Bleak, then why would they light a fire?

Maybe it was a fake. Maybe it was—

"Two kids," Bleak said.

"Where?" Randall asked, craning his neck. Even Ed leaned forward a little, searching.

"Sandbar in the middle of the river, maybe fifteen yards off the bank. No kayaks."

"Canoe," Ed said softly.

"What's that?"

"They had a canoe."

"They don't now." Bleak was still looking through the binoculars, and Matt saw Ed's eyes flick over. The gun rested in Bleak's lap. If Ed reached for it now, he might get it, but then Randall would shoot him. Matt hoped Ed was smart enough to see that.

"Where is she?" Randall asked. *She* being Leah Trenton, Matt figured. *She* being the one they'd come to kill.

"Not present," Bleak answered, monotone.

"Something's fucked. They're alone on the river a mile from the pond and a fire is burning and there's no boat?"

"There's a boat," Bleak said, still unfazed. "But it's not the canoe. An inflatable with an outboard, good equipment. A Zodiac or close to it. Deployment craft." He lowered the binoculars, looked over at Ed, and said, "How'd they get that boat, Ed? Maybe you forgot a few things?"

"I don't know," Ed said. He sounded weary. "I really don't. Look closer; they had a canoe. It's a yellow Wenonah. Sixteen feet. You can't miss it, not on that river."

Bleak said, "I don't overlook yellow canoes, Ed. I assure you of that."

After a long silence, Ed said, "I lied. I'm sorry."

Matt tensed, expecting a punch at best, a gunshot at worst. They wouldn't tolerate a lie from him.

No one struck, though. Everything remained still in the cockpit.

They can't fly the plane, Matt remembered. *He's lucky he admitted to lying up here, because they can't hurt him too bad. But when we're back on the ground...I think they'll kill him then.*

"You're sorry," Randall said. "Well. In that case."

"You flew the boat up here?" Bleak asked.

Ed seemed to hesitate again, then shook his head. "It's stored in the cabin. With the motor. I brought the gas up, that's all."

"And you neglected to mention this until now."

"They were in the canoe when I left," he said. "I forgot."

"A minute ago you said you lied. Now you forgot?"

"I lied," Ed acknowledged softly. "I don't want you to hurt them."

"Your lies endanger everyone. We came only for her. We do not give a damn about those kids. If we did, they'd have been dead long ago. We don't give a damn about the kid in back or even your lying ass. *We came for her.* Now do the right thing, Eddie. Make the right choice for the most humans. Isn't that what you want to do?"

Ed was silent.

"I got no *need* to kill other folks, got no *desire* to kill other folks, but do you think I have a *qualm* about it?" Bleak said.

Ed didn't speak.

"Look at me," Bleak said.

Ed turned to face him.

"Do you think I have any qualms about leaving five bodies in that river?" Bleak asked.

"No." A whisper so faint it was barely audible.

"Correct. But there's a tactical advantage to leaving you alive. There will be less heat behind me if I limit it to her than if I kill a bunch of kids. Think I don't realize that?"

"Fuckin'-A, we realize that," Randall contributed from the back. Matt felt like he just didn't want to be forgotten.

"That's my tactical position," Bleak continued. "Get the woman, leave the kids alive. I don't mind leaving you alive with them, Ed. Not yet. But another lie?" He made a soft, sad sound with his mouth. "Another lie, and I'm gonna begin to feel like there're scores to settle between us. Copy that, Captain?"

"Yes," Ed whispered.

Bleak put the binoculars back to his eyes. Stared for a time in silence. Said, "What's *she* doing, Ed? She hiding?"

"No. I mean—I don't know. But she wouldn't have left them."

"How'd they get in the water?"

"Don't know."

Randall pushed forward, the gun between him and Matt now, its oily black body looking lethal as a snake. "Let me have a look."

Bleak passed the binoculars back. "Pan west from the smoke. The fire is on a gravel bank, but they're out on a sandbar or something in midriver. It's just the two of them."

"Got it. So where's Mom?" Randall said, eyes to the binoculars. "I don't like this. Feels off."

"I know it."

"She's not losing the kids. So—"

"I bet they ran away," Matt said. His words surprised even himself. He hadn't intended to speak; the idea had come to him with such clarity that he voiced it.

Randall lowered the binoculars and looked at Matt. Up close, you could see the spiderwebs of old scars on his cheek and forehead. His nose was crooked, too, like it had been broken once. Or many times. His mismatched eyes were the meanest things Matt had ever seen.

"What's that, boss? They ran away?"

Matt wished he hadn't said anything now, but he nodded. "Maybe. They knew—Hailey knew—that she was...that she wasn't right. Her aunt, I mean. That something was wrong with her. Hailey wanted to get away from her."

Ed said, "I think he's right," in a soft voice.

"Consensus from the hostages," Randall said. "Interesting. How could they have run away? Thought there was a big rescue plan. Thought Nina was on top of her game today."

Ed glanced back at Matt. Matt was grateful for the brief gaze, the glimmer of compassion.

"Because of what he just told you. He's right about that. I could feel it coming off the kids like heat waves last night. They were scared, and they didn't want any part of that cabin. This morning was different. Hailey especially. She was warmer, friendlier. Because...because she wanted to get on the water."

"To run away," Matt said, speaking despite himself.

"To run away," Ed echoed. "Yeah."

Bleak said, "What will Nina do?"

"I don't know."

"Guess."

Ed thought about it. "She can't outpace them on foot. So she'd wait for me to come back. She'd hate it, but that's what she'd do, because it's the smart thing. Once I'm back, finding them is easier. From the air, we could find them." He paused, then added, "We just did."

"Yes," Bleak said. "We just did, didn't we?"

Bleak reached back and said, "Give me those," to Randall. Randall passed the binoculars forward. Bleak lifted them, scanned the river, and said, "There's a little bit of white-water action just upriver from them. Enough to cause a kid trouble. Enough to dump the boat if they didn't know how to use it."

"Or scare them into going to shore."

"Right. But the fire..."

"Yep. You think those kids know how to start a fire?"

"Wondering." He looked away from the binoculars, faced the pilot, and said, "If you forgot to mention that there is another friend on the ground..."

"It was just the three of them," Ed said in a resigned whisper. "It was just them. And the dog. That's the truth."

"They're waving now," Bleak said. "They have their jackets off and they're waving them around at us. Little shits are signaling us for help."

Randall laughed. The sound made Matt squeeze his eyes shut. It was a terrible laugh, one that delighted in the prospect of pain.

"It sure is nice," he said, "that they recognize the plane."

"Isn't it?" Bleak said. "Stroke of luck for those kids. Cold, wet, alone, and then they look to the sky and what to their wondering eyes did appear but our boy Ed, come to end all their fear."

It was the most he'd ever said at one time, and he grew more terrifying with each word. Randall laughed again. Matt kept his eyes shut, even when Bleak whispered instructions to the pilot, and the plane began to descend.

43

Leah's mind was so lost to the run that she was late hearing the plane.

Her legs had taken on the liquid throb that preceded collapse and her breath was coming in red-lined rasps. She ran, she climbed, she stumbled, but not once did she fall, and then the sound of the white water grew clear and she knew she was closing in on the only place she was likely to find them. If Hailey had shot the gap here and kept going, they'd be well out of reach.

Then came the second sound.

At first it seemed to be coming from within her own gasps, a manifestation from the pounding of her heart in her ears. Too late, she recognized it for what it was, and her immediate thought wasn't *Rescue,* but *Threat.*

She stopped running, crouched beside a wind-downed tree, and watched the sky.

She wouldn't be visible even to an intentional searcher. Not here, where the pines crowded and jostled like passengers in an overstuffed subway, not when she was wearing a gray fleece that matched the tree trunks. Tessa's rust-colored coat might be more eye-catching, but the dog looked more like a fox than a domestic pet even up close, let alone from the air.

It's no one coming for you, Leah reasoned as her heart rate decreased and her lungs filled, *it's just someone headed north to fish.*

It was then, as she watched the sky and her overexerted body cooled, that she finally smelled the smoke.

Faint, but undeniable. The wind was blowing out of the west and yet the smoke didn't seem to be riding the wind. If the fire was downwind from her and she could still smell it, it could not be far off.

She was just beginning to consider the possibility that her children had stumbled on strangers along the river when the plane passed overhead and she saw its distinctive red belly.

Ed.

She started to rise and wave. Stopped only because she recognized the futility of that; even if he was looking for her, he wouldn't spot her here. She would have to get out to the river, into open terrain, and even then she'd likely have to signal him somehow.

As she stood, she finally thought to look at her watch: 10:18.

He was back early. Very early. And he was north of the pond.

He knows, she thought with a relief that ran through her like blood. *Somehow, he knows.*

But how?

The canoe. He saw it was gone. He wouldn't have missed that. He'd have passed over and flown in search of it and—

The plane's engine noise changed, and she saw it was descending, the angle steep. Just before the plane vanished from sight, she saw a flashing light on the wings. Navigation lights. She tried to remember if Ed had ever used navigation lights for a remote water landing on a clear day. Why would he?

She checked her watch again. Looked back up at the now empty sky.

It was too early for him to return. He had passed over the pond and carried on north, and his navigation lights were on against the crystal-blue day.

She'd been running at a forty-five-degree angle to the water, targeting a destination as close to the stretch of white water as possible. Now she broke hard right and moved at ninety degrees, pushing uphill through a tangle of underbrush so thick that Tessa vanished from sight. It was harder going but it would take her to the water, and she needed the vantage point.

The hill was steep, and the footing was atrocious. She fought through it, branches lashing her face, a line of blood along her upper lip, and then the hill crested and she could see the water, granite-colored as the clouds pushed in from the west and the pines threw shadows. There was no shoreline, just a ledge five feet above the surface, with trees crowding the banks. She slung herself down on her belly on the stone, brought the Winchester to her shoulder, and lowered her eye to the Leupold scope.

Water and woods, green-gold riffles ahead of the rapids, two massive boulders that tilted like old gravestones.

Nothing else. She was still too far away. The sound of the plane's engine came in a low thrum that told her it was down now, on the water, possibly taxiing, possibly idling. Either way, it was down, and she had no visibility.

She rose to her knees and looked at the woods and then at the river. To make any progress along the shoreline would involve more of the same scrambling she'd employed to get here. It would not be fast. Alternatively, there was the water, which would be cold but swift and open. She'd be exposed only as long as she remained in it. If she could catch one of the tilting tombstones of rock ahead, she would have a secure spot with a clear view of the rapids and the gravel bank beyond.

Tessa whined, as if sensing her plan. The dog that could run for hours did not like the water. She was a hound, not a retriever.

"Stay," Leah said. "Stay, baby. We're fine. Good job." Idle chatter, coming too fast, serving only to make the dog more nervous as Leah unfastened her backpack and dropped it, then strapped the Winchester across her back and cinched the strap tight enough to press her breasts hard against her chest. She picked up the backpack again and held it in front of her, a cushion for impact.

The rushing water that had at first looked so close seemed far off now.

"We're fine," she said again, and this time it wasn't for the dog. Tessa whined and nudged Leah's calf, and though it was a request for attention, Leah took it as the signal she needed.

She leaped from the bank and into the river.

The shock of cold water was almost soothing at first. She was on the surface and drifting with the backpack held out in front of her when the cold came, and she channeled the adrenaline to energy and began to kick. The current was strong enough that she didn't need to do full swimming strokes, just keep her head above the water and let physics do the rest. The weight of the backpack grew exponentially, and her shoulders throbbed from holding it up, but she knew what she was aiming for and she knew the landing would be rough.

Kick and cushion, that was all she had to do.

Her thighs felt strong and her calves useless, anchored by the soaked boots. The weight of the rifle across her back deepened the throb in her shoulders and muscle memory cried out for her hands to release the pack and join the rest of the body in swimming, but she willed it away and floated on, head tipped back, nose and mouth clear, sputtering but breathing.

The water swirled and caught and carried. The tilted tomb-stone rock loomed ahead, approaching faster now, gathering size. She knew that the water was teasing her, though; it wouldn't drive her into the rock but sweep her past it, and then she'd be in real trouble.

And now each kick was achieving less, and each ounce of water that saturated the pack dragged her shoulders lower. She was doing exactly what you should never do in a river: aiming with her head. She should be floating with her feet out and her head back so any collision with rock wasn't led by the skull. She couldn't afford to do that, though; on her back, she thought the current would sweep her past the rock before she could get a hand on it, and then she'd be shot through the churning stretch of white water and right out into the open above the pond, visible to anyone who waited.

A limb scraped her boot, and above her, keeping pace, Tessa barked and barked. If Leah could have drawn a deep enough breath to shout, she'd have told the dog to shut up, please, please, just shut up, but there wasn't enough air for shouting and there wasn't enough time to allow distraction. The water raced and the rock rose and she rode the current and saved her final kicks for the place where she would need them the most.

Just ahead of the rock, the water below her seemed to strengthen, as if outstretched hands had reached up to snag her, a hard pull down and to the right. She kicked then, kicked furiously, defying gravity, fighting up and left, up and left, up and—

Bam.

The impact was worse than she'd anticipated. She'd managed to get the pack up just high enough to cushion the blow, but still her face snapped forward and ripped across the wet nylon, shredding her cheek as she released the pack with her left hand and scrabbled for purchase on the rock, feeling her body turn and the current catch her again, the bloodied face and the screaming shoulder pain not enough, she was going to miss it anyhow, be swept right by.

A handhold, thick as a tennis ball, brushed hard and sharp against her palm.

She held tight. Pulled. Felt the current release her grudgingly, with a final, ferocious swirl around her aching ankles as she pulled free, as if reminding her that she'd won the battle but not the war.

She lay facedown on the stone with the sun on her back. Gasped in, rasped out. Felt the head-to-toe throb of that collision with the rock, her muscles and nerves all yelling out to one another that, yes, they'd gotten it over here too, like neighbors after a lightning strike.

She dumped the pack in a crevice high enough to keep it from being swept away, then pushed her hair back from her face. Her palm swirled with diluted blood. Her cheek had been torn open, and that was *with* the backpack absorbing most of the impact. If she'd hit it head-on…

But she hadn't.

She was right where she wanted to be.

Leah Trenton climbed up the rock and started to free the rifle strap so she could swing the gun around and use the scope. Then her head cleared the rock and she saw that she wouldn't need the scope. She was close enough that they were all in view.

Her children, on a sandbar in the middle of the river, standing with their backs to her and gazing downstream, where a red plane taxied toward them out of Lower Martin Pond. To the right of the kids, a campfire burned on a gravel bank. A gray Zodiac inflatable boat was pulled up on the bank. Who in the hell had been in the Zodiac? And *where* were they now?

She panned right. High, slanted rocks, much like the one she was on. Then trees. She panned farther, scanning the trees, looking for motion. Who'd been on the boat, and who had started the fire? She couldn't imagine campers out here, or at least any who would have walked far from the river. The terrain was too rugged and held no clear allure. Anyone who camped in this part of the Allagash would know better than to leave a fire burning untended.

And yet there was the boat, and there was the fire, and there were her kids—unharmed, standing on the sandbar, soaked but safe, waving at the plane.

She lifted the scope, focused on the plane, then adjusted the zoom with her left hand, bringing the cockpit into focus. The sun glare fell on the right side and the shadows claimed the left, but even so, she could see Ed behind the stick. He was alone. Or seemed to be. No one was sitting beside him. In the back, she couldn't tell. Was that a human crouched behind the seat or just a shadow? She inched higher, the rock like steel wool against her forearms, her cheek stinging and her back throbbing. The gun held level. She felt steady, her breathing controlled, her hands still. Ready to shoot.

She'd never taken a shot at an animal, let alone a man. She'd fired who knew how many thousands of rounds into targets in her early years in Maine, fired rifles and shotguns and handguns of every make and caliber. Convinced herself that she was a killing machine, cool under fire. She would be ready to shoot.

But she did not need to shoot Ed. Had he really come alone?

Too early. You asked him for time. He would have given you time.

Unless the plane's arrival wasn't a threat but an emergency. Maybe he had learned something alarming. Maybe he'd been afraid that the dock was compromised, that his identity had been determined, something. He would've come back fast then.

Flashing the navigation lights. A distress signal. A warning. She couldn't believe it was anything else. She'd flown with him count-less times, and he'd never taken that approach. It was a simple but clear visual cue to anyone on the ground.

That didn't mean the plane was compromised, though. She might have seen the signal but misinterpreted it. Maybe, upon returning to the cabin at the pond, he'd seen that the canoe was missing and had done the smart thing and gone searching for it from the air without pause. He'd been in pursuit of the canoe—in pursuit of them all—when he spotted the kids. He'd put the plane down and come to help.

It all made sense now, it was all vintage Ed Levenseller, observant and proactive, and she felt ridiculous for not realizing it sooner, for risking her foolish float down to the rocks to lie here, rifle in hand. She should stand up and shout to them. Let everyone know that she was here, that she'd come to help, she'd come to help them and tell them the truth.

She didn't, though. She held still and stayed low and kept her eye to the scope and her finger floating near the trigger.

He brought the plane up almost to the sandbar against a cross-wind that turned it slightly, presenting her with a better view of the passenger seat. Empty. Ed's hands were free on the stick, and she could see him adjusting the rudder controls, moving unencumbered, showing no trace of tension. The plane floated about twenty-five feet from the sandbar when he killed the engine.

She frowned. Why hadn't he banked it on the gravel bar?

The kids are alone, the boat is not mine, and the campfire is not mine. He doesn't know what he's getting into.

He opened the door and climbed out. She tracked him, focused but still aware of a distant sickness at having him in the rifle's crosshairs. He stepped down onto the float as the plane drifted, a short but deep stretch of water between him and the kids. She heard him shout, and though his voice was probably full-throated, up here by the rushing water it was almost unintelligible. Had he said *I come in peace?* He was making jokes? Nervous, probably. As unsure of what that Zodiac and that campfire meant as she was.

"I come in peace," he repeated, and this time she heard it clearer, and she saw him raising his hand and making a peace sign. Trying to relax the kids and knowing something was wrong, but not understanding it yet.

The kids stayed on the sandbar.

"Where is your aunt?" Ed shouted. The question was returned to him by the rocks.

If either child responded, Leah couldn't hear it. Their backs were to her and their voices softer than his loud, awkward attempt at humor. One of them must have said something, though, because Ed nodded and stepped farther out onto the float.

"Let's get you home, guys. Get you safe." This was shouted too. Why was he screaming at them from such a short distance? And he still had his hand raised in the peace sign. He kept it up while he turned to look at the gravel bank where the campfire burned.

Scared. Yes, he is scared that something has already happened.

Then he said, "She let you take that boat? Alone?"

Let them take that boat? What was he talking about? He knew it wasn't her boat. He knew that they'd been in the canoe. So what was he—

Signaling. Not a peace sign or a dumb joke. He's holding up two fingers to tell me how many are in the plane. She swung the scope away from Ed, up and over, and refocused on the interior of the plane.

Empty. Maybe she was wrong. Maybe the kids were talking to him in voices she couldn't hear and were lying to him about the boat. It was possible, because they had run away and wouldn't want to admit it, so maybe—

Something moved inside the plane. A quick glimmer, there and gone, but motion. She was sure of it, and sure of more than that.

They'd come with him. Bleak and Pollard. They'd forced him to fly to her. She was absolutely certain, felt it in her blood, felt it in the pulse of the finger she curled around the trigger.

Ed was still talking loudly, still asking about the boat, and now it was even more clear that he was lying with intent, because he was asking if the motor had worked all right, if it had been shaken up on the plane. He was trying to buy time and shout some truth into the woods, hopeful that Leah might be there, listening. Ready to shoot.

And she was.

She reached up with her left hand and twisted the focus knob, bringing the cockpit into the crosshairs, Ed and the floats entirely hidden from view, nothing left but that empty pilot seat and copilot seat and—

A face. A flash of white flesh as the man hidden in the back seat lifted his head.

As Leah pulled the trigger, she saw it wasn't a man.

It was a child.

44

The first round came from an unanticipated source, some-where upriver, and if Dax were the type of man to jump at an explosive sound, he'd have cleared the eight-foot boulder that hid him in the shadows. He was not the jumping type, though, and so he simply leaned back and put his eye to the V-shaped crack in the rock that afforded him a view upriver.

It wasn't a wide angle, and he couldn't see much beyond the white water and the rocks. He leaned forward again, looked at the plane.

The bullet had punched through the fuselage on its left side, ripping a nasty furrow through it, bits of fiberglass and metal scattered to the river like a handful of gold dust.

A warning shot or a terrible shot. One or the other. Nobody with a gun that big—the sound still seemed to echo in the stillness of the woods—was incapable of hitting Ed or the cockpit unless the shooter was beyond incompetent.

Not an ineffective shot, though. It had put things in motion. The kids were screaming and crouching on the sandbar, holding on to each other, and Ed Levenseller had been so scared by the sound that he'd jumped—or fallen?—right off the pontoon and into the river. He sank out of sight, then surfaced, and when he surfaced, he was screaming.

"Run!" he shouted at the kids. "Hailey, Nick, run!"

He was swimming toward them while he shouted, and he never so much as looked back at the plane.

That was a mistake. His back was turned when a man leaned out of the plane with a semiautomatic pistol in hand and fired three shots.

Ed screamed again, but this time it was out of pain and not fear, and then he disappeared below the surface. Still swimming, though. Still fighting against the current toward the kids. There was a slick of blood in the water, so he was wounded, but not yet dead.

Wrong gun, Dax thought, and he felt mild disappointment, because he'd been promised these two were very good. If the shooter had used an AR-15 he'd have been able to make quick work of Ed. Plugging away with a handgun was less efficient.

Dax looked from the water to the plane and saw that the shooter was leaning back into the plane and someone inside was handing him something. A smooth exchange, fluid, and then the shooter was back outside of the plane with an AR-15 and an extended clip.

Excellent. They'd come to party after all.

The shooter—he was white, so that meant he wasn't Marvin "Bleak" Sanders, but the other one, Randall Pollard—swung nimbly down from the cockpit to the float, keeping low and close to the side of the plane. He understood where the gunfire had originated, and he knew that the gunfire was a bigger problem than Ed Levenseller swimming wounded or the two kids screaming on the sandbar. He did not glance at the C-shaped curl of rocks where Dax was positioned, completely sheltered from any threat that didn't come from behind him. Dax didn't anticipate any threats arriving from those deep woods.

Then again, Dax hadn't anticipated the first shot.

He checked his back, watched the pines wave in the breeze, studied the dark wood. There was no sound that did not belong, no motion save the weaving trees.

He turned back to the cut in the rock that afforded his upriver view. He still couldn't see anything. He squinted, waited…yes, there was a glimmer of metal at the top of one of the huge, slanted boulders where the rapids frothed. An excellent shooting location. Too good of a vantage point for an amateur, which meant that the shot must have been a warning, not a miss. What was the point of the warning shot? Leah, he assumed, would have known better than to open the gunplay with a shot that didn't count.

Randall Pollard crouched on the float, the AR at his shoulder, and scanned the river, searching. He would find her in time, but he wasn't going to hurt her, not with that much rock between her and the bullets. He might fire just to fluster her. Dax would.

Ed Levenseller had surfaced again and was gasping out his cries of *Run,* and Dax watched Randall Pollard note him and ignore him.

Again, excellent. The pilot had more value alive than dead. It had been wise to prevent him from reaching the children, but there was no need to kill him. Also, Pollard would need to expose himself for a clean shot at the pilot, and maybe Leah Trenton wouldn't miss twice.

There was no sign of the much-ballyhooed Bleak, which was disappointing. Had he sent Pollard on a solo mission? Or was he simply biding his time, like Dax?

On the sandbar, Hailey Chatfield rose, shielding her brother with her own body, and turned to face the rocks that hid Dax.

"Shoot them!" she screamed. "Help us! *Help us!"*

Dax sighed. He hadn't expected the children to obey their instructions in a moment of chaos, but nevertheless, he'd enjoyed his invisibility.

Randall Pollard turned in the direction of Hailey's shouts, and Dax could see that he was pondering the development. And, no doubt, thinking that he was in a hell of a lot of trouble now, because he was exposed to Dax's position but moving away from it would put him in Leah's line. Oops!

"Open fire," Dax muttered, resigned, as he ducked deeper into the protective granite and Randall Pollard opened up on him with the AR-15.

The sound was nowhere near as impressive as the single, massive blast of Leah's shot into the plane, but the result was annoying—rock chips sprayed into the air and fragments blew into treacherous needles, and Dax closed his eyes and pressed tight to the rock, held it like a lover until the shooting stopped.

Out of ammunition? Probably not. If he's any good, he'd have saved a round or two. He wants to see who's going to poke their heads out.

It would be a dumb way to die, leaning out from behind a rock to take a .227-caliber bullet to the forehead.

It wasn't even a paying job.

Fun, though. Isn't it just a little bit of fun?

It was. It was more than fun, it was *living,* real living in a way so few humans would ever know.

Dax dropped to his knees and grabbed Andy West's twelve-gauge. Lying on his side, he wriggled forward, inch by inch. The silence was broken by a hoarse shout, probably from Levenseller. A cry that was nearly feral, a shout of...no, no. Wait. It wasn't a shout at all.

It was a bark.

Hmm.

Dax stood up behind the rocks and put his eye to the crack that let him look upriver. Leah Trenton's dog was running down the bank, barking and baying.

"A circus," Dax whispered. "That's what this is turning into, my friends. An absolute circus."

He ducked again and slid along the rock, the granite rough on his shoulder, then let the barrel of the shotgun slide out, testing to see if he'd draw any fire. He thought his angle would make him invisible to anyone on the plane, but it was better to be sure of that than to be dead.

No shots came. The baying turned to furious barking, and Nick shouted: *"Tessa!"*

Dax slid out from behind the rock just far enough so that he could see the plane again. Pollard had turned his attention upriver, leaving his back to Dax. Dax could kill him if he wanted to, but what was the point of that? Everything was fine here for now, and it was interesting to watch them all sort it out. You never knew who had a trick you hadn't seen before.

He squirmed out farther, and now the sandbar was in view. The kids were sticking to it, neither of them seeking refuge in the water. Levenseller was between the sandbar and the far shore. He was probably trying to get on the other side of the plane, which would both protect him from Pollard's current angle of fire and maybe draw that fire away from the children.

Positively heroic.

Randall Pollard was down on one knee now, inching up the float and sighting from beneath the plane. A terrific, protected position. From there he could kill Ed if needed and probably get some decent cover fire down on Leah's position, maybe flush her out.

There was a splash, and Dax looked upriver to see that Tessa had leaped from the bank into the water and was now swimming to Ed Levenseller. The dog was not a good swimmer—every awkward, lunging stroke of the paws announced that she was built for land, not water—but her powerful hind legs were enough to keep her snout high, and her fierce determination was enough to drive her toward her friend in need.

Randall Pollard dipped lower, shifted his angle, and swung the AR-15 toward the dog.

It was a wise choice. The dog could not fly the plane, but the dog could cause some trouble. The dog was all risk and no reward. Kill the dog, then.

Absolutely the right choice, and yet … not one that Dax cared for.

He sighed, lifted the Remington—he was still on his back, which meant shooting upside down—and fired a single blast into the water between himself and the plane. The shell blew out of the muzzle with a pleasantly thunderous noise, water sprayed in all directions, and Randall Pollard whirled to face the threat.

And slipped. It wasn't bad—not a full fall into the water, like Levenseller's, but enough that he fell forward and had to catch himself by grabbing one of the struts that held the pontoon float to the plane's body.

Ka-WHANG.

Another round from Leah Trenton, and this one was placed much better; in a blink, the float was empty, and Randall Pollard was in the water.

Hell of a shot.

Dax slid out farther, admiring the moment. Pollard had made the slightest of mistakes, and Leah had made the finest of shots. Her success made the one she'd missed all the more baffling, but nevertheless, she'd recovered well. Pollard floundered and fought his way behind the pontoon, a sheen of blood rising around him like a gas-line leak from a boat. He was hurting, and he was very likely going to bleed out and die, but he'd kept his cool as well as anyone could, remembering to maneuver to a protected position.

It was a pleasure to watch.

Dax looked at the plane, waiting for Bleak. No one moved. The plane rocked in the water, thrown by Pollard's fall and buffeted by the light winds. It was drifting farther from the sandbar, the kids, Levenseller, and the dog. It was beginning to look empty and innocent.

Dax didn't trust it for a minute.

The plane was turning in the wind, though, and he watched as Pollard assessed this and realized what it meant—he was about to be exposed again, with no ability to return fire. If he was smart and physically strong enough after taking that shot, he'd at least try to swim for the shelter of the nearest rocks.

The rocks that currently hid Dax Blackwell.

45

She'd made the second shot count.

Leah slid down the rock, ejected a spent casing, and chambered a fresh round. Her hands were steady but her heartbeat was a rock drummer's dream, had been ever since she'd seen the child's face as her finger closed on the trigger. She'd jerked the rifle as she fired, and it had been enough—by a fraction of a second of fool's luck, it had been enough.

The child was alive and Randall Pollard, may he drown slowly on his way to hell, was shot and in the water. Dying.

Her first kill. She thought she should feel something for that, but she did not. Only relief that one was down, and fear for where the other might be. She could hear the sounds of her children's sobs and her dog's bark and her lover's desperate splashes. A symphony of sorrow, her world fracturing in harmony.

Cool your mind, trust your hands. One down. You put one of them down and there will be one more to come.

Just one? Someone else had fired. An awful shot, one that missed even the plane and kicked up nothing but water, but still, there was a second shooter in play, and she knew that it wasn't Bleak. Bleak wouldn't have taken a shot at Randall Pollard. If he had, he certainly would not have missed.

So who?

Impossible to know. What she did know: One threat was down, and one remained, and then there was an unknown armed presence. She hadn't seen Bleak but she believed he had to be in the plane. With the child.

Who is that kid? He looked familiar. Looked like someone...

Bouchard. The neighbor. The recognition made her squeeze her eyes shut and grip the gun tighter. How had they gotten him? And why?

None of it mattered. What mattered was that he was here now and had to be kept alive.

She flexed her toes and pistoned her body up the rock, wet and cold and bleeding. The wind had shifted and she could smell the smoke from the dying campfire as its burned-out ashes were given fresh, false life from the breath of air. She put her eye to the scope. Pushed an inch higher. Watched the river take shape before her once more.

Ed had reached the shore. He was hanging on to a broken tree limb. She could see blood trailing from his legs. He'd taken one bullet, maybe more. How badly he was wounded, she couldn't say. The strength he'd shown just to make it this far suggested no major artery had been damaged. But how much longer could he go without medical attention?

Tessa was with him, licking his face. Attention, though not medical. Leah pivoted left to right, found the sandbar, and watched her children. They were staying low—smart, even if largely useless, considering how exposed they were—and Hailey was sheltering Nick from the plane's line of fire with her body. Leah felt an anguished, awful pride, seeing that.

Good job, baby. I'll do the rest.

She moved the scope again. Found the rocks from which the surprise shot had come. Studied them and saw nothing, but she understood why—it was a perfect sniper's nest, better even than her own, completely concealed. You weren't going to force anyone out of that spot with distant gunfire. You'd have to come get him.

She moved the scope back to the plane. Surveyed the cockpit, taking care to leave her finger off the trigger this time. She had never understood the term *friendly fire* in a real way until she'd seen that boy's face in her crosshairs.

What in the hell was Bleak intending to do?

Nothing that required him hurrying, she realized. He was performing exactly as his legend promised—unfazed by a firefight gone bad.

The plane was unmoored, drifting farther away, turning in the wind, and she saw that it would soon end up on the shore. Ed's side of the shore.

Inside, no sign of motion.

She pivoted right once more, scanning the water, looking for Randall Pollard's body. She passed over him the first time, and when she swung the scope back and found him, she saw a bright orange rope flicker through the air and hit the water near him. He grabbed it and was pulled toward the rocks in a swift tug, pulled just out of her firing line. She scrambled higher, found him, and fired, just barely overshooting the top of his head as he rode the rope out of sight behind the boulders.

The water frothed red where he had been.

He was still alive, but not for long. The same as Ed, who might not have long either. But someone was there to provide Randall with aid now, and Ed had no one. Time was running out for the parties on both shores, and out in the center of the river, a line of stillness had been created, three points on a shared thread: Leah, her children, and the plane.

Nothing moved inside the plane.

He will wait, she realized with sick sadness. *Bleak will not care who dies and who lives out here. He will wait.*

A shadow passed overhead, and Leah jerked, rolled onto her shoulder, and pointed the Winchester skyward.

A bald eagle, its massive wingspan stretched full, glided by, its raptor eyes seeing all below. The gunfire might have scared it into the air, but the gunfire was gone now, and there was blood in the water. A potential meal. Leah craned her neck and watched it soar, seeking a safer altitude from which to survey the excitement below.

"Tell me what he's doing in that plane," she whispered, but the eagle was gone from sight then, and even its shadow went with it.

46

Randall Pollard was a badly wounded man. As Dax tugged him ashore with the orange paracord he'd found in Andy West's gear, he saw that Leah Trenton's shot had entered Pollard's right leg just above the knee, exited out the other side, and gashed across the top of his left thigh. There was not much left of the femur above the knee.

He was impressed that Pollard had been able to make it this far with that kind of injury.

"Hey, buddy," Dax said, easing the man up onto drier ground as the echo from Leah Trenton's latest miss faded away and silence returned. "How you doing?"

Randall Pollard's mouth opened and closed and no sound came. A fish on dry land. Dax nodded sympathetically.

"It's bad," he said. "But I've got a med kit." He pointed into the pilot's bag, where the first-aid box rested.

Pollard's eyes tacked over to the kit, then back to Dax. "Who?" he said. It took him a great deal of effort, so Dax put a finger to the man's damp lips to keep him from trying to speak again. He didn't need to try; Dax understood the question.

"Take it easy. Don't say more than is needed. I work with the kids out there."

Randall Pollard had eyes of two different colors. Fascinating. Dax leaned close, studied them. Tears ran with the river water along Randall Pollard's cheekbones. Dax wiped them away.

"I worked for Leah—or Nina—the woman with the hunting rifle? But then the girl hired me. So I work for Hailey now."

Pollard stared at him. His clearing mind was not prepared to handle this.

"It's a lot to take in," Dax said. "But the point is, we could be on the same team now. You came for the woman, right? Only for her. Nina. Leah. Whatever you'd like to call her."

Pollard managed a slight nod. The idea of teamwork seemed to inspire him. Excellent. Nobody got out of this world alone.

"Stop the bleeding," Pollard hissed.

"Right," Dax said. "The bleeding is the problem. But what's your partner going to do?"

Pollard's mismatched eyes flicked left and right, tracking Dax, trying to make sense of him. Struggling.

"Is he as good as they say?" Dax asked.

Another nod. "Yeah," Pollard rasped.

"Will he die for you?" Dax asked.

Pollard looked at Dax and then down at his leg. The blood was running hot and bright. Dax had made no move for the medical kit.

"He knows where you are, and that you're hurt," Dax said. "He doesn't know anything about me other than where I am and that I can shoot. So what do you think, will he risk his own life to save yours?"

Randall Pollard was still staring at the roadkill that had once been his right leg. He wet his lips. Spoke slowly. "Doubtful," he said.

Dax nodded. "I appreciate that. It's a hard truth."

"You gotta let him know," Pollard whispered.

"Know what?"

"That you're…you're…"

"Yes?" Dax said, ever patient. It wasn't *his* leg that was pouring blood onto the rocks, after all.

"You're help."

"Oh. Huh." Dax winced, lowered himself into a catcher's squat, and clasped his hands in front of him, the gun pointed down. "Well, this is awkward."

Randall Pollard looked up at him and smiled then. It was tortured and terrible, a death mask, an expression Dax had never seen before in his life and yet one that he understood: Pollard wasn't sure what, exactly, Dax represented out here, but he knew he was not a friend.

"You're missing the point," Pollard wheezed.

"How's that?"

Pollard kept the smile. There was blood in the corner of his mouth now. He seemed more clearheaded than before, as if the pain was receding.

"He won't have to die," he said. "She's not beating him. Neither are you."

"That's real respect for his skills," Dax said. "Nothing false about it. And yet..." He shrugged. "I beg to differ. We're about to settle the matter, one way or the other. A shame you won't be here to see how it plays out."

Pollard's pain-ravaged face changed only slightly when Dax shot him in the eye. The brown one, not the green one. Dax preferred the green eye. It was a pretty shade, one that conjured cool valleys in high mountains.

"Hailey!" Dax shouted. "Hailey, do you hear me?"

No answer.

"Gotta communicate," Dax shouted. "Gotta be a team player."

"*I hear you.*" Her voice trembling and tearful.

"We have a teaching moment," Dax cried as he grabbed Randall Pollard's boots with both hands and shoved the dead man into the water. "In which direction is this bad man floating?"

The river took Randall and swept him away from the rocks, and almost instantly Leah Trenton's big rifle boomed again and a bullet blasted the corpse, a perfect shot, center mass. It drove Randall down into the river and red water rose above him.

"Tell your mom to save her ammo!" Dax shouted. "And answer the question. Which way is that dead man floating?"

Hailey's voice, high but clear: "North! He's floating north! Stop shooting! Everyone, stop shooting!"

The final cry was an anguished sob. Dax sighed and shook his head. He liked the girl, she had unique spirit, but she had so much to learn.

The shooting didn't stop because you asked it to.

He had a feeling that the man called Bleak, who still hadn't so much as fired a round, understood that very well.

47

"Tell your mom to save her ammo!"

Leah lay against the rock, rifle in hand, eye to scope, watching the scarlet streaks on the surface that represented where one of the three men she'd feared most in the world had gone to die with her bullet in his belly, and the question echoed around her, rattled in her mind, the words seemingly impossible, and yet she'd heard them clearly. She knew that.

Tell your mom.

Your mom.

Hailey hadn't contradicted him. Hailey had answered him, whoever he was. She'd answered him in terror but not confusion, even his question about which direction the body was floating. He—and she—both understood the mistake Hailey had made when she'd paddled out of the pond that morning.

They had spoken, Leah realized. Her kids had been caught by someone who knew who they were, and who she was.

Who was *he?*

Someone whose behavior made absolutely no sense. He'd rescued Randall Pollard only to kill him. He'd put the children in harm's way out there and hid himself, then fired a shot that revealed his hiding spot in order to save a dog.

Who in the hell was he?

She was wondering whether she should call out to him, scream a question, because Ed was bleeding on the bank, hurt bad, and her children were trapped in the middle of the river, and if Leah had an ally behind those rocks, she damn well needed to know—

but then the first motion in many minutes came from inside the plane.

It was the child. While she watched, Matt Bouchard crawled tentatively and awkwardly out of the open pilot's door and down onto the float.

He's letting him go? She couldn't believe that. Unless Bleak had been more shaken by Pollard's death than she'd imagined and was willing to negotiate whatever it took to simply get out of this place alive.

Matt Bouchard inched farther out onto the float, and Leah understood then why he was moving so awkwardly.

His hands were bound with a plastic zip tie, and there was a thin rope looped around his throat, the free end trailing back into the plane, back into the hands of a man who could send the boy into the river with a single jerk. A boy who couldn't even fight to free himself or stay above water with his hands bound.

Bleak was in action.

48

M att wasn't sure how long he'd been curled up on the floor of the plane, listening to—and sometimes feeling—gunshots echo around him. Time was a foreign concept now. All he knew was the sound of the shots, the smell of fuel that permeated the cockpit after one of the shots ripped through the body of the plane, and the feel of the fierce, strong grip that the man called Bleak applied to force Matt down as the gunfire intensified. Then, so fast that it took Matt a moment to recognize what had happened, the feel of the rope dropped over his head and yanked tight through a slipknot.

"Now," Bleak whispered, "you're gonna go save some lives, kid. Or lose them all. Up for that?"

Matt didn't answer. He was fighting for tears. He *wanted* to sob, wanted to cry in a way he hadn't in years, a gasping collapse of little-boy wailing, but he couldn't draw them up. Maybe there came a time when you knew that there was no point. That even the small thing inside yourself that could be comforted from crying was no longer able to hear you.

"Boy?" Bleak said, and he tugged at the rope. Thin, abrasive fibers nipped at Matt's neck.

"Yes," Matt whispered. "I'm ready."

"Walk out that door. Feet cut loose, but hands stay tight. So don't fall in the water, right? Gonna sink fast if you do."

Matt nodded.

"Climb down carefully. Don't stumble. Walk out on that float and then start talking. Loud."

"What do I say?" Matt whispered. The smell of the fuel was heavier now, and he thought that he could hear dripping somewhere. A bullet had hit the gas line. Would the next one blow the plane up?

"You say that if she comes down, everyone else stays alive."

The tears he'd been hunting for began to rise, finally. He said, "She won't believe you. No one will. Because you're lying."

Another tug on the rope. The slipknot tightened on his throat.

"I do not lie," Bleak whispered, and Matt could smell his scent intermingled with the leaking fuel. He smelled cool and clean, somehow. Smelled, Matt realized, like deodorant. The knowledge conjured a wild, irrational fear: *He is not sweating! He is literally not even sweating!*

"I want her," Bleak said. "Your job, if you want to stay alive and want those two kids to stay alive, is to be convincing."

A powerful hand pushed on Matt's spine. The hand seemed as broad as Matt's entire back.

"Get out there."

Matt forced himself upright on quivering legs. He stumbled moving from the back of the plane to the front, where the cool breeze funneled in through the open door, and he smelled smoke with an undertone of copper on the breeze.

Blood.

Blood and smoke.

Death waited outside, he was sure. But death waited behind him too. He'd rather be outside. The river wasn't as terrible as the plane.

He made it from the cockpit down to the struts that led to the pontoon float, climbing carefully, while Bleak paid out rope like he was walking a dog on a retractable leash. If he cared about the gunfire, he didn't show it.

"Kid?" he said.

Matt stopped, his head just above the bottom of the doorframe. Looked back up at him.

"Tell the spook in the rocks to come out, too. He might not want to listen, but you're going to need to tell him."

Matt didn't know how to respond to that. Didn't even know what it meant. He nodded, though.

Bleak paid out a little more rope, hand over hand, giving Matt enough slack to climb down.

Down he went. It wasn't far, but the sight of the water frightened him, and his legs were shaking so badly each step felt like one more than he'd been capable of.

He made it, though. Held on to the strut, the metal cold in his palms, then got himself turned around to look up the river. That was where he'd seen Hailey and Nick in the instant before the first bullet hit the plane.

They were still there. Or Hailey was, at least. For a moment, Matt thought that Nick was gone. Then he realized how carefully Hailey was standing in front of him, screening every inch of her little brother's body with her own, facing down the monsters so he didn't have to. It made Matt think of the chalk drawings on the wall in her basement.

She's braver than me, he thought, and right then Bleak said, "Kid, talk."

Matt shouted through dry lips. "Hailey, all he wants is your aunt! He says he won't…he won't…"

He couldn't keep going. Not looking at her and seeing the way she stood like a human shield in front of her brother. She was going to make Bleak go through her to get to Nick. That's how Matt should feel—one last stand was better than none. He knew that Bleak would kill him no matter what he'd promised. If Matt was going to die, why lie?

"He's going to hurt everyone!" he shouted. *"He's going to kill every—"*

The jerk on the rope would have sent him into the river if he hadn't been holding so tightly to the metal strut. Instead it just drew the rope tighter around his neck.

Bleak said, "Just say her name. You tell Nina that Bleak is here. You say that, and you live."

The river ran beneath Matt and made him dizzy. If he lost his grip on the strut, he would fall fast, and drown. He wasn't sure how much longer he could hold on to the strut. His knees were flexing, calf muscles loosening. The motion of the water was the worst; it made him so dizzy. He looked up, searched for Bleak but couldn't find him.

"I hate you," Matt told the darkness inside the plane.

"I know," the darkness answered. "Now say her name."

Matt turned away from the darkness, taking care to keep his head high so the water below didn't disorient him. He balanced on the gently rocking float and faced forward, toward Hailey and into the wind. He could still smell the smoke but down here, closer to the water, the blood was gone. Rinsed clean.

He took a deep breath, and then he screamed.

"NINA! BLEAK IS HERE!"

The force of the scream actually bent him forward, and the plane rocked again, and for an instant he thought he was going over. Then he straightened and clutched the strut with all the strength he had, and balance was restored.

"That was good, kid," the darkness told him with a soft chuckle.

Matt didn't answer. He was waiting for the gunshots to begin.

"Let me go get the kids!" The shout came from Matt's left, and again he nearly lost his balance as he twisted to look. No one was in sight.

"Who is that?" Matt said, but of course Bleak didn't answer. All Matt knew was that it wasn't Randall. This voice was new.

"I'll get in that boat and get the kids out of here," the voice from the rocks shouted. "And the dog." A pause, and then, as if it were an afterthought, "The pilot I don't care about. Settle that however you like. Let me get the kids and the dog out of here and then you can finish your job."

Suddenly a shout came from upriver, a woman's voice, but not Hailey's. *"Who are you?"*

It was Leah Trenton, Matt realized. He couldn't see her, couldn't see anything but dark trees and large rocks and a funnel of swift water topped with white foam that looked like the lace tablecloth his mother put out at Thanksgiving. For a moment, everything was quiet, and then the man in the rocks answered her.

"I'm Doc Lambkin's phone call!"

Wind and water. No voices. Soft whines from the dog on the bank, soft cries from Nick out on the sandbar, tucked behind his sister. Nothing at all from the darkness inside the plane.

Then, sudden as a rifle shot: *"Let him take my kids, Bleak! Let him take them, and I'll come down!"*

Bleak didn't answer right away. Matt wasn't surprised by this. He'd been the man's hostage for long enough to understand that the man thought things over when he could—and even when it seemed he couldn't.

The man in the rocks spoke softer, as if hoping not to be heard by Leah. "There's another plane, Bleak," he said. "North of Roman Island. The pilot is in the cargo hold. You want to fly out, you can fly out with him. Let me take the kids, and then I'll bring her to you."

"Sounds too good to be true, brother."

"I'll do it. She'll do it, too. She knows those kids are going to die otherwise." His voice rose, as if he wanted to be heard by all parties again. "I'm not going up there if she's still shooting, so regardless of your opinion, I need to see her rifle come over the rocks."

The low chuckle came again from Bleak. "Who *are* you, man?" It was the most emotion Matt had ever heard from him, a blend of authentic amusement and curiosity.

No answer from the rocks.

"All right!" Leah Trenton shouted. *"I will give up the gun. Just let him move them out of sight! You want me! You know that. You've always wanted me!"*

The plane creaked and the river whispered. Bleak thought about it. Then he spoke to Matt in a soft voice. "You tell her it's a deal, kid. And then you tell her that you'll be the first to die if she's lying."

Matt shouted what he'd been told. His mind barely registered the words. He shouted that he would die if she lied. The rope rasped over his throat with each word.

"Rifle coming over!" Leah Trenton screamed.

Behind Matt, a rustle of motion rocked the plane as Bleak moved inside, probably getting in a position to watch.

A rifle arced into the air above one of the largest boulders. It rose high, ten feet at least, and then came down in a sparkling tumble, smacked off the boulder, and went into the water.

Almost as if on cue, a man appeared on the far side of the boulders, walking upriver, backpedaling, a shotgun in his hands pointed at the plane.

He didn't shoot.

Bleak didn't either.

The man reached the gray boat on the gravel bank. He put the gun into the boat and then pushed the boat off the shore and into the water and started the outboard motor. He was exposed now but Bleak wouldn't have a shot unless he ventured out onto the floats like Randall had, and Randall was dead. Bleak would have to wait to see what happened or he'd have to come out and fight fair, in the open.

Matt thought that the man in the rocks had understood that the whole time.

49

Leah slid across the rock face like a free-climber, using hand- and toeholds to stay pressed tight against it while she went left to right to the point where she had a view of the Zodiac as the outboard fired up. A slender man of average height was at the tiller.

I'm Doc Lambkin's phone call. Leah's Hail Mary to an old friend on an island three thousand miles away had somehow produced help.

She watched as he banked the Zodiac on the sandbar. He got low then, looked back at the plane, and spoke to the kids quietly out of the side of his mouth. Hailey shifted away from her sheltering position in front of Nick, but she refused to release his hand. They climbed into the boat quickly, flattened themselves against the bottom.

Leah felt a pressure in her chest, watching. The stranger was giving all the right instructions. He'd negotiated well with Bleak, he had promised the right things, and he was playing the firing angles perfectly, understanding exactly where he was vulnerable and where he was not. He would get the children to safety, and then...

Then they would figure out the rest.

Ed was on the far bank, and she still had no idea how badly he was wounded, but he'd made it into deeper cover, crawling back into the pines. Tessa had followed him. Leah could hear the occasional mournful whine from within the brush. Everyone was moving to safety now.

Everyone except Matt Bouchard, another child, another innocent.

As the Zodiac motored upriver, she free-climbed back across the rock face. Reached her pack, unzipped it, and withdrew the snub-nosed Smith & Wesson .38 revolver that was inside. Her backup. Six opportunities to hit from close range. The short-barreled gun wasn't meant for distance, but she was good with it, and in the pocket of her fleece, it would be barely visible. If she got a chance, she could bring Bleak down.

She would bring him down.

She pocketed the Smith & Wesson and dropped down to the far side of the rock, where she could watch the Zodiac approach. Her rescuer guided it through the white water skillfully.

Matt Bouchard was the real problem, and thus Bleak's source of confidence. They couldn't leave him. Other than the hostage, Bleak held no advantage. That was good news for the hostage, but Leah wasn't sure how to save him. She hoped Doc Lambkin's recruit had some ideas.

The Zodiac splashed through a rapid, the stern kicked high, and the prop whined as it caught nothing but air. The man in the black cap guided the Zodiac up through the churning water expertly, reading the current with the eye of someone who knew rivers, and finally brought it in behind the rock where Leah waited. He already had a line in hand. Tossed it to her. A perfect toss, one she caught easily, and then he cut the motor and let her pull them in close before tying them off by looping the line around an outcropping of granite and securing it with a quick hitch.

Leah scooted down the rock and held out her hands to her son.

"I'm so sorry," she said. "I'm so sorry."

Nick was crying. "We shouldn't have left. We ran away and we shouldn't have."

He took her hand and she guided him out of the boat and onto one of the low shelves of rock and held his trembling body against hers, made soothing sounds. How much had he weighed the last time she'd held him like this? Twenty-five pounds? She closed her eyes, breathed in his scent, then opened them and looked at Hailey. Hailey was crawling out of the Zodiac and onto the rock. She was staring at Leah. Scared, but there was something else in her eyes.

"My mom?" she whispered. "Our mom. Is that true?"

Leah nodded, gazing at her daughter over the top of Nick's head. "Yes. I left because I thought it would protect you. It was the hardest thing I have ever done. I loved you—love you—so much. So much. I know you'll never understand that, but I promise your safety was the only thing I ever—"

"Enough family bonding," the man in the boat said.

When she finally looked at Lambkin's recruit, she was shocked. It was the college-age neighbor who'd come down to tell her about the HOA, the one who'd said *Carson* and she'd heard *Corson.*

He smiled, seeing the memory written on her face. "The pond wasn't the liability after all," he said. "But I was close, right? Pond, river, whatever. At any rate, Dax Blackwell here, and it's a pleasure and all of that. Now let's move."

"Doc called *you,*" she said, stunned by what she should've seen on that first visit. He'd looked familiar because he was familiar. A generation behind maybe, but…

"There were two men—" she began, and before she could even begin to explain the men who'd engineered her fake death, he interrupted her.

"My father and my uncle, yes. Small world when it comes to hired guns, isn't it? But we don't really have time to reminisce. That guy back there on the plane, the one with the kid tied up by his throat? He doesn't strike me as particularly patient."

Leah nodded. He was right. They had to deal with the threat.

She kissed the top of Nick's head, tasting the river in his hair, and slid aside. Put her hand on Hailey's shoulder and squeezed hard. "I'll fix it," she told Hailey.

Before Hailey could answer, Dax Blackwell said, "Get into the boat, please."

She saw he'd picked up his shotgun. She nodded and reached into her pocket and withdrew the Smith & Wesson.

"I've got this. I'm good with it too. How do you think we can do it? We need him to let Matt—the kid—go first. Maybe if we flank him. You've got better range, but I can—"

"You can get into the boat and go out to the plane," Dax Blackwell said in a neutral tone. Leah realized the muzzle of his shotgun had swung her way. "That was the arrangement."

She cocked her head, stared at him. Said, "You think I'll need to get close and take the shot?"

"No," he answered, and for a moment she was relieved. Then he said, "In fact, I want you to drop that gun in the water. Right now."

The gun in her hand was pointed down at the rock, and he had the shotgun leveled at her chest.

"Right now," he said again.

"But you...you came to help."

"That's right." Still as calm as if they were discussing the weather. "Things have shifted, though. I work for Hailey now."

Leah looked from him to Hailey. Her daughter was crying silent tears. She looked at Leah with shame and desperation.

"I didn't mean that," she said, sobbing. "I said the wrong thing." She whirled to face Dax Blackwell and shouted, *"I didn't mean that!"*

Dax stayed focused on Leah. Moved his finger to the shotgun's trigger. "Your corpse will be enough to satisfy him, and it'll be easier on me. Make the choice."

Leah remembered what Doc had said about the man who might help her. That it might not be anyone in a white hat.

The face might be boyish, but the eyes held no lies. He meant what he said.

She opened her fingers, and the weight of the revolver was gone. The gun bounced down the rock and into the water and sank.

"Get in the boat," he said.

"No!" Hailey cried. "I didn't mean it, and I want to take it back. Don't hurt her! Don't!"

"I gave you the choice, Hailey. We agreed that she had lied to you, abandoned you, and put you in harm. You made a choice based on that."

Hailey was down on her knees now, still sobbing. "I take it back! I didn't think you'd really—"

"That's not how it works, I'm afraid," Dax Blackwell said with what seemed like genuine sorrow. "We talked about teaching moments, Hailey. This one, while painful, will be lasting. That's important. The lessons that linger are the ones that hurt the most. You made your choice and charted your course. I'm just here to see it through."

"No! I didn't mean it." She spun to face Leah, spit the words in her direction, desperate. *"I didn't really mean it!"*

"I know you didn't," Leah said softly. "Hon? I know you didn't." The wind rose and blew cool air over her face and she looked at her daughter and at her son and then said, "But he's right."

No one spoke. Everyone seemed surprised. Everyone except for Dax Blackwell, who looked pleased. He gave her an approving nod, and she wanted the gun back in her hand then, wanted to put a bullet into his brain. But still...

"He's right," she repeated. "I can't stop the threats. I thought that I could. But I need to let you go now. They won't follow you. I promise that." She looked at Nick, saw his eyes widen with horror. She touched his arm. "They won't. And you can go home. Back to your real home. You'll be safe. I'm so sorry. I am so—"

"So over the time limit," Dax Blackwell interrupted. "Let's get moving."

"Don't!" Hailey shouted at him again, and he sighed.

"I'm doing *your* work, child! A little gratitude is apparently too much to ask for, but at least accept the—"

"Shut up!" Leah shouted as she moved down the rock toward the boat. "Don't poison her with that. I'll go with you, but do not poison my daughter with that! It was *not* her choice. I brought them here. Brought all of you here."

She looked at Hailey when she said the last part, and for a moment time seemed to stop. They locked eyes, and Leah realized what she had just said aloud for the first time.

My daughter.

Leah climbed into the boat. "Do not blame my daughter for my mistakes," she said. Then, looking at Nick: "Do not make my son hear any of this. The choices were mine. Always." She was struggling now. There was so much she wanted to tell them. "I'm sorry," she said. "I love you so much, I have always loved you so much, and I am so sorry."

Dax Blackwell started the outboard and then leaned forward and cut the line holding them to the rock. The boat pulled away as Hailey screamed for him to stop it, screamed for them to stay, screamed that she hadn't meant it.

"Children," he said, "are not easy. Am I right?"

Leah didn't respond. She shouted to Hailey, "Bring that backpack to Ed! Bring it to him, give him the first-aid kit, and he will help. Hailey, listen to me, baby!"

The current caught the boat then, and the rocks whipped past, and her children were out of sight once more.

My daughter.

My son.

"I love you," Leah shouted as Dax opened up the throttle and let the boat gain speed. *"I love you!"*

Part Five

COLD STARS

50

Dax was glad that Leah wasn't the begging or pleading kind. It appeared that she understood her burden. She didn't so much as turn to look at him as he brought the Zodiac around and eyed the plane.

The wind was picking up and it had pushed the plane back into the weeds and shallow water, then spun it. The spin was good for Dax and bad for Bleak. He wouldn't have a clear shot until they were almost up to the plane. Dax was curious how long Bleak would give him to deliver Leah Trenton without shooting but not so curious that he wished to die. The boy was still out there on the float, grasping the strut at if he were stuck at the top of a frozen Ferris wheel.

"Can you fly that plane?" Dax asked Leah.

For a moment, he didn't think Leah was going to answer. At last she said, "I can fly it, but he won't let me."

"Why? He knows you're a pilot."

Her voice was almost emotionless when she said, "Yes. But he also knows that if it is just us, I will crash it, and I will kill us both."

Dax raised an eyebrow. "Excellent point. I'll confess I hadn't even thought of that possibility."

Leah sat rigidly in the bow seat, refusing to look back at him. She was, he thought, pretty damn tough. She was, in fact, more like her daughter than perhaps either of them had had time to realize. A shame, but he thought Hailey might recognize it eventually. When she had a proper chance to reflect on the days she'd enjoyed with her mother, Hailey might extract more lessons than she could possibly imagine right now.

He piloted the Zodiac directly to the open door on the pilot's side. It should have swung closed in the wind, so Bleak must have used something to wedge it open. A smart choice. As they came closer, Dax could smell fuel in the air.

"Good thing I have another plane," he said. "I think you shot this one up pretty well."

Leah said nothing. Her posture, straight-backed and defiant, was just like her daughter's.

He brought them in alongside the pontoon where the boy hostage waited. The boy held tight to the strut and watched them with a mixture of fear and hope. Dax slowed the motor but didn't cut it, so he could push back against the current and hold position. They were in front of the open door now and he could see the black barrel of a rifle pointed at them. Beyond that, he saw the man himself—the famous Bleak.

"Delivery," Dax called. "Just as promised. Same-day shipping, too."

Bleak said, "Tie up the boat."

Dax shook his head. "That would be a poor choice on my part. And if you shoot me now, the boat sweeps downriver, you're going to have to get wet getting it back, and then you'll *still* need to find another plane. The problem is how you're getting out of here."

"I'll find an exit strategy, thanks."

"No doubt. I'm just thinking about the fastest one for you. It's a conundrum."

Bleak laughed. It was soft but audible. Dax liked the sound.

"Here's my idea," Dax said. "You get in the boat. I take us to the plane. If you want to kill Leah at any point along the way, that's fine, but I could make an argument for keeping her alive because she can fly the plane." He raised a finger. "Full disclosure, though: She has already spoken of trying to crash the plane. I don't know about you, but that's not the attitude I like to hear from a pilot after the boarding doors are closed."

"Who are you, bro?"

"We can talk about that when we're out of here," Dax said. "You got any problem with my plan?"

"Yeah. What do you want out of it? This is crazy, what you're doing. You should've cut and run once you were behind the rocks. Instead, you're down here waiting to get shot."

"Incorrect," Dax said. "I'm waiting to get paid."

"Get paid?" The man's voice rose in volume for the first time. "You think I'm paying you? I could lay your ass in that river right now, six shots in you before you blink."

"Absolutely," Dax agreed, "but you still wouldn't have a plane and a pilot. I think you want those. I also don't think you care if I take some of Lowery's money. He was going to pay the two of you, right? You and your partner whose body is at the bottom of the river now."

He watched Bleak very carefully while he said that.

"You're a crazy man," Bleak said. "Type of man gets killed for no reason."

"Your partner was going to be paid," Dax said, "and all I'm asking for is his share. It's a reasonable request. I'm not even utilizing my leverage here. Just being reasonable."

"Leverage? Shit!" Bleak said, and he shook his head, incredulous. It was the most emotion he'd shown. Dax was pleased that he'd been able to provoke it.

"Tell me that's not reasonable," Dax said.

"Leverage," Bleak said and shook his head again. "You really talkin' about *leverage.*"

Dax shrugged. "I'm not asking you to negotiate. I'll ask Lowery. It's not your burden."

"No wonder you're so damn young. There's no way a man who acts like you do gets old."

"Mind if I make one guess about your circumstances on this river?" Dax asked.

"You never stop talking, do you?"

"Here's my guess: Lowery doesn't want *you* to kill her. If he did, she'd already be dead. And the kids, the pilot, the dog. This would have been a zero-sum afternoon if you'd been given that option. Everyone would've been dead but you and me."

That low chuckle again. "But *you?*"

Dax nodded. "Correct. We'd have indulged ourselves in a little showdown, maybe, some pissing contest, but eventually we'd have assessed the situation and realized it wasn't worth it. The rest of them would be dead. He's waiting on her, and he wants her alive. Am I wrong?"

A long beat. "Put down your weapon."

Dax put down his weapon. He had come this far on his curiosity, might as well proceed a bit further. He was dealing with a pragmatist here, a man of unique confidence, which meant a man who would let the situation play out much longer than most. Bleak wasn't worried about losing the upper hand. Wasn't worried about losing, period.

Dax hadn't seen such confidence since his father was alive.

But Dax was confident too. Bleak would have filled the river with the dead and vanished into the woods long ago if that were an acceptable outcome. He was supposed to deliver Leah alive. It was the only thing that made sense.

Bleak slid out onto the edge of the plane and sat with his feet dangling, like a soldier about to jump out of a helicopter. He wore boots and jeans and a white T-shirt. Dax noted that the T-shirt wasn't stained by so much as a drop of sweat. Impressive. The man had a shaved head and dark, observant eyes and was all lean muscle, no body fat, as if he bench-pressed any incoming carbohydrate before he ate it.

He looked at Dax, studying him in similar fashion, and Dax

would've loved to hear what he thought he saw. When he was done assessing Dax, he looked at Leah Trenton.

"Nina." No trace of emotion.

"Marvin," she said, and Dax thought there might have been a tiny twitch in the man's face at that, as if he didn't like his given name. In fairness, he did not look like a Marvin. He looked like a Bleak. You couldn't blame a mother for trying, but the world had corrected her mistake most appropriately.

Bleak lifted the rifle, a modified AR-15 with an extended magazine and an infrared scope, put the red dot on Leah Trenton's forehead, and said, "Pow."

Leah said, "Feel better?"

"I will soon."

She shrugged.

"Ten fucking years," he said. "You out here, me inside. All over now, though."

She shrugged again. She wasn't going to give him a damn thing. Dax liked her despite himself.

"You really got a plane and a pilot?" Bleak asked, looking at Dax again, moving the red dot from Leah's forehead to his. Dax didn't react.

"Yes. The pilot will be a little sore, but he can fly."

"How far from here?"

"Twenty minutes."

Bleak nodded and dropped into the boat beside Leah in a move so sudden and graceful that it was as if he'd always been there. She recoiled, scrambled backward into the center seat. He reached into the plane, dragged a camo backpack down, dropped it into the boat.

"Shotgun," Bleak said to Dax. "Pass it forward. You know how."

Dax knew how. He picked the shotgun up by the barrel, keeping his hands in plain view and nowhere near the trigger, and passed it forward. Bleak took it and tossed it into the river.

"Shirt," Bleak said.

Leah Trenton looked confused, but Dax understood. He lifted his shirt so Bleak could see his waistband. He twisted without being told, showing that there was no weapon in a spine holster, either.

"I'm clean," he said.

"Ankles," Bleak said.

Dax smiled and nodded. Bent at the waist and rolled up the pants on the left leg first—clean. As he rolled them back down, he said, "You won't like the next one as much. I'll go slow."

Bleak didn't speak. Dax rolled the pants up over his right boot, moving carefully as the ankle holster was exposed. A snub-nosed revolver waited there.

"Into the water," Bleak said. "If that muzzle comes toward me, you die."

"Copy that." Dax removed his backup piece from the ankle holster, holding it by the grip with just two fingers, and dropped it over the side of the boat.

"Clip knife in my pocket," he said. "I'd like to keep that, if you don't mind. It has sentimental—"

"Shut up and dump it."

Dax sighed, removed the Benchmade knife that had traveled so many roads with him, and dropped it into the river.

"That's it," he said, and it was. He was unarmed now. Not the best feeling, admittedly, but he was comforted by the reminder that a Blackwell was never *truly* unarmed. His mind was still sharp and his body was still sound and his creativity was peerless.

Nevertheless, he would miss the knife.

"Take us to your plane," he said.

Dax was ready to, but Leah said, "Untie Matt."

"Huh?"

"The kid." She pointed at the trembling boy on the seaplane's float. "You untie him or I will."

"Nobody will."

"Yes, I will. Because what he just said was the truth: Corson wants to see me. You're not killing me until then. So untie him."

Bleak spoke to Dax. "Get moving."

Leah Trenton stood up and moved to the front of the boat. Bleak rose swiftly and slapped her once, a seemingly casual effort but one that knocked her back on her ass and rocked the boat. Blood rushed from her nose. She licked it off her lips, got up, and stepped forward again.

"Just untie him," Dax said. "What are we gaining here? Nothing. And we're losing time."

Bleak and Leah stood eye to eye, one bleeding and unarmed, the other uninjured and with a rifle in hand, and yet they seemed evenly matched in ferocity.

Bleak spun, his hand flashed, and the cord binding Matt Bouchard's throat to wherever it was tied off in the plane's cockpit parted and fell in draped ends. Bleak stepped out of the boat and onto the plane's float, knife in one hand, gun in the other, moving sideways, never offering his back to Dax, which was wise even though Dax had no intention of killing him.

Bleak flashed that knife hand again, and the plastic ties binding the boy's wrists fell away. Without a word, Bleak abandoned his hostage and dropped back into the Zodiac.

"Move," he said.

Dax moved. Leah fell heavily back in the boat as the prop whirled, and Dax brought them around in a circle and headed downriver. He saw Leah staring backward and followed her gaze. Past the plane where the child waited on the float, there was motion in the trees along the bank. Hailey and Nick were creeping through the woods to the place where Ed Levenseller waited with the dog. They were trying to move stealthily, but they were still exposed to gunfire.

Bleak was watching them. He didn't move to lift his rifle,

though. Dax realized he didn't view any of them as threats, not even the pilot. They'd all seen him. They could all testify against him. Bleak had no concerns about a courtroom, not in his current situation, already a fugitive. He intended to become a ghost.

That was easier to do when you had ample resources. Bleak's resources required Lowery's satisfaction. Thus, Leah Trenton lived for another hour. Maybe two.

As Dax piloted them toward Roman Island and the awaiting plane, they passed Randall Pollard's corpse, hung up on a bone-white limb that had snagged his shirt. There was a crater in his gut from Leah's bullet and another in his eye socket from Dax's. His body twisted in the current, as if trying to pull free and sail on. Or sink. Already, the flies had found his wounds.

Dax watched Bleak's face closely as they went by the corpse.

There was no hint of emotion.

They passed the dead man and went on down the river.

51

Leah rode in numb silence, pinned between the two killers, one she'd known for years, and one she'd apparently hired. Each as empty as the other. She'd felt little surprise listening to the one named Dax negotiate with Bleak. She'd reached into the darkness in search of salvation, and who could be surprised that she withdrew only more darkness?

Hailey and Nick were alive. Ed was...still living, at least. So was the neighbor's boy, Matt. Even Tessa.

The innocent ones live on, she thought as she swayed with the boat, pines flying by, the water gray-black beneath gathering clouds. If the innocent ones made it through this day alive, it had gone well enough. She was not ready to die, but she was fine with the choice she had made.

She hoped her kids would remember her like this. Would remember that when she'd had to kill for them, she had, and when she'd had to lay down her own life for them, she had.

Like a mother.

She closed her eyes. So much pain, so much suffering, and always by those who deserved it the least. What world allowed that?

The world didn't answer her, but the wind did, blowing fresh and cold into her face, and she knew without having to open her eyes that they'd rounded the point and come out into the wide stretches of Roman Island Lake.

She wanted to see Lowery before she died. It was the last thing she wished for: a chance to see him face-to-face. What she would do with the chance, she wasn't sure. Spit in his eye, claw at his skin, shout blood oaths? None of it would matter. And yet she wanted it. She wanted that one last thing. The chance to hurt any part of him, however briefly.

She opened her eyes and saw Bleak staring at her, expressionless, his body moving in natural, easy motion with the boat. He should have been cold in the wind and on the water with nothing but that T-shirt, but he seemed as unaffected as if he were resting in the Florida sun.

She turned her head so that she didn't have to look at him.

They were coming up on the west side of Roman Island, and she saw smoke rising from the stovepipe of one of the isolated camps there. Thought about shouting for help but knew better. If she shouted, someone might actually run down to try to help. Then there would be more innocent blood.

Past the island and on out to the expanse of open water on the north side, gray flecked with whitecaps in the freshening wind. Something rested in the water across the way, floating near the cliffs that rimmed a small cove. She squinted.

It was a plane. Dax Blackwell hadn't lied. She hadn't expected that he had, though. He was here for a payday and willing to sell her to the highest bidder. Her own defense, her hired hand. She wondered if Doc Lambkin was dead. All those unanswered phone calls. Yes, he was probably dead. Dead because he'd answered her call. Leah was an infection spreading from coast to coast, a trail of death in her wake.

Kill the source and let it end.

Just let me have a chance to take Lowery with me. He is the ultimate source.

They fought the wind northwest toward the cove, no one speaking, the Zodiac spanking across the chop, and then Dax Blackwell brought the boat around in a shallow arc and came to an idling stop beside the plane.

"Mind tying us off?" he said. "I've got to go free the pilot. Unless you want to."

Bleak gestured at Leah with the rifle.

"You," he said. Just the one word.

Leah moved past him, climbed onto the float, took the line from the bow of the Zodiac, looped it around a strut, tied a hitch. She climbed back down into the boat as Dax Blackwell killed the motor and the world fell silent around them.

"May I go get the pilot without being shot in the back?" he asked. "It would be nice."

Bleak's only response was to lower his rifle by about three inches. Dax Blackwell nodded as if this were a fine display of cooperation, and then he climbed out of the Zodiac, nimbly made his way to the cargo-hold door, and opened it.

A slim, pale man with unkempt hair and wide, terrified eyes above a strip of tape that covered his mouth looked out of the dimness and directly at Leah.

"It's Andy!" Dax Blackwell said, as if greeting an old friend. "Andy, we're going to need you to do some flying now. You game for that, old buddy?"

Dax ripped the tape off his mouth. Thin furrows of blood formed on the pilot's lips. He licked the blood away and looked at Dax.

"Where?" he said.

"Good question," Dax Blackwell answered. "You're improving with that." He turned to face Bleak. "Where?"

Bleak opened the camo backpack he'd taken from the plane. He used only one hand, keeping the rifle in the other. He withdrew a satellite phone. Leah looked at it and thought numbly of the plan that had seemed so plausible just hours ago. The call to Mrs. Wilson in Louisville to arrange for her children's exodus, then finding Lowery on her own terms, fighting him, killing him. How quickly the plan had fallen apart. On Lowery's terms, again.

Always on his terms.

"I think we have to wait for that answer," Dax told the pilot, and he dropped back down into the boat, rocking it and stumbling toward Bleak. Bleak lifted the rifle and popped the muzzle off Dax Blackwell's forehead hard enough that Leah heard the click of his teeth snapping together.

"Sorry," Dax said. "I don't have sea legs like you."

Bleak's finger traced the trigger. He now had the plane and the pilot and thus no more need for Dax, Leah realized, and she waited for the shot.

Bleak removed his finger from the trigger.

"Get in the back," he told Dax, and Leah laughed.

"Funny?" Bleak said, looking at her as Dax slid by, crawling to the stern.

"Yes," Leah said, the taste of her own blood in her mouth. "It is. You've got to ask for permission first, don't you? Not quite sure who you can kill."

"Don't need permission," Bleak said. "Not now, not tomorrow, not yesterday. Keep laughing."

"I will," she said, and she felt a high, dizzy giddiness. Why not laugh? Whistle through the graveyard, as they say. She was on her last breaths. Why not enjoy them?

But Bleak had already lost interest in her. He had maneuvered so he was facing Leah and Dax, but his attention was on the satellite phone. He pressed buttons and then put the phone to his ear. Pause. Then: "I have her," he said. No preamble, no exchange of greetings.

Leah imagined Lowery on the other end of the call. Saw his snow-white hair and his deep tan and his crisp clothes and perfect posture. Saw his reptilian eyes. The eyes wouldn't change when he heard this news from Bleak. He might smile, he might scowl, but the expressions never affected his eyes.

"Allagash River in northern Maine," Bleak said. "There were casualties, and there were witnesses. Time is an issue. I have a plane and a pilot, though. I also have a passenger."

Pause.

"Someone she hired. He wants Pollard's share."

Pause.

"Dead."

Pause.

"Says his name is Dax Blackwell."

Dax's mouth twitched with a hint of a smile. He leaned on the outboard, seemingly having no reaction to the conversation other than mild amusement. Leah thought that he'd be smiling when he died.

"Tell him I left a bill in Montana," Dax Blackwell said.

Bleak ignored that and said, "He told me he was hired by Lambkin to protect her. He wants a bigger payday now. Pollard's share."

"Not a bigger payday," Dax said, as if talking to himself. "There was interest due, that's all. It's a matter of common courtesy."

Bleak said, "He's right here. Right now."

Going to shoot him, Leah thought. *Right here and right now, Bleak is going to—*

There was the sound of ripping tape and Leah and Bleak looked toward the stern at the same time and saw that Dax Blackwell had a gun. It was a Glock nine-millimeter, child's firepower compared to Bleak's, but it was pointed at Bleak's forehead. A tendril of black electrician's tape fluttered from the butt of the Glock, and Leah realized that Dax must have taped it to the transom long before the first shots had been fired. Long before he'd even known that any shots *would* be fired.

The muzzle of Bleak's AR-15 was adrift somewhere between Leah and Dax and the pilot, the trio of threats he'd been trying to keep in check while also handling the phone and balancing on the water. He could try for a shot easily. It was fraction-of-a-second stuff, and yet he was smart enough not to try. He'd have lost.

There was a frozen moment and then Dax spoke softly.

"Put yours down and tell him we're in good shape. Because we are."

Bleak didn't move. Still weighing the odds. Gauging the steadiness in Dax's gun hand. The muzzle of his own rifle was only two inches from being centered on Dax.

The water rose and rocked them and still Dax's gun hand didn't waver.

Bleak lowered the rifle. Put it down on the bottom of the boat, resting near his boot. His eyes never left Dax's.

"Finish the call," Dax said. "We need to get out of here."

"No," Bleak said into the phone. "All good here. It's just…you might want a look at him, is all I'm thinking. He's no trouble for me."

Making excuses for the killing he now could not perform even if ordered to.

Leah looked back at Dax. All of his attention was on Bleak, and no humor was on his face now. That shield of glibness was gone.

"Shoot him," she whispered. "Please. Trust me. He will not—"

"Shut up," Dax Blackwell said quietly.

For money. All of this, for money.

Bleak was still talking into the phone.

"You deal with him when you see him, then," Bleak said. "Sounds good." Pause. "Helicopter. I'll send coordinates. You give me an ETA."

Pause.

"Copy that," he said, and he disconnected the call. Looked at Dax. Said, "Cute trick."

"Could've been a dumb one. Once you saw the pilot was alive, I wasn't sure you'd leave me time."

Bleak nodded. Said, "Ten years inside. Wouldn't have made that mistake otherwise."

"Sure. It's all muscle memory. Comes back to you fast. Don't force it."

Leah said, "Kill him. Please. Just—"

"I'll take the rifle," Dax Blackwell said. "You know how."

Bleak picked it up by the muzzle and held it out. Dax moved the Glock to the back of Leah's head, then leaned past her and took the AR.

"Let's not let things get personal," Dax told Bleak. "It's a job, and money. That's it, and that's all. No egos need apply."

Bleak didn't respond.

"Where we headed?" Dax asked.

For a long time, Leah thought Bleak would refuse to answer. Finally, he said, "You know Three Cross Lake?"

Dax called out, "Yo, Andy! Time to shine. Where's Three Cross Lake?"

The wild-eyed pilot who was tied up in the cramped hold of his own plane looked petrified. He didn't say anything.

"Canada," Leah said for him. "New Brunswick. Middle of nowhere."

Everyone considered her.

"Sounds right," Dax said. "How long?"

"An hour, maybe."

"Terrific. I was hoping for a short trip. Been a long damn day." Dax took the gun away from her head and said, "Go untie Andy. He'll fly, you'll navigate. You and me in the back, the fellas up front. I'd like to keep Bleak in front of me."

Bleak was studying the clouds now, indifferent as an old man on his front porch.

Leah rose and walked past him, resisting the urge to repay him double for that slap that had left the crust of dried blood below her nose. Save that energy, channel that rage. Lowery waited ahead.

She climbed into the cargo hold and untied the pilot.

52

Matt Bouchard remained on the plane for a long time after Bleak was gone. He was still holding on to the strut. He'd never been afraid of the water, but this river was different. He'd seen the water foam red with blood here.

What finally prodded him into motion was the loud barking of the dog. He couldn't see the dog because the plane blocked his view. He let go of the strut and immediately felt a surge of vertigo, but he willed his aching hands to stay down. He had good balance, and he would not fall. If he did end up in the river, he would swim. It wasn't so hard. He was alone and he was free.

The reality of that overwhelmed him. He sank trembling to his hands and knees on the float and took gasping breaths. He was alive, and the awful men were gone. One of them was dead. The other one, Bleak...

He won't die.

But neither had Matt Bouchard. Neither had Matt, damn it.

The dog barked and barked. Matt wiped his face with his hand and began to crawl from one side of the plane to the other. He thought that he could make it without getting wet if his sore hands could grip the struts. He stopped himself then. Said, "Come on, brain," which was what his dad always said when he did something dumb. There was no need to crawl to the other side of the plane.

He could just go through it.

He climbed up and into the empty cockpit. Looked in the back seat. Bleak had taken a small backpack and left several guns. Matt reached down and picked up a handgun. Touching it filled him with an electric fear, but the fear turned to empowerment when he turned and threw it into the river. It sank fast. One killing tool gone.

He threw a rifle in. Then another. Then a shotgun. Working quickly. Only when the last of them was under the water did it occur to him that if Bleak returned, Matt would want a gun.

He didn't think Bleak was going to return, though.

The pitch of the dog's bark changed, went higher, a sound of nervous delight. Matt crawled through the cockpit and opened the passenger door and then climbed down to the float on the opposite side.

The plane had drifted very close to the shore and grounded. He could see the bottom. Knee-high, thigh-high at most. He could walk out.

He looked up the bank and saw Ed Levenseller, the pilot. Ed was sitting up now, his back against a tree. Still alive. The dog was barking behind him. It looked like Ed was trying to talk to someone in the woods.

Matt sat down on the float so his feet were hanging off the edge and then pushed off. The water rose above his knees, but his feet found the bottom. He didn't mind the cold. All he wanted was to get away from the plane.

He waded toward the bank, surprised by the strength of the current. It felt like the water wanted to rush him right back into Bleak's arms. He stumbled on, though, and the shallower it got, the less strength the current had. He was almost out when someone shouted his name.

"Matt! Matt!"

He looked up and saw Hailey standing beside Ed. Nick was with her, and the dog, Tessa, weaved a frantic circuit between all three.

Matt splashed over to them, running now, his legs finding strength. He hadn't believed he would ever run again, let alone toward a friendly face.

When he arrived, breathless, he saw that there was blood in the dirt below Ed Levenseller, and the pine needles were matted with it. Ed had taken off his belt and cinched it around his thigh just above the knee. Ed said, "It's not bad. Really. I'm okay. *We* are okay."

Matt sank down into the pine needles. They all looked at one another. Hailey broke the silence first.

"Where are they taking her?" she said.

"Another plane. Then they're going to go see someone. The man who wants to kill her." The words felt strange; Matt had never imagined saying things like this. "His name is Lowery. All of them knew who he was."

For a moment, there was no sound but Tessa's whine. Then Hailey said, "She told us to bring you the backpack." She was speaking to Ed.

Ed tore the zipper back and rummaged inside, breathing heavily, the exertion clearly hurting him, sweat blooming on his brow. He came out with a first-aid kit in his hand.

The wind picked up and Matt shivered and brought his arms tight against his chest. When he did, he felt the item zipped into his chest pocket. He unzipped the pocket, removed the sunglasses, and held them out to Hailey. "I brought these," he said, and it felt like the dumbest thing in the world right then, after all that had happened to them.

Hailey rushed toward him, took the sunglasses in a trembling hand, dropped down to her knees, and started to cry.

"Thank you," she whispered. She cried harder, though. Matt knelt down and touched her arm. She leaned against him, her body shuddering, and he hugged her. Nick scrambled over to her side, and Matt moved his arm to let Nick slip in close. The three of them sat there and held one another and Ed Levenseller said, "We are fine, guys. We are fine."

He was speaking around a plastic tube that he held in his teeth, something he'd removed from the first-aid kit. Matt realized it was the cap of a syringe. Ed had the needle pressed close to his wound, and his eyes were closed.

"She is my mom," Hailey whispered, her face pressed into Matt's shoulder. "My *mom*."

"I know," he said.

"One of you is going to need to get back on that plane," Ed Levenseller whispered. "And use the radio."

"I can," Matt and Hailey said at once. She looked at him.

"We can," she said.

"Okay. I'll talk you through it." Ed's words were coming with difficulty, but his breathing was steady, and he did not sound afraid. "We'll get help. All is well. All is well."

A sound in the sky then. An engine. They looked toward it. For a while, there was nothing to see, but then a plane appeared just over the trees. Matt thought, *Help got here fast.*

But then he understood.

The plane was heading away from them, not toward them.

They all watched it go, not knowing where it was headed, but knowing exactly who was on it.

Nobody said a word.

53

They flew in silence through the deepening cloud cover, and Dax was grateful for the quiet. He wanted to watch Bleak and only Bleak, but he also had to be aware of the other two. Leah Trenton was in kamikaze mode, which meant her decisions would be very hard to anticipate, and while Andy West piloted his plane without evident distress, he'd had a long day tied up in his own cargo hold.

Beneath them, the land was as desolate as any he'd ever seen. No towns, no roads. Forests and rivers and lakes, the undulating low hills turning it all into a dark quilt tossed haphazardly over a rumpled bed.

Andy West broke the silence to say that he was crossing international airspace and needed to use the radio. Bleak answered before Dax could: "No radio."

That simple.

They were in a small plane flying over an isolated wilderness. Dax didn't fear Canadian fighter jets scrambling in pursuit. He was sure the border patrol had concerns with small planes flying silently, but he'd take his chances today.

Leah Trenton seemed to be studying the plane, familiarizing herself with the controls. Dax observed that with interest. She might yet maintain some hope of survival and escape. Noble, albeit misguided.

Bleak was harder to read. He sat motionless and expressionless and if not for the steady rise and fall of his breaths—he was a deep breather, oxygenating blood and tissue for the next time he'd need it to respond—he could have been a corpse.

He couldn't be in a good mood, though. He had lost his gun and he had lost control. He intended to reacquire both.

Dax watched Bleak and matched his breathing. It was both prudent—a calming mechanism—and intimate. He wanted to feel as close to the man as possible for the inevitable moment of conflict. Bleak breathed. Dax breathed. Together, they waited.

They had been flying for nearly an hour and he was beginning to wonder about the possibility of planes being sent from the Maine Warden Service or the Mounties or whoever the hell would draw the job in Canada. Surely by now the children had found a way to get help. Just as his concern rose, though, the plane angled down.

"Approaching Three Cross Lake," Andy West intoned. His voice cracked on the last word.

"Where do we put it down, Bleak?" Dax asked.

Bleak breathed and waited. Dax sighed and leaned forward, bringing the Glock in behind Bleak's ear.

"Where?" Dax repeated.

"Northern shore. There's a clearing for a helicopter nearby."

"Why?"

"It's owned by a timber company," Leah Trenton said tiredly. "They blocked it to fishing a couple of years back. It's all private now."

"Owned by him," Bleak said.

Leah stiffened. "By Lowery?"

Bleak nodded once. Dax watched Leah take this in. She gave a short, strangled laugh.

"I've been there," she said. "I've fished on his fucking lake."

They came out of the clouds and the lake rose ahead of them with a metallic sheen that seemed designed to warn you that it was harder than expected. Dax spotted the clearing near the shore.

It was maybe an acre, no more, the only break in the woods for miles, and a black helicopter sat in the center. It was easy to miss unless you were looking for it.

"He's already there," Dax said. "Short flight at chopper speeds. So where was he?"

Bleak didn't answer.

"I suppose I don't need to know," Dax agreed, and he sat back in his seat. Leah Trenton was staring at him, and when their eyes met he saw the imploring look. She wanted him to help.

She understood so little of the world, he thought. It was sad, really. He looked away, studied the water. "There's a discharge to the east," he said. "What's that?"

Leah said, "The river."

He nodded. "It's all connected in these parts, isn't it? One massive system."

She ignored him.

Andy West put the plane down smoothly and safely for the second time that day. Dax couldn't complain about that. Nor did he mind the long taxi; it was time to think.

Lowery wouldn't have come alone. There would be a pilot, of course, and there would be a guard or guards. How many of them? Time would tell, but the only certainty was that Dax would be outmanned and outgunned again.

He was tired of that.

"Leah walks with me," he said. "Bleak goes ten paces ahead. No more, no less. Andy, I hope you don't mind staying with the plane."

No one responded.

"There will be guards," Dax said. "Don't encourage them to shoot early. Remember, we haven't gone through all of this just so Mr. Lowery can watch Leah die at someone else's hand."

When Bleak spoke, it surprised them all.

"No guards. Just the pilot. He'll be armed."

"Why would I believe that?" Dax said.

"Because I'm the one bringing her," Bleak said.

It made some sense. If Lowery believed Bleak was in charge, he wouldn't need reinforcements. Dax also suspected that Lowery would want any killing he did to be as private as possible.

Andy West banked the plane on the northern shore and killed the engine. The prop wound down like a tired clock.

Dax nudged Leah with the gun. "There's cord and tape on the floor. Please secure Andy for us, and make sure his mouth is closed. If he objects, remind him that it's more comfortable in the pilot's seat than down in the cargo hold."

Andy West sat back in the seat without a word of objection. Those hours in the cargo hold had probably been very long indeed.

Leah Trenton tore a piece of tape off and passed it to him. "Do it yourself," she said.

"Thanks," Andy said, and he sealed his own lips with the tape. Leah wrapped the cord around him quickly, binding him to the seat, his arms at his sides. She tried to make it look tight while leaving some stretch, but Dax sighed and cinched it tighter, then tossed the slack end forward.

"Do his hands, please," he said to Bleak.

Bleak tied Andy's hands to the yoke. Bleak's knots did not require any further cinching.

"Okay," Dax said. "Leah with me, Bleak ten paces in front. There shouldn't be any shooting. Lowery gets what he wants, I get what I want."

He glanced at Leah, curious if she'd reveal fear or desperation. She just popped open the door and climbed out on the float, then waited for him.

She was ready to see it through, he realized.

Bleak led them to shore. He pivoted right to left, searching for sentries, but he didn't seem to find any. Dax hadn't either. It was a private party.

Once he and Leah reached the shore, Dax switched the AR-15 to his right hand and put the Glock in his left, then pressed the Glock to her spine. She seemed indifferent. Her attention was only forward.

She wanted to see Lowery. He could feel it coming off her like heat.

There was a narrow footpath from the shore to the clearing. A tenth of a mile, maybe. Bleak kept pace, staying ten strides ahead. Leah made no move to break away from Dax. Everything as it should be.

They came out of the trees and into the clearing and there stood J. Corson Lowery.

He was taller than Dax had expected, well over six feet, with hair the color of fresh snow and skin like a cowboy's saddle. He wore a black jacket over a white shirt with jeans and black cowboy boots, looking every bit the part of the wealthy rancher. He had made hundreds of millions of dollars in his life, maybe more than that, and he'd ordered the killings of dozens of men, maybe more than that. Yet there he stood, rich and unrumpled.

Just a job. It is just a job.

They walked across the clearing toward Lowery. Lowery made no move to close the distance himself. He was used to people coming to him. Dax felt Leah's body tensing. Ten years since she'd seen the man. Ten years on the run, a new identity, a family left behind, and still he'd found her. Still he stood here in front of his helicopter, waiting.

You had to respect that reach. That power.

That relentlessness.

All for one bullet that she had not even fired.

Dax saw Lowery's pilot inside the helicopter, and although the tinted windshield limited visibility, he didn't need visibility to know the man was armed.

"Slow up," Dax said when they were thirty paces from Lowery.

Bleak slowed, then stopped altogether. Dax followed suit. They were close enough to hear one another now.

Lowery was wearing a gun in a holster on his hip. He didn't reach for it, but when he looked at Bleak, he seemed confused.

"Where's your gun?" he asked. The first words he'd spoken, and in them Dax could hear both the practiced polish and the faint wisp of Florida cracker that all the money in the world hadn't been able to wash out of J. Corson Lowery's mouth.

"It's right here," Dax said, and he lifted the AR above Leah's shoulder and leveled it at Lowery.

Lowery's hand drifted for the holster. Dax said, "No."

The hand stopped moving. Drifted back.

"The fuck do you think you're doing?" Lowery said. Low voice. Not scared.

"Finding the highest price for my services," Dax said. "You wanted her. I brought her to you. Bleak might've helped, but I did the heavy lifting. I think even he would agree with that."

Bleak didn't speak.

Lowery said, "Who are you, really?"

"Dax Blackwell." The full name left his lips with pride and an aftertaste of something darker.

"You killed one of my men," Lowery said. "Why in the hell did you do that?"

"Everyone criticizes the debt collector for his methods," Dax said. "I've never understood that."

"Killed him," Lowery said again, and his anger seemed impersonal, as if Dax were a mere frustration to be swatted away. "You stupid little bastard."

"He just wants his money," Bleak said, and Dax was astounded that he'd spoken, let alone said *that*. Immediately, he was distrustful and moved the muzzle of the AR to bear on Bleak instead of Lowery. As he shifted, he saw the pilot move inside the helicopter.

That was where the first trouble would come from. He was almost sure of it.

"Just wants his money," Lowery echoed.

"We can even forgo the old bill," Dax said. "Let's not get bogged down in the past. You want her, and I brought her. Pay me."

Lowery laughed. It was an oddly high, delighted sound. "Yes," he said. "Yes, of course I will. Why would I not?" He laughed again, shook his head in disbelief, and then ran a hand back and forth over that coiffed white hair.

Dax was ready when the pilot moved. He swept Leah's legs out from under her so that she fell beneath the line of fire and dropped the Glock from his left hand so he could shoot the AR with a two-handed grip as the pilot swung out of the helicopter door and pointed a scoped rifle at him using the helicopter as protection, nothing visible above the chopper but the rifle and his face.

Dax stitched a line of bullets through his face.

The scoped rifle, unfired, fell a half a second before the pilot did. Dax sidestepped and aimed at Lowery as the old man's hand went for the gun once more. Dax shook his head and Lowery straightened, moving his hand away from the gun.

"That was a bad signal for your shooter," Dax said. "I mean, come on. It's pretty clear that a man with your head of hair doesn't spend much time mussing it up."

He stepped back, clearing room. They were three points of a triangle to him now, Bleak and Lowery on their feet, Leah on the ground. Dax swept the AR back and forth, hoping there was no one behind him. If he'd been wrong—and if Bleak had been wrong or if Bleak had lied—and there were more guards waiting, Dax would die soon.

No shots came. The wind blew soft and gentle in the pines, and no one moved. There was a trace of blood on the wind again. Second time today, or was it the third? So hard to remember.

"Pay me," Dax told J. Corson Lowery.

Lowery turned from Dax to Bleak. His voice was full of disdain when he said, "How did you let this happen?"

Bleak did not respond.

"Sure," Lowery said after a pause. "I'll fucking pay you. Just bring her to me." He looked at Leah Trenton as if no one else in the world mattered. If he'd given a thought to his dead helicopter pilot, it wasn't evident. Leah was crouched in the grass where Dax had dropped her, on her hands and knees, looking up at Lowery. Dax watched her glance to her right, where the Glock now lay in the grass. He understood her idea, and he heard that internal voice whispering the family mantra, *It's just a job, it's just a job,* so he kept silent.

The mantra was right. Dax would have died hours ago if he'd admitted that there were no bullets in Andy West's Glock and never had been. It was hard to hold people hostage with an unloaded gun, though, so you had to convince them to believe the lie.

Clearly, Leah had believed.

54

Leah's only question was whether Dax Blackwell would shoot her. If he fired at her as fast as he had the pilot, then Leah would die.

If he let her go, though…

She looked at the Glock in the grass. Looked at Lowery. He was fifteen feet away. She just needed to make the first shot count. If Dax killed her after the first shot, so be it. As long as she made that one count, she would die knowing her children were safe and the bad man was dead. That was enough.

"How much?" Lowery asked Dax.

"What were you going to give Pollard?"

"Freedom. He got it."

"He squandered it," Dax said.

Lowery shook his head as if he couldn't understand why this intolerable interruption had come along. "Just bring her to me."

"Leah's worth a lot to you, I think. Maybe I'll protect her, and we negotiate a higher price."

"Her name is Nina." Lowery took a few steps closer, and his eyes moved from Dax to Leah. "I'll kill your children now. You realize that, don't you? Before, they didn't matter to me. You've made them matter. So I'll kill them too."

She flexed on her toes, felt the ache of her exhausted legs. She'd already run through the woods today, ridden a river, shot a man. She should be done. Damn it, she should be done.

But she wouldn't be as long as he still breathed.

Lowery spoke to Dax without looking away from Leah. "May

I finish this? You'll find that I'm in a more generous mood when the job is complete. Your father and uncle should have told you that. They'd have been rich men if they'd just honored their word."

Leah started to glance at the Glock again but stopped herself. She knew where it was. She knew what needed to be done. Wait for the right moment. It would come when his attention was fully on Dax. She sensed, somehow, that Dax would command Lowery's attention at least once more. She would have to move fast then.

"Now," Lowery said, "may I draw the gun, and you can keep your rifle on me, and we can both trust that when this is done, money will change hands?"

Silence. Bleak stood, motionless, between Leah and Lowery. She couldn't tell what he was looking at. Someplace beyond all of them.

"You may draw the gun," Dax said, and Leah's execution order was signed. "But whose is it?"

Lowery's hand stopped an inch above the butt of his pistol. "What?"

"Is it Brad's suicide gun?"

Leah almost took her eyes off Lowery and looked at Dax Blackwell herself. The question was that shocking.

"What did you say?" Lowery asked slowly. Still facing Leah.

"I thought it would be poetic," Dax Blackwell said. "After all these years, if you finally put the bullet in her head with that gun...well, pardon me for the question. I was just curious."

Lowery swallowed. "It is not his gun." There was a tremor just beneath his right eye. His skin was very tight, as if over the years he'd simply contracted in on himself, hardening.

"Wise choice," Dax said. "Sentiment is always a risk. Romantics are reckless by nature. A pragmatic man comes in with clear eyes and an empty heart. Brad was probably a pragmatic man. His solution to his own problems, while extreme, was efficient."

Lowery's face whitened with rage, as if Dax's words had drained him of blood. "How dare—" he began, and then he turned to Dax, and Leah grabbed the Glock from the grass.

She grasped it cleanly on the first try, just as she needed to, and she spun back with the gun tracking right to left as her left hand came up to cup the right in a shooter's grip. Lowery turned back to her and his shocked face fell into the center of her aim and she squeezed the trigger before he had so much as reached for the weapon on his own hip.

The flat, impotent click of a dry fire.

Lowery's face, a mask of horror, warmed to a smile.

Leah fired again, and again.

Click, click.

He laughed then. Threw his head back and laughed as he reached for the gun on his hip and said, "Nina, Nina, Nina," and she threw the Glock at him and charged as he cleared his own gun and leveled it at her face and fired. She heard the shot and felt a terrible agony at being so close and yet never even drawing blood. She'd wanted to draw blood.

She was still moving, though, the shot hadn't dropped her, and she could see the shock on his face, could see the fear on his face, and then he was down and she was on top of him, her left hand on his throat as her right fist hammered his lips into his teeth.

There was the blood.

There it was.

She struck him again and again, and then suddenly she was lifted and hauled back, and she still felt no pain. It wasn't until Bleak pulled her away that she realized the gunshot she'd heard hadn't been Lowery's.

Dax Blackwell had shot him in the thigh.

Lowery fumbled for his own gun but his fingers were wet with his own blood and he couldn't draw it from the grass. Bleak held on to Leah, but she didn't fight him, just watched, gasping, as Dax

Blackwell approached Lowery with the AR-15 in hand. He looked older, somehow, the boyish face weathered with sorrow.

"I know I shouldn't have done it," he said, and she had no idea who he was speaking to.

He dropped into an exhausted squat beside Lowery, bracing himself on the rifle. He looked up at Leah and Bleak. Studied them as if hoping for an answer to an unasked question.

"He shouldn't have criticized them," he said. "That was the problem, I think. Up until then...I was steady up until then."

Bleak released Leah and stepped back. Leah looked at him and then at Dax and tried to decide what to do.

Then Lowery lunged up and grabbed Dax's rifle.

Dax Blackwell shook him off with ease, sighed, stood up, and stepped back. He was the only one holding a gun now. The empty Glock lay in the grass and Lowery's sidearm lay in the grass, and Bleak and Leah stood and watched as Lowery bled and hissed in pain. He was trying to speak. Leah could barely make out the words.

"Paid you," he was saying. "Would've paid you."

"I know you would have," Dax Blackwell said. "I made a poor choice." He looked up at the trees and smiled. Then looked out to the lake. "There's a river on the other side of that lake," he said. "The river flows out to the sea. All the water on earth is finite, remember. One drop joins another. They evaporate and fall and join again. Enough time, and rain in Montana will find its way to the sea."

He looked down at Lowery.

"We're all burned-out stars in the end, nothing but dust," he said. "I know this is true, and yet..." A cold smile spread across his face. "And yet still I enjoy the idea of your old, burned-out dust meeting theirs. I love the idea that you'll find them waiting for you somewhere downriver."

He stepped back, and Leah was sure that he would take the

killing shot. Instead, he retrieved Lowery's gun from the grass. He racked the slide, checked to ensure that there was a chambered round, then ejected the magazine. Looked at Leah. His unlined face was hard and his eyes distant.

"You get one," he said. "Use it however you'd like. I'm tired."

He tossed the pistol to her. She caught it, flipped it, lifted it…and watched him take a knee in the grass, leaning on the rifle, the muzzle pointed skyward.

She turned to Bleak. He stood with his arms folded. Waiting.

She took a breath and stepped across the bloody grass to look down at J. Corson Lowery. He parted his lips, and she waited for the offer—how much money did he think she would need? How many promises of protection?

"Let's negotiate," she said, and his eyes brightened at that, because on some level he actually *could* believe his good fortune. There was always one more chance for a man with money and power.

She fired the bullet into the center of his forehead.

Dropped the gun onto his chest.

Silence descended.

After a while, Dax Blackwell looked up at Bleak. "Can you fly a helicopter?"

Bleak shook his head.

"Damn," Dax said. "Me neither. Looks easy but probably isn't." He sighed. "I wouldn't trust that plane for long either. We've burned that one."

Bleak nodded.

"So we figure it out," Dax said. "Such is life." He pushed upright and looked at Leah. "It would be very good," he said, "if we had some lead time. Just a little. Useful for you, too, because you're going to have to explain this dead man, and that will be easier if you have the two of us to blame. I don't think my friend is the confessing type, and I know that I am not."

"You're not walking out of here," she said. "It's miles upon miles of…" She waved a hand at the densely packed woods, the pines crowding each other for light. "That."

"We'll figure it out," he said. He shifted the rifle to his left hand and reached behind his back with his right. Once, this would have made her tense. Now, she simply waited.

His hand came back with a hundred-dollar bill held between two fingers.

"Give this to your daughter," he said. "She wanted a refund. You might caution her about impulse purchases, though. She's quite shrewd when she can control her emotions. I sympathize with that particular challenge."

Leah took the hundred, staring at him, unsure of what to say or even think.

Dax turned to Bleak.

"You've worked with a partner before," he said.

Bleak nodded one time.

"I'm sorry I killed him," Dax said.

Bleak said nothing.

"If you're as good as I think," Dax said, "then you understand that my killing your partner in those circumstances is no reflection of my loyalty in other circumstances."

Still nothing.

"I could use help," Dax said. "I've wanted a collaborator. Sometimes you're born to one. Sometimes it's a longer journey to find one."

Bleak said, "You'd do the talking, I take it."

Dax smiled. "Feels that way, doesn't it?" He pointed at Leah. "I know you came to kill her. I could let you do that, as a gesture of goodwill, but from a marketing perspective, it sends a troubling message if we both kill our bosses, I think."

Bleak might've smiled right then.

"Here's the bargain we'll strike," Dax said, turning to Leah. "We let you walk back to that plane, and you—"

"Give you time. Yes."

"And you put him in the water," Dax finished, pointing at Lowery.

Leah frowned and looked at the helicopter. Hiding Lowery's corpse was a pointless task as long as the helicopter sat there.

"It's not about that," Dax Blackwell said, understanding her thinking. "I just want him in the water."

"All right."

"You said there's a river, right? The lake flows into a river and then on out…" He swept his hand through the air.

Leah nodded.

Dax Blackwell smiled. "I like that," he said. "Let them find him, then. They will, too. I'm sure of it. Family business."

She had no idea what he was speaking of, but she wasn't about to argue.

"And so here we part," Dax said, and then, without another word, he started into the woods. He was heading northeast as if he had a plan, but there was nothing to the northeast but miles of dark forest. They wouldn't be able to hide there. Not for long enough.

He walked on, though, purposeful, without a look back. When Bleak finally followed, he didn't give Leah so much as a glance.

She watched until they were out of sight, then she took hold of Lowery's body and headed for the water.

The plane waited in the dying daylight.

She didn't look at Lowery while she dragged him through the tangled brush and down to the shore. She waded out into the cool water and tugged him along. When it was deep enough to float him, she finally looked at his face again. Blood painted the hollows beneath his cheekbones and caressed the creases of his dead skin. His eyes were open, the bullet hole between them.

She looked at him for a long time, wondering how it all might have been different had she managed to do this years ago. She couldn't conjure the image, though. The past was gone and so she tried to see the future. Glimpses came and went. The house in Camden, the kids in their bedrooms. A house in Louisville, shaded by old oaks, Mrs. Wilson on the porch. The cabin at Moosehead, Ed's truck in the driveway, Nick's laughter in the air.

Too soon to tell, but it was all possible now because of a bullet hole between an old man's eyes.

She didn't want to believe that about the world, but there it was.

She shoved the body farther out into the lake. He drifted and sank, pulled down and away quicker than she'd expected. There was no current here and yet the water seemed to want him.

She turned her back on the sinking corpse and waded out of the chill waters of Three Cross Lake and hauled herself up onto the seaplane's float. She felt fatigue in each muscle and nerve ending, like the ache that followed a terrible fever. It took her two tries to get the door open. The pilot looked at her, tape over his mouth, cord wrapped around his chest and wrists. He couldn't have seen anything that had happened in the clearing, but she could tell he was both astonished and pleased with how things had turned out.

She leaned over and pulled the tape from his mouth. She tried to do it slowly, but he made a sound of pain. Then the sound repeated, and she looked down and saw that he'd managed to get his hands on the headset and turn the radio on. It had been a hard struggle and a pointless one, because with the tape over his mouth, he couldn't say a word.

She said, "Those knots will take me a minute."

The pilot said, "Your children are on the radio."

"What?"

"Everyone's looking for us now," he said. "They don't know it's my plane they're looking for yet, but they're out there. Your children are okay, though. I heard them. I heard your daughter's voice. She's on the radio now. Explaining where they are."

"Mind if I borrow that?" Leah said, picking up the headset. "I'll deal with the knots in a minute."

She put on the headset, dipped the microphone to her lips, and spoke.

"Hailey, Nick? It is your mother. You are safe."

ACKNOWLEDGMENTS

Thanks to the great team at Little, Brown and Company—it remains a pleasure and a privilege to work with you all. Josh Kendall leads the way. Sabrina Callahan, Craig Young, Terry Adams, Bruce Nichols, and Michael Pietsch are wonderful, enthusiastic champions. And Sareena Kamath, Ben Allen, Karen Landry, Karen Torres, and so many others actually make the product go. I'd be remiss if I didn't thank copyeditor extraordinaire Tracy Roe, too. (And I wouldn't be myself if I didn't toss in that last comma just to exasperate her.)

Richard Pine and the team at InkWell Management couldn't be better, and I'm fortunate to work with Angela Cheng Caplan on the film and TV side. I can't thank Erin Mitchell enough, particularly for allowing me to outsource my working memory to her. It's very refreshing. Gideon Pine provided wonderful notes. Tom Bernardo kept the great questions coming. Appreciate you both. I'm grateful to my family and friends, who always encourage me along the way, and to all the booksellers and librarians who have supported my work with such kindness and enthusiasm. And to Christine: always, all ways, grateful.

ABOUT THE AUTHOR

Michael Koryta is the *New York Times* bestselling author of sixteen novels. His previous novels—among them *If She Wakes, Those Who Wish Me Dead,* and *So Cold the River*—were *New York Times* Notable Books and national bestsellers and have won numerous awards. His work has been translated into more than twenty languages, and *Those Who Wish Me Dead* was recently adapted into a movie starring Angelina Jolie, Tyler Perry, Nicholas Hoult, and Jon Bernthal. Koryta is a former private investigator and newspaper reporter. He lives in Bloomington, Indiana, and Camden, Maine.